An Average Man

By Robert Hugh Benson

Once-and-Future Books

For more fiction by Robert Hugh Benson, visit
www.benson-unabridged.com

An Average Man was originally published in 1913

ISBN: 978-1-60210-008-4

Cover by R. L. Brohawn

Table of Contents

Foreword to

An Average Man

"Hugh Benson can never describe a house where there is not a second footman." Possibly intended as a snide comment on Monsignor Robert Hugh Benson's presumed snobbery and social pretensions, that snippet from a letter to the Rev. C. C. Martindale, S.J., Father Benson's official biographer, is proven wrong by *An Average Man*, perhaps the finest and most incisive commentary on social pretension and snobbery ever written. This is all the more surprising when we realize that Benson was himself a member of the highest echelons of British society. He was a son of the Archbishop of Canterbury, a personage who, in religious terms, is second only to the reigning monarch, with a social position to match. There was no question about Benson being in any way socially "pretentious."

Not surprisingly, Benson strips bare the altar of the false god of social pretension and caste with such dexterity, sensitivity, and even kindness that some readers might miss the biting satire. In this novel, however, Benson comes as close as he ever does to treating his characters badly, even exceeding the near-cruelty evident in an earlier novel, *The Conventionalists*. Percy Brandreth-Smith, the presumed hero and example of an "average man," in contrast to the ubiquitous sincerity of Benson's villains and most other characters, is portrayed as a self-deluding narcissist who, had he stopped to think for even a moment, could have halted his downward plunge into meaninglessness at any time.

It was this utter meaninglessness and lack of purpose that (if anything could be said to do so) outraged Benson. A firm believer in "breeding" and the British caste system, he had, nevertheless, internalized the idea of the servant leader as a basic principle of private and public life. In Benson's eyes the aristocracy of England, no less than its clergy and public servants, were there to serve those "lower" than themselves as well as the whole of the common good. This was, in fact, their sole reason for existence.

Unfortunately, that idea seemed to have gotten mislaid somewhere along the way. Benson saw the upper classes of his day as hollow shells, with nothing holding them together except a firm reliance on convention and unquestioned secular dogma.

Father Benson saw Edwardian country house life as the culmination of a process that began with the Reformation. The process had actually begun much earlier, with Henry VII Tudor's introduction of the idea of divine right into a formerly democratic England. The English Reformation was, in fact, virtually unique in that it was brought about largely because of the personal desires of Henry VIII, not because there was any popular demand for such an overreaching change.

Most objective authorities acknowledge that the vast majority of the people of England were perfectly happy in the Catholic Church, despite the need for some genuine reforms, and that the Reformation was forced on them against their wishes. Having largely been stripped of property by the policies of Henry VII, the "stingiest man in Europe," the English — to say nothing of the Irish — were ill-equipped to resist the "stripping of the altars" and the confiscation of what remained of widely distributed property when Henry VIII came to the throne. As the astute Protestant commentator William Cobbett noted, "The 'Reformation' has impoverished and degraded the main body of the people of England and Ireland."[1]

The direct results of the Reformation were not, then, religious indifference or heresy (despite the break with Rome), although these were certainly indirect and inevitable fruits of the change. The most debilitating effect of the Reformation was, on the contrary, the creation of a class of purposeless drones, a relatively small class that owned the vast bulk of the productive capacity of the British Empire, an empire that, in Benson's day, encircled the

---

[1] William Cobbett, *A History of the Protestant Reformation in England and Ireland*, 1826, §§ 350-351.

globe. It was, in terms of territory, wealth, and sheer power, the greatest empire the world has ever seen.

It was also an empire in which incredible wealth existed side-by-side with unbelievable poverty. The astounding wealth-gap of today, while dwarfing that of a century ago, is less obvious, if only because stop-gap social welfare programs have somewhat ameliorated the condition of the poor in developed countries.

At the same time, however, the lot of the poorest of the poor in the undeveloped or developing countries of the 21st century has become worse than could ever be imagined in Benson's day. Advancing technology has so diminished the value of human labor as an input to the productive process that the wealthy and super-wealthy can satisfy their wants and needs easier and cheaper with technology instead of the human labor of a vast army of servants or non-owning employees.

Benson evidently believed (erroneously) that returning the upper classes to a purpose in life would prevent the disaster that he saw looming over the world. A return to the solid practice of Catholicism would, he seems to have felt, reintroduce the philosophy that drives the concept of the servant-leader. Of course, this would also be true of a return to any religious or ethical system based firmly on a sound understanding of natural law, but Benson saw this philosophy most clearly taught — and supported both philosophically and spiritually — by the Catholic Church.

Not that a personal conversion to proper principles is not a necessary first step in the restructuring of the social order that, as popes Leo XIII and Pius XI made clear, is the only hope for civilization. A sincere dedication of one's self to something larger than the mere self is also necessary to maintain the personal conversion and provide the incentive to restructure the social order. By itself, however, all a personal conversion does is inculcate a spirit of religious priggishness and pharisaical superiority over the presumably less-enlightened. This was a danger of which Benson was constantly aware, and against which he continually guarded himself.

The dangers of spiritual pride were all the more apparent to Benson as the result of his unfortunate and quickly

ended relationship with Marie Corelli and Frederick
Rolfe. These were two literary and social *poseurs* who
were convinced that they had private revelations superior
to those taught by traditional religions. Once Benson realized this, he cut the connection immediately and never
looked back. He was pursued ever after by the sneers and
attacks of this proto-"New Age" pair of charlatans, the
mildest of which included accusations of hypocrisy and
even homosexuality, for neither of which there exists any
evidence other than the accusations.

In *An Average Man*, Percy Brandreth-Smith is presented with opportunity after opportunity to give his life
meaning. Rejecting each opportunity in turn, he succumbs
to the lure of an utterly purposeless existence. While he
manages to convince himself that he is acting "like a gentleman" at every turn, it is clear even to the most casual
reader that he is only acting like a complete cad. He re-
places purpose and meaning, with social and material
pride. This leads to complete spiritual indifference. In one
stunning display of near-absolute depravity and intellectual dishonesty, Percy uses his stated intention to enter
the Catholic Church to terminate an inconvenient relationship with a young lady (convincing himself he is a
Great Martyr), and later makes it clear that he has no intention of going through with the conversion in order to
retain his new social position and wealth.

Even Percy's one kindness to Mr. Main — a man who
sacrifices everything to accept all that Percy has rejected
— costs him nothing and is ultimately completely ineffec-
tual. Percy sees the favor he does for Mr. Main as an example of *noblesse oblige* . . . on which (characteristically)
he fails to follow through, leaving Mr. Main worse off than
before.

Mr. Main — we never discover his first name (at least, I
am completely unable to recall it) — is, perhaps, Benson's
greatest creation. He is, among other things, the surest
answer to anyone laboring under the delusion that Benson did not understand ordinary people.

Mr. Main is appallingly ordinary, so much so that he
seems at times a repellent creature. Even the descriptions
that Benson gives of him seem intended, at first reading,

calculated to turn the reader against him. He is, in today's terminology, a "Loser" with a capital "L." He has
never succeeded at anything, and it is painfully clear to
everyone except Mr. Main himself that he never will. He
is so pathetic that situations that would send most of us
into paroxysms of fury against the gods, fate, "the system," — whatever — leave him thanking God for his good
fortune. He considers his colossally selfish and shrewish
wife a blessing, and bears with her unbearable criticisms
of him with more than the patience of Job.

Adding more insult to injury (if possible), it becomes
very clear that a great deal of Mr. Main's lack of success
up to the opening of the novel is due in large measure to
the fact that his wife is clearly "unsuitable" — a *suitable*
wife being absolutely necessary to the advancement of a
clergyman in the Church of England. Marion Main (she is
given the dignity of a first name) has alienated everyone
in their little suburb of London, especially her husband's
religious superior, the extraordinarily kind Reverend Mr.
Bennett, Vicar of the local Anglican parish. After Mr.
Main's conversion to Catholicism (at the worst possible
time, of course), Mrs. Main immediately begins taking
steps to alienate her husband's new co-religionists.

With all that (and much more), Mr. Main is magnifi-
cently, if quietly, heroic. He holds up under adversities
that would have crushed a less "average" man. Benson
brilliantly juxtaposes the heart-wrenching case of Mr.
Main, who rises to every challenge with a stubborn perseverance although he lacks the material, intellectual, and
social resources — though not the spiritual — to maintain
him, with that of Percy Brandreth-Smith, who either begins with or gains every possible advantage — and who
quickly gives way under the least pressure. Adversity
makes no inroads on Mr. Main's faith, while worldly success and advancement destroy Percy's.

This is only to be expected, for two equally important
reasons. The first is (as I noted above) Benson seems to
have been convinced that only a sincere and honest return
to the practice of the Catholic faith by the upper classes of
England would save them from what he saw as a doom
hanging over them. *An Average Man* contains Benson's

harshest satire on English upper class society by showing
Percy's almost immediate loss of faith as soon as he gains
worldly advancement, and the growth of Mr. Main's the
worse his life becomes. Only the Catholic Church (so Benson seemed to believe) could give purpose to people who
appeared absolutely convinced that the height of individual and social development was to do absolutely nothing.

The second reason is that Jesus did not come to save the
upper classes alone, however much they might construe
the Holy Trinity as a very elite group of English aristo-
crats ("God is an Englishman . . . probably educated at
Eton" as one humorist put it). As Benson reminded people
in the opening passages of *The Religion of the Plain Man*
(1906),

> The book is intended for the "man in the street," who,
> after all, has a certain claim on our consideration,
> since Jesus Christ came to save his soul. This man in
> the street, like myself, is entirely unable to discourse
> profoundly upon the Fathers, or to decide where
> scholars disagree in matters of simple scholarship. . . .
> Now this kind of intellectual attainment seems a poor
> equip-ment for the pursuit of salvation; but it is un-
> doubtedly the only equipment that many of us have,
> and it is God that has made us and not we ourselves.
> Therefore if we believe in God at all — at least in a
> God of mercy or even justice — we are bound to ac-
> knowledge that this equipment is all that we actually
> require. To tell me that because I cannot infallibly
> pronounce upon an obscure sentence of St. Cyprian's,
> I am thereby debarred from making up my mind
> about the necessary truths of the Christian religion, is
> to represent my Maker as unjust and capricious. I am
> only capable of that of which I am capable.[2]

Thus Mr. Main, for all his lack of material success, his
dullness, his unintelligence — is the obvious victor in a
struggle that ends up destroying Percy, for all his newfound wealth, social position, and advantageous marriage.

---

[2] Robert Hugh Benson, *The Religion of the Plain Man* (1906),
Chapter I.

Benson seems to have intended Mr. Main as a sort of mirror to his own career, a kind of horrifying "might have been," a bullet dodged. This was not, however, because Benson thought of himself as specially favored by God. Mr. Main represents the opposite of everything that Benson was, while everything that happens to Mr. Main could, under less favorable circumstances, have happened to Benson himself. Mr. Main's conversion to Catholicism is, speaking in worldly terms, a complete disaster. Benson got off lightly, and knew it. As he has a priest tell a potential convert in *The Religion of the Plain Man*,

Three hundred years ago we could have offered you great things: the hatred of all who heard your name; the contempt of those who were loudest in their love for England. We could have offered you the Tower as your prison, chains, stinking dungeons, the rack, the whip, the gallows, the hangman's cauldron. Now we have no more than the chips of Christ's cross to tempt you with; a little sneering and lifting of eyebrows; a little good-humored laughter; a few remarks about 'intellectual servitude'; a little smiling pity over your medievalism, your materialism, your lack of the sturdy British spirit, your superstition and your fear of the priest.[3]

Benson escaped even that. As he related in the story of his own conversion, *Confessions of a Convert* (1912), "I must acknowledge with the greatest gratitude that the charity with which I was treated by members of the Anglican communion in general simply astonished me. I did not know that there was so much generosity in the world."[4]

Nevertheless, Benson was fully aware of that to which he *could* have been subjected. *An Average Man* marks the first of two appearances of Mr. Railton, an apostate Catholic priest, a man whose history included leaving the Catholic Church as well as his ministry, and marrying within a week of doing so. He appears again by intimation in Benson's posthumous novel, *Loneliness?* (1915), as an

---

[3] *Ibid.*, Chapter VII, 1.
[4] Benson, *Confessions of a Convert* (1912), Chapter VII.

exemplar of intellectual dishonesty and religious hypocrisy. In *An Average Man* he has made a career of attack-
ing the Catholic Church in books and lectures, making a
very good living at it.

Railton is a bully, both physically and intellectually,
and (like most bullies) obviously a coward, as demon-
strated by the fact that he spews forth in great detail
about the presumed "sins" of the "Romish" Church —
"sins" that he, as a priest, knows full well are either extremely twisted half-truths or outright lies — in venues
where no defense of the Catholic Church is possible. The
lies are so blatant that Benson's numerous Protestant
readers would have had no problem seeing their utter fal-
sity.

Percy, flushed with his newfound religious enthusiasm,
quite properly refuses to listen to such trash. He has no
responses to what Railton declaims with such an appearance of authority, but he instantly divines the man's interested motives. Percy later meets a less rational and
much more easily refuted attack, and fails to discern his
own interested motive in his failure to defend the Catholic
Church. Ironically this is after he has been through the
greater part of a course of instruction in what the Catholic
Church actually teaches, and is presumably well-equipped
to respond to such attacks on their own ground. Instead,
he weakly acquiesces in emotional condemnations of the
Catholic Church made by a girl who has heard Mr. Railton lecture. Not even the much-vaunted English upper-
class worship of "fair play" inspires him to give the devil
of the Catholic Church its due.

It is thus in *An Average Man* that Benson creates — for
him — a new kind of character: the religious hypocrite.
This signaled a new direction in his satire. He still
seemed to be convinced of the sincerity of the great mass
of men, even those who came across as the most arrant
villains, such as Topcliffe in *Come Rack! Come Rope!*, published the year before *An Average Man*. Still, he began in-
serting religious hypocrisy into his stories, both times
(oddly enough) in the person of Mr. Railton, who may
have been based on someone of whom Benson had personal knowledge. It forms a minor theme in both *An Av-*

erage Man and *Loneliness?*, while (had he lived longer), it might have been the major theme of a novel.

Interestingly, all the religious hypocrisy, while admittedly rare in Benson's characters, is on the part of Catholics, former Catholics, or those seeking instruction in the Catholic faith. No Protestant minister or devout member of the Protestant laity is ever depicted as anything other than absolutely sincere — however shallow or erroneous Benson might believe the sincerely held beliefs to be. Even his *poseur* characters (such as the incredible "Chris Dell" in *The Sentimentalists*, 1906) are absolutely sincere in their ridiculous posturings and poses — which is the chief danger in them, as Dell's attempted suicide makes clear.

One satiric jab that the reader might miss due to its extreme subtlety is that, after his conversion, Mr. Main is described as dressing in a way that could be a caricature of Mr. Railton's clothing, possibly a private way Benson had of indicating a change of religion — and of highlighting the difference between the two cases. Mr. Railton's apostasy — due to completely self-interested motives — brought him wealth and fame, while Mr. Main's conversion out of conviction resulted in nothing but disaster.

One more piece of subtle satire is that the church where Percy goes to take instruction in the Catholic faith is "St. Francis'," and is staffed — naturally — by Franciscan friars. Percy's own failure to persevere in his intention to become a Catholic is emphasized by the fact that by the end of the novel he has accepted everything that Saint Francis rejected, and lost all that Saint Francis gained.

An Average Man thus ranks as one of Benson's best novels, which (in a bit of appropriate irony that might have called forth a wry smile of appreciation from the author) has been almost completely overshadowed by his more "sensational" works. It is an "ordinary" novel about "ordinary" people that is far from ordinary.

— Michael D. Greaney, editor

An Average Man

Part I

Chapter I

(1)

It was noon in the City of London,[1] and the many-sided space on which look the Bank of England, the Royal Exchange and the Mansion House seethed as usual in a strangely disciplined confusion. The pavements bubbled like twisting streams; between the toppling omnibuses figures, hatless yet smartly dressed, dodged and turned; Jewish-looking persons, handsome and otherwise, moved briskly about and talked with gestures; pale women, trim and tired-looking, glanced this way and that on the edges of the pavements; underground passages discharged continual groups and units; taxicabs hooted and slipped by; policemen held up hands, dropped them again and took two majestic steps; a grave person in a swallowtail coat of the color of crushed strawberry eyed the crowd from the pavement in front of the Bank; the visible world roared and boiled and shifted without advance and without retrogression; and the invisible world of affairs beat steadily and orderly at this central heart of British commerce, under the cloudy September sky.

A large proportion of those who came and went so busily had every right to be there. Old men with gray beards, bright eyes and hooked noses; middle-aged men with hats on the backs of their heads, large waistcoats, and heavy watch-chains and tight trousers — persons of this kind, who care a great deal about moneymaking and nothing at all about anything else — who think in planes of moneys and investments — are, perhaps, as harmlessly employed in the City as they could well be anywhere; but there were young men there too; some bronzed with their summer holiday, some white-faced from lack of it; some with the

---

[1] The "City" of London, frequently referred to simply as "the City," is the business district of London, approximately one mile square and a separate political entity from the rest of the metropolitan area.

build of soldiers, erect and smart; some lithe and quick as
athletes; some sturdy and square — these seemed extraordinarily out of place. Two, in particular, looked it,
and felt it, and were actually saying it, as they came
swiftly across from the direction of Threadneedle Street,[2]
and made their way to their regular lunching-place round
beyond the Exchange.

"I got back on Saturday," said one; "only a fortnight —"[3]

"I got back last night," said the other. "Wouldn't waste a
Sunday in town."

They were two such young men as may be seen twenty
times over at such an hour and in such a place by any re-
spectably intelligent observer, say, from the top of an om-
nibus in so long a time as that vehicle occupies in halting
at the corner by the Bank. They were both top-hatted,
both wore tightly- buttoned black morning-coats — one
with a braid edging, and the other without — gray trousers, well-polished boots and white shirts. They walked
briskly out of step, side by side, leaning slightly forwards,
beginning sentences on one side of a perambulant finan-
cier, and, after passing him, finishing them on the other.
Their hair was beautifully brushed, and one — he that
wore the braiding — was just now withdrawing from his
sleeves the white paper sheaths with which he had protected his cuffs during the morning's work. So far the differences were small; both followed precisely the proper
convention; and even the differences that remained were
not very startling.

Reggie Ballard was the taller of the two, fair-com-
plexioned and blue-eyed, not at all handsome, but quite
wholesome looking. He lived with his mother and sister at
Wimbledon; he was twenty-two years of age, and had been
in the shipping office of Jenner and Jenner since he was
sixteen; he now enjoyed an income of ninety-five pounds a
year; he was quite harmless, quite intelligent, and with

---

[2] Sort of the Wall Street of England. The Bank of England, established 1696, is known as "the Old Lady of Threadneedle
Street" from its long residence there.

[3] Fortnight — "Fourteen Nights" or two weeks. The word comes
from the Celtic habit of counting time in nights rather than
days. A "sennight" is a week or "seven nights."

faint undeveloped artistic tastes of which he was a little ashamed.

It follows, therefore, that Percy Brandreth-Smith was the shorter of the two. The first thing one noticed about him was the extremely pleasant darkness — the more vivid in his boyish complexion — of his eyes; and the second, the agreeable curl in his dark hair. Beyond these things one did not notice a great deal unless one made a point of it. He was a year younger than Reggie; he was paler, he was squarer; and he wore at this moment, chiefly because he was hungry, a rather dissatisfied expression.

No one in the world, however, can become wholly conventional before he is thirty years old. Even the constant passing, for nearly three-hundred days in the year, of mahogany swing doors with plate glass panels, the mounting of four steps, the pushing open of another double door, and the sitting at an American desk[4] for six hours out of every twenty-four, of such days, dealing in the one case with ships that ply to and from Australia and elsewhere, and in the other with the mysteries of the cocoa-trade — even these things cannot wholly obliterate the divine image in less than fifteen or sixteen years.

There was, therefore, in each of these young men still one open channel that gave upon real existence. In Reggie it led to Religion — he had actually gone so far as to be received into the Catholic Church three years ago; in Percy it led to Romance about the female sex and to vague dreams about leisure and wealth. There was no excuse for Reggie; it was entirely uncharacteristic of his upbringing, which had been sweetly but rigidly Evangelical; there was some excuse for Percy, because there actually was in existence a Mr. Brandreth — his mother's great-uncle — who was possessed of real country estates. These two, then, had still their dreams. Reggie meditated with his subconscious self, as he sat at his desk and made calculations for Lloyd's, on things like the Monastic Life, or his duties as acolyte in St. Francis', or his private altar (with ten candles) at home; Percy, dozing in his train from Liverpool

---

[4] This appears to be a desk at which you sit in a regular chair, as opposed to a podium behind which you stand or are perched on a high stool.

Street on his way home, woke up to eye-scurrying female figures, and imagined what it would feel like to have a manservant and to go out shooting. In a word, the duty of them both was to mind other people's business, and their relaxation to think about their own.

(2)

It is a tolerable definition of a bore that he is one who talks about himself when you want to talk about yourself; but the transposition of the sentence is not always true. A bore, certainly, always does that; but he who does that is not always a bore.

At the end of lunch, for instance, when the two had lighted cigarettes, Percy was not finding Reggie a bore, although Reggie was talking hard about himself, and Percy seriously wanted to tell Reggie more about his own holiday at Yarmouth and a girl he had met there. But Reggie was really being interesting, even on such an amazing subject as a Popish Friar — a personage whom Percy had hitherto thought to have ceased from existence about three-hundred and fifty years ago. (He did not actually say so; but he did go so far as to say he had thought there were none in England.)

"Why, my dear chap," cried Reggie (so far as a discreet undertone can be a cry), "there's a whole batch of them down at Forest Gate — and . . . and . . . heaps more everywhere; besides at St. Francis'. I've only just discovered St. Francis': it's in Kensington; and they've taken me on there as acolyte: I have to wear a brown habit, you know; and I'm going to be a Tertiary."

"Well . . . about this . . . this chap you were talking about?" said Percy, completely bewildered, and trying not to appear so.

"Father Hilary, you mean. Well, he's amazing. You should just see the crowds. He's preaching all September; and he preached in May too. He's quite young, you know; he's not been a priest more than two or three years, and he's been at their house in Wales till a year ago."

"I don't like sermons," said Percy. "It seems to me that you can worship God, if you want, just as well in the open air. And down at Yarmouth, for instance —"

Reggie waved his hands.

"Oh, Lord! Blue dome, and birds as choristers — I know that stuff. Lord! Don't talk such rot! And Father Hilary —"

"But what does he do? I don't understand." (Percy was sufficiently pricked by this summary to feel a little annoyed.)

"Preaches, my dear man; preaches! The real thing, you know; not the kind of stuff you hear in your beastly churches; but the real thing. Why —"

And Reggie went off into a torrent, while Percy drew solemnly upon his cigarette and thought what a queer chap the other was.

Hitherto Percy had resisted all his friend's enticements. They had discussed religion, of course, as solemnly and judicially as every other subject in heaven and earth. Percy had stood up for the Church of England; he had said that he didn't like candles and incense and fuss: he liked a plain sung service (and might have added, with attractive tenor parts in it); and Reggie, on his side, had become incoherent altogether on that mysterious scheme of faith and art and life that the world calls Roman Catholicism. Percy had had it all his own way; he had quoted dicta of the vicar's which Reggie had been unable to answer; he had assumed the sensible, restrained, unfanatical pose which is so hard to storm; he had spoken of Nature, and the Great World and the Heart of Humanity, and a reasonable National Church; he had hinted of Science and vague Agnosticism — which he did not apparently find incompatible with his Church; and all that Reggie had been able to do so far was to wave his hands and describe pieces of ceremonial that he liked, and to quote texts whose force Percy instantly evacuated by references to Higher Criticism and Later Additions. Neither, of course, had known anything whatever about the subject that they discussed; the only difference between them was that Reggie used more or less firsthand observations of his own, and Percy secondhand arguments of other people.

But today Percy was a little impressed. It was plain that something had got hold of Reggie, which, hitherto, the other had dismissed as part of the general character of Queer Chap; and this Something had at last solidified in a preacher, who had the additional suggestive fascination of being a Friar. . . . Well: a preacher made statements that could be tested; it was not a matter of subjective impressions. Why should not he, Percy, do as he was asked, and confront this Friar from a pew? (He would be able to get the proper arguments to use to Reggie afterwards from his own vicar.)

"But I shouldn't know how to behave in a Cath — a Roman church."

"Why, my dear chap, I'll put you up to that in five minutes. Lots of Protestants come, anyhow; and nobody notices them."

Percy drew three last whiffs from his cigarette and laid it down.

"Do Protestants, and Anglicans,[5] really come?"

"My dear man, after the sermon last Sunday a good third of the congregation stumped out. They'd only come to hear him. The church was simply packed. People standing in the aisles all the time."

Percy stood up.

"I think I will," he said. "I'll tell you tomorrow."

He drew out his watch.

"Good gad! . . ."

And he was gone.

(3)

Percy had his innings later in that afternoon over a cup of tea and another cigarette, and enjoyed himself enormously on the subject of Yarmouth and the girl he had met on the pier. He gave his confidences under difficulties, since a lean and satirical-faced young man caught his eye from time to time, from beyond the small marble-topped table where he sat with a glass before him. But he got the main points of it out.

---

[5] Percy, the Church of England adherent, is careful to distinguish between "Protestants" and "Anglicans" whom many in the Church of England refer to as "Anglo-Catholics." Reggie, the convert Catholic, doesn't bother — to him, anyone separated from the unity of the pope in protest over any doctrine or belief is, *ipso facto*, a "Protestant."

No; he had not actually spoken with her; but he had bowed to her, on the occasion of their fourth encounter on the pier, and she had returned his salutation.

"You know," said Percy, in an earnest undertone, "it wasn't just one of those ordinary things. Lots of chaps do that, I know; and girls like it — girls of a certain kind, I mean — tobacconists' assistants and so on. But this one was quite different."

He explained the differences. This girl had a real mother with whom she walked sometimes, and a brother who looked a decent sort of chap. He had seen her reading, too, one day, a novel from Mudie's.[6] . . . There was all the difference in the world.

"And this isn't like those old affairs," said Percy. "I was a young fool then; I know that well enough." (He sipped his tea and assumed a mature air.)

Reggie listened, nodding and smiling. He was an excellent confidant for this kind of thing: Percy had found that out long ago. He never betrayed confidences; and — more subtle still — he never outraged them by sneers or incredulity; he listened patiently; and . . . and seemed to understand, Percy thought.

For Percy, in the eighteen months of their acquaintance, had had at least three sets of such confidences to impart. There had been the pale typist, with the intelligent eyes, five years older than himself; the aristocratic attendant in the A.B.C. shop[7] on Ludgate Hill whom he had believed to be of gentle birth; and there had been the desperate affair of the chorus girl who had turned out to be an excellent wife and mother. For Percy was as shy as such young men

---

[6] "Mudie's Select Library," established by Charles Edward Mudie in 1842, exercised a virtual monopoly over popular literature in England in the 19th century. Mudie would only purchase "Three Volume Novels," making the "Three Decker" a symbol of middle class respectability, and a fruitful subject for satire from such diverse commentators as Captain Frederick Marryat and W. S. Gilbert. The girl Percy talks about is thus presented as a virtual paragon of Victorian respectability, embodying the superficiality of the milieu.

[7] The "Art and Book Company," a chain of stores in the early 20th century.

usually are: he had not actually spoken yet once to any of the divinities, except, indeed, to order tea and buttered bun, with a meaning air, in the ordinary course of business, of the lady in the tea shop; all his experiences had been of the purely imaginative order, as romantic as the dreams of a child, and as harmless. Actually to have bowed, with a beating heart, to his last idol, and to have had that bow returned, distinguished, sincerely enough to his own mind, this engagement of his heart from all others that had preceded it.

Both these young men were, therefore, quite good and quite innocent. They were perfectly aware that a good many of their fellows were not; they listened, in the ordinary way of business, to talk and to the recounting of detailed histories the very outlines of which would have horrified their good mothers; Percy, at any rate, had nodded and assented to such conversation with an air of complete and world- hardened experience. Yet each of them alike felt infinitely more at his ease in the company of his friend than in that of those other acquaintances; and, largely through such community of experience, the two little by little had fallen into the way of lunching together when the hour could be arranged, and even, once or twice, had visited one another at home. Each talked, therefore, to the other with the extremest confidence of those intensely intimate things that lay at the heart of each, while the World of Business roared round them, as the solemn tide surges over the rock-depths where the shrimps lie at peace.

"I must be going," said Reggie, at last. "See you on Sunday, anyhow."

He tapped with a coin on the table and caught the eye of an attendant.

"Then what about —" said Percy knowingly.

"Well, look here: you'd better be at Kensington High Street, by the booking office, at half-past ten."

"But, good Lord! —"

"Mustn't be a minute later," said Reggie firmly. "Place is packed by twenty to. But I can see that a seat is kept for you till the quarter. And if you're at the booking office at Kensington at half-past, I'll meet you there myself."

"But I never said —" began Percy slowly.

"Rot! Of course you're coming. So long, then."

The satirical young man eyed them both over the edge of his emptying glass. He was a thorough businessman.

Chapter II

(1)

Engggland has a wonderful central heart, but its circulation is not of the best, for all that. For, though the City leaves nothing to be desired, as a City, its suburbs leave a great deal to be desired as suburbs.

Now there lies one such suburb, about eight miles north of Liverpool Street, named Hanstead; and the parallel between Hanstead and a chilblained finger is quite a tolerable one. It is quite conscious of London; half its male population goes up to the City every morning and back in the evening, and its female population goes up at least once a week, especially at sale times; and the notice boards outside its news shops announce editions of the evening papers scarcely half an hour behind Kensington itself. But the drawback of Hanstead lies in the fact that it has also a terrible individual life of its own: it has its own Society; its own debating club; its lawn tennis courts; its public opinion; its mayor; its church, and its self-consciousness. There is even a weekly *Hanstead and Beeling Gazette,* that publishes long accounts of flower shows and church functions, and who decorated which stalls, and who presided at the organ or rendered the tenor solo on what occasion — for the Church looms very large indeed in the social functions of such districts. Sometimes it reports sermons in full, or speeches properly interpolated with applause or laughter or dissent; and refers in at least every number to one or other of Hanstead's respected citizens. The rest of the paper is chiefly occupied by advertisements, and the political complexion of the whole place is resolutely Tory.

The difficulty of Hanstead, then, lies in its double nature. It is part of London, and, simultaneously, it is Hanstead. If it were frankly a town — good; a newcomer would plunge, no doubt, into its life and identify himself with its interests. But in Hanstead, as it is, the moment he would do this, he runs a danger of becoming suburban and provincial; he must be familiar with quotations from the City, and must pretend to disappear now and again for some social affair in Kensington or Bayswater. On the other hand, if he is frankly a Londoner and speaks too much of his friends in these high quarters, he falls under the suspicion of being a snob and of despising local society. It is an exceedingly delicate position for all except born diplomatists or unscrupulous liars.

Dr. Brandreth-Smith (who had married his cousin Miss Amy Brandreth twenty-two years ago) had long since abandoned any pretensions to be anything but a citizen of Hanstead. For one thing, he had ceased to go up to the City except on special occasions; for another, his wife resolutely regarded herself as an exile.

He was a small, silent, harassed man, with a few hobbies on which he had learned to hold his tongue, such as the collection of certain families of dried herbs and the profession of Liberalism in politics. His house stood in the High Street — a little old Georgian building, with sections of two Corinthian columns supporting the roof of a little porch, with three white steps going up to the front door and wire blinds in the windows. There was no particular reason why he should look harassed; his practice was regular, if small; his wife had a little money of her own; and he had only a son and a daughter — Percy and Helen. Percy had quite a good place in the City, and sang tenor in St. James' choir; Helen was at present an art student in Kensington, and would presently, it was hoped, teach drawing in Hanstead High School. Dr. Brandreth-Smith had probably saved quite fifty pounds a year for the last ten or twelve years, and had no objective secret reasons for unhappiness. He was quite conscientious; he was a church warden[1] and held the plate; the Vicar supped at his house about once a month. The only thing that was the matter with him was that he was bored.

Mrs. Brandreth-Smith, too, was a little unhappy-looking, but she had better reasons for it. Twenty years ago she had thought herself something of a personage, and had not hesitated to say as much. For she was sprung, really and truly, from quite an important county family in Sussex. She had made this quite clear to every-

---

[1] An office similar to an usher.

one; she had a blotting-book in her drawing room with Marston Park inscribed in faded gold and Gothic letters on its top cover. But somehow or another, the vague expectations she had both formed and disseminated, had faded into nothing. Her father had died, without a sign from Marston Park; and old Mr. Brandreth, her great-uncle, had still lived. The quarrel which all the world expected to be made up, grew more rigid as time went on: not even one dead pheasant reached Hanstead House as a symbol of peace; and it had been conveyed to her, firmly and unmistakably, by the mere lapse of years, as well as by rumors that floated down to her from time to time, that old Mr. Brandreth's adopted son would inherit every penny and every acre when the old man died.

So the poor lady had given up talking about Sussex county society at Hanstead garden parties, and, really, she had little else to talk about. She had a repressed appearance, and was rather tightly dressed in black, always. Her house was perfectly proper in its appointments: her husband had his consulting room (reached from outside through the old stable yard, disguised); Helen had her studio (in the ancient coach house, also disguised); Percy had his big bed-sitting room at the back; and she had her drawing room, with stiff, but perfectly good furniture, and the wire blinds, of course, in the windows, to prevent people looking in. Mrs. Brandreth-Smith ruled this household with the help of two maidservants, adequately and completely, and her children were just a shade afraid of her.

(2)

It was to this house, then, that Percy came home a little before sunset, carrying his small black bag. It was not an inspiriting place to which to return from the City, though the High Street still retained, like a middle-aged woman who had once been pretty, faint traces of freshness. There still ran a real little stream of clean water through the gutters; there was a triangular space of grass left at the junction of the roads, surrounded by chains and posts. But St. James' Church of Bath stone[2] and brick struck a defi-

---

[2] Oolitic limestone, particularly suited for building purposes.
The Empire State Building in New York City is faced with Ooli-

nitely town note; and the Mayor, a stout man, in his
shirtsleeves (for he was one of those people who have no
nonsense about them), was talking to Mr. Barnes, the
black-clad undertaker, opposite his own cast-iron railings.
(It was the Mayor's supreme object to leave his domain
more up-to-date than when he had first assumed respon-
sibility for its government; and he had almost succeeded
in pushing through his design of abolishing the triangle of
grass, and of substituting for it a stone drinking fountain
with chains and cups complete, and a raveled space about
it, commemorative of Victoria the Good.)

It all irritated Percy; he did not know why. Again and
again in the City he thought of Hanstead as a country retreat — (there were, in fact, several walks that could be
taken through fields and nursery gardens) — and again
and again, as he returned to it, he found it to be a suburb
after all. Its reality failed to fit in, as did its imaginative
picture, with its own dreams.

Above all, he was irritated today, since his summer
holiday was but just ended, and an entire autumn, winter
and spring intervened before the next. He was getting
broken-in nicely, but the process was not complete. Fifteen or twenty years hence, he no doubt would be comfortable; it would seem to him no longer a hardship to
have to spend nearly all his daylight hours in an office; it
would have become inevitable and familiar. But at present he still reared now and again at the touch of the bit
and the grip of the lunging-rein. . . . A motor tore by as he
fitted his newly acquired key into the lock beneath the
Georgian portico, and he looked with a kind of resentful
hatred at the bound up, nodding heads that vanished over
the rim of the back in a cloud of dust.

Percy was, too, it must be remembered, in the purely
sentimental phase of love — in love, that is to say, in such
a manner, that he thought of the face of the girl at Yarmouth whenever he was not thinking of anything else.
Sunset, therefore, made him have a strange sort of yearn-

---

tic limestone from the quarries in southern Indiana. It is sometimes called "Bath stone" in England due to its use in many of
the buildings in the city of Bath, a popular resort and historic
town dating to Roman times.

ing feeling towards nothing in particular; gave him visions
of a boat sailing over pink seas with himself and another
within it; made him want to go and sit by himself in church
and listen to organ-playing. He had not got further than
this: he did not really think of marrying this girl. In any
case, how could he, on an income of eighty pounds a year,
fifty of which he dutifully paid over to his mother? . . .

He fell, therefore, into a frenzy of irritation when, as he
was hanging up his coat behind the door in the inner hall,
he felt himself slapped sharply between the shoulders.

"Don't do that, Helen!" he snapped. "You know how I
hate it."

She was a pleasant, smiling girl who faced him, dressed,
of course, in art-green, with a neck cut much too low and
crimped, apparently, round a piece of elastic. Her feet,
too, looked needlessly flat in her low heel-less slippers,
and her wrists were rather red. She was frankly and con-
fessedly artistic, and said so continually.

"You needn't be shirty,[3] old man," she said.

Helen's pose, at this particular time, was that of the
Reckless Bohemian. Girls who live at home in Hanstead,
with a Georgian portico over the door and wire blinds on
the windows, must do something. She had tried being
soulful and yearning, but, with uncommon good sense,
had soon recognized that this was out of date. So she had
shifted her attitude. She had continued to dress — well —
as she dressed; because it was convenient and unmistakable and (she thought) rather attractive; and she had
learned to talk slang, as a girl always does learn to talk it,
of just the wrong kind, ceasing to present the deportment
of a lady without acquiring that of a gentleman.

Percy liked Helen quite: he was bound to, in
self-protection; but he had begun lately to understand
that their ideals were quite different. Helen yearned for a
studio in Chelsea and a female companion; Percy, for a
country house and a distinguished wife.

"You've got a choir practice tonight," she said. "Mr.
Main came in to tea to say so."

Percy grunted.

---

[3] A very slangy way of saying someone is being irritable — from
the starched shirtfronts presumably worn by fussy old men.

"What time?"

"Half-past eight. Sooner you than me."

Helen, of course, had added to her pose just now — or, rather, had found to be an essential part of her pose — the attitude of the Independent Thinker.[4] She went to church unwillingly, and talked desperately about Nature, and the Religion of the open air, when her parents were not present. Percy had imbibed a little of it from her too, though he would have died sooner than confess it.

He grunted again. Then he went upstairs. He must do some of his work, then, before dinner.

(3)

The church looked bleak and uninviting as he turned in at the west door a little after half-past eight. It is one of those churches that not only seem to be, but actually are, turned out complete by about three firms at a given sum. One firm built the fabric; one supplied the organ, of its number four specifications, and a third furnished it, down to the low ironwork screen with brass and copper flowers in the pattern. It had absolutely everything necessary for divine worship, and had nothing in it of any interest whatever. It was paved with shiny encaustic tiles, each of which bore a sacred monogram or an ecclesiastical device; the same devices were repeated in stencil upon the chancel walls; a shiny oak communion table, with a shiny brass cross upon it, two shiny candlesticks (with shields) and two shiny vases, stood at the eastern end. Its pews were of shiny pitch-pine, and the choir seats of pallid oak. It possessed, of course, a peal of tubular bells, and at given intervals a retired colonel protested in the *Hanstead and Beeling Gazette* against the ringing of these for more than ten minutes at a time, or at an earlier hour than half-past seven.

When Percy came in, a little late, the hanging gas chandeliers in the chancel (resembling celestial crowns in enamel and brass) were lighted, but the rest of the church was dark, and the company of singers — boys in front and men behind — stood in the light, with their books before

---

[4] An atheist or an agnostic, depending on how confused the holder of "independent" opinions happened to be.

them, like the inhabitants of a rather shoddy heaven. From every quarter about them glimmered points of brass — from the retable of the altar behind, the candlesticks of the organ on the south, and the low screen to the west. In the midst stood the Vicar, with a high desk before him and a small baton in his hands.

"Now once again," he said. And Gadsby's *Te Deum* in C burst forth afresh as Percy slipped into his place, after a nod from the conductor, and opened his music.

The weekly choir practice was always a vague pleasure to this young man. He had an excellent ear for music and a tolerable voice for a chorus; and it was a pleasing sensation to him to stand here at choir practice in his ordinary clothes, and on Sundays in his surplice and cassock, and be off in full cry in some such piece as Gadsby in C. It gave him a sense of unity and strength and melodiousness. The choir had lately been promoted from Anglican chants to "services"; they had acquired three already, and had even ventured on Stanford in B flat last Easter Day. But the result had been such that it was determined to wait another year before venturing on it again.

The Vicar was, of course, the director of the choir, as of everything else. In appearance he was a genial, rubicund man; in doctrine he was moderate; and in character he was the kind of man who honestly believes that, in virtue of his office, he ought to control everything with which he was connected. He controlled things quite well too, without genius, indeed, but with plenty of talent. He had quite a good taste in harvest decorations; he had been very particular with the church furnishers that nothing "tawdry" should be supplied; he sang a tolerable bass; he preached what he called "bright" sermons and conducted "hearty" services; he had plenty of conversation for social occasions, such as the choir outing, the Band of Hope tea and the Mothers' Meetings. He was an Oxford man, and wore, therefore, a red hood that was very effective. He always, if grammar permitted it at all, said "one" instead of "I." His wife was as helpful as himself; she was of an unfailing brightness and perseverance; she managed to play the organ sufficiently well for weekday services and for a hymn or two at early celebrations; and she governed her household — including her single boy Clement (who in the holidays sang treble in the choir) — with tact and discretion. She even managed to keep on tolerably friendly terms with poor Mrs. Main.

For Mrs. Main was the difficulty of the parish, on its social side. She was the wife, as need hardly be said, of Mr. Main; and Mr. Main was the middle-aged curate with ritualistic tendencies, severely repressed. He stood now — the poor man — by the side of Mr. Tempest, the organist; for he had no voice and the least possible appreciation of music, and contented himself with turning over the music when Mr. Tempest violently bowed his head in that direction. He was a melancholy-faced man, with long, pointed jaws, heavy eyebrows and bald temples — all of a dusky complexion; and he was nearly everything which the Vicar was not. He had no small conversation; he had no taste; his sermons were the last word in dreariness; he could never take the lead anywhere at anything. It was, indeed, reported in the parish that it was only at the earnest solicitations of the bishop that Mr. Bennett kept him at all. Yet no one could deny Mr. Main's efforts; he was ruthlessly conscientious in visiting his district, and called upon the sick every day; he was always punctual, always patient (even when he was treated with scarcely disguised disdain by the less Christian members of the choir) and always dreary. Yet three or four queer people in the parish liked him particularly.

But his wife was the difficulty. They had no children, and all the energies of the pale little fiery, bitter woman had poured themselves into the channel of social ambition. It appeared to her abominable that her husband should be a curate still at the age of thirty-eight, and that he should be able to furnish towards their joint income only one hundred and forty pounds a year. She fought gallantly and furiously; she was dressed at least as well as the Vicar's wife, and her drawing room was amazingly correct — even down to the detail of a "silver table," with articles under the glass worth at least thirty shillings[5] all told. But her energies escaped now and again into unfor-

---

[5] Approximately US $6.00 at this time.

tunate channels . . . there had been one or two scenes . . .
she was not on speaking terms with at least six or eight of
the wives of her husband's sheep. Once there had been a
scene even in the Vicarage drawing room itself. . . . But
these things are best forgotten. It was eighteen months
since the last scene, and they had been in the parish three
years — ever since the church had been built and conse-
crated.

(4)

"Once more," said the Vicar. "And I think one should
take that 'Make them to be numbered with Thy saints' a
little slower. . . . Like this."

He sang the phrase emphatically through, waving his
baton mechanically.

"Like that," he said; "a little more solemnity."

He bent a severe eye on Tommie Mann, who was giggling.

"Now, Mr. Tempest, please."

He rapped professionally with his baton on the desk,
and once more the *Bourdon* boomed out under Mr. Tempest's left heel.

Percy was getting warmed up by now. Dinner had been
as usual — rather a silent meal, with his father har-
assed-looking as usual, his mother severe and correct, and
Helen rather tiresome. Percy had flamed up once at some
piece of slang more outrageous than usual, and had been
gravely rebuked by his mother.

"I can't think," he had said, "why it is that women try to
be like men; they only succeed in being cads."

"That's not a nice thing to say," said his mother. And
Helen had turned white with anger.

But now Gadsby in C was doing its genial work. It is not
a profound composition, but it is hearty and optimistic
and sufficiently melodious. It deals, in the *Te Deum,* for
instance, with the deepest mysteries, and renders them
innocuous. It includes heaven and earth and all that is in
them in a pleasing and polished frame, about a foot
square, so to speak.

So Percy cried his tenor part aloud, next young Mr.
Barnes, the undertaker's son, who eyed him sideways to
catch his note at doubtful moments; watched the Vicar's

controlling hand and countenance; regarded Tommie Mann vindictively; glanced at Mr. Main's black silhouette and the fuzzy gleam of his eyebrows against the organ candles, and began to grow more content. Gadsby in C was going better every time: it would be almost ready for next Sunday.

It is strange how in a state of intense attention the background of thought becomes more active. So Percy, concentrated on his notes, taut on the high ones and relaxed on the low ones, followed, easily and interestedly, his own interior affairs. The gas lit chancel, the white walls, the pallid oak book-rest, the encaustic tiles — all these things which he saw or felt or fingered served as a frame to his more engrossing business — the girl at Yarmouth and the friar of Kensington. Then he suddenly remembered that if he kept his promise to Reggie he would not be singing Gadsby in C here next Sunday morning, after all. Next he remembered that Rule IV of the choir — in the little typewritten schedule that hung up in the choir vestry — stated that in case of a foreseen absence from the choir at either of the Sunday services, notice should be given to the Vicar at least before the preceding Friday evening. And, thirdly, he wondered what the Vicar would say if he told him the reason. . . .

"I think that'll do for tonight," said the Vicar presently. "I mean for that music. We've still got the Harvest Festival — Caleb Simper. Will you get out the music, please, Mr. Main?"

While the curate creaked across into the choir vestry, the Vicar continued his comments, though in the subdued tone appropriate to the sanctuary.

"The basses, I think, were not quite sure of themselves in the fifth bar of the second page. One wants it a little more pounded out, as one said before — a strong, resolute lead — 'Lord God of Sab-a-oth.' It is very effective sung so. . . . (Thomas Mann, if I have to speak or look at you again, I shall send you away from the practice.) . . . And, by the way, one wanted to say a word about the vesper hymn last Sunday evening. It was not quite soft enough in the last bar or two; it ought to fade away, as one said last week, into silence, so that the congregation scarcely know.

. . . Perhaps one might try it over, Mr. Tempest, if you
have the music there. . . . Oh! Here is Mr. Main with the
music. Perhaps one had better get on with the Harvest
music. There are not many more days before Thursday
week, and we have the bishop this year, one must remember."

The Harvest Festival was, of course, the supreme feast
of the year. As early as Monday morning the more solid
decorations began to come in — a couple of loaves of
bread, for instance, six feet in length, gigantic vegetable
marrows and boxes of apples. These were all sent relig-
iously on the following Monday — the bread a little stale,
of course; but, as Mr. Bennett said, "One cannot have everything" — to the local hospital; and, after all, the First
Great Commandment comes before the Second. Special
music was always rendered on this festival, all about corn
and wine — although the Vicar was very nearly a teeto-
taler — and oil; and there was always a special preacher,
usually an Oxford friend of the Vicar's. But on this occasion a suffragan bishop was to be present and to preach;
and Mr. Bennett was, of course, more anxious than ever
that all should be as it should.

(5)

It was nearly ten o'clock before Mr. Simper's anthem
was perfect, the music collected again by Mr. Main, and
one of the gas chandeliers turned out. The choir dispersed
in twos and threes, the boys, of course, running before
they reached the door, scuffling as they went out, and interrupting the Vicar in his conversation with Mr. Tempest. He turned sharply, but too late.

"I shall have to speak to Mrs. Mann," he said. "I am
sure that was Tommie again."

The boys were his one trouble connected with the
church.

One by one they approached the troublesome age, and
one by one justified its name; only the very meekest of
them survived confirmation and remained in the service
of the sanctuary: the rest lapsed into brightly-colored ties,
and might be observed by their pastor on Sunday evenings talking to female acquaintances of their own age in
Hanstead High Street instead of coming to church. Mr.

Bennett had even ventured to wonder whether, if confirmation were not administered to them a year or two earlier than fourteen, more might not be retained.

However, he dismissed the thought of Tommie for the present, bade Mr. Tempest goodnight, and came down from the chancel to find Percy waiting for him.

"May I speak to you a moment?"

"Certainly, my boy, certainly." He turned.

"You'll put out the lights, Mr. Main, won't you, and lock up. Please put the new music out of the boys' reach."

"Come along to the Vicarage," said Mr. Bennett genially. "I haven't seen you since your holiday."

The Vicar, as has been said, was an absolutely conscientious man. Honestly he cared more about his church and the conduct of the services, and the music, and the behavior of his flock, than about anything else in the world. Further, the suburbs seemed to him the key of the situation: hold them, he was accustomed to say, and you hold the whole country. He was especially careful, too, for an analogous kind of reason, to be very cordial and hearty with all his young men; they, too, seemed to him another key of the situation; and he had been deeply disappointed when, after advertising for a curate who should be "good with men and boys," Mr. Main only had been forthcoming. But he did his best; he had a club with real billiard tables and smoking permitted, for all church youths over seventeen; and he was careful, too, for his own part, to be sympathetic and friendly with every young man who would permit such advances. Finally, he was meditating a guild of St. George, but, so far, had taken no action, from a faint suspicion that such a society might become more high church[6] than he liked; the very word "guild" had a suggestive tone about it. But he had determined to speak to the bishop next week. . . .

He put his arm through Percy's as they walked together down the little graveled path, and began inquiries as to Yarmouth.

"You found a good church there, I hope," he said, "and plenty of bathing?"

---

[6] That is, too many of the external trappings and internal doctrines of the Catholic Church.

Percy reassured him on these points. (He was becoming a little doubtful as to how much he would reveal as to his plans for next Sunday morning.)

"So important, my dear fellow," continued the Vicar, latching the gate behind him with one hand and still retaining Percy with the other, "so important not to take a holiday from religion too. . . . You went alone, I think?"

"I met one of our chaps there," said Percy.

"That's right; that's right. (Ah! Goodnight, Mr. Mayor, goodnight to you! . . . And you made other friends too, I daresay."

Percy literally could not get one word in on the very small matter on which he wished to speak. The Vicar made sympathetic and helpful observations so continuously that interruption was impossible; and it was not until they had gone up the dark garden path of the Vicarage, and the key was being produced at the end of the Vicar's watch-chain, that any mention was made of it at all.

"You wanted to see me, my boy. . . . Come in, come in; and you shall have a cigarette in the study."

Mrs. Bennett was waiting for them there, and a jug of cocoa steamed by the study fire. She was an almost perfect vicar's wife, in character, manner and appearance; her own father had been an excellent clergyman in the north, and her training was complete. She was a kindly woman, fresh-colored, bright-eyed and quiet; she had been slim, but was growing mature; she was always quietly and nicely dressed; she reverenced her husband as a "priest" and loved him as a man: she did her duty perfectly and contentedly; and had not an enemy in the world, except, perhaps, poor Mrs. Main.

"Here's Mr. Percy," said the Vicar, "come in for a cup of cocoa and the cigarette. . . . Yes, my dear, the practice went off beautifully. I think we shall do very well. Where's Clement?"

"My dear, you forget what time it is. It's after ten. I sent Clemmie straight off to bed."

"That reminds me," said the Vicar. ("Sit down, my boy, and make yourself at home.) That reminds me I must speak to Mrs. Mann about Tommie. That boy's getting very troublesome. One can't have that sort of thing in the choir. And he's in Mr. Main's confirmation class, too."

While the gentle, harmless gossip went on, Percy nursed his cup of cocoa, which he did not want, and fingered an unlit cigarette, which he did. It was a regular Vicarage study in which he sat. There were the books, behind brass latticework, the writing table with a couple of books open upon it, the three or four Arundel prints,[7] the side table littered with account books and parish magazines, the worn carpet, the bright wallpaper. The very room was a symbol of its owner, and the wife made it complete. It stood for a harmless and quite useful life — beyond reproach, active, philanthropic, and fairly studious. It was quite conventional, of course; but the world would soon explode unless there were conventions to hold it together. . . . It was like Gadsby in C.

"And there was something you wanted to say?" said the Vicar suddenly, setting his cocoa down, and glancing almost imperceptibly at his wife.

Percy made haste to get it out. He understood what the glance meant.

"Oh, yes: but it was nothing important," he said. "It was only that I've promised to go to church with one of our chaps in Kensington next Sunday, and shan't be able to be here."

"Ah! Yes," said Mr. Bennett indulgently, "you'll be missed in our new music; but there! We can't expect — What church are you going to?"

"I . . . I forget its name," said Percy — speaking the truth, however, at that moment.

---

[7] "Arundel prints" were cheap reproductions of religious works by the famous masters. They are now highly sought-after collector's items, a bit of unintended satire that probably would have delighted Benson.

Chapter III

(1)

Mrs. Smith was one of those people who are always entirely occupied with occupations which to a very large extent they invent for themselves, and believe that Providence has laid upon them. In her case it was the superintendence of her household which took her time.

Now the care of a smallish house resembles a telescope. It may be reduced to a very small compass and yet remain intact; or it may be prolonged to an almost incredible extent. In the case of Mrs. Smith it was prolonged through practically the entire day.

She was down always at least a quarter of an hour before breakfast, for a general survey, and that she might reprove Alice if the staircase wasn't "done." Then she made the tea and lifted the metal dish covers to see what lay beneath them. Then she dispensed the tea when her family appeared, and took her own food.

But it was after breakfast that the real business began. There was a fixed hour for interviewing the cook and sending, through her, reproving messages to the tradesmen. There were then accounts to be done, and a thousand other small affairs, of which she could have given no very clear description afterwards, and yet affairs which undoubtedly did occupy her till noon. It was then time to begin the extras, so to speak: it was then that she wrote letters, if there were any to be written, and glanced at the paper, if anything was happening in the world in which she took any interest, if not, she scanned the Ladies' Page. After lunch there was a pause, in which she supposed herself to rest; as a matter of fact, she spent the time till three in small mysteries of dress of which I am not competent to treat. At three she issued forth — usually alone, sometimes with Helen — again on household business, with an occasional call upon a lady as resolutely conventional as herself. She returned to tea; and immediately afterwards went about her business once more, connected, usually, with household stuffs in some manner —

curtains were to be inspected and drawers opened — at
any rate, she was busy, either upstairs, where she might
be heard opening cupboards, or downstairs with her sew-
ing. Then came dinner; then the nightly visit to the
kitchen again; and then a short social repose with her
husband and children. Exceptions to this daily course
were made on Tuesdays, when it was known that she was
"At Home"[1] from four to six.

Such a day was blameless, if not actually meritorious —
at least, from the point of view of its subjective strenu-
ousness. She certainly did not injure anyone else — there
was no time — neither did she sit with her hands before
her. But it never even occurred to her that to live entirely
in order to live was open to question on any grounds at
all. She was a good and a just mistress, even if a little
strict. Brasswork was well polished in her house; the var-
nished boards in her floors shone; the food was adequately
cooked. She complained a little, but not excessively, of the
time her duties took; she said there were so many things
she would like to do, if only she could fit them in; but she
could not probably have named any of them more precisely, nor did she ever show any inclination towards any
pursuit or interest beyond that involved in household
cares. She was an excellent housekeeper; the one pity was
that she had not a wider sphere.

Now and then her old dreams visited her. She felt, and
with perfect justice, that her faculties had not fair play in
a small suburban house; and she was quite aware that if
things had fallen out ever so little differently, she might
have had two houses, one in Wilton Crescent and the
other in Sussex, in which to exercise her powers. It
seemed to her extraordinarily perverse that these king-
doms were to fall one day into the possession of a single
young man — not of the best reputation — whom her
wealthy old relative had adopted and made his heir — a
young man who had not, as she said to herself in moments of ancestral bitterness, a "drop of Brandreth blood
in him" — at least it was to be hoped not.

---

[1] That is, available to receive visits from friends and neighbors.

But she was quiet and self-repressed — except with the servants, whom she ruled like a despot — she said little or nothing of these things to others; at least, she had not said them for several years. But the blotting-book inscribed "Marston Park" was still a symbol to her of ideals that once had been more vivid.

(2)

"The bacon was not crisp enough this morning," she remarked in the kitchen at ten o'clock on the day after the choir practice.

"No'm?"

"It was cut a little too thick. You will find it a good plan to dry it well in the oven before frying it."

"Yes'm."

"About the beef we had yesterday. . . . That will make into rissoles for Sunday breakfast. The doctor likes them. Will you remember that? He likes it better than mince."

"Yes'm."

There was quite a quantity of things to mention this morning. She held a little written list of them in her hand, with the shiny red-covered account books; and she went through them promptly and decisively. There were so many, in fact, that she thought it better at the end to leave it for the cook's guidance. Then a long disputation had to be held about Wingate's bill. Wingate's mutton was certainly tenderer than Johnson's; but a halfpenny a pound extra charge — well, was a halfpenny a pound extra. It must be laid before Johnson, then, that his prices were satisfactory, but the quality of his meat not so satisfactory. And, simultaneously, it must be laid before Wingate that the reverse proposition was true in his own case.

Then there was the matter of the servant's laundry that must be ventilated. She had been quite clear, she said, on the amount allowed weekly for this item; yet, continually that amount was exceeded. Neither must there be any diminution in smartness in their public appearances. She allowed ample, she said — ample — for all that was required. Would Mrs. Martin kindly see to it that these reforms were made; she must simply decline in future to pay for more than the stipulated total.

It was ten minutes to eleven this morning before she re-entered the drawing room, where a little pile of household books had to be looked through; and she sat down at them immediately, opening as she did so the famous blotting-book in order to get out the pen she used for red ink. And it was at this moment that once more the train of thought came up of which the faded Gothic letters on the cover of the book was the outward symbol.

There were so many things whose difficulties would be solved, if she only had what was hers by right of blood, if not of inheritance.

There was first Percy.

Now she was content with Percy up to a certain point.

He was a steady sort of boy who never gave her any real anxiety; he was decently educated; he never did anything outrageous: his behavior in the City seemed satisfactory; and so on. But she was perfectly aware that he would not quite have passed muster, say, in a Pall-Mall Club, or at Marston Park. He smoked a certain kind of cigarettes, for instance, of which the little paper case, containing five, displeased her; and he would leave these little paper cases about. He brought home with him occasionally certain types of comic papers which might be all very well for mere clerks — papers which, indeed, anyone might read without harm — but which were not the kind of literature one would expect to find lying on the table of a highly refined drawing room.[2]

Again, there was Helen. Now Helen was a Suburbanite pure and simple. Her very eccentricities — her loose frocks cut square at the throat, her passion for Art, her slang — were all part of the great Suburban System; that is to say, when Suburbanites were eccentric they were always eccentric in this sort of way: there was no more real originality about such unconventionalities than about the most conventional of conventions.

Yet what was the use of finding fault, when she had no positive alternative to offer? It is true that she had succeeded in abolishing *Comic Cuts* from the drawing room table, and in forbidding Helen to wear sandals; but she

---

[2] Such as a three-volume novel from Mudie's Library.

found herself unable to suggest anything else to take their place. Yet she knew at the very bottom of her soul, with a passionate though repressed conviction, that this kind of thing would simply die of inanition in such a place as Marston; she would simply not have to speak; other things would substitute themselves.

For she knew, by a kind of traditional instinct, that these things marked a certain social station — that stratum in which she lived — like a man up to his knees in a quicksand, hating and resenting it, yet unable to extricate himself. She knew that the blotting-book came from simply another realm altogether — a realm from which she was wrongfully excluded.

Lastly, there was her husband.

And here again she had no kind of right to complain; and she knew it. He was a kindly, peace-loving man, who attended to his profession with sufficient care and competence to be able to provide her with an income adequate to the scale on which they lived; he was very moral indeed, and religious enough to be a church warden. Yet there were tiny habits into which he had long been drifting, which she disliked intensely, yet could not remedy. After all there was no final reason why he should not breakfast on Sunday in his dressing gown, nor why he should not put on comfortable carpet slippers in the evening, instead of tight and shiny shoes; there was no actual crime committed by a man who did not seven days in the week shave before breakfast. Yet she knew it was all wrong; she knew that men of the social caste to which she desired to belong, to which, in fact, she did belong by right of blood, simply do not do these things. They might perhaps drink rather too many whiskies-and-soda in the evening, and so forth; but these things do not stamp you. But carpet-slippers and dressing gowns do. . . .

Well; the whole thing would be cured automatically by the possession of a place like Marston. Helen would develop the right kind of eccentricities, and Percy the right kind of conventions. And she knew her husband well enough, too, to be certain that he also would take his ease and seek his comforts along higher lines than those of

Hanstead. Or, if he did not of himself, she knew very well that she could make him.

But she wanted leverage, so to say. She needed big surroundings to which she could appeal, a household whose standard would be self-supporting. She was confident — not out of arrogance, but simple self-knowledge — that she would be adequate to such circumstances; and that the same perseverance and fidelity which caused her to dominate the cook and rebuke tradesmen would be equal to ruling a butler and seeing that even gamekeepers did their work.

Such was her course of thought this morning, as she added up household books, and wrote the totals, at her Davenport, with a firm and unerring hand.

(3)

Mrs. Bennett, the Vicar's wife, looked in that afternoon, just as Mrs. Smith was preparing to issue forth, no other visitors having appeared. And here again the hostess was aware of hardship. For Mrs. Bennett, described (and with sufficient justice) as the "kindest woman in the world," took, of course, her proper place in Hanstead, and therefore in her husband's church warden's wife's drawing room.

She took occasion to explain, for example, with the kindest motives in the world, certain little points about the imminent visit of the bishop.

"We shall be so very glad to see you at tea, Mrs. Smith, if you can come, and the doctor too, of course, if he can get away. My husband is most anxious that as many of his parishioners as possible should meet the bishop."

Mrs. Smith said that she would be delighted.

"I am terribly afraid that some may not care to come. People seem very frightened of a bishop somehow."

Mrs. Smith hastened to express her surprise at such timidity. She at least would not be frightened; and it would be as well for Mrs. Bennett to recognize that.

"Then about tea," said Mrs. Bennett. "We shall have a stand-up tea, of course. The bishop won't have much time. It won't be a regular parochial tea party, you know; otherwise, of course, I shouldn't ask you."

Now this was tactless from its very tactfulness. A "parochial tea party" meant a festivity hardly removed from a
Mothers' Meeting. It was surely unnecessary then to say
that Mrs. Smith would not be asked to such an entertainment: the very highest social figure among the guests
at such a function would only be on the level of, say, an
ironmonger's wife. Persons of distinction would mark that
distinction by waiting upon the guests, instead of sitting
down with them. So the iron touched once more the little
raw spot on Mrs. Smith's soul.

And so it went on. Mrs. Bennett, good woman, desired
nothing better than that all her guests should be completely at their ease when they came; so she took the
greatest possible care, again with so much tact that you
could not help seeing it, to inform them without, as she
thought, appearing to do so, of the little things that would
be expected. For instance, as the bishop would have so little time, it was important that everyone should be punctual, or else they might miss him; and, for the same reason she hoped that no one would have to leave before
half-past five. This was her way of conveying that the
bishop must not be treated like an ordinary guest; his
company must be there both to greet him and to speed
him when he retired upstairs. And all this, in exact proportion to the amount of information conveyed, was so
much gall to Mrs. Smith, who really did, as a matter of
fact, know quite well how to behave to a bishop.

Finally, still with the same overflowing kindness, Mrs.
Bennett commended Percy's singing in church.

"My husband says he would hardly know what to do
without him. It's so difficult to get young men to come to
church regularly."

And again Mrs. Smith perceived, as in a vision, how
Percy to Mrs. Bennett's mind was just a young man who
might be expected to stand about, if he were not in
church, at street corners in heavy creaking boots and a
buttonhole.

But she repressed herself nobly. She had been learning
to do it, poor lady! For many years past; and she purred
and she nodded and she assented; and her heart burned

dully within her. Marston was but a dream, after all; like a fairy tale to a child.

Chapter IV

(1)

The nine-seven train from Hanstead is one of the events of the day. In a hundred homes at a hundred breakfast tables its name is sounded forth on six days out of the week. Wives remind husbands that they have only four minutes before the nine-seven will leave the station; husbands sharply remind their wives when the eggs have not arrived that they have only fourteen minutes before the nine-seven is due. In appearance it resembles all other trains, except in that it has hardly any third-class carriages at all; but in significance it stands alone — at least in Hanstead. It is due at Liverpool Street at nine-thirty-eight, and is approximately calculated, therefore, to enable those who travel by it to be in their offices before the clock has finished striking ten.

It was on the Thursday morning that Percy so nearly missed it, and, in consequence, was forced to leap into a third-class non-smoking carriage, as the train was half-way up the platform. Such things had happened to him before, but it was especially annoying this morning, as he had not had time for a cigarette, and, since the nine-seven stopped nowhere on the way, would be unable to have one at all, except an unsatisfactory one on his way to the office. Another annoying incident was that as he sprang in, and the guard banged the door behind him, he tripped violently over a bag and fell full length along the floor.

He turned savagely to apologize to a woman of whom he had just been aware — the only occupant of the carriage — and was completely taken aback.

"I am so very sorry," said an exceedingly melodious voice. "It was entirely my fault. I do hope you're not hurt?"

Percy made haste to reassure her, and, such was the impression she made upon him, further to inform her that it was wholly his own stupidity. For he was aware, even in that agitated moment, that this was about the prettiest girl he had ever set eyes on. He had expected an anemic typewriter, or a portly slum-woman; and, behold, here sat a girl, about his own age, dressed charmingly and neatly,

with mysterious effects about her costume which he could
not analyze; pale, but with glorious eyes and pretty lips
parted, it seemed, with genuine anxiety and sympathy.

"It's really nothing at all," he said again. "I ought to
have looked where I was going. And it's my own fault, too,
for being late."

She smiled, watching him with amused and appreciative eyes as he dusted his knees free from sawdust.

"Forgive me," she said. "But you've a lot more on your
elbows. Yes, you'd much better take off your coat. You'll
never get it off unless you do."

Percy hesitated, agreeably aware of her pleasantly
friendly interest.

"Well, if you don't mind," he said, conscious that his
shirt was irreproachable.

"I shall be distressed if you don't," she said, smiling
again.

Percy was very deliberate in the process that followed,
aware of a curious excitement. He took off his tailed coat,
pulled up his shirtsleeves daintily, and began to brush off
the sawdust with his fingers. But it was not very successful. He was aware that the girl had moved, but did not
venture to look at her till she spoke again.

"You'd better have this brush," she said, holding one
out. "It's lucky I had one in my bag."

It was a beautiful brush, with an ivory back and a
monogram which he could not make out.

"Thanks, very much," he said.

"It's only fair," she smiled back at him. "You know, it
really was my fault, although you are so dreadfully polite
about it."

As Percy re-endued himself with his coat, pulled down
his cuffs and settled himself opposite her, he was wondering whether it would be proper to go on talking. Hanstead
was terribly rigid on certain kinds of etiquette.

He decided to ignore Hanstead.

"This train's always on time," he said. "Worse luck!"

"You come by it often?"

"I come by it every day," said Percy; "and it's just ten
minutes earlier than it need be."

Ah!" said the girl.

Certainly she was surprisingly pretty, especially when she spoke and her whole face lighted up in a subdued kind of laughter. Her eyes were not only splendid, but they were kind too. Her lips moved deliciously when she spoke, showing very white teeth indeed behind them; but they relaxed, when she was silent (thought Percy), into a kind of melancholy. Her hair was as dark as possible, without being actually black, and was done up in a massive kind of way, quite new to Percy, but completely satisfying. But, above all, there was real charm about her. People often have features — a nose or ears, for instance, in the less marked instances — that have nothing to do with expression — features stuck on, so to speak, without any vital connection, so to say, between them and the personality that uses them. But in this girl there was none of that: she was entirely alive, and every speck of her told. Her very hat and shoes and gloves seemed entirely hers. (Of course, the fact was that she was quite perfectly dressed; but Percy did not understand that.) Her voice, too, seemed completely under her control, as pliable as a violin, and her enunciation strangely perfect.

He tried in vain to elicit facts about her.

"Do you come often by this train?" he asked, with flare of audacity.

"It's the . . . the third time," she said.

"You live down this line, I expect?"

She seemed not to hear.

"How stupid of me!" she cried. "I've never suggested your having a cigarette. Do, please. I'm sure you smoke!"

"Well, but —"

"My dear boy — I don't mind it at all. I — I . . . . Shall I tell you?"

Percy tingled all over at her phrase.

"Do tell me!"

"Well — I smoke myself sometimes, when I'm alone."

Percy began to feel a desperate dog; he did not quite know why.

"Now do have one of mine," he said rather familiarly, drawing out his thin little silver case.

She shook her head.

"I couldn't dream of it," she said. And there seemed to fall between Percy and her a sudden impenetrable wall of ice.

He drew out his matchbox and lighted up. Then he determined to attack again.

"You didn't tell me whether you lived down this line?" he said.

She looked at him with a cool, odd look, and the ice wall grew piercing cold: he understood that he was presuming.

"The point is," she said, "whether this train will arrive up to time. I've got to be in the Strand by ten sharp, and I don't want to take a taxi unless I must."

"Sure to be in time," said poor Percy. "It always is unless there's a fog." (Interiorly he was scourging and lashing himself for his presumption. What an ill-bred ass he had been! Dense, pigheaded boor!)

She seemed to understand his self-reproaches, and her eyes grew kind again.

"You see, I'm quite new to this line. I've always lived in the Croydon direction — at least, for the last three years, and I've just moved. And the Brighton line —"

And the two went off into severe discussions and comparisons. But Percy's heart grew warm again within him at the thought that she lived now, at any rate, on the same railway line as himself, and that he might, if he were fortunate, travel up with her quite often. He wondered whether it were possible that she could really be in business. . . . Certainly she did not look like it. Once he thought of the Yarmouth girl, and bitter laughter rose in him. He was as one who has climbed a snow-peak, and looks back in disdain at the steaming valleys from which he has come. The Yarmouth girl indeed! Maud was her name! . . . Maud! . . .

(2)

Percy's business application was quite appreciably affected all that morning by his experience in the train.

It has been said that he was susceptible, but even he knew that this particular romance was different from the others. The only difficulty was that each new romance seemed so. But the quality seemed different. One may be deeply affected by both Beethoven and Tosti; one may even shed tears over Tosti and not over Beethoven; yet there is no question, even to a very moderate musician indeed, as to in which lies the deeper profundity. It was so with Percy in this particular experience. The thought of the Yarmouth girl had made him cross under certain circumstances; he had even attempted to write a few verses upon the moonlight on Yarmouth seas; but though he could not conceive of the thought of the girl he had met in the train ever making him cross, or of his own attempting to write verses to the music of the rolling wheels through which they had talked together, he had no question at all in his mind on the point that this was as the deepest romance he had ever encountered. I do not mean that he analyzed it all, in the very least. He analyzed nothing — least of all himself. But he was just aware of her, as of music, during the whole of that morning: he talked with his fellow clerks; he added up his columns: he carried in checks to be signed; he stood patiently on the Turkey-carpet behind the mahogany table while his chief signed the checks. And the whole while her presence was with him, as a perfume or a strain.

Yet he had arrived at no further facts about her at all. She had told him absolutely nothing, except that she lived on that railway line; he had no clue to her name, or her occupation, or her friends, or her home — beyond the clue of a monogram which he could not read, but which, on consideration, he thought bore a G somewhere in the midst of the silver tangle.

(3)

He consulted Reggie at lunch, but with great diplomacy and aloofness.

"By the way," he said, "I traveled up with a girl this morning, and couldn't make out what she was."

Reggie looked his inquiries over a sandwich.

"Very pretty indeed," said Percy, with a superbly dispassionate air. "Very well-dressed and all that, and had a little dressing-bag. But third-class."

"I thought you had a second season?"

"Yes, but I had to get in anywhere. Only just caught the train, and tumbled over the bag. Well, we got talking. Nice girl! But I couldn't make her out. Traveling alone;

quite poor: had an engagement at ten: always lived near
Croydon till lately. So I suppose she comes up to town
every day."

"Typist," suggested Reggie.

Percy shook his head.

"Too well-dressed — too cheerful. Not that sort."

"Milliner?"

"My dear chap, she was a lady."

"Give it up," said Reggie. "You want Sherlock Holmes!"

It perplexed Percy a good deal, and the more he thought
of it the more he was perplexed. No profession with which
he was acquainted seemed to fit her at all; and yet he had
an idea that she was not of independent means, chiefly
because she had such an exceedingly independent air.

He did his work quite badly that afternoon. Drowsiness
was always the enemy after lunch, and drowsiness, rein-
forced by violent preoccupation, was irresistible. He received a rebuke from the bald head-clerk. And he went
away at last to Liverpool Street, without any tea, in the
vague hope of meeting her again on the platform.

(4)

Percy was in two minds as to whether or no he should
let out at home, as if unconsciously, that he meant to go to
a Catholic Church on Sunday. Honestly he was not quite
sure as to the attitude of his parents towards that ancient
denomination: it was not discussed; there was no Catholic
Church at all in the neighborhood; there was no particular reason why it should be discussed.

There was nothing tonight in Hanstead to take him
away from home. On three nights out of four there usually
was something — either a choir practice, or a
whist-drive,[1] or a social evening, or an amateur concert. It
was an extremely sociable place, within limits.

He ran into Mr. Main as he came up the High Street.
Mr. Main was walking very fast as usual, with his trousers turned up and a flat hat on his head of such a cut as
to make it appear as if he had no crown to his head at all;
and he turned his eyes from side to side as he came, in a

---

[1] A social event at which progressive games of whist, a card
game similar to bridge, are played.

manner which his critics called underhand, but which, as
a matter of fact, arose from nothing except a shy self-
consciousness. Mr. Main was always afraid of saluting the
wrong people and of neglecting those who saluted him.
Percy waved a hand towards his own hat in a manner calculated to show respect, yet not adulation, and Mr. Main
waved back to him from across the street.

Aha! Good evening to you!" cried Mr. Main.

"Going to have rain!" bawled Percy.

"Aha! Yes, I think so," cried Mr. Main.

Percy was beginning to be old enough to feel compassion
for Mr. Main, and to understand the dreariness of the
poor man's position. People were rude to the curate sometimes; there was no question of that. The Mayor never
dreamed of giving him more of a salute than he gave to a
tradesman, though he took his hat entirely off to the
Vicar. Even as Percy turned round at the door to find his
key he heard a remark bellowed at the curate down the
street by a hobbledehoy,[2] and saw Mr. Main still walking
very fast, swinging his umbrella with an air of obviously
assumed unconsciousness. Poor Mr. Main! And with that
wife of his too!

The dining room in Hanstead House was as correct as
everything else in it. It was papered in dark red, with a
dark red carpet. It had a mahogany sideboard with a mahogany wine-cooler that was never used, underneath it. It
had a black marble clock in the middle of the black marble mantelpiece, flanked by two semi-recumbent bronze
female figures. It had a large engraving of Luke Fildes'
"The Doctor" over the mantelpiece, and two oil portraits
on the other walls. There was a writing table between the
windows at which a letter could be written in emergen-
cies. It was all perfectly comfortable and quite dull, and
entirely what a dining room should be. The woodwork was
all painted a chocolate brown.

It was here that the four sat down to dinner at half-past
seven — Mrs. Brandreth-Smith with her back to the windows, her husband opposite to her, with his back to the
fire, and the children on either side. Helen was in a new

---

[2] A gawky, adolescent boy.

dress, very Greek-looking indeed, with sleeves cut short at the elbows. They were waited upon by Alice, a perfectly correct-look-ing maid with an anxious face.

Of course, there was nothing at all to talk about. Nobody had any news; everyone knew everyone else's experiences perfectly. Helen talked a little about a new student (female) she had had tea with that day. The doctor made some remarks about the Mayor's scheme for the Queen Victoria fountain; Percy observed that he had seen Mr. Main just now; Mrs. Brandreth-Smith assented to what was said and kept a roving eye upon the table and Alice. No one was dressed for dinner, really; there was no conceivable reason why they should be: the doctor wore his frockcoat: Percy, a short black jacket and waistcoat over his gray trousers; his mother wore a black satin bodice over her black cloth skirt.

And then, suddenly, by one of those coincidences that really do make it appear as if one mind can affect many, Helen opened out on a piece of gossip, just as the bread and butter pudding was set on the table.

"I saw a Catholic priest in the High Street tonight," she said.

"How do you know he was a priest?" asked Percy.

"One of the Irish boys called him 'Father' just as I went by. He was asking his way to Sloan's End."

Sloan's End was one of the little corners of the parish that grieved the Vicar's heart, since it was inhabited chiefly by Irish who entirely refused to come to his church, and who, on Saturday evenings, were sometimes a little noisy. Besides, they wouldn't salute him in the street.

"I didn't like the look of him," said Helen judicially. "He didn't look like a gentleman."

The doctor roused himself.

"Sloan's End? Oh, yes, there's a woman dying there. That'll be what brought him. I must say these priests look after their poor wonderfully."

"Well, I didn't like the look of him," persisted Helen.

"And I don't know what they want to bother dying people for. I'm sure I shan't want a clergyman to come and see me when I'm dying. It seems to me a stuffy sort of thing to want."

"Hush, my dear!" said her mother.

It was a very typical evening for these four. They drank soup made out of a shin of beef; ate some shoulder of mutton with boiled potatoes and cabbage, and bread and butter pudding, some cheese and some apples. Plates were taken away and other plates substituted. By each plate stood a tumbler and a red wine glass. The doctor drank a single glass of sherry, and Percy a bottle of fizzy beer; and when dinner was over, and Alice had filled up each wine glass with water, they all went away to the drawing room and sat grouped about the thick black mat that lay before the fire. Percy spread out his legs and smoked a single Virginia cigarette; the doctor took up *The Nation*,[3] which, as an earnest Liberal, he read through every week and regarded as an oracle; Mrs. Brandreth-Smith, when she returned from her nightly visit to the kitchen, opened her work basket and began to sew; Helen fetched a large drawing board and propped it on the arms of her upright chair. Each of them made a small remark now and then of no interest whatever. Percy, looking rather moody, first decided to say nothing about his excursion on Sunday till it was all over, and then gave himself to pondering over the girl he had met in the train.

It was a typical evening. None of them, except perhaps Helen, were really interested at all in their occupations. Yet upon them all had descended a Scheme of Life that

[3] At the time *An Average Man* was written, *The Nation* was a Liberal Party newspaper. It was founded in March 1907 by the radical journalist H. W. Massingham. In the First World War Massingham changed *The Nation* from a Liberal journal to supporting Labour, switching from a newspaper supporting political democracy, to one supporting economic socialism, and agitated for a negotiated peace. John Maynard Keynes headed a group that purchased *The Nation* in 1923. As Keynes was believed to be a supporter of the Liberal Party, Massingham resigned. Later in the 1920s after Keynes's socialism became evident, Keynes suggested that *The Nation* merge with *The New Statesman*, edited by his friend Kingsley Martin. Over the next decade *The New Statesman & Nation* formed the opinion of England's intellectual elite.

gave them no choice except to submit — a scheme which tightened its grip on them every month that went by, and was gradually crushing out every elastic instinct that they possessed. The doctor doctored because it was his profession; his wife managed her household because it was her household; Percy went up to the City and did accounts, because there was nothing else for him to do; and even Helen, though just now she did rather enjoy what she believed to be an artistic life, would presently find that even that was no more than a convention; her Greek costumes would cease to seem odd or bold; her ideas of art would become formulae which, having learned rigorously, she would teach to others with equal rigor. There was no spice in life anywhere, no sting of conviction, no ardor of enterprise. The one soul among them who had real competence in her work was the mother, and she had no scope. There was everything necessary to Life, except Life itself.

Chapter V

(1)

Outside, in the warm September sunshine that cut half across the narrow street opening downwards out of the High Street, Kensington, a steadily increasing drift of vehicles choked the thoroughfare; and the crush was further aggravated by the stream of pedestrians that grew, circled and eddied round the church door. The church was nothing to look at. The end that abutted on the pavement was a façade of white brick, gradually darkening under London smoke. It had a wide, low west door, over which stood in a niche a stone statue of the Poor Man of Assisi, and above that again a large oval-topped window of clear glass. Two shallow steps led up to the door. It was quite an ugly place, but quite simple; it had Poverty visible all over it.

The clock from St. Mary Abbot's higher up struck the half-hour. A minute later the doors shook and then opened, revealing a smiling young man in a brown habit. The crowd swayed and surged forward, and began to disappear within the dark opening like a stream sucked under an arch.

Within, in the big bare house behind the church, Father Hilary was preparing for his sermon. He was in his cell on the first floor, and that cell contained precisely the following articles and no more:

A low bed, covered with a brown blanket, stood along one wall. A table stood by the window, holding writing materials, a thick book of ms. notes and a Bible. In the corner furthest from the bed hung a curtain of red serge, and, behind it, Father Hilary's second habit and a few clothes such as he wore out of his monastery. Finally, there was a chair drawn up opposite the black iron radiator, and in it sat Father Hilary, quite motionless, with closed eyes. There was no washing apparatus in the room — all such things were done in the public lavatory across the passage. The room was lighted, when necessary, by a gas burner that projected over the radiator. There was no carpet, there were no curtains. There was nothing else at all in the room, except a crucifix over the bed.

He remained quite motionless with closed eyes until the clock below struck three strokes. Then he opened his eyes and stood up.

He was close upon six feet tall. He was dressed in the brown frock of the Capuchins, with its long hood and its cord, and his bare feet were in sandals. He could not have been more than twenty-six or twenty-seven, and his light brown beard was silky and soft. But his eyes were the most remarkable feature of his face, very large, very wide open, and of a startling sunny blue. So he stood a moment, his lips still moving, with the abstracted look on his face not yet gone. Then he went across his cell, opened the door and went out.

The corridor outside was as plain as the cells within. There was nothing in it at all from end to end, except two radiators and a statue in a wooden niche. He went along this corridor and turned down the stairs; pushed open a swing door, went down a couple of steps, passing on his right a door set wide into the garden at the east of the church; walked along another passage or two, up some more stairs, passing on the way, in silence, another figure dressed like himself, and found himself in a little upstairs choir, with lances windows looking straight out upon the high altar. There he knelt down again and remained motionless.

Father Hilary had had a singularly uneventful life. His mother was Welsh, and he had helped her in her little Cardiff shop out of school-hours until the age of fourteen. Then he had offered himself to the Capuchins, had been accepted, and thenceforward had vanished entirely from the world until just before his profession eight years later. Then he had come home again for a vacation, and to consider himself, and to recover from an illness that threatened him. He had recovered, and gone back again to the novitiate in North Wales. Four years later his mother, at great cost to herself, had traveled north from Cardiff with all her luggage in a single bundle; had been present at his ordination to the priesthood, had kissed his hands and received his blessing; had assisted at his first Mass and received Holy Communion from him. Then, in an ecstasy of pain and happiness, she had returned to her shop in Cardiff, and had seen him no more. But she knew that she had for a son a priest and a friar. . . .

A year or two later Father Hilary had been sent to London, and here the surprises began. For within six months after his first sermon he had a reputation sufficiently great to draw at least a third of his congregation from other parishes, and six months after that special tickets had to be issued whenever he preached.

But the surprise chiefly lay in the fact that the matter of his sermons was not at all original: he was never hailed as a thinker by anyone at all. It is true that reporters had tried more than once (in vain) to get an interview with him; but that was out of sheer curiosity. He never said anything particularly profound or startling; he was never cynical, never epigrammatic. He knew nothing at all of the world, in the ordinary sense of the word; but he appeared to know a great deal about the next, and spoke as if he lived there — which he probably did. The charm of him apparently lay in his amazing and overwhelming simplicity and the personality that lay behind it. Certainly he was sensational in the pulpit sometimes; that is to say, he called certain practices Sins, and named them by their names. But he did not always provide even such sensationalism as this. For the most part, he preached about the Love of God and the Passion of Jesus Christ and the joy of renunciation — such sermons as might be preached — up to a certain point — by Salvation Army captains. He bore himself quietly in the pulpit, using only such gestures as were obviously natural to him. And yet — here were these motors, these polished broughams, this crowd of foot passengers. Here was the church beneath him already humming like a hive; here was Brother George holding up a cord at the end of the center aisle and Brother Francis dancing to and fro on his sandaled feet in a hopeless endeavor to crowd seventeen hundred persons into a church built for fourteen hundred. And meanwhile Father Hilary kneeled alone at the lances window upstairs, staring out at the wooden altar, the wooden gilded candlesticks and the little white-curtained tabernacle.

(2)

For the last twenty minutes Percy had been like a cat in a strange room. Every fiber of him was alive and sensitive: he smelled the peculiar smell of rich ladies — furs and silk and eau-de-cologne; he listened to violently whispered expostulations from seat-holders before and behind, and the endless rattle of footsteps on the bare wood-paved aisles; he felt the pressure of a stout lady on one side and a lean man on the other, who sat forward with his elbows out; and he eyed incessantly every detail of places, persons and things that were within his vision.

Of course he was chiefly absorbed by the lay brothers and the altar. The altar he did not think much of: it was only of very common stained wood, and the wooden, gilded candlesticks had no particular brilliancy of outline or color. Between the candlesticks were two large white earthenware vases filled with artificial flowers. It seemed to him to be (as, indeed, it was) very cheap and common. There was nothing else sensational in view — except occasionally a friar, as Brother Francis darted up the aisle with a new convoy. But he had seen two or three statues on the way up to his place, that he had dismissed with the same epithets as those which he applied to the altar — one of a friar with a labeled money-box in front of him, and a child in his arms — all of evident plaster; and one of a barefooted woman in a confusing dress of black and brown holding some kind of gilded object in her hands.

But the lay brothers were the point. They were no statues; they were living facts, here, in Kensington, in the twentieth century; real human beings who were dressed in brown robes and had real bare feet. It appeared to him incredible. . . . He craned in his place once or twice to catch a sight again of Brother Francis' bare feet. . . .

The chief emotion he had, at present, was that of oddness. He was not awed, he was not frightened, he was not fascinated, he merely found it all very odd. By the time that the organ began to play he had begun to propound a theory to himself — namely, that the dress of friars was really no more than a kind of cassock which they wore in church in order to make a sensation; at other times, probably, they wore coats and trousers like other people.

Through that door, there, where a face occasionally appeared, and whence, once, a complete friar issued forth, life was probably very much what it was elsewhere. It was incredible that people really lived, here and now, in Kensington, in the kind of way in which (he understood) friars and monks had lived in the Middle Ages. It was probably, he thought, rather like college life. Dim memories of comic pictures began to come back to him — of red-faced friars and barrels of wine; of smoking dishes in a refectory; of stout abbots with miters. Obviously that kind of thing must have stopped long ago . . . it had been put an end to by Henry VIII, he thought.

The organ rose louder; a door opened somewhere; and then to his amazement, Reggie, also in a brown dress, with a very short surplice, came out with a taper. He seemed quite at home, thought Percy, and highly self-conscious; he went up to the altar, performed a curious movement there, and began to light the candles. Then once more he disappeared; and an instant later out came a little procession with three men in white and shining robes in the midst. . . .

(3)

It is not necessary to say more, as to the effect of the first part of the Mass upon Percy, than that he grew more bewildered and more repelled every moment. It seemed to him the most confusing, the most unintelligible, and the most meaningless ceremony he had ever looked upon. These three men went to and fro without cause and without excuse. No sooner had they formed one figure than they broke it again; now they were in line, now in single file; now one turned round to bellow an incoherent gabble of words; then, turning, he ducked again in an absurd manner. It seemed to Percy that the half had not been told him of the superstitious mummery of Rome; it was not even pleasing to human senses; and as to its acceptability before God —!

Percy compared it with the service that he ought to have been engaged in himself — the service proceeding at this very moment, in far-away Hanstead — this dark, cheap altar with the gracious brass-glimmering white stone east end of St. James'; these posturing, mouthing

men with the Vicar in his clean surplice and Oxford hood
and white stole, and Mr. Main in his no less clean surplice
and his Durham hood; this bellowed unintelligible Latin,
with the well-turned sentences of morning-prayer and lit-
any. Above all he compared the murmurous, incoherent
roaring of the hidden men's choir with his own dear
"Gadsby in C." . . . And he had expected so much: he had
expected almost to have to guard himself against the se-
ductive strains and the languorous harmonies and the so-
norous Latin and the nerve-entrancing perfumes. He had
expected a dark, jeweled sanctuary, an hieratic celebrant
splendid in mystery and cloth of gold. He had heard endlessly of the glamour of Rome and the plain, honest simplicity of Anglicanism. . . . Well, if this were glamour, he
preferred simplicity.

When at last the three white men retired to the side
and sat down, Percy leaned back in his seat with scarcely
an illusion left.

He paid no great attention to Father Hilary at first,
when that friar first appeared in the pulpit. Certainly he
looked a fresh, decent sort of man, thought Percy; and he
listened, scarcely aware that it was this man whom he
had come to hear, to an endless and quite unintelligible
series of notices. He heard a list of names read out with
the mention of certain days on which "the Holy Sacrifice
would be offered" for this and that individual: some observations on something called a "novena" and something
else about an "indulgence" that "could be gained on the
usual terms." He pricked up his ears a little at this.
Reggie had told him that an indulgence did not mean a
paid-for permission to commit sin; but it seemed as if this
sounded uncommonly like it.

Finally Father Hilary laid the book aside and faced the
congregation. There was first a rustle, and then a deep,
absorbed silence. Then the friar uttered these words:

"I am sure that neither death, nor life, nor angels, nor
principalities, nor powers, nor things present, nor things
to come, nor might, nor height, nor depth, nor any other
creature shall be able to separate us from the love of God
which is in Christ Jesus our Lord. Words taken from the
thirty-eight and thirty-ninth verses of the eighth chapter

of the epistle of Saint Paul to the Romans. In the Name of the Father and of the Son and of the Holy Ghost. Amen."

Chapter VI

Alittle after half-past twelve Percy Brandreth-Smith pushed his way patiently out through the crowd, detached himself from the stragglers on the pavement, and set out to walk eastwards. He had told them at home, after a very diplomatic mention of the fact that he was going to hear a preacher in the West-end whose name he had forgotten, that he would get something to eat for himself, and wouldn't be back till tea. So he had three or four hours to himself.

His first determination was that he must walk, fast and far. Eating must take care of itself. Perhaps he would have something later on; perhaps not. At any rate he could not face Reggie just now; he had half-intended to suggest their lunching together. But that was impossible. He must be alone; he must sort himself out. . . .

For that thing had happened which does occasionally happen at the reading of a book, at the meeting of a new friend or at the hearing of a sermon. That thing had happened to Percy which appears at first to be an entire overturning of the whole scheme of life, to be a revelation of a completely new set of facts whose existence had never been suspected.

. First, he had never in all his life heard a sermon which in the smallest degree resembled that to which he had listened just now. Sermons, up to that point in his life — since he had experience only of the most moderate of Anglicanism — had signified the reading of some manuscript pages or, at the best, the delivery of a discourse with the help of notes, sometimes tolerable in its interest, sometimes intolerable in its dullness. These sermons had been sometimes the careful exposition of a sentence of Scripture, with a moral exhortation at the end; sometimes they were descriptive and drew pictures of scenes in the Holy Land with a group of unconvincing persons, who tripped over their long robes (if stained glass windows were trustworthy), in the foreground; sometimes they were argumentative settings forth of doctrines that never erred through the immoderateness of their demands upon the mind, and all ended with a moral exhortation.

This sermon had been entirely different. There was no manuscript; there was no application at the end beginning with some such sentence as: "And now, my dear brethren, let us see how this all comes home to ourselves here and now." It had been a steady rapid utterance, even conversational at times, dealing with familiar old facts indeed — but dealing with them in a wholly different way; treating them as if they were as much facts as tables and chairs and as real as falling in love; not as if they were a series of propositions, true indeed, but true as the higher branches of mathematics are true or the simpler formulae of chemistry — true apart from what all human beings know as the experiences of their conscious life.

Secondly, these truths appeared to be part of the very fabric of the preacher's own life. The Love of God, on which he had preached — that Love which hitherto Percy, as a good boy, had taken for granted much as he took for granted the distance from the earth to the sun — appeared, instead, to be as much a fact as the sunlight on earth. It was conditioned for us and presented to us, the preacher had remarked, in the life of Jesus Christ; in fact, the text said as much. It is therefore not only by the imitation of Christ but by actual union with Him that this Love becomes and remains the driving force of the soul. It sounds bald, put like that; yet bald was the very last word that could be applied to the enunciation by Father Hilary. For it appeared to Percy, as he listened, that this extraordinary personality in the pulpit, this tender face, those radiant, serene eyes, and this clear, artless voice — all these things through which that personality had seized upon and affected him from the very moment that the text was finished, were what they were because they lived and moved and drew their being from precisely that which was the subject of the sermon — the "Love of God which is in Christ Jesus our Lord."

It was this personality, of course, that had done the work. There was not one single thought in the sermon — except a few at the end — on which Percy could not have passed a theological examination a week ago. These few at the end, however, had interested him intensely: for it appeared from them that there was in the Catholic Religion a system of what were called Sacraments — sacraments that sounded, somehow, quite different from those "two generally necessary to salvation" with which he was acquainted — by which this union with Jesus Christ (which, in its turn, meant a union with the Love of God) could be promoted and consummated. This was what had been said; but it was the personality that had mattered — the personality in which these things seemed embodied, like sunlight in clear water.

Briefly, then, that had been his experience. But it meant enormously more to him, psychologically. That had happened to him which can, as has been said, only be described by saying that it appeared to him as if his whole life had been turned upside-down. All the things that had seemed to him important, appeared now unimportant — his office work, his home — little imaginative dramas that he acted to himself. And all the things that had seemed unimportant — religious doctrines, the way he behaved, his attitude towards people, and, above all, towards the Personage whom he called God — these appeared vital, overwhelming and entrancing.

The event that had happened to him is called, sometimes, Conversion. . . .

(2)

Halfway up the Long Walk in Kensington Gardens he began to be able to formulate some of those things to himself; and to see how completely values had been changed for him. Up to that point he had been aware of nothing except that something seemed to have emerged from himself whose existence he had not previously even suspected — emerged, as a slender winged creature emerges shivering and iridescent from dark water into warm sunshine. And this creature began to shake out and unfold its wings, and colors to throb and mature in every part of its body.

If he had been questioned closely at this point, he would have said that the Person of Jesus Christ had become real to him, as suddenly as if a picture had come alive. The preacher had told him nothing on the matter which he

had not known before; but it appeared to him as if all he
had known had been but a mask. Now the mask was
dropped. This new Person had qualities he had not previously dreamed of. He was no longer the pained, meek Person he had thought Him . . . He was huge and virile and
infinitely tender . . . He was everything that was worth
anything. . . . He was the Heart of all color, the Melody of
all music, the Perfection of all shape, the Essence of all
sweetness . . . Another name for Him was the Love of God.
. . . The Love of God was not, then, a bland, impersonal
atmosphere, after all: it was a Person without the limitations of Personality but with all its reality . . . . And this
Person stood now in the midst of a System which previously Percy had called "Romanism." . . . He thought he
began to understand this now. The ceremonies he had
seen were still as unintelligible as ever; but their very un-
intelligibilities had become as significant as court etiquette. They were, taken by themselves, as foolish as the
gestures of a signaler with a flag, until it is perceived that
they have a purpose; then, even though the purpose is not
known, nor the message, they become oddly eloquent and
attractive. It all meant something. He saw that now.
Whereas the very intelligibility — the intellectuality, so to
speak — of his own Anglican worship — the fact that he
understood and followed every word of the Book of Common Prayer; the complete reasonableness; the weighed
sentences; the careful and expressive intonation of the
reader's voice — all the plainness and intelligibility of
these things suggested that there was nothing expressed
by them that the intellect could not apprehend, and therefore nothing that could be abjectly worshiped. It was like
passing from the study of a Republican President, to the
antechamber of a crowned and anointed King. . . .

Then Percy began to see that the whole of life was different forever and ever. He might have to go on doing the
same things; he had no alternative program to suggest;
but they could never be the same. He began to perceive,
incoherently at first, and more clearly later, that the
"things" he did had become, simultaneously, of infinite
value and weight and of no importance at all. It did not
matter what he did, or what the outer details of his life

were, so long as they were permissible by the New Law; it mattered vitally and eternally why and how he did them. . . . This is a cold and passionless analysis of what was, as a matter of fact, now making this boy's heart to beat and his nerves to tingle.

As he considered these things, still walking as on springs, he saw people go past him: couples walking together; three children with a nurse; a rider or two far across the meadows; a boy in a frilled collar throwing a stick for a retriever to fetch. He heard the usual sounds: the roll of wheels, voices, the soft wind in the evergreens. He was conscious of the sunlight on his face, of the breeze on his left cheek; he looked down at his own feet moving below his knees. And these things, too, appeared to have become new. . . .

He thought of the preacher's face sometimes, pallid against the dark pillar, lit by the eyes; of the intonations of his voice. It seemed astonishing to him that the whole world did not know of all these things.

For Percy had no struggle of the intellect at all. The words he had heard and the statements and arguments — (though these had been very few) — found no intellectual obstacles in the boy's mind. He had never even questioned the main dogmas of Christianity: he had accepted them always, since they had been taught to him. So there was no intellectual struggle. It was simply that the great bare structure that he had called Christianity — an affair of poles and ropes and frames, barely disguised with a few sentimental wreaths here and there — had blazed out into fire. There had been no damp doubts to check the conflagration. It had all flared up into glory together, vast and triumphant and dominant.

So his mind went round and round, retreading in its own steps without fatigue. It is as indescribable as falling in love. It is more indescribable, since it cannot be reduced to terms of flesh and blood or of a materialistic philosophy. It comes to some, in a measure, under other aspects; it comes in the Quaker meeting house and at the penitent form of the Salvation Army; but it comes to none with the same vastness of appeal as in Catholicism — to none with the same simultaneous assault along every line

of human nature at once — along the intellect, by the way
of theology; along the heart by the way of the affections;
along the Will in the name of Obedience. He dimly saw
this. He understood that there was an enormous Creed
which he would have to master — if, indeed, this way was
for him; a discipline of the heart and a training of the will.
He saw that History played its part, and philosophy, and
things to eat and drink, and prayers to say. He saw that
there was no part of common life which would not have to
be affected.

Then he put all this away. This was not his business.
Besides, the thing was too great altogether, and also not
great enough. There was only one thing that mattered —
more real to him than the sunlight which was its symbol
and the breeze that was the illustration of the Way of the
Spirit — the Love of God which is in Jesus Christ our
Lord.

(3)

He had reduced his raging turmoil of happy bewilderment to some kind of coherence by the time that he got
into the slow Sunday train for Hanstead, and he looked
upon his fellow-creatures now with a completely unconscious contempt.

These people — this group of loud-voiced young men in
black coats with buttonholes; that dismal family party of
father and mother and three children — all this strange
jetsam that the Sunday tide throws up in the terminal
stations; the bleak-looking woman selling *Lloyd's News*
behind a counter — these people did not understand at
all. He felt like a dragonfly looking down on grubs that
had once been his fellows. . . .

He had arrived at some sort of coherence. First, he must
be entirely different at home. Now that the "Love of God
which is in Christ Jesus" had displayed itself, he must
give up once for all that tiresome, critical, prickly attitude
that had grown on him of late. But, of course, he would
give it up: it was gone already. It was unthinkable.

Next, he must be exceedingly conscientious about his
work . . . he must not draw pictures on the blotting paper
any more. . . .

Next, a certain entire plane of imagination must cease. It had ceased. It was unthinkable. Fourthly, he must say his prayers always . . . not less than a quarter of an hour every morning and evening. Fifthly, he must go to Evening Prayer after tea — (that reminded him; he hadn't had any lunch: he had walked all the way to Liverpool Street instead) — and sing in "Gadsby in C."

Sixthly, he must convey to his family — one by one if possible — where he had been and . . . and what had happened to him.

These things, then, he pondered, looking dreamily out at the stations where the train stopped, sitting all alone in a third-class carriage, with his hands pressed between his knees. He thought once or twice of the girl over whose bag he had tripped last Thursday, though from an infinitely remote distance of emotion; and wondered whether she knew all about those things too. . . . He supposed not. . . . He pictured himself telling her. . . . He wondered whether he could make her understand. . . . He supposed not.

Anyhow, it did not matter. He understood, at least.

Chapter VII

Helen had gone out to tea with an artistic friend, and, retiring upstairs with her afterwards, had sat on the hearthrug of her friend's bed-sitting room, and discussed the narrowness of the world, of Hanstead, and of religious people in particular.

"Did you ever know such a place?" she said. "Very nearly all the only people of our sort are entirely wrapped up in St. James' and the Vicar. Of course, Father's a church warden, and that makes it worse for me. . . . I . . . I *hate* church."

The friend cooed sympathetically.

"Then there's Percy," went on Helen discontentedly. "He's in the City all day, and I do think the City absolutely deadly. And then when he's at home he's always busy, and when he isn't busy he's singing in that beastly choir. It's only the music he cares about, you know: he isn't a bit pious, really; but it's just as bad as if he was. Oh! he's a good boy: I know that. I sometimes almost wish he wasn't."

Then Helen launched out into her gospel. It was the convention of unconventionality; and there is nothing more conventional. The ideal life appeared to her to consist in living in a particular sort of house, almost precisely the opposite of the house in which she happened to live: there must be a great deal of whitewash in it, and red tiles, and rough- cast, and copper fireplaces. There must be large bare rooms, with floors stained with permanganate of potash,[1] and rugs on the top of it. It must have divans; there must be leaded lights in the windows, and doors of stained deal; there must be a large "studio," with plaster casts on a shelf all round it. There must be little oak beds in the bedrooms and a green-tiled bathroom. There must be an orchard all round it, with anemones in

---

[1] An efficient and cost-effective antiseptic, often used in treating fungal infections. It has the unfortunate side-effect of staining the treated area purple.

the grass in springtime, and a stream running through it, and a perpetual liquid sunshine.

"I don't want a big house," she had said modestly, "with estates and responsibilities, and . . . and . . . *mariages de . . . de* — what's the word? . . . Oh! Yes — *convenance*. All that's as stifling as a suburb. I don't want any servants at all, or horses, or motors. I wouldn't use them if I had them. No; just a *little house,* of the right kind — artistic, you know."

The details of the life to be lived there were a little vague. She, and the ideal friend with whom she must live, must, of course, cook for themselves and wear Greek-looking costumes: they must be fearless artists and paint what they really saw: they would recreate themselves with gardening and housework, and the reading out of books that were bound in olive-colored leather. They must never go to church. They must find their religion in the clean, innocent things of earth and water and air. It was all immensely spiritual and unspeakably superior.

She did not say quite all this, but this was more or less the vision behind her speech, and the friend listened rapturously. Helen illustrated it by references to what it must not be, taking the awful examples of such households as that of the Vicarage or of Mr. Main's. These stood to her (with her own home) as types of Philistinism; they were respectable in the wrong way; they were religious and conventional.

"I can't conceive what the inside of that man's mind is like," she said, referring to Mr. Main's. "I picture it like the inside of a station waiting room." (Her friend gasped at the brilliancy of the comparison.) "It's got useful seats to sit down upon, and a square table in the middle, and a time table on the walls; and no fire; and a bottle of flat water and a glass on the chimney piece. And it's absolutely dreary and drab-colored. I wouldn't be that man for . . . for nuts. And then Mrs. Main lives there always, you know."

There was a pause.

Mrs. Main may be said to be the one person whom Helen really hated — whom she hated so much that she seldom said so. She was, as has been said, a little, bitter, fierce woman, rather hollow-eyed and tragic, and a very great deal more capable than Helen suspected. But the reason Helen hated her was because the elder woman ignored her as if she were a child, and refused to admire or to sympathize. She had been quite rude to her once at least, in this kind of way.

"Well — and about the Vicar?" said the friend, who was of the adoring kind, and thought Helen in great form this evening.

"The Vicar?" reflected Helen, staring into the little coal fire and stroking her ankle. "Oh! He's like a little new drawing room, furnished by contract. It's all quite complete, down to the oil pictures of waterfalls and the blue mat and the proper books in the revolving bookcase. He's a bright little man, and quite competent in his own little way: he knows a little about everything; but Lord! The futility of it all. It doesn't amount to anything."

And then Helen began on theology, until the tubular bells began to peal outside.

(2)

She got to church a little late with her friend, and slipped into a seat near the door. It was considered proper for her to go, since her father was the Vicar's warden, and she was not yet emancipated enough to refuse. Her mother was quite resolute on the point, and when that was so there was no more to be said.

As a matter of fact, too, she rather enjoyed it, since she had an unequaled opportunity there for despising (in a youthful and comparatively harmless manner) everyone in sight. She despised the Vicar in his Oxford hood, the curate in his humbler Durham hood, the choir in their surplices, and the congregation, of whom she saw little this evening except the backs of their heads. She despised the white stone and the bricks and the ironwork and the candlesticks and the altar-frontal. It all seemed to her conventional and narrow and meaningless and Philistine: she thought with an exquisite superiority of her ideal house amidst its orchards.

It was during the *Magnificat* (to "Gadsby in C") that she first noticed Percy, and was surprised by the look on his face. She hadn't seen him since breakfast, and he looked, she thought, a little tired or overwrought. Perhaps he had walked too far, she thought . . . . Really he looked rather nice, though, in his surplice up there in the choir stalls — rather distinguished, with his clean profile, his curly dark hair and his dark eyes. . . .

Mr. Main preached, all about Ahab. She attended in a kind of fierce contempt for about five minutes, marveling that any man could be so dreary, could say such banal things and avoid with what was very nearly a kind of genius a single interesting or attractive thought. His jaws moved solemnly in enunciation; his eyes were downcast; his hand, trembling a little, appeared at regular intervals and turned a page. Then she half-closed her eyes and began to think about copper fire-hoods.

The Vesper hymn (sung kneeling) betrayed her very nearly into sentimentalism. The windows were all but dark; there was just a glimmer behind them like the light of a dying fire; the gas burned with clear radiance; the surplices shone; the brasswork sparkled; while from the organ, heard in pauses and short intermediate passages, came the sound of aerial bleating, with a tremolo, as if ten thousand goats wailed together from a distance of five miles in luscious, languorous harmonies.

Then Mr. Bennett elevated the alms-dish, as if in sacrifice, and sang a blessing.

Percy joined her as she waited in the dark evening outside. The others had gone on home.

She had forgotten all about his looking tired, and greeted him with genial friendliness. But the instant he spoke she remembered.

"Yes, I've had a good time," he said. "We've got half an hour before supper. I wish you'd come a little walk. I've got something to tell you." He spoke with a curious solemnity.

"But —"

"I want to tell you before I tell Father and Mother, and I must tell them this evening."

She was silent. This was a completely new side of Percy.

(3)

All through supper she kept on glancing at him when he
wasn't looking, in complete bewilderment. She did not
even yet understand one half of all that he had tried to
tell her as they picked their way in the dusk through the
nursery gardens on the north of the High Street. It
seemed to her incredible and very nearly indecent. But
she had controlled herself: she had spoken in short sentences rather breathlessly; and had nodded for assent. He
had had a burst of humanity at the end.

"I expect this seems to you hopelessly foolish. . . . Well,
so it would have to me yesterday."

"And you're going to tell them tonight?" she asked after
a silence.

"Yes," he said. "What d'you suppose Mother will say?"

She shook her head. That was the point in both their
minds. Their father could be managed; but they were not
so sure about their mother.

All this appeared to the girl, then, simply unintelligible.
She was aware that such things happened to people of the
lower classes — these strange, emotional, almost inhuman brainstorms; and she had been no more puzzled by
these than by other habits of the same class, such as getting drunk and singing loud on Bank holidays. But that it
should take Percy, her own brother, like this! (That was
the phrase she used to herself. He seemed to "have got
them badly," she said to herself.) That he should speak
about God and Grace and a new life! It was all jargon to
her.

But the crisis would come, she knew, when he told all
this at home. He would have to be more explicit then; he
would have to make some kind of a coherent defense; and
what would his mother say?

He was silent during supper, except when he was directly questioned. Once, when his father asked him outright where he had been all day, he answered that he
wished to tell them all about that afterwards. And he had
said this in a manner that made both his parents look up
at him and then down again, and say no more.

He was surprisingly brisk and useful at supper. He had
their plates on the sideboard, and the cold sweets ranged

before his mother, with unusual speed. He passed the
sugar before he was asked, and had his hand on the bell
push before his mother told him to ring for hot water. And
all through his face was of the same steady paleness
which Helen had noticed in church, and his brown eyes
were soft and bright. Certainly he "had them very badly."

The moment came when his mother had sat down in the
easy chair in the drawing room, and his father had taken
up the Sunday paper and immediately laid it down again.
It was evident that they too were aware that some kind of
a revelation was coming. Helen sat far back out of the cir-
cle of light and watched.

Percy poked the fire with great deliberateness.

"A little more coal," said his mother.

He put the coal on; lingered a little over its bestowal.
Then he suddenly laid the tongs down, went straight to
his chair opposite his father, and began, as if in desperation.

"It was a Roman Catholic Church I went to today," said
Percy. "It was the first time I've ever been in one, to a
service at least. I went with Reggie Ballard."

There was silence.

Helen saw her father's face, first downcast with pursed
lips, glance sharply up at his wife. It was a very little and
melancholy face, of a dusky complexion, with little discreet whiskers. He made no movement after another
glance at his son's face and away again. She looked at her
mother. That lady also was motionless, with rather a rig-
orous look in her face.

Then Percy burst out all at once, leaning suddenly forward, with his hands gripping his knees. An extraordinarily tense look was in his eyes and the lines of his mouth.

"It's no good," he said. "I can't beat about the bush. The
fact is that I was entirely knocked over by the sermon. It
wasn't the least what I expected. . . . All I know is that I
was knocked over . . . once and for all. It was a monk who
preached, at least a friar. Everybody's going to hear him:
the place was crammed. Well: I was knocked over. I . . . I
suppose you'd call it conversion. All I know is that everything's perfectly different. Everything's changed. I . . . I
understand now what religion's about. I . . . I didn't be-

fore; at least, not in that way. I . . . I see everything now, for the first time. That's . . ." (he hesitated), "that's all."

He threw himself back in his chair, and his face fell into shadow.

No one moved for a moment. Helen's heart beat so furiously in her ears that it seemed as if there were no other sound in the whole world. Then she heard her father clear his throat, in the little rasping way he used, when he did not quite know what to say.

"Well, my boy . . . I . . . I'm very glad to hear that . . . that you think religion will mean more to you now. But . . . but I wish you'd told us it was a Roman Catholic church you were going to — eh, Mother?"

"I know, Father; I ought to have. I'm sorry."

"Well: I'm glad you've told us now. That's something. I . . . I hope I'm broad-minded enough to recognize that there's good in all religions. . . . And . . . and what do you mean to do?"

Suddenly Helen perceived for the very first time in her life that her father had his limitations — not limitations that he chose to have, but limitations which he could not help. She perceived that there were larger things in the room than her father, and that he saw this too. The doctor suddenly became small to her. It was an odd sensation. . . . But her mother had not yet spoken.

"How do you mean, Father?"

"Well, my boy, I hope you don't want to become a Romanist yourself. That I . . . I shouldn't approve of at all."

There was no answer for a moment.

"Your mother and I —" began the doctor.

"I really haven't thought about that much yet," said Percy. "It had occurred to me. But . . . but that wasn't quite the point with me. . . . I . . . I only thought I'd better tell you straight out what had happened."

"Yes, my boy; that's quite right of you — very honest and straightforward. I'm . . . I'm glad that it's gone no farther yet. Eh, Mother?"

His wife drew a breath and expelled it again. And simultaneously Helen perceived by a quick inexplicable intuition, that the situation was far beyond her mother too. There was no question about it. Percy dominated everyone there, or, rather, the forces that he had brought with him into the room entirely beat down and practically eliminated the forces for which his parents stood. It was like a wind blowing suddenly through a little parlor. . . .

"Percy's done quite right to tell us," said Mrs. Brandreth-Smith. "I of course hope with your father that it'll go no further. I think it's just a little sentiment, and no more; natural, perhaps, in a boy." She stopped.

"A good talk to the Vicar'll set all that right," said the doctor.

"And a little thought and consideration," chorused his wife more emphatically.

It was a great relief to the tension of Helen. The situation had been so completely abnormal, so wholly unexpected, that she had not been able to form any conjectures, even, as to what would happen. Her parents, in spite of her pose of emancipation, still stood to her as the sky stands to the earth — presenting indeed one side of her to a protective and final kind, but having another side of which she knew nothing. They had been symbols to her of finality — especially her mother — the authoritative embodiment of human life so far as she had experienced it; they were (so to speak) the emblems of Church and State to her: they were always the last infallible court of appeal. She would no more have dreamed, really, of setting up her studio against their wishes, than she would have contemplated an elopement. They were the background and walls and roof of existence.

And now, though she did not entirely realize it yet, she had had a glimpse that there were forces and powers and principalities beyond them; that they were not the sky, after all, but moved beneath it, like herself. They seemed infinitely smaller than they had ever seemed before; she saw round them and beyond them; and it was Percy, of all people — or, rather, Percy's incredible situation — that had wrought this revelation. Finally, she was vastly relieved. So far as she had expected anything, she had expected a painful scene, and denunciations and threats. It would have been terrible, but in keeping with her scheme, if these had been uttered. And now she saw that they would not be used at all; and that her parents were really human like herself.

Then Percy leaned forward again; and she saw his face strangely working.

"Mother," he said, "— and Father too. I . . . I can't tell you how grateful I am. You have been as kind as possible. I'll . . . I'll do anything you ask me . . . now that I know you'll let me follow my conscience. I'll see anybody you like. . . . I'm ever so. . . ."

Then Helen drew a whistling breath of pain and bit fiercely on her lower lip, for she saw Percy's face suddenly break into tears.

"That's all right, my boy; that's all right," said his father tremblingly. "There! There!"

His mother said nothing.

Chapter VIII

(1)

Percy awakened next morning straight into his new joy. Of course the thing sounds ridiculous; but the fact remains that there is no happiness in the world comparable to that of the experience known as Conversion. It is as if the world had come tenderly alive; as if the sky had grown transparent and gracious faces looked down; as if the rooms and streets of common life were on a sudden thronged with friends; as if, above all, a brilliant light, warm and radiant, had started into flame within the soul.

Naturally all this has to materialize in small actions as well as in great.

Last night when Percy had gone up to his room he had first written a letter to Reggie — not very long, but eloquent. He had told him briefly that he had been "knocked over" by the sermon; he asked him to meet him for a cup of tea at five o'clock tomorrow, and to come down with him to Hanstead for an hour or two at least. He had told him, too, that everything "seemed quite different." This letter he proposed to leave at Reggie's office on his way through the City.

Then an idea had come to him; and he had gone to a little Japanese cabinet he had on the top of his bookshelf, and after opening two or three drawers had found what he was looking for. It was a little brass and black wood crucifix he had picked up in the street one day. It seemed to him that this would be helpful as a kind of focus for concentration. He had tacked this up, taking care not to make too much noise, over the side of his bed; and had knelt down before it to say his prayers with an extraordinarily intense pleasure. (He had thought of Father Hilary, and the crucifix that had hung on the pillar by the pulpit.)

And now, on this Monday morning, he awoke a little before seven, and lay looking at it.

"The Love of God which is in Jesus Christ our Lord. . . ."

At a quarter-past seven he got up, and knelt in his pajamas, with his elbows on the bed, for a quarter of an hour, staring at the crucifix. His thoughts went round and round, dwelling now on the material of the brass and wood, now on the Thing for which it stood. He said his ordinary prayers over three or four times. . . . He was cold before he was done; but his heart burned like fire. Certainly "everything was quite different."

Breakfast was almost a sacramental meal. He felt both elated and reasonable. He had had a long talk with his father last night; had heard mention made of the doctor's "position as a church warden"; had enthusiastically assented to this; had given full consent to his father to tell the Vicar everything; had said that he thought it quite unlikely he would want to become a Roman Catholic; had promised to take no explicit step without informing them at home.

His sense of elation and reasonableness were at full pitch this morning. He felt he had acted frankly and courageously. So he rang the bell for the eggs, and cut bread on the sideboard, and took plates away with an alert and zealous attention. His parents and Helen regarded him; but said little.

It was astonishing how friendly he felt to all the world as he went along the High Street to catch the nine-seven. Everyone seemed a brother; he took off his hat — right off — radiantly, to Mr. Main, who came out, melancholy as ever, from the churchyard after reading morning prayers. He greeted the stationmaster with a loud cheerfulness, although up to the present he had borne a certain grudge against that official for not treating him with sufficient deference.

He bought no halfpenny paper this morning. He felt it would be a tiresome distraction. He was sufficient company to himself.

So all day the elation continued; for it appeared to him that drudgery over accounts was no longer drudgery; it was as sacramental as everything else. He did it with a strange delight.

(2)

"My dear chap!" whispered Reggie earnestly. "I can't tell you —"

He broke off; there was no more to be said; but he shook with excited sympathy.

Percy fetched his cup and a sponge cake to the little round table in the corner behind the pillar where they could talk unheard; and began. (His hands trembled a little.)

"Well," he said. "It's as I told you. It's just. . . just knocked me over. I don't know how to put it into words. But you understand, don't you?"

Reggie looked at him, nodding a little.

"Well: I want to know," continued Percy, "what's to be done next."

"See Father Hilary," said Reggie.

Percy hesitated. Then he took a bite at his sponge cake.

"But that means my becoming a Catholic, doesn't it?"

"That's what you mean, isn't it?" cried Reggie with round eyes.

Percy perceived that the thing was more complex than he had thought.

"I don't exactly see why," he said slowly. "It isn't the Church I want. It's . . . it's . . . ."

"My dear chap, you don't understand! You can't possibly not be a Catholic now! I thought that was what you meant."

Reggie's face had a look of dismay on it. Of course he hadn't understood in the slightest. It had seemed to him that, when Percy had said he was "knocked over," he had meant of course by Catholicism.

"Look here," said Percy softly, glancing round the white pillared room to make certain he was not overheard. "You remember what the chap preached about. Well, that's what it did for me. . . . And I don't quite see where Catholicism comes in. Surely —"

"Look here," said Reggie in his turn. "Will you come and see Father Hilary? He'll put the whole thing far better than I can. Are you afraid of your people?"

"No: it's not that. I've spoken to them. They were awfully decent."

"Well, will you let me speak to Father Hilary?"

There was a pause.

Percy did not know exactly how far the priest was
bound up in his new experience. It had been by the personality of the man that he had been captured, but it appeared to him that he had immediately been handed on,
by him, so to speak, to this new and astonishing world of
religion. At the same time he could not even think of the
priest without a thrill. . . . He seemed to him a kind of radiant demigod, a glorious personal gateway to unimaginable things. It appeared incredible that he could really
talk with him in the flesh.

"Do you think —" he began.

Reggie made an impatient movement. He felt like a
fisherman whose fish sulks at the last moment.

"Look here, don't hedge," he said. "Will you come and
see Father Hilary?"

"Yes, I will," said Percy almost defiantly.

"I'm glad you've spoken to your people," said Reggie, after a pause for refreshment. "And I'm extraordinarily glad
they took it so well. I had rather a bad time with my
mother, you know."

"Oh! My people are all right," said Percy. "You see that's
always been their line. They're Church of England, but
they aren't bigoted."

"Lots of people say that," said Reggie with an air of un-
bounded experience. "But when it comes to the point, you
know. . . . Now let me tell you about Father Hilary."

For the next ten minutes Percy listened. He felt like a
child introduced to the society of friendly giants or fairies.
He heard all about the life of friars, about vows and discipline and the rest. It did not seem to touch common life at
any point at all; it appeared a kind of ideal existence in
another state of being. It presented itself to his imagination as an embodiment of the new world to which his own
interior experience had given him access. It was as if a
child, having for the first time seen a fairy, was informed
minutely of their ways and haunts and etiquette. It was
as if doors opened all round in what he had previously
taken to be impenetrably confining walls.

It must be remembered that clerks in offices, who have
been educated in grammar schools and live at home, suf-
fer under extraordinary disabilities. Up to the present,

with Percy at any rate, the world had been a very somber, materialistic kind of thing. The realities were things like breakfast, and nine-seven trains, and ledgers and moneymaking: these were the brutal undeniable facts; other things were dreams and fancies. Gadsby in C and girls at Yarmouth or in the train were the nearest he had ever approached towards the gates of Romance: he had fastened upon those things as safety valves through which a little of his rapidly lowering interior energy of imagination might escape. Gadsby in C, in fact (with the girls), stood to Percy for that for which Greek costumes and copper fireplaces stood to Helen. And now wide and glorious gates had rolled back and sunlight and music streamed through them: he thought he saw worlds within worlds; and now, again, from Reggie's talk, he understood that the vision was a fact; that there were men like himself who lived beyond those gates, who found religion as practical and as solid as moneymaking and morning trains; men whose objective lives and occupations were the embodiment of all this newly discovered glory.

"You're coming down to Hanstead, aren't you?" he said suddenly.

"There's no need. Besides I can't. I must get home I've got to call at the friary on the way, too."

"Oh! ... Well, perhaps that would be better; and —"

"Oh, yes; I'll see Father Hilary tonight. Perhaps next Saturday afternoon we can see him."

(3)

It was a distinctly odd atmosphere in which Percy found himself this evening — or which, perhaps, he generated. And upon him too, as upon Helen last night, there began to come a sense that his parents did not quite know how to deal with the situation, that they found it very unusual and puzzling.

He mentioned at dinner that he had seen Reggie Ballard and that he was hoping to see the friar himself on the Saturday afternoon; and these statements were met with a certain blankness. His father pursed his lips and frowned a little, but not at all unkindly: his mother nodded once or twice, as if it were just what she had expected. Obviously they proposed to behave as well as possible.

In the drawing room, however, the doctor made a little gentle attack — quite mild and quite kind.

He was holding the *Nation* in front of his face, and suddenly laid it down.

"Well, my boy," he said, "if you must go to see this . . . this priest, you must go. I wouldn't interfere with your liberty for anything. But . . . do you think it quite wise just now?"

"Why not, Father?"

"Well, you see, you're excited and worked up. And you must remember that these priests are very highly trained. They're very clever and quick, you know."

"Are they?"

"Yes, my boy. It is the one thing they're trained to do — persuade . . . er . . . sensitive people like yourself. They have years of training, you know. I can't help thinking you'd be wiser if you'd wait a little."

Percy shifted in his seat.

"But, you know, I don't at all see why I should become a Catholic: and, in any case, it's a long business. It means months of instruction first, Reggie says."

"Well, I'm glad to hear that, I'm sure. . . . But . . . but don't you think you might go and have a good talk to the Vicar first."

Percy began to see light. It was obvious to him that his father had been round to the Vicarage already. He put the question straight.

"You did see the Vicar, then, Father?"

The doctor also shifted in his seat.

"Why, yes; I went round just to have a word this afternoon . . . your mother thought I'd better. He . . . he was very kind. He said he'd be delighted to be of any service to you that he could."

"Well: that's very good of him. I'd like to talk it over. Of course I would in any case before doing anything. But I think I'd better see Father Hilary first. And I'll promise to ask the Vicar anything that puzzles me."

"Very good, my boy, very good."

And the doctor took up the *Nation* once more.

(4)

Percy went to bed unusually early. He was honestly tired, for one thing, with all his emotions; and, for another, there was the crucifix waiting for him.

He stood looking at it a minute or two. He turned away, and then wheeled round, to see it again suddenly. The sight gave him extraordinary pleasure — that little dark emblem against the pale wall.

He took it off its nail presently and carried it round, trying it here and there in other places. Then he had an inspiration.

He laid it down, climbed on to a chair and got down from the top of his wardrobe a box containing quantities of small miscellaneous ornaments — such things as photograph-frames and china animals — things which he had rejected from the adornment of his walls. He found at last what he was looking for — two tiny tin candlesticks, saved from a Christmas tree of a year or two ago, with an inch or two of pink candles still in them. These he set upon a bracket over the head of his bed, where he usually kept a candle and matches. Then, with infinite care, he drove a tack at the right height above them, hung the crucifix on it, and stood back. The effect was even beyond his expectations; above all when he lighted the pink candles. It looked exceedingly devotional.

Then he knelt down facing it, to say his prayers.

Chapter IX

It was on the next morning that Percy again ran across the mysterious Lady of the Train.

He was buying a halfpenny paper at the north end of the platform when the train came in. The boy hadn't got change ready, and the result was that Percy had once more to run. As he tore past the third-class carriages, he suddenly saw her looking out. He hesitated, felt himself flush, and then turned back and opened the door.

He lifted his hat.

"Good morning," he said. (He quite understood that he must not say "Miss.")

Obviously she was pleased to see him. She smiled swiftly and warmly, and all the melancholy of her face vanished.

"So here you are again," she said. "Good morning."

Honestly, Percy was not a coxcomb. Of course, he wondered, as all young men of his kind wonder, what kind of effect he produced upon people; but he had not, as a matter of fact, the least suspicion of how easily they got to like him. The truth was that Percy was very true to type — a type that is not very common. The first thing people noticed about him was his curly hair, his dark eyes and his clear complexion; and the next thing they noticed was that his character seemed to correspond, in that he was a natural, clean, simple boy. Certainly there was no overpowering personality about him; he did not compel. Yet neither was he obviously weak: his chin was well formed, his lips were decided, and he had a very frank, straightforward look in his eyes. But he was not self-conscious about it. It was precisely the absence of self-consciousness that made him so pleasant. He had a good taste in dress, and his manners, on the whole, were excellent and even rather engaging.

"I saw you at the window," he said, with a pleasing candor.

"That's very nice of you," she said, smiling again. "I mean it was very nice of you not to hurry past. You go up every day, I suppose?"

"That's it. I'm in an office."

"Oh! . . . Don't you hate it?"

"Yes." (Then he remembered that he had resolved not to hate it, and grew confused.)

"I mean, I'd sooner do other things," he said.

Persons of Percy's temperament find it usually quite impossible to be secretive about things in which they are passionately interested; and he talked rather abstractedly as the train went on. Of course, he wanted to tell her all about Sunday; and he was trying to frame a reason for telling her, satisfactory to himself. Of course he got that reason pretty soon: he perceived that it was his duty to bear his witness. He did not notice that she was watching him; and presently he broke abruptly in.

"A big thing has happened to me since I saw you last," he said suddenly.

"Really?"

Common sense for a moment restrained him. He saw vividly what a very odd thing it would be to talk about his soul, in a train, to a girl he had only met once before in his life. But his fervor was hot on him, and he resolutely trampled common sense down. But he flushed with the effort.

"Yes," he said, "I went to church on Sunday in . . . in a Roman Catholic Church."

She looked an inquiry. If he had been sharp, he would have seen that the brightness rather went out of her face. But he was thinking about himself just then.

"And . . . and I was bowled over by the sermon. I . . . I never dreamed in all my life —"

"Oh! You've found religion," said the girl.

He looked at her quickly, and the flush died out of his face. The coldness was quite unmistakable; it was, to all intents, a sneer.

"Yes," he said bravely. "I have. Why do you say it like that?"

All conventionality was gone now. Up to the present they had played counters with one another; now it was honest coin.

"Because I haven't found it," said the girl sharply. "At least, I suppose that's it."

"But —"

"I simply don't know what it means. I thought I did once — at least I thought I'd found it in somebody else. I was married in Church, you know —"

She stopped suddenly. Obviously she had said more than she meant. Percy's heart leaped and stood still.

"You're married?" he said.

"I didn't mean to say that," she said hurriedly. "But it's true. I was married. I'm not now."

"I suppose —"

"No; he's not dead. I divorced him six months after my marriage. He was what's called a religious man."

Her bitterness was like frost in the carriage. Her face had changed: her splendid eyes were veiled and hard: her red lips were like a trap.

The train was screaming through a junction; and Percy turned his face mechanically to look out. He watched the faces on the platform whirl past in white lines. Then he turned again; and his heart blazed suddenly with Quixotism. It seemed to him that he saw his task. Here was a sorrowful, tormented soul, embittered by treachery, a soul that had turned against God and man . . . .

"I don't care in the least," he said earnestly. "I . . . I'm very sorry. It's exactly people like you who want religion. . . I . . . I wish you'd let me help."

For the first moment he thought she was going to laugh.

"Do you know what I am?" said the girl, looking at him with an odd searching expression.

"How do you mean?"

"I mean my profession. Well, I'm an actress. There! That generally puts religious people off."

"But —"

"Oh! I'm in a perfectly respectable theater: and I'm a perfectly respectable person. I'm rehearsing at His Highness, — a problem play, don't you know."

Percy did vaguely know; and asserted that he understood perfectly.

"But that doesn't shock you —"

"Shock me! Why, good Lord —"

Then her face relaxed again; and the smile came back. It seemed to Percy that she was quite the most beautiful person he had ever seen. And now that he knew her story — at least, the dramatic and sensational part of it — her appeal to him was enormous, as it would be to all young men such as he. It appeared to him wonderful that he should have encountered such a soul in his newfound strength.

"I . . . I wish you'd let me talk to you," he said. "I . . . I believe I could help. I don't mean I myself; but . . . but I could get somebody —"

She shook her head — smiling faintly.

"You couldn't. Nobody can. You know — I was rather religious once, and that makes it all the worse."

"I . . . I'm certain I could. Look here, may I come and call upon you?"

The head-shaking continued. She looked out of the window a minute or two without speaking. Then she turned again.

"Give me your address," she said. "But I won't give you mine. You're . . . you're a dear boy."

(2)

She was very silent at the rehearsal that morning.

The play was of the usual modern kind known as a Problem play, which means a drama that plants its feet firmly along the very edge of the Ten Commandments, particularly of one of them that occurs towards the end. Such a play as this gives the keenest sensations of pleasure to people who are chiefly preoccupied in ordinary life with that kind of subject: and the best of it is that it can always be defended along highly philosophical and human lines. The principal persons of the play were in love with other persons than those whom they had promised to love — an old situation which brought about some very pretty and new scenes. There was one particular such scene in the passage of a country house towards the end of the second act that was very problematic indeed.

It was the third act, however, that was being rehearsed this morning; and the girl whom Percy proposed to "help," had not more than a sentence or two to speak.

She had done her talking just before the previous curtain. So she sat apart just off the stage, and said nothing to anybody. Two or three friends came up to her, and rapidly went away again. She was obviously in something of a temper.

When her cue came she sat still, completely unaware that the entire party was waiting for her.

"Now then, please —" called a voice impatiently.

Then she sprang up suddenly and went on.

"Not like that! Not like that!" wailed a voice from the gloom of the stalls. "Please remember that you're supposed to be brokenhearted. Surely you haven't forgotten —"

She flounced out indignantly. (She had very much of a "temperament"; it was her "temperament" in fact that had won her this fairly prominent part.) Then she came on again, the very picture of brokenheartedness.

On the whole she did very well; and the bald man, with no nose to speak of, who happened to have written the play, complimented her. But her temper was ferocious; she snapped like a chained dog at every living being except her theatrical superiors. She flatly refused to go and lunch with her dearest friend, and gave no reason at all except that she didn't want to.

As the last lines drew to an end, a rather shabby-looking man in trousers with a red line down the seam, came up and stood in the wings; and, as she moved off, he came up to her.

"A note please, Miss. And Mr. Marridon's waiting for an answer."

She took the note without a word; opened it and read it. Then she tore it up and let the fragments flutter down from her fingers.

Then she said, quite clearly and distinctly: "Tell him to go to hell!

(3)

She knew quite well that there was an element of pose in all this attitudinizing; but she did not know how much. Such pose as there was consisted in representing these

various personages — herself, Percy, her ex-husband, Mr.
Marridon, in certain roles more clearly defined than the
facts warranted. She herself was the disillusioned, embittered woman, who had drunk eagerly of the cup offered
and found it poison and rottenness: Percy was the ardent
boy whose simplicity attracted her, in whom, as by looking in a child's face, she might find forgetfulness: her ex-
husband was the traitor through whom disillusionment
had come; the Hon. James Marridon (who had, as a matter of fact, pestered her a good deal with little notes and
whose invitations she had once or twice accepted) was the
tempter who would disillusion her still further.

Her temperament was essentially dramatic: she was not
interested in people or things, unless she could group
them. Generally she grouped them sufficiently accurately;
but in any case, if they were once grouped, she threw herself with zest into her own part. There was no harm in
her: at least she meant none: there was no malice. But the
danger lay (as always in such cases) in the temptation
that her puppets experienced, to play up to her lead. Mr.
Marridon, for one, went away in precisely the mood she
would have wished. He received the message as it was
originally given; and stamped off in a rage, pulling his
moustache fiercely. He also remarked: "Curse the
woman!" quite in the accepted manner.

And Percy, too, unconsciously, took up his role with
equal promptness. His head, too, was full all day of the
help that he proposed to give her, though he felt rather
more manly and protective than she had contemplated.

And she herself, as she put on her hat and cloak in the
dressing room, preserved a rigid silence. Was it conceivable, she asked herself, that the way out really might lie
along the road that Percy had represented? Since her own
disillusionment she had preferred to label all religious
persons as unchristian; to thank God that she was not as
these Pharisees. Certainly she had suffered at the hands
of a man who professed religion; and, of course, to one of a
pigeonholing temperament, the short cut to generalization
lay in a contempt of all religious professions for the future. But the new pose appeared even more attractive:
she knew nothing whatever about Catholicism except its

gracefulness. Might it not be something of an idyll, if she could find her peace by its means? . . . She pictured herself at confession.

But she was not insincere in all this. She was, on the contrary, entirely true to a temperament that happened to be dramatic, and to a youthfulness that was certainly not at present her fault.

She went away in the same moody manner at the close of the afternoon rehearsal; and down again to the cheap little flat she inhabited near Ponder's End. She had settled on her about a hundred a year from her parents, now deceased; she lived alone and did her own cooking.

So she let herself into the flat; glanced at a couple of letters inscribed with her stage name that also was her maiden name — Miss Gladys Farham — made herself some tea, and settled down to an emotional evening. She was scarcely aware that in a private drama it is not only one's puppets but oneself too who occasionally grows into the part assigned by imagination.

Chapter X

(1)

It was with extraordinary excitement that Percy came up the stairs from Kensington Station and saw Reggie waiting for him at the top. He knew that the Friary was not ten minutes' walk away.

Hitherto he had not spoken to the Vicar. He had gone to the last frantic choir practice on the Wednesday night; he had sung, in a stifling atmosphere of vegetables, on the Thursday night, and had watched, through a kind of bower, the bishop preaching on the Lessons of the Harvest; he had even gone into the Vicarage to meet him afterwards, and had had the privilege of offering him a plate of seedcake, on the hearthrug. Caleb Simper had gone tolerably, and Gadsby in C excellently.

But he had not discussed anything with either of his pastors. Obviously they both knew the crisis through which he was passing; for the Vicar had patted him on the shoulder with particular attention as he actually held the plate of cake towards the bishop; and Mr. Main had looked at him, and, still more, not looked at him, with a peculiar sort of expression. But he had held to his determination to consult Father Hilary first. And now the day and hour had come. He had lunched at one o'clock sharp in an A.B.C. shop, and had come immediately on to Kensington, whither Reggie had preceded him.

High Street wore a dreamlike look to him as he came out into it. People did not seem quite real. It was unimaginable that they could be content not to be going to a Friary. . . . He was quite silent as he walked, listening to Reggie explaining in an important undertone that Father Hilary could not give them long, as he had to be in his "box" at half-past two. He did not even ask what this signified.

As he stood by the door of the Friary he had a fierce impulse to run away. The flat, dull face of the house appeared to him sinister. Reggie looked at his awestricken face with pardonable elation.

"Just talk straight out to him, won't you?" he said. "He's as nice as he can be. I shall leave you alone with him in the parlor, you know."

Percy nodded; his face was resolute, if pale.

A minute later he found himself in the "parlor," eyeing the retreating brown back and the bare heels of the brother who had shown them in. It was, indeed, fairyland come true. He looked round the parlor: it seemed to him astonishingly commonplace. The walls were distempered a faint green, with a mechanical key-pattern border four feet up; there was a table, with a wax crucifix under a glass case upon it; there were three rush-bottomed chairs, a strip of old carpet, and a shelf with three or four faded books in it: and nothing else. It was pleasant to find it so poor; but he wondered why it need be so ugly. He thought with a faint amusement of Helen's views on copper and stained wood.

"This is their kind of drawing room," said Reggie in an arch undertone.

Then the door opened and Father Hilary came in, smiling and holding out his hand.

(2)

"I understand entirely," said the friar, twenty minutes later. "And it's as satisfactory as it can be. So many inquirers, you know, begin by being drawn by the externals — the system, so to speak. Now that's one way, certainly; but I don't think it's the best. Yours seems to me the best (if I may say so). With you it's the interior things first. The other will come later."

Percy swallowed in his throat, and nodded.

The situation had developed very swiftly indeed, since Reggie had departed (with a discreet air of proprietorship) twenty minutes ago, leaving Percy in a state of profound disquiet and terror.

First, there had been the astonishingly easy friendliness of this priest. There was no stiffness, no pose, no rigidity of propriety about him at all. Percy had half-expected signs of the cross to be waved at him, oracles uttered, and even perhaps threats or warnings. Or if not these, he had thought that the friar would be insinuating or silky or disingenuous. (It must be remembered that this boy's acquaintance with Catholicism was entirely drawn from literature.) But, on the contrary, Father Hilary had been exactly like everyone else, only far more accessible than most; he had not patronized the boy at all; he had talked a little, fluently and charmingly, until Percy's frozenness began to melt; and then he had begun, gently, to question him.

Next, the priest had seemed to understand him even before he had properly explained himself: he had put into words, once or twice, precisely what Percy was feeling very much better than Percy felt himself capable of putting it.

Thirdly, so far from urging him to become a Catholic instantly, he had told him what a very serious step it was; how much consideration it needed; what a respect, he must remember, was due to his parents and their wishes — "short of offending God," the priest had said; and, finally he had remarked that a course of instruction was absolutely necessary, and that this instruction would in any case occupy not less than four months or so, and perhaps a great deal more.

"And even if you put yourself under instruction," the priest had added, "it would not commit you in the least. If, at the end, you felt that you were not entirely convinced of the truth of the Catholic religion, it would be your duty to draw back."

The psychological effect of all this on the boy's mind was very considerable; yet not so considerable as he thought. For what had been done to him was that his own position had been analyzed, and the analysis laid before him; and this, by a very persuasive and simple man. Certainly one or two further points had been made clear, and one or two of his misconceptions corrected, so that the chain of his thoughts was better linked up. But no more than this. . . . And now he perceived that conviction was further advanced than he had dreamed. Up to half an hour ago he had believed that he was inclined towards Catholicism, but not at all convinced; now he thought he saw that he was practically convinced; but not altogether inclined towards it.

"Well," said the friar after a pause, "I'll give you one or two books. Will you read them, and then come and see me again — say in a fortnight?"

"Yes," said Percy.

Then Father Hilary looked at him with sudden gravity, and the twinkle died from his eyes.

"And will you remember to pray regularly for light and strength? That's really the point, you know." He stood up.

"Reggie Ballard told me you'd like to see the Friary. We might go straight through the house now, and then end up in the church; and you can join him there."

(3)

The Friary made an enormous impression on him.

It must be remembered that all this was, to him, like an initiation. The fact that there actually were Englishmen, like himself in birth and experience, yet unlike him in that they lived a life under circumstances which he believed non-existent since the Middle Ages; that these Englishmen wore habits and sandals and were called friars; that they dined in silence; that they were bound by vows; that they had shaven heads; that their religion — and that the Catholic — was more real to them than banks or stock-exchanges or fluctuations of the cocoa-trade or nine-seven trains — well, he had known this in a kind of subconscious way; and now for the first time he saw it with his eyes, not under the slightly dramatic circumstances of a church, but in plain whitewashed passages, bare cells, and all but empty refectory. And it was one of them who was actually his guide; against whose habit he brushed as he walked, whose sandals flapped and creaked beside his own well-polished boots, who explained these mysteries to him in a matter-of-fact undertone. More than all this — it was this man who, from the high pulpit last Sunday morning, had drawn up the veil which every year had thickened between Percy's eyes and the Real.

"This is the refectory," whispered the priest, motioning him through a door.

It was a long room, with stained deal joists visible in the ceiling, paved with wood-blocks, and furnished in a manner that recalled to Percy certain pictures in Christmas numbers of the illustrated papers. Round the entire room, with breaks here and there, extended long, narrow, spot-lessly-clean wooden tables, on trestles, with a continuous bench attached to the wall behind them. On these tables lay the simplest possible articles — in each place was laid a brown mug, a knife and fork, a wooden spoon, a brown water-bottle and a folded napkin. Between each two places stood a cruet-stand with oil and vinegar. Opposite the door, in a little recess, stood a high pulpit with a shaded gas burner above it. On the extreme left, on the wall, hung an immense crucifix, blood-stained and weary-looking. On the extreme right an open door showed the tiled wall of the kitchen.

"That is the pulpit," said the friar. "One of the fathers reads from that during meals. We don't talk at meals, except on certain days."

"What does he read?" whispered Percy.

"Well — always from the Gospels first; and then some other books — 'Lives of the Saints,' and so on."

Percy had an imagination, and he was using it strenuously. He ran his eyes round the room, picturing the hooded figures, each in his place, the Father-Guardian (as he had learned the Superior was called) beneath the crucifix; he perceived the leisure and the wideness and the slow, deliberate dignity of the action called dinner, under the grave voice of the Reader. . . . He contrasted it with the dining room of his home, and the pictures, and the red walls, and the slight stuffiness, and the talk, and the figure of anxious Alice changing the plates.

"I expect you'd like to see a cell," said Father Hilary as they came out again. "I've got leave to take you to mine. But I must just show you the room where we have what's called Recreation, first."

"What's that — Father?" said Percy with sudden courage, as they went along the bare corridor.

The friar smiled frankly.

"Well; it's rather a trial to some of us at first," he said. "It means that we all have to sit round and talk, whether we want to or not. But it's very important. No monastery can go on well that neglects it."

"Why not? I should have thought —"

"Yes: I know. But without it, you know, you might get cliques, and special friendships, and so divisions and so on. — Well, here it is."

This too was an almost bare room. But it had a billiard table at one side, covered with a cloth. Round the fireplace was a great semicircle of wooden chairs. There were a few religious pictures on the wall, and, on a bracket, over the mantelpiece, was a plaster image of St. Francis. An immense black cat uncoiled himself with majesty where he lay on the seat of one of the chairs, and began slowly to stretch every muscle of his being, meanwhile displaying the interior of his mouth in a gigantic and deliberate yawn.

"You're looking at the billiard table," smiled the priest. "Everybody does. But I assure you it's not touched once a week! An old lady insisted on giving it to us. She said she was sure we must be so dull."

He stooped to scratch the cat under the chin. The cat was, at that instant, just finishing his stretch, and the point of his great tail was ending in a quivering crook: he interrupted himself to incline his chin to the skillful finger. Percy glanced at the friar. He was smiling with that curious radiant contentment that the boy had noticed so often.

"What's the 'Box'?" said Percy suddenly. "Reggie told me you had to go —"

"Oh! He meant the Confessional. Yes: I've got to be there in ten minutes. Saturday's our heavy day, you know. . . . (There, Tom!)"

"How long —"

"Well: I shall get out about nine, I suppose."

"Do you mean that people will go on coming till nine o'clock, from half-past two?"

"Why, yes," said the priest gently. "It's one of our great feasts tomorrow."

"And do you all take it by turns?"

The friar smiled outright.

"We've got eight confessionals in church," he said. "They'll all be full."

It was beyond Percy altogether. He could only imagine that each confession must take at least half an hour. . . .

He was going to ask as they turned; but he was distracted by seeing another friar go past in the corridor, raising his hands slightly to his head in salutation.

"That's Father-Guardian," whispered the priest. "He's going to church now — I must make haste."

The cell was the last straw; and there was no more spirit left in him. Or, rather, the new spirit, suggested by imagination and inflamed by what he had seen, surged up dominant and victorious. (The cat, who had preceded them with an air of a complete stranger, leaped on to the bed and proceeded to drive his claws into it, as if marking time.)

He looked at the narrow brown-veiled bed with the black crucifix over it; the coverless table, the upright chair, the curtain; and he understood that this was the home, deliberately chosen and obviously loved by the great simple preacher who stood by him. The vision had been dawning on him — as indeed it does dawn upon some souls — of a life entirely different in externals as well as in motive, from that which he had hitherto known and from that which the world considered normal and sane; a life simple indeed, but simplified by leaving most things out rather than by adding a few things on; a life of real poverty but of dignity as well; and, above all, a life inspired by the new motive whose driving-force had manifested itself to him for the first time hardly a week ago.

And the sight of the cell finished it. He had thought that there would be a few intimacies here — a photograph or two, a snug neatness, marks of an individuality, signs that a separate person and not the mere member of a community inhabited it: and there were none. This was the sanctuary of one who was a pilgrim on earth, as he professed to be, who looked for no city here as his home, but for one to come. (The cat was the sole domestic touch.)

The sight seemed to him to cause a sort of snap in his imagination, as of a last rivet or cog fitting into its place, completing the perfect adjustment of the whole.

He stared on it; and said nothing.

(4)

"Well," said Father Hilary, five minutes later, in the little passage outside the sacristy. "You'll remember, won't

you, about the books I gave you just now. And you'll come
again today fortnight at the same time?"

"Yes, Father."

"God bless you. Pray for me."

Percy could not speak. He gripped the little parcel given
him just now in the cell upstairs, and held out his hand.
The friar took it, smiling. Then Percy went out into the
church, swiftly and dazedly, and down the aisle — aware
of what seemed to him an unusual number of people — for
such an hour, he thought — kneeling in church.

At the door he found Reggie beside him, and, reassured
by his presence, turned and looked up the church. Then
he understood why so many were there. Each group, he
saw, was gathered near one of the curious structures,
ranged along the sides of the building, as he had noticed
them last Sunday. The figures were very quiet; but, as he
looked, Father Hilary came out from the sacristy door,
down the aisle, and turned into one of the little wooden
erections. Two figures — a man and a woman — followed
him closely, and themselves disappeared behind curtains
on either side.

"Saturday afternoon, you know," murmured Reggie dis-
creetly.

"Well?" said Reggie, when the two got outside at last.

"It's . . . it's amazing," said Percy, with an intense solemnity. "To think that all that —"

"I know; I know."

"I saw everything," said Percy "— everything. Even one
of the cells . . . A cat came with us."

"And that goes on all the time," said Reggie. "I meant —
well — all of it."

Percy was silent as they came up into High Street.

Before him there unrolled itself the usual spectacle of
Saturday afternoon. The great shop-windows were shuttered for the most part, and there was a holiday air
abroad. Young men on bicycles scudded hither and
thither; girls in twos and threes paraded past him
arm-in-arm. The air was full of the solemn roar of wheels.

And this was considered ordinary normal life, thought
the boy. . . .

"I'll tell you what it is," he said; and then stopped.

Chapter XI

(1)

"I tell you I shall do exactly what I please with my own work," hissed Mrs. Main, as white as paper. "You're only a curate; you'll never be anything else: and . . . and it's not fit that I should live as I do. At any rate, I don't choose to."

He shook his head. His face was pinched and miserable, and yet resolute.

"It's impossible," he said again.

"You can't stop me," she cried.

The two were in the little dining room of their lodgings at tea. Between them, on the round table, stood the black japanned tray with imitation Derby tea-things. About them were the mean, low walls, papered in green with a stamped dado; and upon these were the large photogravures with which Mrs. Main had covered their nakedness. There was a veneered sideboard, with an electroplated biscuit tin — (a wedding present ten years ago) — reflected in the small beveled mirror: blue plush-like curtains stamped with lighter blue flowers hung over the windows: a hanging gas chandelier, not yet lighted, hung from the ceiling. Upon the mantelpiece of black imitation marble was a bronze-imitation clock: two Japanese fans flanked this on either side, and two photograph frames, in silver as thin as paper, held these in position: an imitation Turkey carpet covered the floor, and imitation-mahogany chairs, with imitation leather seats and backs, supported the bodies of the husband and wife. A gas fire, with imitation logs, burned blue and yellow on the hearth. It was an imitation room altogether, rather like a rather nice room, and yet not really like it at all. It had been furnished by their landlady, under stress of Mrs. Main.

Mr. Main was aware that another crisis was come on him; but it had come with such suddenness that he was dazed by its virulence. For the last six months he had enjoyed comparative peace. His wife had been engaged in her room, during this time, for most of her leisure, with what she called her "writing"; and the clergyman had been so relieved by the absence of the unpleasantness with which he had to deal when his wife had been less occupied — the eternal malicious gossip that he had to assimilate in spite of himself, the lacerated feelings he had had to soothe, and even the apologies he had had to make once or twice — that he had even encouraged his wife to "write," saying nothing of the occasional discomfort of his meals or the spasmodic attacks of nerves that she experienced, rising, apparently, from the intentness of her occupation. She had told him nothing of her subject: he had had not the faintest idea of what she was engaged upon; even — poor man — he had laboriously played up to her mysteriousness and joked feebly and domestically upon her Secret, when she was in a good temper.

And now the secret was out.

She had come late to tea that afternoon, and had burst into the room in a state of extraordinary and infectious excitement, bearing with her a large brown-paper parcel. For the time she looked almost like the girl he had married ten years ago; her pale cheeks were flushed, her eyes shone: she had seized her husband round the neck and kissed him twice.

"Guess!" she had cried. "No, promise first you'll tell nobody till I give you leave."

Mr. Main had endeavored to play up: he had hastily wiped his chin on which a crumb had lodged itself, and been astonished and delighted. Of course, too, he had given the promise.

Then she had told him; and his delight had merged itself in his astonishment. For he was informed that she had been to see the publisher with whom she had left her mysterious manuscript a week ago; and that great man had actually told her that his reader had advised him to accept it. He could not give her very high terms; but he was willing to advance her twenty-five pounds as an installment of the smallish royalties he proposed. He had promised to have the agreement drawn up and sent to her immediately; and, meantime, Mrs. Main might take away her manuscript for the two or three small alterations she wished to make before it was sent to the printers. He must have it back in a week at latest.

To say that Mr. Main was astonished is a very poor description of his state. He had regarded the publication of printed books — other than parish magazines — with the same kind of feelings as he regarded the performance of an opera or the erection of a church. Persons of distinction and genius did do these things no doubt: for here in the world were operas and churches and books. But that it should be his wife — that it should be the fiery, moody creature who sat over her desk all the morning, and fractiously locked up her manuscript at dinnertime — that it should be Marion Main who was about to publish a real book, appeared to him incredible.

For a few minutes, of course, he asked questions about irrelevant details — the name of the publisher, the proposed binding of the book, and its name. She had answered tempestuously, meanwhile cutting the string of her parcel with a butter-knife, and tearing it from its bandages.

"It's to be called 'A New Arcadia'," she said. "Here it is. . . ."

He had turned the written pages feebly and irresolutely, smiling as he did so. Of course he was delighted — as an old man is delighted by a dream that he is a child again. . . Twenty-five pounds in advance too! . . . .

"What's it all about?" he said. "My dear!"

She had kissed him again, and torn the parcel away.

"Now I'll give you bits to read," she said.

He sat there obediently, reading, while she poured out tea and drank it, explaining between her gulps. Her high spirits filled the room like electricity. She nibbled a fragment of dry cake, and left the rest.

. . . . Then, little by little, point by point, the facts began to dawn on his mind; and he understood what his wife had done. She had taken Hanstead as her scene; and she had drawn in, ruthlessly and unmistakably and — (the worst of all was) — with a real skill, the principal people of the place. The Vicar was there; his wife was there; the Mayor, the undertaker, the rival butchers, the stationmaster; and every soul of them was grotesque and absurd:

they were elongated shadows of themselves; their virtues were like noses distorted hugely; their little faults were as monstrous humps. But even this was not all; for the woman had spared no one and nothing; she had taken the very kindnesses shown to her, and caricatured them; she had presented the Vicar's wife, for example, in tears of mortification and wounded pride, drawing, out of drawing, a scene at which Mr. Main himself had been present, out of which his own wife had not come very well, and in which the Vicar's wife had behaved with a pathetic and emotional kindness; she had described with horrible minuteness the furniture of the houses to which she had been admitted as an intimate; and a slightly ridiculous photograph or two that hung in the Mayor's parlor. She had, in a word, as it seemed to Mr. Main, betrayed every confidence shown to her, and returned evil for good. She had described the Vicar's Oxford intonation . . . she had sketched, quite admirably, the suffragan bishop in the bowery pulpit. (This was an addition recently made.)

At first he had hesitated to allow even to himself that he was right. He had ventured on a question or two.

"My dear, is not this a little like the Vicar's house?" he had said at one point: and she had nodded back at him with tight lips and dancing eyes.

"But this is exactly what Mrs. Barr said to you at her Christmas party!" he said later.

Again she had nodded, apparently in the highest spirits.

Presently he had laid the papers down; and his face was full of perplexity and pain.

"They'll all recognize it," he had said.

"That's exactly what I hope!" she had cried; and he had seen the cruel glee in her face.

"It's impossible, my dear, simply impossible. You can never publish this. It would be intolerable."

And then the horrible crisis had precipitated itself. She had snapped back; he had repeated his views; she had gone white and red: she had snatched the papers from him; and stood up. Then she had sat down again, glaring at him and away again.

(2)

"You can't stop me," she cried again. "It's settled." He too was pale now; his lips trembled; his patient eyes were scared and determined.

"My dear, as a clergyman's wife —"

She uttered an indescribable sound of disgust. Her temper dominated her like a storm. The whole of her bitterness, growing now for years and years, during which she had seen the social ignominy of her husband even increasing with his age, during which she had seen younger men preferred before him, during which she had quarreled first with one and then with another of those who pitied her yet could not conceal it — this bitterness seemed to culminate now in one white-hot blast.

She leaned forward, clasping her bundle tight. Her hat was pushed back, and her face looked white and venomous in the dying light that fell on it from the window.

"A clergyman's wife!" she said, seeming to spit it at him — "Yes, that's what you're always telling me; and that's what I'm always trying to forget. Do you think if I'd known what it was, I'd ever have married you? . . . Do you think I've got no soul of my own? . . . that I haven't got a life to live as well as you?"

"My dear —"

But her energy swept him silent.

"You've got yours — such as it is — and I suppose you like it, or you wouldn't live it — with your confirmation classes and your visiting and the rest of the . . . the bloodless nonsense. And I'm going to have mine! You're . . . you're just as much a woman's husband as I'm your wife. . . . I tell you I'm going to live . . . and I've found my life. My first book accepted. . . . I knew it would be: I knew I had it in me. And if you think I'm going to suppress this just because a few old cats and suburban bouncers won't like to see themselves as they are — why you're mistaken. What else is all novel writing but a picture of life —"

So she swept on, justifying, denouncing, defying: her energy was tremendous. And he sat miserably beneath it, holding on with a terrible kind of patience, his poor face contracted, his eyes winking rapidly and continuously, his

lips shaping little sentences, in rehearsal for when he
should be allowed to speak.

"That's my last word," she cried at last. "Now what have
you got to say?"

She threw herself back in her chair, silent, fierce and
resolute.

He lifted his eyes.

"I must ask you to listen to me," he said. "I have listened to all you have said. . . . You do not understand
what you are doing. No novelist that I have ever heard of
— no writer of any repute at all — would dare even to do
as you have done. I know they take characters from life,
sometimes; but they disguise them; they take them out of
their surroundings. You have not done so. I tell you —"

Her lips opened sharply as if to speak. He glanced up;
but she said nothing.

"Well; that is the first thing. It is not honorable nor . . .
nor Christian. You may not like these people here: about
that I say nothing. But at least they have tried to be kind
and pleasant to us both. And you have drawn them unmistakably — their little ways, their homes. . . . It is unmistakable. Why that scene in the Vicarage —"

He looked up again, hoping from her silence that he had
touched her. But she nodded sharply as if in recognition
and glee.

"And I say it is unchristian; because you have drawn
them unkindly: you have made them ridiculous. . . . Oh! I
know it is very clever: I know you are very clever, Marion,
my dear." (His voice shook a little in his desperate attempt to conciliate.) "But that is not the way to use the
gifts which God —"

She jerked her head; and again made a little sound of
contempt.

"And have you considered me . . . ourselves?" he said.
"You would make my position impossible here. I should
have to resign. I tell you that if that book goes back to the
publisher, I shall be obliged to go straight to the Vicar and
tell him —"

"You promised you wouldn't," she snapped suddenly.

"I didn't know then —" began Mr. Main helplessly.

"But you promised: you promised," she cried, leaning forward again. "That was exactly why I made you."

"Ah! You thought then that I should object?"

"I thought perhaps you might," she said coolly.

"Then I shall consider it my duty —"

She was on her feet in an instant; and her eyes blazed.

"What! You'd tell him! And you know perfectly well that I could have done the whole thing without telling you at all! You know that! Well; do it, and break your promise. I shall know better next time; and — and it won't stop me, and'll only make it worse. Why —"

Neither of them had noticed a ring at the doorbell, and voices talking; and the tap on the door came unexpectedly. They were silent.

"Come in," said Mr. Main in something of a quaver.

The door opened a crack.

"Young Mr. Smith's in the other room, sir. He wants to see you."

Mrs. Main gathered up her papers in silence. The door was still open.

"Marion," said the clergyman in a very low voice, "we must have another talk. Shall we have time —"

Her face silenced him as she went to the door. At the door she turned.

"You had better see young Mr. Smith here," she said in a voice of ice. "I shall want the drawing room."

(3)

· Mr. Main was still shaking interiorly as he brought Percy in and directed him to a chair. The scene he had just passed through, with the thoughts of its possible consequences, still obsessed and dominated him. He asked the young man whether he had had tea, whether he would smoke, by sheer effort of will, and he knew neither then nor afterwards what Percy answered. He made a little vague talk too about the evening's drawing in, and even regained self-control enough to go across and draw the imitation brocade curtains over the darkening windows nearest the fire and light the gas. But his mind still whirled with Marion, with her white eager face, her bitter sentences, her mischievous intentions: half a dozen sentences and arguments sprang to his mind, which he re-

membered he ought to have used: he was tormented by
the doubt as to whether or no he ought to break his promise and tell the Vicar of what impended. Perhaps it would
only make it worse — as she had said.

Once more, too, a certain other doubt occurred to his
mind which, six months ago, had been the torment of his
life. . . .

It seemed to him, then, struggling with these violent
distractions, that the interview halted strangely; and he
put it down to himself. Percy sat, obviously ill-at-ease, on
the edge of his chair, twirling his cap; he held a cigarette,
but it was already gone out. He had said "Yes" and "No"
and "Just so"; and had added that he wished to come and
ask some advice. And Mr. Main had said "Yes" and "Just
so," pumping up his assent through a storm of wholly
alien thoughts. Then there fell a silence; and then Percy
approached a little nearer to his object.

"I'm troubled about religion," he said. "Perhaps you
heard —"

The curate jerked himself a little more upright and ordered his thoughts to heel.

"Any service that I can be —" he said. (He told himself it
was disgraceful that he could not put his own affairs out
of his mind.)

"It's . . . it's a very serious matter," said Percy.

"Mr. — er — Smith, you must forgive my apparent inat-
tention. I've just had some bad news, and —"

"Shall I come another time? I'm so very sorry to hear —"

"No, no, I . . . I assure you there's no need. It was only
for a moment or two. Please go on, Mr. Smith."

Mr. Main felt his own man again now that he had made
that little admission. Percy sat back in his chair.

Percy didn't quite know why he had come to the curate
first. The Vicar was obviously the right person to consult,
and certainly would have to be consulted sooner or later.
Yet, on his way home this evening the boy had suddenly
determined to break the ice in this way. He had always
had a kind of compassion for the curate: he was perfectly
aware of Mr. Main's position in the place — a position of
vague but quite real indignity as an oldish man, still under authority, without any social prestige whatever. He

had had, even, certain qualms of pathos with regard to
Mr. Main; he had wondered whether he himself had not
been off-hand with him once or twice. . . . So it had appeared to him suddenly this afternoon that he would pay
him the compliment of a spiritual consultation; it had
even occurred to him as quite conceivable that the suppressed and rather furtive-looking curate, who wore short
trousers and swung his umbrella to show that he was at
ease, might understand the situation better than his
prosperous superior who was always so certain and so effective in all that he undertook. Percy was in a very tender mood himself: he felt he would prefer vague sympathy
to bright and well-cut advice. (Besides, he knew precisely
what the Vicar would say, beforehand.)

"Well," he said at last. "It's . . . it's about the Roman
Catholic Church."

He had no sooner said these words than he perceived
that something had happened to Mr. Main. A moment before. the clergyman had been leaning a little forward with
his long knuckly fingers together in a pathetically profes-
sional attitude, his long melancholy face twitching a little,
and his feet twisted together beneath his chair; but at the
utterance of this sentence he appeared first to jerk to a
new attitude, and then to freeze.

"You . . . you mean," he began. "I didn't know it was that
— I had thought —"

"I . . . I mean," said Percy, "that I think I shall have to
become a Roman Catholic. I've . . . I've been to see a
priest; I've read a book or two he gave me. . . . I don't see
any answer to it. I want to know what it is."

Mr. Main rested as if petrified.

"I can't help it," went on poor Percy; "my father knows
all about it. He doesn't like it, of course; but he's been awfully nice about it. Of course I shall have to go and see the
Vicar. But . . . but I thought I'd like to come to you first,
Mr. Main. I hope you aren't awfully shocked."

"No; no. . . . Go on. From what the Vicar said, I gathered
— Go on, please."

Then Percy poured it out.

He was a little astonished at the extraordinary iciness
of the other; he had expected an anxious kind of flustering

at the worst: but his own warmth carried him along. He told him all about the sermon, all about his visit to the friar, and as much as he could remember of the books. He said he wanted to know what the Protestant answer was to this or that argument. Once or twice he hesitated, as if to receive the answer: but the curate nodded and murmured to him to go on.

And, at last, he got out his deepest secret of all — his conviction that he too must be a friar; that it was the most perfect life on earth, that there was no other life conceivable for himself.

"Of course I know," he said, with solemn prudence, "that I'm quite young yet and so on. And I shan't tell my people that, yet. But I thought I'd better be quite open and straightforward."

He was flushed with his own enthusiasm, and looked across, waiting for an answer.

Then it came.

Mr. Main stood up abruptly, went across to the hearth and leaned his head on his hands, with his face away from the boy. Percy observed his shapeless-looking trousers, the polished gleam on his shoulders. . . . He contrasted the figure with that of Father Hilary. Then he wondered why the other did not speak; and as he wondered the curate turned round.

His face no longer twitched, but there was a curious strained look in it.

"My boy," he said, with wonderful tenderness, "you must go to someone else. You must go to the Vicar. I . . . I could not advise you rightly."

"But —"

Then Mr. Main did an astonishing thing. It was what the Vicar would have done in the first five minutes; but from this man it was as uncharacteristic as eloquence. He came a step nearer and put his long hand on the boy's shoulder.

"No," he said; and his voice was strangely decided, yet perfectly kindly. "Please do as I say. I could not advise you well. I — Please go to the Vicar."

(4)

When Percy had gone the clergyman went back to the
dining room and stood a long time on the hearthrug, fin-
gering a little china mandarin on the mantelpiece, making the head nod and then checking it again. Then he sat
down, in his armchair, and remained motionless, staring
into the gas fire.

Chapter XII

(1)

There are few differences in this drab-colored world so startling as those between various kinds of minds. One man, after a glance at a fragment of bone, will reconstruct Hercules; another, after the entire skeleton stands before him, will even then question whether it is Hercules at all. One man will by intuition discover, or believe himself to have discovered, an entirely new philosophy; another will spend laborious days in working out a sum, with the help of the most prosaic of all faculties, and, even then sometimes will get it wrong, or, what is worse, doubt his own accuracy.

' Now Percy had fallen in love, head over ears, with that extraordinary society called The Catholic Church. He could have given extremely few, and, to the scholastic theologian, perhaps, very inadequate reasons for his conclusions. Mr. Main, on the other hand, had for the last two years and a half been piling up very solid reasons indeed for a conviction that that same Society had a claim on him such as none other had, and, simultaneously was doubting his conviction.

It had begun in a little unimportant incident that had aroused his interest. Then he had taken up a book showing a great many plain reasons why no man in his senses ought to join the Church of Rome, and his discomfort had increased. Then he had read one or two more books on the other side, and had again run back to his Anglican fortifications. So it had gone on; and for the last few months he had resolutely laid aside all reading upon the subject and had thrown himself instead into feverish activities of visiting and confirmation classes: he had even made small evening engagements to coach a spectacled youth, of the grammar school type, in trigonometry. Yet in that strange under-self of which psychologists have begun to talk so eloquently, a certain process, he was aware, still continued — a process that caused him, at certain moments, a distinct physical sensation in the diaphragm — on such occasions, for example, as that of reading in church certain words about building a Church upon a Rock, or of catching a glimpse of a cleric in a rather abbreviated overcoat and a trilby hat. It was a sensation as of being slightly bruised immediately beneath the breastbone — such a sensation as people experience when the lift in which they stand suddenly begins to move downwards.

(2)

The Vicar had been so exceedingly discreet about Percy, that Mr. Main, until the unhappy interview in his own dining room, had been firmly under the impression that the young man was merely suffering under one of those fits of agnosticism that attack the adolescent Christian almost as punctually as scarlet fever or measles attack a child.

"Young Percy Smith's in trouble about his faith," the Vicar had said to him one evening after choir practice. "One must not forget to pray for him."

Mr. Main, too, had been so discreet as to ask no further questions: he had nodded his head with compressed lips, and, as soon as he had returned home, had entered Percy's name on a little leaflet which he carried in his prayer book. . . .

And now the disclosure had been made; and the sensation of a bruised diaphragm had returned with such violence as to promise a considerable stay. His discomfort was increased by a conviction, against which he strove courageously, that Percy's confidence was meant as a Sign.

Now let it be clearly understood that Mr. Main was not yet convinced (or at any rate, if he were convinced, he did not know it) that the Church of Rome was right and the Church of England wrong. He was still able to repeat to himself with sincerity — even though of a rather feverish nature — quite a number of statements, each of which, if true, completely demolished the claims of the Pope over Mr. Main's conscience. He still could assure himself that these claims were entirely founded upon certain forged Decretals; that more than one Pope had authoritatively taught heresy; that *Petros* and *Petra* meant entirely different things; and so on. (These statements, and others like them, can be found in abundance in any modern work on the Roman controversy.) And, as he sat this evening staring into the fire, one part of his mind busily repeated them. But it was in the other part of his mind that the trouble lay (that part which energizes physically, as has been said, in the region of the diaphragm) — and, since it is entirely untrue that the average man cannot think of two things at once, Mr. Main sat silent and compressed and miserable, while his inner self conducted the conflict.

"It's impossible," murmured Mr. Main, half-aloud, presently, shaking his head. "I could not, in any case. Marion. . . ." And then he was off again, contemplating those reasons which really most affected his action, and which he knew ought not to affect it at all.

Marion, indeed, loomed very large in the poor man's life — far more large than any wife has a right to loom. She was there always, as the east wind is there, and that strange bitter atmosphere which indicates it. There was hardly an incident which he did not interiorly refer to her. If he stumbled in reading the lessons, he wondered whether she had noticed, and, if so, whether she would say something disagreeable afterwards. When Tommie Mann misbehaved under his eye, he wondered whether Marion would think that he ought to lean over and press him firmly and kindly on the shoulder. When his sermon went better than usual, he wondered whether, possibly, she would be pleased. He knew this kind of attitude was all wrong, and that no human being in the world ought to count for so much in the life of any man — and especially of a clergyman. Yet one is none the less liable to irritability in the east wind, however much one may assert that an immortal soul ought to be impervious to atmosphere conditions.

It was Marion, then — the Marion-element, so to speak — that oppressed and burdened him now.

He began, for the tenth time, yet for the first time, perhaps, with full deliberation, to contemplate the effect of his conversion to Rome, on the Marion-plane. First, he would have to tell her. . . . Then he would have to give some kind of reasons for the step he proposed to take, and listen to the kind of scorn in which she was so proficient. Then — (Mr. Main forced himself on in a kind of desperation) — if he really took the step, it would mean having to pack up their furniture and go away; and where? And how could he possibly earn his living, and hers? He had perhaps sixty or seventy pounds saved; and he might make a little more by selling some furniture. And then there would follow an entirely different kind of life — a life, too, that would certainly be more sordid, even than this — in smaller rooms; and all with Marion. . . .

Mr. Main sucked in his lower lip and bit it hard, screwing up his eyes tight, as if in neuralgia. He was still smarting from his recent encounter with his wife: she appeared to him now as wholly lurid and bitter. It appeared to him inconceivable that he could give her such an emphatically solid excuse for being really disagreeable.

(3)

The last glimmer of light had faded completely outside, and the windows presented rectangles of chilly blackness. Now and again a step sounded on the pavement outside, and once a cheerful and shrill whistling grew out of the distance and faded again, as a boy went home. It seemed to Mr. Main as if life were a complete blank, as hopeless as the empty street. There was no gleam anywhere to relieve its dreariness.

He had sunk now far below the realm of activity: his mind did no more than stare upon the pictures which his imagination sent past it. Now an array of Anglican arguments went by — very positive and clear and upright, like drilled men marching. Now a flare of half-seen lights — Catholic arguments — lit all into a confused and suggestive crowd of fire and darkness. Now Marion, with a contorted face, said bitter things, such things as she had said an hour ago in this very room.

"I wish I had never married you. — You are selfish; you think only of yourself; never of me. —You shall not spoil my life. — I have as much right to live my life as you have to live yours" — things that always had a deformed kind of truth within their bitterness.

And the world might be so splendid a place; he saw that well enough. If Marion still were to him what she had been for the first six months of married life; if she still retained even a reflection of that radiance she had worn in

that glimpse of Paradise called a Honeymoon — when
they had had, he thought, no secrets from one another;
when they had knelt together, like children, each night, to
say their prayers, and he held her hand and, at the end,
had blessed her with a solemn joy; when he had awakened, morning by morning, an hour before she, and had
lain there in a kind of tranquil ecstasy, knowing that this
was his dear wife, before God and man; when he had been
able, by the help of his religion even to think of her death
without despair, so utterly, he had believed, were they
two one for both time and eternity. . . .

Ah! if she were still like that now! If only he could go
now to the other room, and find her there turning to meet
him as he came in; and if he could but tell her, simply and
tranquilly, of his trouble; and they could pray over it together, and resolve to follow God's Will together wherever
it might lead them. Why, he could face anything, if only
she were on his side, or at least not against him!

She had been so sweet during those first months. She
had told him, more than once, how sacred the relationship
had seemed — the more sacred since he was an ordained
priest of God. She had even gone so far once as to say that
it seemed to her that a clergyman's wife had access to a
kind of double sacrament — one in matrimony; and the
other in the priesthood of her husband. He had explained
to her then, carefully and laboriously, that she was not
quite correct in what she said; and that a wife could not,
however holy and perfect the matrimonial bond, really
share at all in her husband's priesthood. She had smiled
so delightfully, then, and said that she had not really
meant it, but that she liked to think it.

Or, again; he remembered a day when she had asked
him something about the Church of Rome; and he had
solemnly explained to her exactly in what points that
Church was unscriptural. First and foremost there were
the claims of the Pope; there was the "mutilation of the
Sacrament"; then there was the Invocation of Saints, for
which, he had told her, there was no scriptural authority
at all; and he had added a few more points beside. She
had said that it was quite clear to her now: and he had
answered that the Romanists were, of course, still our fel-

low Christians, and had quoted a line or two from Keble about our "fallen sister."

Well; if she were still in the very least that Marion whom he had married, with what a simple ease he could go to her and remind her of their conversation, and tell her how his opinions were changing. Of course (he made haste to assure himself), he would add that he was not yet in the least convinced; but that he thought it his duty to say that his mind was not quite so certain as it had been; that they must talk it all over together, and he would explain exactly what points they were that troubled him; and they must pray over it together.

His eyes began to smart a little as he contemplated the picture, and its hopeless remoteness. . . . And, if the prospect of telling her was difficult, how infinitely more difficult the prospect of doing it.

He leaned forward, presently, and looked at his watch. It was not yet seven. The spectacled boy was coming at half-past for his trigonometry, and supper would be as usual, at nine.

He had had a sudden idea that he would like to go to the church for a few minutes, and see whether a little praying there would clear his mind. But, as he stood up, the door opened suddenly, and Marion came in.

(4)

"He's gone?" she said in a sharp questioning tone.

She had closed the door behind her, and remained standing before it, with the table still between them. The unshaded gas shone straight on her white sharp face, as she stood there in rigid dignity.

"Yes, my dear," said her husband mildly, also standing. "He went quite an hour ago."

"What have you been doing here?"

"I have been thinking," he said quietly.

She came a step nearer, as if with sudden impetuousness.

"I'm not going to give in," she said. "I hold to every word I said just now. But I want to know what you're going to do."

"I have not yet decided."

She looked at him with a kind of expectant hesitation: her eyelids flickered a little. Then she came resolutely forward and sat down.

"Sit down too," she said. "I can't bear to talk to anyone standing up: and we must just talk this out."

"I have Dick Mortimer coming at half-past," he said.

"There's half an hour yet," she said sharply. "Please sit down."

He did so.

"Now I want it to be perfectly clear," she said, "that I am going to publish this book. (Wait till I've finished, please.) You do not seem to consider that money is of real importance to us both. If it were not for the money, I might possibly consider postponing its publication for a little — until we leave this place, for instance. I don't suppose we shall live here forever. But we want money: and we don't want to touch what we've saved. Supposing you lost your curacy here, for instance, we should be quite destitute. How much is there in the bank?"

"Between sixty and seventy pounds, I think."

She made an impatient sound.

"There!" she said. "And I thought it was nearly a hundred! Well: all the more I must publish this book while I have the chance. It might not be accepted again. How shall we get a holiday next year, I should like to know! And I want a new dress."

He said nothing.

"Well; I am going to publish it, and at once. Let that be quite clear."

She paused, as if for a remonstrance: but again he said nothing.

"Well?" she asked sharply.

"I am listening to you, my dear."

"Well; why can't you tell me what you mean to do?" she snapped. "It isn't very civil —"

He lifted his long hand, and half-closed his eyes with the expression that she always found trying; but she stopped.

"My dear," he said, "I was waiting for you to finish. . . . Well; I have not yet decided what I shall do."

"What can you do?"

"I might decide to tell the Vicar — in spite of the promise I gave when I did not understand the circumstances. (Please do not interrupt me, Marion.) Or I might . . . I might find it necessary to leave Hanstead."

"Leave Hanstead? And where would you go?"

One strain of Mr. Main's nature cried aloud within him that now was the moment to begin to prepare the way — to hint at his trouble. But the rest of him, including what is known as Prudence, urged him to do nothing of the kind — to wait till one crisis was passed before provoking another.

"I . . . I do not know," he said undecisively. "That is why —"

"It's perfect madness!" she cried. "How can you leave Hanstead unless you've got work elsewhere? And what work are you likely to —"

But then even she stopped in her brutality, so agonized was the look in the long solemn face that was turned to her under the gaslight.

Mr. Main swallowed, audibly, in his throat.

"I cannot bear very much more of this," he said; and his voice broke piteously in the last two or three words. "You do not seem to consider —"

He made a loud grotesque choking noise, and hid his face in his hands.

Chapter XIII

"Percy, my boy," said the doctor an evening or two later, as the young man walked into the sitting room after hanging up his coat in the hall. "Percy, my boy; I want you to come round with me to the Vicarage after dinner."

"Oh! To talk things over?" asked the boy rather wearily. He was tired with his day in the City: there had been a little overtime, and every hour had been strenuous.

"That's it," said his father.

There was a look of a slight suppressed excitement in the doctor's face, but so slight as very nearly to evade notice. Percy just perceived it; and then thought no more of it. His mother sat silent at her davenport.

It was a heavy starless night as they set out about nine o'clock. Doors and windows were for the most part cloaked; and the street was almost completely dark except for the light cast by the street lamps.

"Is it anything particular?" asked the boy, aware again that his father's very silence seemed suggestive.

"No, my boy, no: at least — Well, your mother wished you to hear the other side from . . . from one who knows. The Vicar suggested it."

"Oh; just that then —"

"That's it," said the doctor rather hurriedly.

They were obviously expected. Steps came immediately across the hall in answer to their ring at the Vicarage door; and it was the Vicar himself who opened to them.

He greeted them almost effusively; and again Percy noticed an air of unusual excitement.

"Come in," he said. "Come in. . . . Good evening, doctor; good evening, my boy. Mr. Railton's quite ready."

It was not possible at that moment to ask who Mr. Railton might be. Plainly he was some sort of a controversialist, and Percy prepared himself for the fray. His weariness seemed gone; there was communicated even to him a touch of the excitement that plainly affected the others.

Later he fancied that there had been something a trifle sinister in this excitement.

The study was lit as usual with its shaded lamps. As Percy followed the other two in he noticed that Mrs. Bennett was not there; but that there sat in the deep chair by the fire a heavily-built man, clean-shaven, slightly bald, dressed in dark clothes. So much he saw in the light of the lamp, but no more. But, as the door was closed by the Vicar, he saw that the man had stood up, and that his face was in shadow.

"This is Mr. Railton, doctor . . . Doctor Brandreth-Smith. . . . And this is the young man, Mr. Railton."

Percy found his hand taken an instant later by the stranger, and could see his features more clearly.

He was a rather heavy-faced man, going gray about the temples: and there were lines about the corners of his mouth and of his eyes. He wore a stand-up collar, with straight edges in front, and a broad black tie that hid any sign of a shirt about his throat. His hand was large and firm and well-cushioned.

The Vicar, still obviously rather perturbed, bustled about, setting them all in their places. Percy was placed in the deep chair opposite the stranger's; his father was near him, and like a kind of umpire, the Vicar settled himself in an upright desk chair, as if to arbitrate between the disputants. No refreshment — not even cocoa — was mentioned. The hour was evidently too pregnant.

"Now, Mr. Railton," began the Vicar, leaning forward and clasping his hands over his knees, "*In medias res*,[1] if you please. I have told you the outlines. This young man here has been much taken by a friar — Father Hilary — in St. Francis', Kensington; and wants to become a Romanist. It is only fair that he should hear both sides. He is most reasonable — most reasonable," he repeated, looking up at Percy approvingly. "He wants just to hear both sides, I am sure — no more than that; and . . . and it is his father's hope, and indeed of all of us, that when he has done so he will be content to remain where he is — where

---

[1] "In the middle way"; to Anglicans a way of describing a church that they believe to be neither Protestant nor Papal.

he is, in our dear old Church of England. Now, Mr. Railton, if you please."

There was a moment's silence, the Vicar glanced up again at the stranger, and then at Percy. Then the big man began.

"Well — er — can you give me any reasons, Mr. . . . Mr, Smith — I mean solid theological reasons for wishing to make this change? I suppose you would scarcely allow that . . . that the mere attractiveness of a Franciscan is a sufficient reason for separating yourself from the religion of your parents?"

His voice was rather impressive: deep and a little husky; and with an odd ring of a kind of authoritativeness in it. He kept his eyes down as he spoke.

Percy moistened his lips with his tongue. He was quite sure now that he did not like this man. There was a certain domination about him; but it repelled rather than attracted. He felt entirely different towards him from that which he felt, for example, towards the Vicar. He was conscious of an air of oppression.

"Well," he began, "it's rather hard to put it into words. I . . . I haven't had many talks yet with Roman Catholics. I . . . I think I should find it rather hard to put into words."

There was dead silence. Percy felt this would never do: he really must marshal an argument or two.

"It . . . it was the idea of sacraments that first began —"

This was too much for the Vicar. He almost wailed out a protest.

"But, my dear boy, surely you have heard all that again and again from the pulpit here: we Anglicans, you know, have the sacraments just as much as the Romanists. Surely you know that!"

"I know," said Percy, warming up a little. (He felt he could talk so much more easily to the Vicar.) "I know. But . . . but it sounded different somehow, when Father Hilary preached about them. But that's only the beginning —"

"But —" burst out the Vicar again; and then he realized that they would never get on like this. "Well — my dear boy, finish your statement; finish your statement, and then listen to what Mr. Railton has to say."

So Percy began again.

"It was that that began it," he said — "that's to say after I began to think about it. And all I can say is that it really did sound different. I know that we've got Confirmation, as well as Baptism and Communion; and . . . and Absolution —" (He paused again and glanced tentatively at the Vicar: he was really not quite sure whether this was a sacrament or not, according to Church of England theology. But Mr. Bennett only nodded his head, half-encouragingly, once or twice.) "Then there are Matrimony and Orders — if those are sacraments." (Again he was not quite sure of his ground.

He had lately looked through the Thirty-Nine Articles with some care, and felt a little confused on the point.) "And then there's Unction. . . . Oh! No, we haven't got that, have we?"

The Vicar cleared his throat.

"That is in abeyance," he said firmly. "But it's not necessary to salvation in any case."

Percy passed on.

"Well; but all this seemed so much clearer when Father Hilary preached. . . . I don't know why, but it did. But that's only the beginning."

Again he paused; and again the heavy figure opposite him was silent and motionless. The Vicar leaned back as if in despair.

"Well," began Percy again; "after that I read some books and talked to a friend; and it seems to me that the texts about St. Peter settle it."

"Which texts, please?" came the steady voice from the deep chair.

"Well — the *Thou art Peter,* and *I will give thee the keys* — for one."

"And what about, *Get thee behind me, Satan?*"

"That was when St. Peter said what was wrong, wasn't it?"

"Then St. Peter can say what is wrong? And if so, what becomes of his pretended Infallibility?"

There was a curious ring, as if of a strongly repressed violence in the voice. It pricked Percy into a more alert mood. A faint thrill of resentful defiance went through him.

"Of course he can say what is wrong, but not when, as the Catechism says, he speaks to the whole Church on a matter of faith, as Pastor of all Christians."

"Well; go on, sir."

"That seems to me the point," said Percy. "Of course there are others, but —"

"But you have not yet told us how, even if Christ did give to St. Peter the prerogative you suggest, you go on to prove that it was handed on to his successors."

"It's like the kings of England," said Percy feebly.

"Nor how is it that so many saints and doctors, whom even you would allow to be so, have lived and died outside the communion of Rome without any notion at all that they were outside the Church of Christ."

"I don't think that is so," said Percy, once more pricked into defiance by the growing contempt and patronage in the other's voice.

"You will find that it is so, if you will consult impartial authorities," said the stranger, in whom a kind of glow seemed steadily to be rising, warming up his voice with something like suppressed passion. "Nor have you told us how, if all this be true, you can reconcile with it the lives of some of the monsters of iniquity who have sat in Peter's chair; nor, if the Truth is so mighty and must prevail, the Roman Court of today — and indeed of all days — has always been so bitterly opposed to all intellectual progress or liberty. Nor again how it is that, if this be the Church of Christ, the countries under Rome's domination have always been the most backward of all European lands; nor why it is that the Church of Christ tramples down the liberties of men, and crushes their instincts, and breaks or forbids domestic ties. . . . My dear young sir, you have not yet touched the fringe of this question. . . . Now listen to me —"

The glow had waxed to a white hot passion, so swiftly and overpoweringly, that while the man spoke, he dominated the room. It was extraordinary how it transfigured him; and how, too, the others seemed, so to speak, shrunken to nothing. His face was still in shadow, yet it seemed as if it burned; his eyes were pools of shadow, and the lines about his mouth like gashes. His great voice vibrated like a harp; and his words poured forth without hesitation.

"Now listen to me —" he cried. "Here are you, my young sir, proposing to change the religion you were brought up in, to sever yourself from your family, and to deliver yourself over, bound hand and foot, into the power of a Church of which you know nothing — absolutely nothing — a Church which has been the enemy of all progress and enlightenment since the day in which its rulers, mad with ambition, first seized on words of Christ — which He may or may not have spoken — and tortured them into a system to bolster up their own domination. There is not an honest theologian or scholar in the world — even Romanist scholars (if there are any!) — who will not confess that nine-tenths of the Papal claims are built up on forgery and ambition. I tell you that there is no doubt on the subject at all. I have studied these things as you can never hope to study them. I know the system as you cannot possibly know it; and I tell you it is lies, lies, lies from beginning to end. And it is this Church to which you are thinking of submitting! I tell you that you will rue the day, bitterly, when your eyes are opened and you see the truth — bitterly, when you understand for what you have exchanged your liberty and the love of your friends and your own self-respect. The texts you quote mean nothing — at least nothing of the kind that you pretend. I could point you to a dozen texts, or omissions, that militate against the Papal claims, for every one that you can quote for them. But the root of the matter does not lie in texts: it lies deeper: it lies in the character of every man — in the choice as to whether he will preserve his liberty or sacrifice it; whether he is strong enough to walk alone, or weak enough to rely upon a false authority that cannot perform what it promises."

Percy leaned back, dazed and bewildered, as the other ended.

Yet the whole of his being was in protest. He knew with a conviction which he could not, intellectually, in the least justify, that this assault was unfair and one sided. He had heard it before, though not in one blistering torrent, nor driven in by the power with which it was now forced at him; and he knew well enough that its apparent strength lay in the circumstances and air of its delivery, rather than in its contents. Yet he did not know what to answer. He could not meet force by force: and in his despair he was aware that his whole soul had, so to speak, set its teeth in obstinacy, and was more inclined by the tirade towards his growing convictions rather than away from them.

"I . . . I don't agree —" he began.

"Don't agree!" thundered the other. "What do you mean by that? I tell you there is no other point of view tenable by an intelligent man. Do you suppose you know more of the subject than I? Why, I tell you—"

He stopped, as if on the edge of an indiscreet disclosure. And in that instant there flashed on Percy's mind a conviction that came to him like an inspiration. He remembered to have seen this man's name before, somewhere, in some paper or pamphlet: he understood, or began to think that he understood, something of the reason why this man's personality at once evaded and dominated and repelled him. And a huge wave of wrath rose up in him, such as he had never experienced before in all his life — a wave that he kept suspended from breaking, by a violent effort of will, until he was sure.

He was on his feet without knowing it; and a tremendous determination was in his voice.

"Mr. Bennett," he cried. "Who is he? I will know. I think I do know. . . . Who is he?"

The Vicar too was on his feet, tremulous and deprecatory.

"My dear boy, my dear boy — now why all this —"

"I will know," cried Percy. "Tell me — who is he? I'll . . . I'll never trust you again if you don't tell me —"

He felt a hand on his shoulder from behind; but he whisked fiercely on his heel.

"Let go, Father. I'm not a child. I tell you, I will know."

There was dead silence.

The stranger sat motionless in the deep chair; his elbows rested on the arms of it; and his hands met across his mouth; his eyes were in shadow, and seemed expressionless.

Percy was shaking all over. Never in all his life had so strange a passion seized him. It was like some amazing intoxication of the spirit. He gripped himself with his whole will, and went straight across to the door, and stood there with his hand on the handle.

"Mr. Bennett," he said, "if you are going to treat me like a child, I . . . I shall behave like one. If you do not tell me who Mr. Railton is, I shall leave this house and never come into it again. But if you will tell, then, if I am wrong, I will apologize; and if I am right, well, I will promise still to hear anything you have to say — as soon as he's gone or at any other time. . . . Now, will you tell me?"

"Doctor," cried the Vicar piteously. "Percy, my dear boy —"

Percy stamped, without knowing it, and gripped the handle more tightly.

"Will you tell me?" he cried. "Is Mr. Railton the ex-priest, and the anti-Catholic lecturer?"

There was silence.

Then as conviction solidified, the boy cried again:

"Is he the ex-priest, who married a week after he had left the Church — who — who —"

He stopped. He could not go on. The strange passion was on him again, shaking and tearing him. So he stood a moment, waiting for an answer. Then he wheeled and went out.

(2)

"There, my dear," said Mrs. Bennett soothingly. "Now you've had your cocoa, just tell me all about it quietly."

It was nearly eleven o'clock on that lamentable night; and Mrs. Bennett, it appeared, had been the only person who had behaved at once adequately and tranquilly. She had entirely refused to be present at the portentous interview in the study, and even to entertain Mr. Railton to supper.

"If you think it right to have him, my dear," she had said, "I must not say a word to dissuade you. But I had so very much rather not meet him. You know it was not a very pleasant story. I daresay he's a very good man now, as you say; but somehow I can't quite forget —"

"That seems to me not quite Christian —" interrupted her husband.

"I daresay it's not," she said peacefully. "I am a very poor Christian, I know."

So it was settled. The Vicar went down to the station to meet the lecturer and entertained him at supper, saying that his wife was not very well and begged to be excused. (This was sufficiently true: she really had a cold.) And Mrs. Bennett sat upstairs, retaining at least so much humility as not to condemn her husband for doing a thing which, personally, she disliked extremely; and listening to the subdued voices. Then the study door had banged beneath about half-past nine, quick steps had gone across the hall, and then the hall door had banged too. Then there were confused noises that made her sit upright listening even more acutely; again steps ran across the hall, to and fro; and then a loud lamentable talking in her husband's voice. Then the footsteps of at least two people had passed through the hall and gone out. And then silence.

It was not till nearly eleven that her husband had returned alone, and come straight up to her where she awaited him, in such a state of agitation that she had led him straight downstairs again, forced him to put on his slippers and to drink two cups of cocoa before consenting to listen to any connected story. Then at last she had bidden him unburden himself.

"It has been terrible, terrible," moaned the Vicar. "You were quite right, my dear: I should never have had such a man. . . . He, he spoke very well indeed, though I did not quite agree with all that he said; but even then I began to get a little nervous. And then Percy guessed who he was; and there was a dreadful scene; and —"

She looked up patiently.

"Please begin at the beginning, dear; I don't understand at all."

He told her, with tolerable intelligibility; describing the scene, and Percy's violence, and his exit. Then it seemed that the doctor ran after his son, leaving the Vicar alone with the lecturer, who immediately demanded some kind of apology for the insults to which he had been subjected. The Vicar had given him these, abundantly: he said that he was horrified and ashamed at such a scene, and to think that a guest of his had been so treated.

Then Mr. Railton had demanded the same of Percy, and desired to be confronted with him; and the two had gone down to the doctor's house through the dark.

There, again, scene had followed scene. Percy had locked himself into his room, and refused to open. There had been an agitated consultation in the doctor's room at the back of the house, with Mrs. Smith present. (Fortunately, Helen had gone to bed early.) And, in the middle Percy had appeared; and had finally used words which might conceivably be construed into an apology, saying that he regretted having shown so much violence; and that it was not for him in his undecided state to lay down the law quite so furiously as he had done. . . .

Well, at last Mr. Railton had gone, still white and angry, but apparently pacified; and there had followed again another interview with Percy.

"Yes, my dear," said the Vicar. "He did finally promise to come and talk the whole matter over again. But it has been terrible — terrible. I have never had such a scene in my life. I . . . I had no idea that the boy had such strong feelings. You were quite right; I should not have had such a man, even in so good a cause. I fear it has had quite the contrary effect to what I had hoped."

His wife laid her hand on his knee. "And now you must go to bed," she said gently.

Chapter XIV

Father Hilary smiled, not in the least ironically, but with an engaging frankness.

I'm quite sure you needn't be scrupulous about that," he said. "You tell me you want to be a Religious. Well, no Religious Order in the world would accept you until you'd been at least a year or two a Catholic. So there's no kind of reason to distress your people yet. You see you may easily change your mind yet. And your people have been so good to you, in giving their consent to your coming to me for instructions, that you mustn't upset them still further."

"I shall never change," declared Percy.

"All the better," smiled the priest. "But I assure you that no one can be certain of that, least of all yourself. . . . You were telling me about the Vicar, though. Tell me what he said, after the time you had with Mr. Railton."

"Oh! it was just as I thought," cried the boy. "Certainly he gave me one or two things to read that I couldn't exactly answer. But he kept on patting me on the shoulder, and telling me to cheer up and that I should be all right soon! He . . . he was awfully kind, you know; but of course he can't bear my becoming a Catholic. I've brought one or two things on paper I want you to answer for me, if you'll be so kind."

They were sitting in the same bare little parlor round which Percy had rolled his eyes so expectantly a month ago. Things had gone with him extraordinarily smoothly, considering the position: he had had his interview — in fact three or four interviews with the Vicar, besides the fateful one already described — and at least a dozen serious conversations with his parents. But everyone had behaved beautifully: they had shaken their heads at him, telling him that he was too young to judge of such matters, that he had been influenced by a subtle priest, that it was all an emotional fit that would pass; but they had "played the game" as Percy expressed it to Reggie. The Vicar had put controversial points before him with an air of sublime

assurance, telling him that no scholars — literally no
scholars at all — could defend the Papal position; but then,
obviously this was what he believed; and, if so, equally obviously it was his duty to say so. Mrs. Bennett had smiled
at him regretfully and spoken of the beautiful services of
the Church of England; Mrs. Main had eyed him with
sharp-eyed interest once or twice; a choirman had asked
him whether the report was really true. Helen had regarded him with wide-eyed amazement. But they had all
"played the game"; and Percy was sincerely grateful. It
seemed to him astonishing that so great a transformation
could have taken place in four weeks. Then he had known
nothing and faced nothing but an emotion. Now the world's
scenery had shifted as if under some invisible and gigantic
force; and he sat here for his first instruction. It was exactly as Mr. Bennett had feared. The violent scene with the
ex-priest had increased, instead of diminishing, his resolution.

He pulled out his papers.

"One thing more before we begin, Father. How long will
the instructions take?"

"That depends entirely on yourself," said the priest.
"How often can you come?"

"As often as you can have me, Father."

"Twice a week?"

"Why, certainly."

"Well, if you can keep up twice a week, and meantime go
to Mass on Sundays — in fact, live as a Catholic — I
should say five or six months would see the end of you."

Percy's face fell.

"As long as that?"

"Yes. . . . You see it isn't simply the instructions themselves, though these take a good time. But it's the testing
of your perseverance. You must make perfectly sure that
it's more than a fancy."

"But —"

"My dear boy, don't think I think that. I don't, for a moment. I'm as convinced as I can be that you're a perfectly
genuine case. But, you know, I'm not infallible; nor are
you. We must test ourselves well, in such a big thing as
this. . . . It is a big thing, you know. The biggest."

There was a pause.

"Well, let's have the Vicar's objections," said the priest, smiling.

Father Hilary had been very agreeably surprised indeed by Percy's account of the interview with the ex-priest.

It had seemed to him extraordinary that the boy should have been so affected, and, still more, so enraged by such an encounter.

"I . . . I can't understand it, Father," Percy had said in a sudden burst of confidence. "I . . . I felt as if I was drunk or drugged. It seemed to me so mean to use such a man; but that wasn't all. There was something in the man himself. . . . Who was he? Was he really ever a priest?"

"Oh, yes," said the friar tranquilly. "He was a priest. He left the Church about eight years ago."

"Are the stories true about him?"

"I think it's best not to say too much," said the friar. "It is true that he married a week after he . . . he left the Church."

"But his vows!"

"Yes?"

"He broke them?"

"Why, yes. It's a free country," said the friar.

"And he lectures against the Church?"

"He began lecturing a month after his marriage. He makes his living by it, I suppose."

Percy sat silent looking vaguely out at the dull London sky, against which stood out the brick gable-end of the poor church.

Then the friar suggested a little Catechism.

(2)

Sensational incidents happen, as often as not, without even the rumor of a warning. Occasionally, indeed, they are led up to: the orchestra begins to gather its forces, the kettle drums to throb, the strings to tremble, the double basses to roar, till the supreme bellowing crash is inevitable. But in at least as many cases there is no warning at all. The thunderbolt falls on a spring morning; or the gun goes off as it hangs on the wall.

Percy was as normal as a proselyte under instruction ever can be, as he went home that Saturday evening. He had all his plans serenely fixed: he was to hear Mass in St. Joseph's at half-past ten, and to go to Benediction with Reggie, at the Oratory, in the afternoon. Then Monday would begin again as usual with the City; he was to go to Father Hilary again on Wednesday after office hours; and so on, and so on, for six months. And about Easter he would be received into the Church.

His fervor had lasted quite satisfactorily. It was perfectly true that the world had changed for him in the most fundamental way possible. Things were still entirely different, because the center of them all had shifted from himself to someone else. The bewilderment had almost wholly left him, but the Fact remained. He continued to act from this new center; and the difficulties that in nine cases out of ten besiege such a transference were practically abolished for him by the smoothness with which, on the whole, his friends had accepted it.

He thought sometimes of the girl he had met in the train, and had had, indeed, a day or two in which he had to adjust his thought of her to his new ideal of the Religious Life. But even this was not a severe struggle: he was not, so far as he knew, at all in love with her, and he was very completely in love with the life of a friar. He wanted to see her again; and he assured himself that he could help her more than ever now; but, so far, she had not written; and he was helpless.

It was not at all extraordinary that the life of which he had caught a glimpse in the Friary had attracted him so violently; chiefly, because it was completely the opposite of the life he had hitherto unwillingly led. But this, honestly, was not the only reason. In the midst of the clean silence of the place, the austere dignity of the friars, the unanxious poverty, he perceived a Presence that was its heart. Religious matters, and doctrines, and all the rest, fitted in now with a completeness he had never before perceived: choir practices and parochial activities and early celebrations and Gadsby in C — all these things were good and harmless enough, natural expressions and accompaniments to the sober moral religion he had known in Hanstead; but he felt there was a great deal more here in Kensington. The difference between the two was as the difference between the imitative life of a child and the self-originated life of a man, between liking and loving, between gentle warmth and a fiery heat. The change for him, therefore, was not merely an interior one; but he had found, he thought, an exterior frame too for the new passion of his life.

Here then was Percy Brandreth-Smith, as he stepped out of the train at Hanstead. Certainly great things had happened to him; the world had opened to him like a flower from a bud. . . . He was changed inside and out; he was to be a Catholic about Easter; he would begin to prepare himself, still in the same old setting at home, for the further life that in a year or two would be his in the Franciscan novitiate. That was his program.

(3)

He put his latchkey into the door, and stepped in.

The first thing he noticed was that the drawing room was dark. This was quite unusual. He lit the gas himself, and looked vaguely round. Then he went across to the dining room. This too was dark; but the table was laid. Then he wondered whether everyone was up in his father's study; so he went up there, and there was no one. He called for Helen, but there was no answer.

As he came down again, a little uneasy, he heard the door from the yard into the house open, and then the swish of a servant's dress.

"Alice," he called.

She whisked up from the back, looking rather guilty.

"Where's everybody?"

"I don't know, sir. Mrs. Smith said they'd be back for dinner."

"Are they all out?"

"Yes, sir; they went out after the mid-day post — the doctor and Mrs. Smith and Miss Helen, all together."

She hesitated.

"I think there was a letter, sir."

There was evidently nothing to be done; but it seemed exceedingly mysterious. He went back to the drawing room and walked about a little, relieved that, at any rate, nothing serious had happened — at least nothing that his own imagination could conceive. But what in the world could it be, that had suddenly snatched all three of them away without a word or message left for himself? It didn't seem as if it could be illness or death of any kind.

But he had not very long to wait.

He was beginning to doze over the *Nation,* when he heard the latchkey in the door; and he was in the hall to meet all three of them as they came in.

"What's up?" he said.

No one answered him for a moment. There was an air of intense and suppressed excitement in the faces of his mother and sister so far as he could see them. His father was still detaching his key from the door: then he turned.

"Ah! My boy," he said heartily; "come into the drawing room and we'll tell you."

With his own heart beating, Percy followed the three in. His mother had drawn off her gloves and was warming her hands at the little fire. Her face had a very odd tense look, and Helen was radiant.

"It's a piece of very astonishing news," said the doctor, smiling too. "Can't you guess?"

Percy shook his head.

"Well, you know who your old great-uncle James was?"

"Yes."

"Well; he's died. Last week. And your mother inherits everything."

"Everything?"

"Yes. That adopted boy of his disappointed him, it seems. So the lawyers told us this morning. And your mother comes in for the lot."

"What does that mean?" asked Percy.

"Well — Marston Park; a house in Wilton Crescent and from ten- to twelve-thousand a year."

Percy sat down.

End of Part I

Part II

Chapter I

(1)

Throughout the first time that the vague splendors, in which, as in a sea of glory, Percy's imagination had moved since the first announcement, became materialized and tangible, was as he drove up to Marston Park with his father halfway through November.

He had had glimpses before of his altered circumstances, but glimpses that dissolved again. There had been an air of undreamed of opulence in the house in Wilton Crescent where he had gone to wait one day for his mother, and where in the shrouded drawing room he had sat listening to the voices of his mother and of mysterious men whom he had later identified as house decorators. He had looked, as in a trance, at some photographs of Marston and had listened, with parted lips, to the raptures of Helen, who had been down there with her mother for a couple of days. But these hints and implications had faded again in the familiarity of the City life which for a month longer his father wished him to continue. Long conversations with his father — the announcement to him that at Christmas his allowance of three-hundred a year would begin, and, with it, his duty of getting a knowledge of how to manage an estate — these things had failed to do more than give his imagination vast and vague materials on which to embroider impracticable schemes. These schemes were precise enough, down to the tiniest detail: they included the building of a chapel at Marston of a particular architecture, a proposal of immediate marriage to the girl in the train, and simultaneous with this latter, a rehearsal of the scene when he should leave Marston and become a Franciscan friar. But they were in the air; they were sheer flights of imagination; they resembled fairy stories which the relater knows to be untrue: for he was still without the solidity of experience. He knew that all must be in reserve until he had seen Marston and, so to speak, tasted it between his lips. The Franciscan-friar scheme was resolutely put on a shelf until this was done; but he would have said, at this period, if he had been directly questioned, that he still intended to carry this out.

There was only one thing, perhaps, that had helped really to bring the fantastic change that had come to him into the realm of reality, and that the discernibly altered bearing of his employers and fellows in the office. There was a deference paid to him, and a readiness to overlook slips on his part that was exceedingly gratifying. He had responded to this by an increased carefulness that was a great satisfaction to himself. It seemed to him that, of all his friends, Father Hilary was the only one who did not understand. That priest, on the revelation being made to him on the occasion of the next instruction, had smiled and congratulated him courteously, and three minutes later was explaining the doctrine of Indulgences.

(2)

"The lodge gate," said his father, as the brougham that had fetched them both from the station drew up suddenly and the footman leaped down from the box to ring the bell. Percy peered from the window. They had driven up from the deep valley beneath, and were now, it seemed, near the crest of the rolling hill, in the midst of a deep country lane. The village, Percy understood, was over on the other side.

It was the lodge at which he looked, a solemn Grecian building, resembling a small temple, on the upper side of the great iron gate, with three steps leading up to the portico. A woman ran out, with deference in every movement, rolled back the gates on their tall stone posts each surmounted by a rampant beast, and the carriage moved in. A small boy regarded the carriage gravely from the lodge door. Percy solemnly bowed his head as the woman curtsied.

And now the glory of the park began its display. Above and below the carriage road it stretched in great luxurious curves and slopes, dotted with groups of giant trees; far away to the left and in front ran the gleam of water which he knew to be the famous trout-stream. The splendor of late autumn was over everything, and golden sunlight. Rabbits skipped into the bracken as they passed:

the chuckling of pheasants sounded from the deep woods whose nearer fringe stood high against the sky to the right. A stable bell began to ring far away in front. . . . A man in gamekeeper's dress came into sight, walking with his gun, and, as the carriage passed, saluted deliberately.

His father was talking now and again as they drove on; but Percy listened with but half his attention. With the rest he was soaking up impressions. This was all his, practically; and would be actually his one day. Here he could walk with his gun (when he had learned to shoot), no man forbidding him; he could fish in that stream; he would ride under those trees. . . . He would come in the motor along the drive, and be saluted at the gate. . . .

"We're just right for lunch," said his father. "Your mother put it off till two on purpose. This afternoon I want you to come round with me. Have you any knicker-bockers? Your mother —"

Percy nodded.

"I bought them on purpose," he said. "Ah! Is that the house?"

They were passing into a belt of trees and undergrowth; and there, seen dimly between the stems, was a mass of gray buildings.

"The carriage-drive goes right round to the west," said his father. "We shall see better presently. . . . There."

And then the trees were past, and the south side came into view.

(3)

It was a noble house that old William Brandreth had built for himself in the reign of Queen Anne; which sovereign herself, it was related, had stayed with him there at least twice. The main entrance is to the west of the square forecourt, of which two sides — the servants' quarters and the stables respectively — face one another across a lawn round which runs the drive; a third side is open, and from the fourth the grand front of the house looks straight across down the slopes and the lower terraced gardens into the valley beneath. It is this fourth side which gives a real classical nobility to the whole, sufficient to draw appreciative Americans from London. It is, literally, in the grand style. Three rows of tall windows, surmounted by a pilastered parapet, are broken by a Corinthian portico to which rises a flight of a dozen shallow steps. Within this portico, beyond glass doors, lies the central hall from which a stone staircase branches up to the gallery on either side, from which open out the stately rooms.

It was in this hall that Mrs. Brandreth-Smith (as she now announced herself on her new cards) was waiting for her husband and son. She was standing by the big fireplace, and came forward to kiss Percy.

"You look cold, my boy," she said.

Percy had scarcely seen his mother at all during the last six weeks. It had been a time of furious activity. There had been the house in Wilton Crescent for which the repainting had to be settled, and then countless inspections and arrangements had to be made down here at Marston. She had come and gone like an intent whirlwind, with Helen whisked reluctantly in her wake. Mysterious persons appeared and reappeared in the little house at Hanstead; notes and telegrams were as leaves in autumn: Percy would leave home in the morning and come back at night to find his father alone again. He had scarcely expected such competent energy as she had shown. But now, even in the moment of greeting, he perceived that she had assumed another attitude. She seemed to have blossomed in amazing ways.

There was first her dress. He knew nothing of dress, but he perceived there was an appearance of stateliness — of black silk and jet and lace, not so tightly fitted together as her older costumes. There was the way she carried her head, a shade higher and a trifle on one side. There was her voice, that had in it a vague drawl. He did not exactly analyze these things, but he perceived them. As she kissed him she left her hand for an instant on his shoulder in an unusual manner.

"We'll go into lunch at once," she said. "There's Helen coming."

The impression of a subtle change in his family grew on his mind during lunch. It was a great room in which they sat, tall and white paneled, with a high marble mantelpiece, elongated-looking portraits — one of Queen Anne herself, over the mantelpiece, particularly drew his attention — and vast mahogany furniture. Three men waited on them — one, the butler, resembling a very respectable dissenting minister of the old school, chin-bearded and tight-lipped, in broadcloth; the two others, young men, with a great severity of face and correctness of demeanor. These were servants of old Mr. Brandreth, who had consented to remain at any rate for the present. But even more than these, Percy regarded his family. He noticed now that his father was in a surprising gray tail-suit with khaki spats, Helen in a tailor-made dress of tweed with a shortish skirt that had nothing whatever in common with the Greek style, and his mother as has been described. No one said anything about these changes, and this made them the more observable. Everything, somehow, seemed different. The feel of the tablecloth over the rounded edges of the table was opulent and solid: the silver was amazingly bright; even the taste of the food was suggestive. The very family looked unusual. Percy found himself, almost unconsciously, playing up to his part: he nodded, with drooping eyelids, to a decanter of sherry that appeared in the air by his right shoulder: he leaned forward and took an apple nonchalantly when he had finished cheese. The talk too was slow and stately: there was no quick glancing here and there of his mother's eyes; no sudden nods and sharp directions. All went smoothly and adequately like a huge noiseless machine. Coffee came round with a silver tray on which was a silver box of cigarettes and a silver spirit lamp. Percy lit a cigarette without a word. Then the men went out. It was impossible to conceive a greater contrast than all this, set beside Hanstead.

"Your father wants you to go round with him this afternoon," said his mother. "You have knickerbockers and a Norfolk jacket?"

"Yes," said Percy.

"You'd better put them on, I think. It's wet in the park."

"What are you going to do, my dear?" asked the doctor.

"Helen and I have some calls to return. We must go to the Marridons first, I suppose."

Helen lowered her eyelids a little and tilted her head.

"I suppose we shall soon get over all that," she said.

Her mother turned on her; and Percy saw in a moment a kind of set and almost fierce intentness break out through her calm.

"Helen," she said, "we shall not soon get over that, as you say. You must remember that these things are your duty now: and I shall expect you to do them."

The start for the round of calls was a great affair.

Percy had been upstairs to change, and had tried to take his room quietly. It was of incredible size, opening out of the gallery, in the angle near the stables, and looked straight out westwards. His pair of suitcases had vanished entirely, and he had rung to have them brought up. One of the severe young men, named James, had silently, on being questioned, opened wardrobe doors and drawers and displayed the contents of the suitcases lying there as if it had been their eternal home. He kindly explained too the mystery of the little curtained cupboard where two pairs of boots, a pair of pumps and another of carpet slippers reposed in state.

"Oh — ah!" said Percy. "You might put out my Norfolk suit and my thick boots, will you?"

James did so instantly, in silence, while Percy looked out of the window in an abstracted fashion. (He felt he was doing it rather well.)

"Anything more you require, sir?

"Er — no thanks," said Percy.

When he had changed — pausing during the process to finger some new polished surface of wardrobe or table that caught his eye — he came down again, conscious of a certain suitability in his dress, and yet more of the splendid solidity of the house, the solid white stone stairs under the deep Turkey carpet, the massive banisters, the dignified space and calm of the great hall where Helen was putting on her gloves by the fire. She grimaced in a friendly fashion as he strolled up to her with his hands in his pockets.

"Got to go calling," she said. "Wish I was you!"

"Who are you going to call on?"

She nodded to the great polished table against the wall: and he went and looked at the cards in the Chinese bowl.

"Lord Marridon . . . Miss Marridon," he read from two at the top; and at the corner "Cleaver." He turned again on her, with a sudden happy warmth at his heart.

"What d'you think of it all? Rather fun, isn't it?"

She grimaced again, cheerfully.

"Oh! It's got points," she said. "But I do bar this —"

She stopped as the rustle of her mother's dress came out of the drawing room.

Her mother was more stately than ever. Her bonnet nodded with various shining bits of jet: her mantle was rich; her face was severe and stately.

"Well? You've found your way about?" she said.

"Oh! Yes — I say, Mother —"

"Yes?"

"Who's that?" He indicated the portrait of a gentleman in a fawn-colored suit over the fireplace. The gentleman sat at a table, apparently out of doors, in a great chair. In the distance, under a thunderous sky, was Marston Park itself, looking very white and new.

"That's old Mr. Brandreth," she said; "who built the house. Queen Anne stayed here, you know."

"Oh —; and, I say, Mother?"

"Yes?"

"What about shooting? I've never shot, you know."

"You must learn," she said shortly. "Your father tells me the woods are full of pheasants."

"What about a gun?"

"You must get one. We'll see about that."

Percy was astonished and even awed by her adequateness. Certainly she had expanded with her fortunes, *pari passu*. There was a masterfulness about her that compelled admiration. Already it was plain that she was to rule in a new kind of way. The boy began to perceive that his father even must now take second place — that he had already begun to learn his assigned part; that the gray-tailed suit and the khaki spats were the result of his first lessons, and that Helen and himself too must prepare themselves for school. They were all to be resolutely "county";[1] there must be no appearance of the *nouveaux*

---

[1] That is, to the manor born, fitting in naturally as if from birth.

riches about them; they were of the Blood, and, if they were but recently come into their own, this was no reason why they should show any signs of unfamiliarity with their responsibilities and privileges. The solemn walk round this afternoon, the solemn calls that the ladies were to pay in the two-horse brougham that already waited outside the Corinthian porch — these must all be done in the proper manner.

The actual departure was as awe-inspiring as all else.

The doors were gravely set open by Underhill — the butler of a dissenting appearance — and a footman came through the swing door at the back of the hall bearing a fur rug. Mrs. Brandreth-Smith sailed forward rustling and down the steps: Helen with one giggling glance, and then a deep sigh, followed her. Percy went out after them, interested, and placed one booted leg on the low pedestal of the steps, to observe his mother the better. The carriage door was closed; the long-coated footman, with a black band round his dark blue sleeve, darted round the back and ascended the box beside the habited coachman: Mr. Underhill bowed slightly from the waist; the mistress of the house waved a gloved hand from the window, and the brougham rolled off.

(4)

There is nothing like a hot bath for the stimulating of thought; and as Percy, about seven o'clock that evening, lay at full length in the white-tiled bathroom whose door was next to his own, his mind moved like a smooth-running wheel.

The bathroom itself was perfection. It was tiled throughout — walls, floor and ceiling. The bath edges were of marble, and the interior was of a tender blue-green enamel (he glimmered through the clear water like a nymph), the fittings were of the brightest nickel; and a great open kind of rack supported warm and dry towels, above nickeled hot water pipes, within reach of his hand when he should choose to stand up.

Since tea he had sat with Helen in an extremely charming room on the ground floor, looking out on to the south lawns, named the "school room," still in his Norfolk suit; and the two had talked endlessly. . . . About seven he thought he would go up and dress, so as to have a knock at the billiard balls before dinner, but had been unable to resist the suggestion of James, whom he found in his room laying out his new dress clothes, that perhaps Mr. Percy would like a bath, and should he (James) turn on the hot water, sir? Here, then, he lay, soaking. The pleasant heat thrilled toes and knees and fingers; and, as has been observed, stimulated thought to an astonishing degree.

His primary emotion was one of an intense and excited pleasure at the realization of his dreams. This afternoon he had been round the park with his father, accompanied for a part of the way by a deferential gamekeeper, and had viewed with delight the pheasants clucking in the undergrowth, the stretches of turf beneath the trees, the long vistas of the "rides" in the woods, the roofs of the "Home Farm," the stubble fields against the sky. It was astounding to look upon these things from a proprietor's point of view — to know, for instance, that he was to learn to shoot and ride, that he could ask Reggie Ballard and his other friends to come down and see him do it. For, as has been said, he had dreamed of these things: he had felt, by a kind of instinct, that he had a right to them; he had envied people in motors and large houses: he had woven visionary fabrics of all that he would do if he were rich too. . . . And now the Prince would enjoy his own again.

His secondary emotions concerned his larger plans for the future. It had dawned on him soon after the arrival of the first news that he was now free in a new kind of way — that he could marry, for instance, practically, at his own will. Now he understood better how vast was this liberty. He need calculate no longer on ways and means. He was to have three hundred pounds a year of his own, at once, as a bachelor: of course, if he married, he would have more. And he and his wife, he supposed, could live here.

Now there clashed with such schemes as these his little idea about being a friar. He had not, up to the present, actually renounced that ideal. Certainly it had retired a little; but, as he lay here now, tingling with exercise and the delicious sting of the hot water, it came and looked him in the face once more, and seemed to him not so attractive. It must be remembered that he had not, to the best of his knowledge, swerved in the faintest degree from his new religious convictions; he had exulted, vaguely, this afternoon, in the thought that this might be made a Catholic estate one day. But, seriously, it began now to be suggested to him that the complete change in his fortunes might really be an indication of another vocation altogether. He began, in a word, to think of his Responsibilities; and when a young man begins to think of his Responsibilities and the serious call to a secular life that they may involve, his conscience needs watching. Might it not be, he thought to himself, that a Higher Life, for him, was to settle down here quietly and unsensationally, to learn the duties of his estate, to . . . to marry and have children; to build, in time, a Catholic chapel here, and have a chaplain? . . . Could he not accomplish more? . . .

(He turned over on his side in the delicious water.) This must seriously be thought about. He must consult Father Hilary. . . . He was glad that he had not, so far, actually mentioned to his parents or Helen, his desire to become a friar.

Chapter II

(1)

H e awoke next morning to find James in the room, drawing back the curtains, and a little tray by his bedside that held a cup of tea in a little pink cup, two slices of bread and butter on a little pink plate, and two letters.

"It's a quarter to nine, sir," said James.

Percy turned over a little more in bed and picked up his letters. He knew the handwriting of Father Hilary, but the other, re-addressed from Hanstead, was unknown to him; he turned the second over once or twice, conjecturing about it, as the human way is of one who has not a large correspondence. Then he opened it; and saw that the address was that of His Highness' Theater.

Dear Mr. Smith," he read,

"I wonder if you would care to come and see me here on Monday next. I think you said you'd never been behind the curtain of a Theater. Well, we have our last rehearsal on Monday afternoon, and ought to finish about five o'clock. I wonder if you would give me a cup of tea afterwards and see me to my train. You said once that you thought you could help me.

"Yours sincerely, Gladys Farham."

He read it again, and a strange excitement began to work in him. Obviously she knew nothing of his change of fortune — (how should she?) — Yet she seemed to want him. . . .

He lay so long that his tea grew cold; and it was not until the stable bell beat the quarter-past that he remembered and emptied the cup. Then, as he got out of bed at last, the second forgotten letter fell to the ground. He tore this, too, open. It bore the Franciscan device, stamped in white, and the address of the Kensington Friary.

"Dear Mr. Smith,

"I know you won't mind my saying that I am afraid we shall not be able to get through the instructions as soon as we hoped, unless you can arrange to come a little more frequently. I quite understand that you have a great deal to do just now; but I wanted just to say this for fear you should be disappointed. You told me you were to settle in the country sometime this week. Do you think you could come up regularly for one afternoon each week? Or shall I make inquiries as to whether there is any priest in your neighborhood to whom you could go? God bless you. Pray for me.

"Yours sincerely in Xt.,

"Hilary, O.S.F."

Percy had a pang of shame. The implied reproach was perfectly just. He had not been to Father Hilary for nearly three weeks. Yet how could he be expected to go, considering all that he had had to do? He must see whether something could not be managed next week — on Monday, perhaps.

The same splendid and leisurely air was as manifest at breakfast, as at lunch and dinner yesterday. There was a vast urn of embossed silver looking to Percy as if straight from Aladdin's cave. There were enormous spaces everywhere — between the four at table, across the table, and between the table and the sideboard on which no less than three silver dishes simmered over little blue flames. There were also cold pheasants. The doctor was still in his gray-tailed suit, with pumps instead of boots and spats; Helen in a blouse and serge skirt, and Mrs. Brandreth-Smith in a morning costume of vague splendor. The great windows gave a distant misty view of rolling woodland and park that was all part of Marston.

As Percy helped himself to marmalade he opened on his subject.

"I think I must go up to town on Monday, Mother," he said. "There are two or three things — I can be down again in time for dinner."

"Haven't you brought everything with you?"

"Well; there are some riding things I might as well try on. And . . . and I ought to go and see Father Hilary again."

She compressed her lips slightly. Her husband rustled his paper.

"Father Hilary, eh?" he said, glancing up.

"Yes," said Percy.

His father sniffed, ever so slightly.

"Well," said Mrs. Brandreth-Smith, after a pause. "Helen ought to go up too. You might go up together. Could you catch the four-fifty down again?"

"I . . . er — I thought of the six-ten. I've got someone I want to see about five."

"That's rather late. Couldn't you make it earlier?"

"I'm afraid not," said Percy with a certain finality in his voice.

"Well —" her voice died away, as of one who would decide it later.

(2)

Dr. Brandreth-Smith was doing his utmost to adapt himself to his new position; and he found it not very easy. But there was one thing that he understood clearly, and that was that all must be done under the direction of his wife. It astonished him how clear was her vision of all that he must be and do. It was she who had decided on the gray-tailed suit; she who had insisted, a month ago, on a small notice in the *Times* that in future the name of "Brandreth-Smith" should be substituted for that of "Smith"; she who had issued commands as to the redecoration of the house in Wilton Crescent. And she had further schemes too. Inquiries were to be made as to whether there was any military force provided by the Secretary for War which would give him an opportunity of being addressed as "Major"; letters had been written to the Secretary of the Primrose League.

One other point, too, had been discussed at length — the problem of Percy and Catholicism.

Now the doctor had religious convictions; or, perhaps they were better called adherences; and they were of the peaceful undefined sort that have no quarrel with others: they were not, that is to say, sufficiently objective or positive as to exclude others that were, as a matter of fact, incompatible with them. (This quality is called Charity at the present day.) Therefore, in the old life of Hanstead he found no great difficulty in bearing with his son; such difficulty as existed was social rather than religious. It was exactly this social element, then, that had waxed great with his change of fortune. No one had precisely said anything to him on the point (except his wife, and she very vaguely); nor had he to anyone else. But the consciousness was there that a conversion did not fit properly into the new juncture.

The situation precipitated itself a little after breakfast. His wife came to him in the smoking room where he was vaguely examining the *Times*. (He had intimated to the *Nation* that he would not renew his subscription at the close of the year.)

"About Percy," she said.

"Well, my dear?"

She wandered to the window.

("That lawn isn't properly kept," she began.) "Well; can nothing be done? It will make an exceedingly bad impression if Percy doesn't come to church with us here. Do you think it would be best to speak to him again?"

The doctor stood up and parted his coat tails over the fire.

"I've been thinking that myself," he said. "Do you think perhaps we had better speak at once? Or . . . or leave him a little. I understand that he can't be received into the Roman Church for three or four months yet."

She swung the tassel of the curtain fretfully.

"Well: do as you think right. . . . Yes, I think you are right. I'll do what I can with little hints here and there," she said. She broke off. "There's Andrewes from the farm. I sent for him to come up about the milk."

She rustled swiftly across the room again. At the door she stopped.

"Mr. Martin's much worse, I hear. Do you think perhaps, if he dies or resigns, Mr. Bennett would care to accept the living? He's a good sensible man, without any fads, you know."

"I think that's a very good idea of yours," said the doctor briskly.

(3)

To Helen, too, changes had come; and, since she was youthful, she found no great inconsistency in assenting to them.

The first thing she had dropped clean was her ancient view of New Art. New (and rather cheap) Art was all very well when there was not much money: whitewashed walls, and rush-seated chairs, and a thin copper hood over the fireplace were all very well when one had only thirty pounds a year for dress and personal expenses: besides, one could make some of the things oneself. But when one fell suddenly into the entire and sole possession of two beautiful rooms, covered as to the walls with expensive peacock-paper, with all the woodwork painted in glossy impenetrable cream-white as hard as enamel, filled with really good furniture upholstered in heavy stuffs; when all the fire-instruments and the fenders were solid brass; when a large number of new dresses and shoes and hats and gloves appeared at her mother's expense, with even a little jewelry; when there were two green riding-habits, a mare on which to ride, riding lessons, a maid, an allowance of a hundred and twenty a year, and practically all necessities found, the ethereal ideals of New Art fell like rags about her.

Her new pose was not yet fully arranged. Bright visions and glimpses came and went — glimpses of distinction, and wide-leafed hats, and slowness of speech, and Gainsborough hats. But she was not sure. . . .

Meanwhile it was all excellent fun. She had greatly enjoyed, in spite of her airs, the solemn calls of yesterday.

They had been to the Rectory on the way back, to inquire; but the event had been the call at Cleever, and her share in the grave conversation with Mabel Marridon in the drawing room of that big house. This girl had seemed quite charming, and rather impressive in her extraordinary ease of manner. It was, in fact, Mabel's pleasant simplicity, with what seemed to be a framework of a very firm character beneath, that had tended to mar her own Gainsborough ideals. Mabel was not at all Gainsborough: she was just very fresh and rather pretty. . . . At the end Lord Marridon had himself come in, a thin dry baldish

man whose skin appeared creased and powdery, in a tight
light suit with a large black tie; and, in spite of Helen's
attempt to appear tranquil, she had been entirely aware
that to speak to a real lord for the first time in her life
was something of an occasion. But she had behaved quite
well, though she had found herself a little tongue-tied;
and the whole experience had done a good deal to confirm
and establish her, interiorly, in her new position. She bore
herself with a certain sprightly dignity all the evening;
and rejoiced secretly within.

She was arranging her books this morning when Percy
strolled in with an air of such complete detachment that it
was at once evident he had come for a purpose. He
mooned round a few minutes, made a suggestion or two,
and then sat down.

"About Monday," he said. "Do you really want to go?"

"I must," she said. "Mother —"

"Well; can't we be independent? I don't want to keep you
hanging about."

"You needn't. The later train will do perfectly for me.
What do you want to do?"

"I've got to see Father Hilary for one thing; and there
are one or two more things."

"Well. All right!"

"Well: back me up with Mother, will you? If you don't,
and if she makes a fuss, I shall just miss the train, that's
all."

She nodded.

"I'll back you up all right," she said. "But what a lot of
mystery!"

Percy frowned.

"I won't be managed," he said. "Mother means to rule
everything. Well: I'm going to have my way. That's all. . . .
I say, Helen."

She planted her fresh pile of books safely, and knelt
down to sort them.

"Yes."

"Anybody said anything about my becoming a Catholic?"

"Do you mean lately?"

"Yes."

She shook her head.

"No."

"Well, because I'm going to, you know." She looked at him with lifted brows. "Why, of course you are! I didn't know —" Percy got up.

"Well; I mean that all this doesn't make any difference at all to me. I thought I might as well say that at once: so that if Mother or anyone says anything, you can just tell them straight out. That's all." He marched to the door.

Chapter III

(1)

It was with extraordinary excitement that Percy, standing in a little obscure lane off the Strand, pulled the bell of the stage door, and waited.

He had had an hour's instruction from Father Hilary this afternoon, all about the Grounds of Faith, and had found it very difficult to keep his attention fixed. He had also explained to him that for the present he simply could not promise to come up to town regularly every week; but he would do his best at keeping Mondays free. He had said no more for the present about his wish to be a friar. He reminded himself that it was hardly fair to consult just at present one who was himself a friar: he must allow time to settle, and to consider his new responsibilities: these were very important, he thought. Just now, however, the point was Miss Farham.

It must here be confessed that the thought of "helping" Miss Farham was not his principal consideration. (He found it necessary, in fact, to remind himself that it was a consideration at all.) Rather his entire emotions were occupied by the romance of seeing her again, and under these strange and kindling circumstances; for the Stage, as to all young men of his temperament and condition, was to him as mysteriously alluring and suggestive as a fairy story to a child. He had solemnly discussed it, again and again, with Reggie and others; he had ruminated upon it alone; he had read a few little books upon it and their revelations had added to his excitement. And now here he stood at a stage door, with a right of entry. (He remembered with piteous contempt his previous mild adventures in regard to the matronly chorus girl.)

"Miss Farham," said Percy, trying to appear natural, as soon as the shabby man in shirtsleeves opened the door.

"By appointment?"

"Yes." (Percy handed him his card which he had ready.)

"Jim, take this gentleman upstairs to Miss Farham."

A small boy appeared, eyed Percy for a moment, and then led the way up the tiny spiral staircase that went up almost immediately behind the door.

Percy's heart beat, as he followed: he pulled out his cuffs a little and arranged his neck in his collar. He caught a glimpse once of a furnished room and smelled the smoke of a cigarette and heard male voices conversing. Then a girl stood aside in an angle to let him go by as he rose still higher; then again he heard voices — this time female — and heard the clink of tea cups. Then the boy, glancing at the card he carried, called out: "Mr. Brandreth-Smith," and indicated a half-open door. Percy went in, and saw Miss Farham within a yard of him.

It was a queer comfortable-looking little room in which the three women sat over tea: there was a bright fire in the tiny grate, bright wall papers, bright gas. Photographs hung everywhere; there was a kneehole table near the curtained window, a sofa along one wall, on which sat a very stout lady and a very young-looking girl; the tea table, set with a curious collection of thick cups and a large plate of buns, stood before the fire.

Miss Farham herself was in a Windsor chair. She stood and gave Percy her hand; smiling.

"Why this is kind of you," she said. "And you really found your way here. Let me introduce you —" (she announced names which Percy instantly forgot again). "Sit down —" (she pulled out another Windsor chair from the wall). "Have some tea. It's just been sent in."

Percy was in a whirl of embarrassment: he put down his hat and gloves and stick, and then trod upon them as he sat down. It was the gaze of the stout lady, he thought, which confused him, and it was the more confusing, since he could not keep himself from wondering whether she really thought that anybody else ever for a moment thought that the bloom on her cheeks and the luster of her eyes were natural. It appeared to him for a wild instant that she must put on these adornments as she put on her hat, without even dreaming that any could conceive that they were really part of her person. And why was there tea here, when he had made all his beautiful plans to take Miss Farham out to a very particular tea-room that he knew of? And was the extremely young girl a relation of anybody present?

There was a silence. Then Percy said that it was just beginning to drizzle as he came in; and he would take only one lump of sugar, please.

He did not recover himself properly till the two strangers went. This they did just as his mouth was rather full of bun, so that his farewell suffered in articulation. But he was promptly at the door to open it; he closed it behind them; and then his excitement steadied down to a still intensity.

She was looking absolutely charming, and her friendliness was like the warmth of the fire. And it seemed to him that her slight air of melancholy was the greatest charm of all. She was without hat or jacket — in itself this was a suggestion of pleasant intimacy: her piled hair shadowed her face a little, and her great eyes shone bright and kind and rather sad; her costume conveyed nothing to him except grace and beauty. . . .

"Sit down comfortably," she said. "Tea came in as usual. . . . You're a little early, you know. . . . Still now it's here, we needn't pretend it isn't."

Percy did not speak for a moment. The charm of her was amazing. It was all that he remembered from his very parenthetical interviews with her before, all that his imagination had meditated upon; since, set here in this pleasant little room, under what appeared almost domestic circumstances, it concentrated itself on him as never before.

"It's . . . it's delightful to see you again," he said.

And how kind of you to ask me here!"

"And what have you been doing since I saw you last? Any more news?"

Percy drew a breath.

It was exactly his news that he had most counted upon for his effectiveness in this interview; and he had wondered how in the world he should introduce it. Here was his opportunity. Yet, for the sheer pleasure of anticipation, he played with it. And the knowledge of his reserve forces gave him a curious ease and masterfulness.

"Yes; I have a good deal of news," he said. "But —"

Her eyes sparkled with amusement. She was half-turned to him, and looking at him with a kindly tolerant interest that was really very pleasant.

"I can guess," she said. "You're a Catholic now."

"Not yet. But I want to know your news first."

Her face changed again to a gentle melancholy.

"Well; we've finished rehearsals. I'm tired to death of it. We open tomorrow night. Don't let's talk about me. I want to know your news."

"In a minute," he said. . . . "But, look here; why did you suddenly ask me to come and see you? Is anything wrong?"

She looked at him a moment.

"Nothing more than usual," she said. "I thought I'd like to see you again, that's all. Are you sorry?"

Now it is most necessary to remember that, as has already been observed, there was no harm in Miss Gladys Farham: there was only a dramatic temperament. She had begun, as has been described, to place Percy on her own private stage in the role of *ingénu,* and herself (in that particular drama) as the weary woman of the world. She had quite enjoyed this for a while, until she had become more interested in her own objective part at His Highness'; then she had largely forgotten him, and now had happened to remember him once more. There was really no mystery about her at all, though she thought that there was a great deal. She mistook her moods for phases of insight or gusts of genius.

For all her superficiality, however, she distinctly liked Percy; and now that she saw him again in the flesh she liked him even more than she remembered. For Percy really had a charm of his own, just as much as she had: he seemed manly and pleasant, and, now that he had cast off his embarrassment, natural as well: he was quite nice to look at, and he was very suitably dressed. Finally, what was to her a very real attraction, he was very evidently attracted by her. . . . Her friendliness to him was very far from being insincere.

Percy did not answer her last question. He put down his cup and crossed his legs.

"Have a cigarette," she said; and pushed him a box.

"And you've no more news?" he said, taking a cigarette with great deliberation. (He felt he was doing it all very well.)

She looked at him for an even longer moment than before.

"Well, you're a clerk," she said — "No: I'm not going to be brutal: but I know what being a clerk means. It means . . . well . . . at the most eighty pounds a year at your age. So you won't be foolish enough to misunderstand me when I say I'm badly in debt. . . . Don't move, please, and" — (her eyes turned fierce) — "don't dare to think that —"

Then her face softened again. She was completely and triumphantly deceiving herself as to her emotions: she really thought herself quite genuine at this moment — and yet prudent too.

"Well," she said, "I owe exactly ninety pounds. Now cheer me up, please, and tell me it doesn't matter at all. That's all I want to hear. Besides, I've got jewelry worth fifty, at least."

Percy was not a fool: he perceived, even in this instant of excitement, that she was perfectly sincere in her frankness; and, further, that to offer her a loan was quite impossible. But his heart beat thick when he realized how all this heightened the drama of his own revelation. . . . Conjectures and visions — up to now only half-allowed as possibilities — flared before his mind.

He paused a moment to be certain of his voice.

"I assure you it doesn't matter at all," he said. "Is that reassuring enough?"

She smiled at him wearily.

"Thank you very much. And now what's your news?"

Percy beat off the ash of his cigarette delicately into his saucer.

"I'm just coming to that," he said. "Well: I'm not a clerk any more."

"What! Have you had a fortune left you?" (She laughed a little.)

He nodded slowly. She sat bolt upright, all alive with interest, and her smile went.

"My people have, at least," he said.

"Do you mean —? How much, if it isn't rude?"

"A couple of big houses and about twelve thousand a year. . . . And . . . and I'm the only son." (He could not help adding that.)

"Good Lord!" said Gladys Farham.

(2)

This girl would not have been human if certain thoughts, hardly glanced at up to the present, had not presented themselves very insistently indeed during the next half-hour. But she was not in the least mercenary, in the ordinary sense; she liked money and she hated debt; but that was all. So she resolutely put these thoughts on one side every time they came; and distracted herself by a very gallant attempt indeed to talk with vivid sympathy. She appeared to bubble over with altruistic excitement; she screwed up her face in delicious appreciations as Percy revealed more and more of his newly acquired glories; she laughed with admirable glee; she gave him brilliant bits of advice: she blankly refused to discuss herself at all.

"I'm not interested in myself any more," she said. "Go on about you. What nice big things do happen to you! First Religion and now a Fortune. They aren't supposed usually to go together, you know."

So Percy went on, kindling as he went. He talked gorgeously of the sense of liberty that he felt, of his release from City slavery; of his newly-ordered gun; of his three-hundred a year. It all burst out tumultuously and triumphantly, under a feminine sunshine such as he had never experienced before: he glowed before himself as a kind of a hero. For he perceived, subconsciously, that her attitude towards him was subtly changed; she called him a "boy" once or twice — ("to think that a boy like you") — but the faint sting of patronage was gone. He felt himself magnificent and protective. He had come a little bit out, and she had gone a little bit in, like the people in a weather-house.

And then, he forgot himself in his intoxication.

"Look here," he said, "I'm sure you're not a bit conventional. Why not?"

Her face fell a little, so sharply that it was as if she spoke.

"Yes?" he said.

"Go on."

"Why not have a loan for a bit, or let me buy the jewelry and give it back to you—my father gave me —"

Then her whole aspect changed. She was leaning towards him, her eyes a-sparkle a moment ago, her lips parted: now she was drawn up and rigid.

"Oh! I'm sorry you've said that," she said with dignified disappointment. "It's just spoiled it all."

He burst into dismayed apologies.

"I . . . I . . . only meant — I'm fearfully sorry. I thought perhaps that — I'm fearfully sorry, you know."

She was looking down in a grave sorrow. There came a tap on the door. She looked up —

"Come in."

The same boy who had shown Percy upstairs came in with a card.

"The gentleman's waiting," he said; and eyed Percy while she took it, turned it and read a message on the back.

"I'll be down in five minutes," she said. "I think you told me —" she went on, glancing at the little loud ticking clock on the mantelpiece, and then down at the card again.

Percy waited till the door closed behind the boy.

"Miss Farham," he said, "I'm entirely sorry. . . . I ought to have known. Will you forgive me?"

She turned her head to look at him as she stood up. (Percy too rose: the clock marked ten minutes to six.)

"Of course I forgive you," she said regretfully. "Perhaps you didn't know that that was — well — quite an impossible thing to say. But, you know, it makes all the difference —"

Percy was at once bewildered and ashamed. Obviously he had done something terribly wrong; and it seemed to him an additional crime that he really did not even now quite understand its enormity. She had seemed so frank and simple and comrade-like. (And how splendid she looked now in her dignified regret! The gaslight shone iridescent in her hair, and her eyes were large and sad in shadow.)

"Oh! But I really didn't understand. Don't say that it makes all the difference. Miss Farham I . . . I —"

Then she smiled; and it was like the coming of dawn to the poor boy's eyes.

"Well: I really think you didn't."

She put out a hand: he took it, and held it while she spoke.

"There — we'll not speak of that again. But you understand, don't you, Mr. . . . Mr. Brandreth-Smith, that that kind of thing mustn't be said. Money spoils everything, you know."

She withdrew her hand.

"There," she said.

Percy still hesitated.

"Can I . . . can I do anything more? Get a cab, for instance?"

She turned again to him; and said with a kind of brisk frankness:

"Oh! no thank you. A . . . a Mr. — A friend of mine has just sent up his card. He'll look after me, thanks. Goodbye, Mr. Brandreth-Smith. Come and see the play, some night, won't you? . . . And . . . and I do congratulate you, you know, most tremendously."

(3)

She kept Mr. Marridon waiting, though, even before she finally dismissed him.

When Percy had gone she still stood on where she was on the hearthrug, and stared over the top of the clock at her own reflection in the mirror.

Honestly she did not know which was her real self in all the personalities that seemed to crowd up and claim her through her own mirrored eyes. . . .

Of course she had acted just now: she had assumed the quiet disappointed indignation which she knew was proper, not feeling half of all that she had manifested. Yet did not her deliberate assumption of it render it her own? And she had forgiven Percy, interiorly, long before she had said so. . . . He was such a boy, anyhow!

And of course she was aware that his significance was considerably changed for her since his announcement: his news had invested him with a kind of dignity. After all, she reflected wordlessly, money is power and power is an attribute: it must surely be taken into account then. . . .

And how like a boy not to have said a word about that of which he had been so full last time — his religion and his desire to "help" her! How like a boy! and how charmingly natural! Oh! she had fenced with boys before; and affected to despise them, and, indeed, actually despised them too for their woodenness and admiration: and she had fenced, too, with comparatively mature persons — such as this Mr. Marridon — and snubbed them and been disdainful — all except with the one whom she had unhappily married three years ago at the very beginning of her stage career. Things had gone swiftly after that: she felt that she knew the world and all its complications inside out.

Yet she stared at herself now in the glass, and all her worldly wisdom seemed useless: she stared at herself and thought still about Percy; and . . . and wondered.

Ten minutes later she rang the bell sharply. The boy who came perceived that she was unusually severe.

"Tell Mr. Marridon I . . . I can't see him after all. Tell him I'm dead tired with the rehearsals today. Say I'm sorry to have kept him waiting. . . . No, don't, I'll just see him for a minute up here."

For she was just a trifle afraid of Mr. Marridon, in spite of all her disdain.

Chapter IV

(1)

Percy's first essay at shooting in the open air was a very exciting business. He had already learned in the shooting school how to hold a gun, and had received a few instructions, three out of four of which he had immediately forgotten; but he was, for all that, sufficiently confident to feel happy, as he came down on the great morning of which Farquharson, the gamekeeper, had been previously warned. Percy's own gun was not yet arrived from town; but it was understood that Farquharson's would do.

Scene One, so to speak, was his appearance in the hall at twenty-five minutes past ten, where his father was reading the *Times* by the fire, and Helen was waiting to see her brother start. His mother also sailed out of the morning room so soon as she heard Helen's excited comments.

"What are those funny little leather things for on your shoulders? And why aren't they the same color as your jacket?"

Percy explained loftily that these were to prevent the gun from wearing out the jacket.

"Oh! I see," said Helen. "But I don't see why they shouldn't be the same color as the cloth."

"He looks very well," observed his mother. "But why have you turned up your collar?"

Percy shrank from saying that he had done so before the wardrobe glass in his room just now, in order to give himself a reckless and weather-beaten appearance. He said he thought it would be cold.

"Nonsense. Turn it down: it looks ridiculous."

Percy felt rather bitter at this inspection. Women, he reflected, like being looked at; men don't. At least so he assured himself interiorly. He turned down his collar.

"And why don't your spats come down further? They look silly like that," observed Helen.

"How stupid you are!" cried Percy. "They aren't spats at all. They're — I forget the name; but they're just to prevent wet and things getting into the boots."

"Oh!" said Helen.

"Farquharson's just come, Madam," remarked Underhill, suddenly appearing through the door that led to the servants' quarters.

Again Percy was annoyed. It was he who ought to have been addressed, he thought. After all, it was he who was going out shooting.

"Tell him to come round this side," he said loftily.

"Nonsense, my dear; he's got the ferrets with him. (Tell Farquharson Mr. Percy will come round at once.) Then you'll be in to lunch, Percy, at one; to tell us how you've got on."

"Mind you hold your gun straight," cried Helen after him, as he went down the steps.

Scene Two was the progress to the Place of Death.

Percy did not like to ask that he might carry the gun; though he thought it was scarcely sportsmanlike not to do so. And Farquharson seemed unduly overloaded. He had a heavy canvas bag over one shoulder, out of which came the sound of violent scratching, and occasionally a squeak. A cartridge-bag was strapped over the same shoulder; and over the other he carried the gun.

"Looks a good gun," said Percy genially.

"Yes, sir. Good old gun. But old-fashioned, sir. Hammer gun, sir."

Farquharson was a brief and abrupt kind of man, and with a very masterful and competent air. He was sturdily-built, and tramped emphatically, rather than walked.

"Many's the bird I've killed with that gun, sir."

"Oh! Have you?" said Percy. "Well: I . . . I hope I shall."

There was silence for a little.

It was a genial and boisterous sort of day, and quite cold enough for Percy presently to turn up his collar once more. The sun came out now and again from behind the flying clouds, and painted sudden vivid patches of color on the winter woods and the brown of the fallen leaves.

"The mistress said it was to be rabbits today, sir," remarked Farquharson suddenly.

"Yes; I . . . er . . . I thought I'd better begin with that."

But Farquharson would not take the hint.

"But I don't suppose the mistress would mind if we had a try at a pheasant, later on, sir. That is, if you make a good job of the rabbits, sir."

"I . . . er . . . don't expect I shall be up to much," said Percy, anxious to prepare the keeper for the worst

"Don't say that, sir. We never know till we try, do we, sir?"

The place of destiny was a large burrow at the very edge of the woods. It resembled in shape half a saucer, tilted at a sharp angle; and this saucer of sandy earth, Percy presently made out, was honeycombed with holes.

The keeper set down the writhing bag at the foot of a tree, and Percy took up the gun which the other had just leaned against a tree trunk.

"How bright the barrels are!" he observed, after an inspection down the muzzle.

Farquharson looked up abruptly.

"Never do that, sir, if you please," he said sharply. "That's not the way to look down a gun. Down the breach, sir, if you please."

Percy felt that he hated Farquharson very much indeed.

The opening of the bag presently distracted him. He had never in his life, so far as he remembered, seen ferrets before, and was intensely curious to know what they looked like. Obviously he dared not ask.

When at last one little primrose-tinted creature was drawn out, moving its small hand-like paws irresolutely in the air, he was relieved to see how small it was. He stepped forward to stroke it, very kindly.

"That's not safe, sir, if you please," said the keeper, drawing it away. "Bite your finger as soon as look at you, sir. There, you beauty!"

He himself stroked it craftily on the top of its head and neck.

"But you can do it," protested the boy.

"Yes, sir; because I know just how to hold him, sir. Savage creatures, ferrets. Otherwise no use to us, sir."

Scene Three now began.

The two ferrets were first dropped somewhere down the slope, where they writhed slowly about, peering this way and that, as if they were short-sighted. Farquharson scrambled back, loaded the gun, put it carefully into Percy's hands, and began to instruct him in a rapid whisper.

"No hurry, sir, no hurry! Don't get excited. Ferrets aren't gone to ground yet. . . . No, sir; they'll find their way in directly. Never you fear. And, sir, the rabbits may bolt anywhere. I can't tell you more than that. But they won't face the open, sir, if they can help it. They'll bolt round to the left most likely. And you must shoot quick, sir, before they're underground again, sir."

"But how do I know which way to look," protested Percy, "if I don't know which way they'll go?"

(He felt somehow that the affair was not being managed as he had a right to expect from a paid gamekeeper. How on earth could he take proper aim, too, with all those tree-trunks in the way?)

"That's just it, sir. Got to be sharp, sir. . . . Ah! There's one! Too late, sir."

The world appeared to Percy, suddenly to spin; for a real live rabbit had bolted out a few yards away, and vanished again like a jumping croquet ball over rough ground, in another hole, round to the left, as Farquharson had said.

"I . . . I . . . I didn't see him properly," said Percy agitatedly.

"Not so loud, sir, if *you* please. Or you won't see no more."

It was nearly five minutes before Percy discharged his gun. Three more rabbits appeared during that time, but in each case, seemed, of set purpose, to take an unexpected line. The first, most unfairly, went to the right; the second looked out, regarded Percy with cocked ears with such an expression of disapproval that he was paralyzed; and then, deciding, it would seem, that he was not worth looking at, vanished noiselessly. The third, most unfairly of all, made straight for the sportsman, missed him by a yard, and disappeared into the woods behind, leaving

Percy turning violently round and round, and inquiring what had become of him.

"Too late, sir. And you mustn't swing your gun round like that, sir; or you'll be shooting somebody one of these days."

The actual firing of his first shot consoled him a little, and did the rabbit no harm. A very fat one suddenly lollopped out of a hole some twenty yards away, paused, went on a few yards and paused again. At that moment Percy decided to pull the trigger, but about two seconds before he actually did so, the rabbit also decided to make another move. A quantity of yellow dust flew into the air out of a molehill by which the rabbit had sat just now, and, what with the noise and the excitement and the kick of the gun, once more Percy found the world a blank.

"Well done, sir," came the low hearty voice of Farquharson.

"Where's the rabbit? Did I . . . did I . . . hit him?"

"No, sir; but you got off the shot beautiful, sir. Better luck next time, sir."

Percy's first rabbit was scarcely as creditable to him as he would have wished.

A very, very young one came out, not eight yards away, and lay still, trembling. Percy took aim and fired.

"I got that one, anyhow," he cried.

Farquharson said nothing. He tramped down the slope, picked up the tiny body, and came back with it. Then he put it under the bag. Percy waited for congratulations; but they did not come.

"I . . . I got that one all right," he repeated.

"Yes, sir."

"It . . . it looked rather small," said Percy, beginning to be doubtful.

"Do very well for the ferrets, sir," said Farquharson, making the best of a very poor job.

There were moments that morning, however, when Percy was in a kind of ecstasy of self-contemplation — moments when, waiting for Farquharson to pick up the ferrets, or to coax out a loiterer with shrill squeaking noises made by his lips, the boy leaned against a tree, with one boot over the other, the gun held in an easy manner, ready for a shot which obviously would not be called for; and thought what a fine figure he presented. Here was he, after all, in his own park, attended by his own gamekeeper, and shooting, or at least prepared to shoot, his own rabbits. That man there, in the velveteen coat with the square-whiskered face, on all fours in the sand and making noises like a harmless maniac, was his servant who called him "sir," and was paid to do his bidding and teach him shooting.

The contrast was almost incredible, between the assured dignity of this position and the genteel ignominy of himself a few months ago, when he ate a hurried breakfast in a mean room that smelled of eggs and marmalade, and ran to catch the nine-seven in order that he might spend the rest of the day in doing things which he did not like, for inadequate pay, at the command of a bald head-clerk who had not an aspirate in his alphabet.

What would his old friends think of him now — Reggie, for instance — if they could see him, here, leaning against a tree, with his feet crossed, while his gamekeeper fished for his ferrets who had been hunting out his rabbits for him to shoot — or, at least, to shoot at: if they could realize what the whole life was which made such pastimes possible, in which such pastimes, in fact, were only a very small incident!

Reggie! — He considered him for a minute or two. Reggie was now, no doubt, at this very moment working feverishly at his job, in order to get to a good stopping place in time for lunch. Then the lunch itself — a poor sloppy kind of meal in a dark restaurant underground — a hasty Cinderella cigarette; and then back to the collar again, and the Australian shipping lines. . . . By the way, that weekend plan hadn't come off yet. It had been difficult to arrange for the first week or two after his own arrival at Marston; and now — well now — he was not quite so sure as to whether it would do. It was a little difficult for the imagination to fit Reggie comfortably into Marston life, even for Sunday. His evening waistcoat would probably be cut wrong, or he would omit to bring evening shoes; or he would wear a white tie and a swallowtail coat at dinner instead of the dinner jacket and black tie that

Percy had thought the correct thing under the ordinary
Marston circumstances.

And yet Percy did very violently wish, not to see Reggie
at Marston, but for Reggie to see him there: and the two
things appeared to stand or fall together. He might even
take Reggie out ferreting for an hour before dark, if he
came down by the early train — or, rather, take Reggie
out to see him ferreting. He might leave an august message with Underhill.

"Mr. Percy is out shooting in the park. Would Mr. Ballard be kind enough to go out and join him in the park?
One of the men will show Mr. Ballard the way."

(2)

The Slaying of the Pheasant, the climax of this glorious
day, was performed, as was but right, at the close of the
sport, half an hour before the dark came down in earnest.

He had been back to the house for lunch, with two rabbits to his account, besides the small one that had been
hidden under the ferrets' bag.

"I got three," he said, as soon as he had a decent opportunity at lunch. "Farquharson's brought them in. At least
he's bringing two. He's keeping one for the ferrets." (He
did not give a more detailed description.)

"How many did you shoot at?" asked Helen brutally.

Percy looked at her in contempt.

"I didn't count the cartridges," he said.

"I expect there were too many," commented Helen, who
seemed in a tiresome mood.

They had visited some more burrows after lunch; and
Farquharson gave a small exhibition at one of how the
thing really should be done.

"They'll all swell the bag, sir," he observed, after the
fourth cartridge. "That's six altogether, sir. Not at all bad
for a first day, sir."

A faint twinkle in Farquharson's eye enraged Percy. Did
the man take him for a child?

"Keep those four separate," said the boy. "You shot
those, you know."

"Very good, sir," said Farquharson.

The assault on the pheasants was made after a singularly poor performance on the part of Percy, at the last burrow. There were so many rabbits that he shot wildly.

"Better try at a bird," said Farquharson. "Nice little lot in the covert on the other side of the river, sir. P'raps, better luck with a bird. Birds want thinning, sir."

"Right," said Percy.

He was placed, upon arrival at the covert, in a little treeless hollow, fifteen yards from the thick rhododendrons that crowded up under the birches and beeches.

"Just there, sir," said Farquharson. "I'll go round behind and beat. Don't fire into the covert, sir. Wait till they rise."

Ah! This was the real thing!

Here he was, a gentleman of wealth, actually shooting expensive pheasants. Farmers, and people like that shot rabbits. . . . Every pheasant on the other hand cost its owner he thought he remembered from some book, at least one and sixpence.[1] Or was that a stag? No: a stag was a hundred pounds. Well; anyhow a pheasant was very expensive and rich. And he was going to "knock them down," just for fun; because it was his pleasure to do it.

The thought of Gladys Farham suddenly recurred to him. He wished she could see him here . . . or Father Hilary. No; Gladys Farham would be better. She'd understand better what sort of person he really was, in his shooting suit, with his little gaiters and his leather patches on the shoulders, and his own gun — well, not his own gun, but at any rate his gamekeeper's — *his* gamekeeper's. She'd respect him more then; and . . . and see how manly he was, gripping his gun, standing with his feet, a yard apart, among the bracken. . . .

A loud crowing brought him back from visions to facts. But he was too late. Already a gigantic creature was mounting high over his head, making such a disconcerting noise that action was impossible. And even while he hesitated whether to fire or no, a similar crowing broke out in entirely the opposite direction. Really it was impossible to shoot when they came out like that! — Two, almost to-

---

[1] One shilling and sixpence, or approximately 30¢, a little over an hour's pay for a highly-paid working man.

gether, in opposite directions. . . . Why couldn't Farquharson manage it better than that?

He turned savagely again to the covert, whence came
now plainly the sounds of heavy footsteps over dead
leaves, the tap of a stick against bush-stems, and a low
truculent kind of voice. He fixed his eyes resolutely upon a
perfectly clear patch of sky, between two feathery tree-
tops, determined that the pheasant — if there happened
to be another left, should pass that way. And, for a wonder, he was right.

Again came the crowing, mingled with taps and shak-
ings; and, an instant later, there, right in the very patch
of sky he had fixed upon, rose a form, dark in the evening
light, monstrous and formidable.

He fired; but the form was gone behind the feathery
treetop on the right. He fired again, desperately and
wildly; and, from the covert beneath burst out the figure
of Farquharson, as if he were mad, running to the right.

Percy shouted an incoherent question. For a wild and
horrible instant he thought, somehow, that he must have
shot Farquharson in the face; but a genial, if also incoherent, answer came back; and the keeper vanished behind a
slope in the ground.

Percy turned round; and there, not twenty yards away,
stood Mabel and Helen.

(3)

Oh! But it was delicious to walk back with these two,
particularly after Farquharson, breathless but respect-
fully triumphant, had returned with a large dead cock
pheasant in his hand.

"Beautiful shot, sir," panted Farquharson. "Second bar-
rel got him fairly. Now that's your first pheasant, sir; ain't
it?"

, Really, it was very nearly as good as having Gladys
Farham there. It was actually in the very moment of triumph, too, that they had come up.

"How well you did it!" said Helen admiringly. "And, oh!
Percy, you did look so nice there against the rhododendrons, with your gun."

"I shot vilely, though," said Percy, desiring to be contradicted, as he tramped beside the girls, carrying his gun, too, this time, like a sportsman.

"Why did Farquharson run like that, if the pheasant was dead?" asked Helen.

Percy didn't know. He turned and repeated the question to Farquharson, who tramped behind.

"Bird not quite dead, sir. Winged, sir."

Helen hissed with pain.

"Oh! How horrid, Percy! Do kill them straight out!"

"You don't suppose I wounded it on purpose?" snapped Percy.

How pleasant, too, to see the lights of the great house, kindling in window after window. There was tea waiting, and a hot bath. And Mabel would be at tea. That would be very nice. He liked Mabel rather.

Chapter V

(1)

It was a morning of considerable excitement when Helen went for her first ride with Mabel Marridon.

She had had her lessons in town — as Percy had had his in the shooting school. For the first three or four lessons Percy had accompanied her, but after a couple of falls on his part, it had somehow got itself arranged that they should go separately. She had learned all the tricks, there in the large blue-atmosphered riding school which had so peculiar a smell of tan and saddles, and had taken to it with some address. Then she had ridden out three or four times with the second coachman close behind, and had distinctly galloped — really galloped — up a nice soft grass ravine where it was practically impossible to lose control of her mare. She had returned with an ineffable air of contentment and competence.

The morning on which, it had been arranged, she was to be called for by Mabel, was one of those soft winter days of sunshine and general dampness under foot. Eleven was the appointed hour; and, by a quarter to, a little group had assembled in the hall, all the members of which, except Helen, pretended to be there by accident. For, far beyond that romance which Helen frankly admitted — the romance, that is to say, of going out for a real ride in the country (beginning in your own park), on your own mare, in your own riding-habit, with your own groom who had received explicit instructions to keep properly far behind — there was besides evidence of really having taken a proper place in county society when a girl of one family lately arrived, goes out for a *tête-à-tête* expedition with another girl of her own age who is the daughter of a neighboring peer. The very slightness and informality of the matter shows its security.

So Percy was there, in pumps and knickerbockers, with his hands in his pockets, looking at the illustrated papers on the top of the Jacobean chest; and Helen's maid was there, giving little earnest pulls to her mistress' habit to ensure its proper hang; and her father was reading the

Times by the hall fire and glancing over the top of it; and her mother was there, pretending to be anxious in one direction, when she was really anxious in another.

"I don't want you to go too much on the highroad," she said. "I don't think Jennie likes motors much."

"Mabel said she'd show me a bridle path all the way — (oh! Don't jerk so, Charlotte) — all the way to Cleever."

"Helen! Let Charlotte put that straight at once. That skirt doesn't hang at all well. I must see about sending to have it altered."

"It fits perfectly, Mother. What's the time, Percy?"

"Just gone the quarter," he murmured from over his papers.

"Oh! Mabel said she'd be here by eleven sharp."

"And don't be out too long," continued Mrs. Brandreth-Smith, approaching once more the subject with which she was principally concerned.

"No, Mother."

"Mind you don't forget about bringing her in to lunch," she went on, with an admirable air of absentmindedness, reaching the goal on which she had set her heart. (It seemed to her exceedingly proper and pleasant that Lord Marridon's daughter should drop in to lunch quite naturally; and she had determined not to be disappointed. But girls were so silly and forgetful.)

"No, Mother. . . . There! I hear her horse." And Helen tore herself free from her maid's attentions.

(2)

But it was, honestly, romance that most occupied her thoughts, as she rode out with Mabel five minutes later, and through the swinging iron gate on to the grass; and, again, so soon as Jennie had done the little dance proper to every mare of spirit when her hoofs first touch grass.

"I . . . I don't ride very well, you know. D'you mind not cantering just yet?" she said with an attractive candor.

Mabel's little pointed face dimpled up with sympathetic humor.

"You shall set the pace," she said. "But you've got a lovely seat."

The nature of the romance was, as has been explained, the sense of lordliness and possessions and ease, and of doing real country things in the right way. In her feminine way she felt, to the full, those emotions, which, in a masculine way, moved Percy as he contemplated his well-ordered room, and James' respectful face, and Underhill's bent back, and his own shining gun and his homespun suit. It was delicious, she thought, to go out riding like this, with another girl, on a well-bred mare through pretty scenery. The sky was softly blue; the dead leaves smelled charmingly; the park-cattle clanked their bells very pleasantly in the distance.

Mabel looked different somehow on her chestnut horse, in her blue habit: she appeared more masterful and adequate, and appeared to manage her mount without paying any attention to it. Helen felt her, more than ever, to be her own superior; and this rather increased her own attractiveness, since, if she had had a fault it had been that of laying down the law a little too positively to adoring friends.

"I wish I could ride as well as you," she sighed presently.

"Oh, you will directly," said the other, smiling; "you only want practice. . . . (Don't dance, Jack!)"

Helen presently became immensely interested in the relations between her own mare and Mabel's horse. They were out in the woods by now, and were for the first time riding very close together between the coverts.

Up to the present the two animals had been showing off to one another — (rather like their mistresses, in fact) — each pretending not to be aware that there was another of their kind present — shoving and pulling desperately to take the lead. Now they began to pay attention. Jack begun by putting his nose tentatively out into the direction of Jennie. Jennie responded by a disdainful toss of her head away from him. Then Jack edged closer, pressing against Helen's habit; and Jennie, more contemptuous than ever, sidled swiftly away, turning her hind quarters inwards, and an instant later Helen said "Oh!"

For it had appeared to her for one confused instant that there was no stability anywhere; her hat was jerked forward, her hands went forward into the air, and she found herself looking at the ground beyond Jennie's flattened ears. The beast had whisked round and kicked sharply.

"Oh! You beast!" said Helen. "I say —" (She tried to shake her hat straight again.)

Mabel laughed delightfully.

"I saw she was going to do it. It was all my little brute's fault for poking in where he wasn't wanted."

"Did . . . did she kick you?" asked Helen, settling herself down again.

"No: we moved away in time. You sat it very well."

"It's the first time she's ever kicked," said Helen.

This was all very friendly and simple and pleasant. Jack and Jennie provided an ample field for a better mutual understanding between the two girls. Helen became more and more interested, not only in the minds of the two horses — in their curious little manifestations of surprise or attention or resentment — in the way the pointed ears moved, now back, now forward, and again (when there were two things to be attended to, such as a rustling in the undergrowth and a mistress' remarks) one forward and the other back — but also in Mabel's comments.

"Look," she said. "That means that Jennie wants to know what's making all that noise in the brushwood: she's getting ready to shy if a dragon comes out, but she knows perfectly well there isn't one. Speak to her."

"Jennie," remarked Helen, "attend to me."

The right ear clicked back for an instant, and then cocked forward again.

"You see," said Mabel.

They reached presently a rising knoll in the woods, bare of trees, with the ground falling steeply beneath on three sides. Below, the delicate filigree of birches sloped away down to the carriage drive a hundred feet lower.

"Let's let them look at the view," said Mabel.

The two horses stood like statues, when once it was made clear that that was what was wished, turning attentive eyes this way and that. Indeed, it was a good view. A sharp valley was beneath them; rhododendrons fringed the glimpse of white road that was in sight, and the gleam of water which was all that could be seen of the long swan pond. Heather clothed the opposite slope, interspersed with birches; and birches again stood out, feathery and delicate against the soft blue sky.

"Those are the trees of Cleever," said Mabel, pointing with her whip beyond the end of the twisting valley. "We just cross the road at the end of this ride, and then get into the woods again."

"That's where Percy's going to shoot, isn't it?"

"Yes: if he'll come. But my brother's away: and there won't be any shooting till next month."

"He's only just learning, you know," said Helen.

"So he said. He said he wouldn't come till he was a bit better."

Jennie drew a long meditative sigh, and beat one dainty foot on to the springy earth.

"Poor dear!" said Mabel. "She's bored. She's looked at the view quite long enough, thank you."

(3)

"You see," began Helen, half an hour later as they turned homewards again in the Cleever woods, "you see Percy's an . . . an idealist."

They had talked Percy with breaks and parentheses ever since his name had been mentioned — Helen discussing him with something of a lofty air, and Mabel listening, with an occasional question or two. He was a very obvious subject for conversation under the circumstances. But Helen had not yet mentioned that he was undergoing instruction with a view to becoming a Catholic: her parents' attitude towards that proposed step had made her doubtful as to whether she had better speak of it. So she called him an idealist, instead. She thought that rather subtle.

"How do you mean?" asked Mabel with puckered forehead.

There is no end to the solemnity with which girls will discuss high matters when they are alone together. When they grow older, they learn that humor is more graceful.

"Well — he used always to be falling in love," said Helen. "Oh! not really, you know; but as boys will. And now it's . . . it's —"

Mabel glanced up questioningly.

"It's religion," said Helen firmly. And then discretion overcame her again. "He's very much interested in religion," she ended lamely.

"Really? In what way?"

"Oh! He thinks a lot about it. He doesn't talk of it much. But he's got a crucifix in his room, you know."

The questioning lines between Mabel's eyes came down into a distinct little frown.

"Oh!" she said, with a clear tinge of disapproval in her voice.

"Yes, I know," said Helen hastily, thankful that she had not said more. "I don't like that sort of thing either. Religion seems to me a much more spiritual thing than . . . than that kind of thing."

Mabel nodded emphatically two or three times.

"I'm very glad you think that;" she said, with exceeding gravity. "We're . . . we're all rather low church you know — at least —"

Helen made haste to agree, with reservations.

"Yes; so'm I; so long as it's not the Revival kind of thing and being saved. I hope yours isn't that sort?"

She glanced at her friend with a look of slight anxiety.

Mabel smiled again, without a trace of disapproval.

"That's exactly what I think too," she said. "My father's very old-fashioned, you know. Just Church of England. And I'm the same, except that I don't like dogma much."

Helen was far too serious and awed to see anything at all incongruous in the thought of Lord Marridon being a pillar of dogma. She was pathetically anxious to please. She had been, almost unknown to herself, throughout the whole ride, interiorly adapting herself to meet this girl's views. It was very reassuring to her to hear Mabel's religious opinions.

"I'm so glad we agree," she said earnestly. "I say —"

"Yes?"

"May I call you Mabel?"

The girl's face lit up with an exceedingly compelling friendliness.

"Why, of course!" she said. "What else — Helen?"

(4)

The same kind of emotion that descended from time to time upon Percy, as he contemplated some picturesque evidence of his own new importance, fell upon Helen, as in a kind of ecstasy, as they came out again from the lower woods and saw the great house smoking before them high against the sky.

It stood there, in so perfect a situation, as to seem inevitable; as if the eternal hills themselves had been set there to await the coming of Marston; the walls of the enclosed gardens cut the sky to the left; the high trees that sheltered the south finished the picture on the right; and, in the midst sat the august house itself, seen slightly from one side, built on a foundation (it seemed) of immovable terraces, and crowned with elaborate chimneys above the leads.

And in all this, she had now an intimate part; and she was riding as an equal with a girl of her own age, of an unspeakably weighty social position, and she was to call her Mabel, and Mabel was to call her Helen; and they were to meet again and ride together again at least twice a week; and Mabel had said how pleased she was that Helen had come to Marston.

Percy strolled out behind Underhill on to the steps as they came up.

"Well? Had a good ride?" he asked.

(He really looked very nice, thought Helen, in his knickerbockers, and bareheaded.)

"Splendid. Jennie went like an angel on springs."

Then his mother appeared too, beaming with motherliness and hospitality.

"Well? Have you had a good ride?"

"Lovely, Mother."

Lunch was an unqualified success. Mabel bore herself beautifully, with just that mixture of dignity and girlishness that was proper. Her manner was perfect. And Helen and Percy sparred pleasantly, the one about shooting and the other about riding; and Mabel turned laughing eyes from one to the other. And Mrs. Brandreth-Smith bore herself without a sign of severity, and completely succeeded in hiding her extreme anxiety that Mabel should really be at her ease; and her husband twinkled sedately in the background, and made a suitable remark about Lord Marridon, and never once made a false step.

"You really had a nice time, my dear?" asked Mrs. Brandreth-Smith benevolently, as she and Helen turned on the steps after watching Mabel's habit disappear among the trees.

"Lovely, Mother."

"She's a very nice girl indeed. I hope you'll make great friends. I heard you call her Mabel."

"She told me to," said Helen.

Chapter VI

It speaks very well for Reggie Ballard's simplicity that within a week or so of his hearing the glorious news of his friend's fortune he had, honestly, ceased to envy him.

The news had been conveyed in a solemn and august manner, in the same teashop where so many other confidences had been exchanged. Hither he had come, at the lunch hour, a day after Percy's first learning of the facts, in obedience to a note that gave no hint of the tremendous disclosure that was to be made — to find his friend looking rather rigid and severe from beyond a little marble topped table. There was no one else in that corner of the room.

"Well, old chap," said Reggie, "what's the trouble? Another —"

He broke off, struck by the terrific gravity of the other's face. Banter, he perceived, would not be in place.

"What is it?" he asked again, sitting down.

Percy opened his lips, and closed them again. Then he tried once more.

"It's a very big thing indeed," he said.

Reggie glanced at him a little anxiously.

"Good or bad?"

"I suppose most people would call it good," pronounced Percy.

"Well, then —"

"I had better tell you straight out," said Percy. "But you understand it's between you and me." (This was the phrase he had already used five or six times that morning to various acquaintances — to all, in fact, whom he could buttonhole for a sufficient space of time. There had been two in the train, and three or four later.)

"Right you are," said Reggie. "Can I order lunch first, by the way?"

"The news won't take a moment," said Percy in a rather high voice. "It's only that my people have been left a fortune, and two places — one in town and one in the country; and that I shall leave the City in a week or two."

It need hardly be said that Reggie's lunch was not ordered till after an interval of at least ten minutes. Details had to be told — as to the exact amount of the fortune, the manner of its coming, the circumstances under which the news had been received. Hands had to be grasped in congratulations; and little broken sentences uttered, expressing amazement and joy and wonder.

"What a time you'll have," said Reggie. "And — oh! I say — as it'll all be yours some day, you'll be able to make it a Catholic estate."

Percy nodded gravely.

"That's the chief reason I'm pleased," he said, really believing it with one part of his consciousness. "We must make some plans together, Reggie!"

Reggie beamed.

The general lines of those plans, then, had been immediately sketched. Percy was careful to say that of course nothing could be done at present; that he must feel his way; that he must learn all about the estate, and the rest; and he reminded Reggie that there was no entail of any kind; that it was all his mother's property, and entirely at her disposal.

"We must be very careful and not talk too much," he said — lowering his voice a little, as a stout man with a gold watch-chain came in and sat down not far away.

And Reggie felt himself, with a glow of pleasure, to be moving amongst high politics and laudable conspiracies.

(2)

Envy had, of course, succeeded to his generous glow; and it appeared to Reggie more than once during the following days that Providence really had been a little ill-advised in transporting Percy to such paradises of wealth and influence, while he, Reggie, still had to devote his powers to the shipping business. A long letter from Percy the next Monday morning, full of suggestions and hints, did not greatly allay his envy; for, among other proposals — all of which, however, were carefully and prudently guarded — was one that Reggie should come down very; often indeed for weekends, in order to pursue his acquaintance with the Brandreth-Smiths with a view perhaps, some day, to becoming some kind of agent to Percy when he should come into his kingdom. Most of the suggestions were of this gloriously vague and roseate kind, yet the very glory of them, however vague, was not soothing: it seemed to Reggie singularly unfair that Percy should be able to throw off such proposals so royally, and that he himself could only gape and wonder at them.

Well; Reggie was a good boy, dutiful and conscientious, even if a little limited; he went to confession like a man, acknowledged that he had given way on five or six occasions to the Sin of Envy; and then resolutely embraced his own lot. He would be a friar, he told himself once more, so soon as circumstances made it possible, and thus avoid entirely the realm where pecuniary ambitions reign.

The prospect of weekend visits, however, still remained to console him. Percy had been very distinct about this, and had even suggested setting aside a room at Marston which Reggie was to consider his own, and to which he could "run down" whenever he felt inclined. The sheer glory of this had been to him like sunlight. Weekends, so far, had been spent, nineteen times out of twenty, at Wimbledon. At least he had slept at Wimbledon as usual, and, after a furious day at St. Francis', Kensington, had returned there for a late supper on Sunday night. To have then a place in the country to which he could go when the humor took him — a place, moreover, of the magnificence of Marston — this, even in prospect, was glorious. A letter had followed later, however, from Marston itself, telling him that just for the present the plan must be postponed; there were so many things to be arranged that Percy did not quite like to add this other; but after Easter, at any rate, it must be done.

Then the weeks had begun to slip by, and not even a single isolated visit was suggested.

A certain resigned depression fell upon Reggie one Saturday afternoon towards the beginning of December, as he made his way homewards.

First, it was a wet day, and, having found two omnibuses entirely full, he had had to walk more than he liked in his City boots; and next, determined to get home as soon as he could, he had postponed lunch, and was, in consequence, in a state of rather low vitality.

As he trudged along, therefore, there came to him with particular poignancy, a vision of the contrast between his own and Percy's lot. He did not know much about country houses — in fact, he knew really nothing of them at all, except what he had seen, as a tourist, on one or two show days at important places. But he knew enough to picture to himself their extraordinary comfort, their spaciousness and their atmosphere of leisure. On such a day as this, for instance, he supposed that Percy would either be shooting, in proper outdoor clothes, with a macintosh, or, if he were indulgently inclined, would spend the afternoon in a billiard room, in slippers, with as many cigarettes (of the best Turkish quality) as he wanted, and a roaring fire. At any rate the inhabitant of a country house would be his own master, under perfectly comfortable conditions, with a practically infinite series of independent and lordly days to follow; while he, Reggie, must be content with about forty hours of peace (of which about sixteen must be spent in sleep), passed in a house in a small road at Wimbledon, before taking up once more the grind of the City.

"One is taken," he considered, once more with a touch of bitterness; "and the other left."

It was not a very nice little house in which he and his mother and sister lived together. It was quite new; and everything, therefore, had a way of going wrong; the new wood of the doors gaped and let drafts through; smells rose from the kitchen with an astonishing poignancy; and the partitions and floors were so thin that a person on the first floor walked upon what was, practically, a sounding board to the room below.

Mrs. Ballard was a little round-about lady, who wore a little red velvet bow in her cap on Sundays, who read a sermon aloud to herself when she could not go to church, and was entirely and impregnably certain that her own point-of-view, on every subject, was the only one. She had been a most excellent mother to Reggie and Mamie, educating them at the cost of severe self-sacrifice, and placing them, when they were old enough, in what she considered to be excellent social positions: Reggie, as has been seen, was a clerk; and Mamie, of course, was a typist.

It was this very serenity and contentment of his mother that Reggie found so hard this afternoon. There was a little cold beef and pickles for his lunch, with the remnants of a bread-and-butter pudding — all set out from the cupboard within ten minutes of his arrival and of his announcement that he hadn't had anything to eat. Mamie, he was informed, had said before leaving that morning, that she would probably not be back till late.

Even the little back room, which was called a "breakfast room" and used as a dining room, seemed unusually pinched and meager after his dreams of Marston. It was quite nicely and properly furnished. It had an enlarged photograph of the late Mr. Ballard over the chimney piece — (his profession had been that of an engineer) — the chairs were mahogany and horsehair; the curtains were clean and decent; the fire-irons and fender were of the highest polish of which black-lead is capable. It was all distinctly within the margin of propriety; it was sufficient and adequate and conventional; and it was kept so by continual economy and carefulness and self-sacrifice. Mrs. Ballard was determined, as she said to herself sometimes, that her children "should have a nice home to come back to."

Yet Reggie felt terribly discontented today. Honestly, he was not envious of Percy; even though it was the thought of Percy's opulence that suggested his own discontent. He was displeased, not that Percy was happy and free, but that he himself was not; and he did think that Percy might have fulfilled his weekend promises before now. Today, for example, how pleasant it would have been to have caught the one-twenty from London Bridge; he would very nearly have been at Marston by now.

"There's no letter for me, I suppose," he said rather gruffly, as his mother pushed the bread-and-butter pudding within his reach.

"No, my dear. Were you expecting one?"

"I thought there might be one."

"You can finish the pudding, my dear. I've got a Swiss-roll for supper tonight."

Reggie said nothing.

"I don't think I'll go to the early Mass tomorrow," he remarked presently. "I'm tired."

Mrs. Ballard's face assumed a controlled expression. She had yielded to her son's conversion with an Evangelical's distress; but she was not going to take back her generosity.

"As you wish, my dear."

(3)

He was carving a little deal panel for his *prie dieu*[1] when Percy's letter did actually arrive. He had his "things," as they were called, in the cupboard of the real dining room in front, which was, in fact, the room where all three sat in the evenings. The "drawing room" was seldom entered, except if one of them was not quite well, or when visitors came, or for tea on Sundays.

These "things," all kept upon two special shelves, combined the most diverse articles. (Mamie had her "things" on two higher shelves.) At present they were chiefly bits of white wood, with three chisels, bought in a pawnshop, and some designs on paper; there was also a broken rosary that Reggie proposed to mend as soon as a bit of decent wire turned up; three or four frilled little cards with pious pictures on them; a lump of incense; and a paint-box, and an account book. He had got out a selection of these articles on to the table, as soon as it was evident that the rain was not going to leave off, and had set himself to finish his conventional lily, which, when completed and stained, was to form part of a small reredos[2] which he desired to affix to his *prie dieu* in his bedroom. Mrs. Ballard encouraged such occupations, in spite of the aroma of popery which seemed now so inseparable from her son's ambitions, out of the excellent desire of keeping her boy at home. She had the most lurid views of the fate of young men who "went out" too much when they were off duty.

He got up the very instant that the letter rattled on the oil-cloth of the little hall, so preoccupied was his subconsciousness with the thought of Percy and Marston; and

---

[1] Kneeler.
[2] A screen or decoration behind the altar in a church.

as he came in again, the letter was already out of the envelope, and he reading it. But his air was such as he fitted
the letter back into its envelope, and both into his pockets, that his mother made a remark from over her mend-
ing.

"What is the matter, my dear?"

His lips tightened.

"Percy Smith wants me to go to a theater with him."

"When?"

"He doesn't say."

He bent again over his carving.

Yet within there was a storm of resentment; and his
mother knew it: and he knew that she knew it. But she
was puzzled as to what in such a letter could have made
him angry: she did not know that Percy had once more
said that the weekend plan must be put off for a bit, as
they were having hardly any guests at present; but that
Reggie and he must do a theater together some time: and,
how was Reggie, and, how beastly the City must be in the
weather they were having!

Mrs. Ballard had sufficient tact to say nothing at all for
a minute or two; but she had not enough tact to be silent
any longer, and, still more, not enough to avoid the subject of Percy altogether.

"And how is he?" she asked, after the pause. "Seems all
right," said Reggie shortly. Mrs. Ballard laid down the
sock upon her lap. "What is the matter, my dear?" she
said. "Nothing," said her son.

(4)

He got better, however, after supper.

Reggie was quite a little person; and there simply was
not room in him for large sinister emotions; there was
only room for the clean and elementary Christian virtues,
though even these could not rise in him to very heroic
heights. There is at least that advantage in not being
great souled, that, so long as actual meanness is not permitted, practically nothing else except what is fairly
wholesome can find any room at all. And Reggie was precisely of this type; he could not bear to be envious or resentful for long at a time, because he found it so very uncomfortable; it was actually easier for him — as it was for

his mother in her desires to make a nice home for her
children — to sweep such things out as soon as possible,
and put the furniture in its proper place. Nothing was, at
present at least, on the grand scale with him at all: his religion precipitated itself in little carved *prie dieux;* his virtues in being as nice as he could be at home, and in doing
his work in the City honestly and conscientiously; his ambitions, in being some day, perhaps, a real friar like Father Hilary.

These are not qualities that will shake the world; but,
after all, there is the best authority for believing that they
are of considerable importance in the world that is to
come. . . .

So Reggie, after eating some more cold beef and the
Swiss-roll which his mother had mentioned; after inquiring from Mamie whether she wasn't tired; and after fetch-
ing, on his own initiative, his mother's knitting from her
bedroom — felt better, and decided, after all, to go to St.
Francis, for the eight o'clock Mass.

Yes; he would write a nice letter to Percy, without any
of the ice-cold irony which he had at first contemplated;
and he would call him Old Chap; and say how ripping it
would be to go to a theater with him.

Chapter VII

(1)

It was not till the third week of the run that Percy managed, all unsuspected of a deeper motive, to get a couple of stalls for *A Gentleman of Fortune*. (He worked it in with a visit to a "shooting school" where he had arranged for lessons.) He went with Reggie Ballard.

Reggie's affection for Percy was tinged now with a distinct accession of awe. At an early dinner at a restaurant (for which Percy of course paid) he expressed this vaguely. He supposed that Percy would soon obtain a church near Marston.

"My dear chap," he said, "what a time you will have! And what a lot you can do! Seen Father Hilary lately?"

"Saw him this afternoon," said Percy.

"When are you going to be received?"

"Don't know."

Reggie proceeded then to pour out his own news — scraps of ecclesiastical matters, tales of the City, and Percy appeared to listen.

Percy seemed a little distraught this evening, thought the other. His eyes were bright and restless and he was a trifle paler than usual. But his dinner jacket was beautiful; and he had two stripes of braid down the outside of his trousers: he also wore a small pearl in the center of his shirt-front, and had a real opera hat in the cloakroom with his long pale coat. And there corresponded to these glories an unusual air of detachment.

He was not at all confidential. Certainly he related (with just the suspicion of a drawl) the glories of Marston, in answer to his friend's questions; and spoke of the shooting school where he seemed to have met with great success this afternoon. But the subtle air of intimacy was gone. A great excitement, however, took its place, as, at twenty minutes to eight, he desired a taxi to be called and the bill presented. With awe and envy Reggie watched the

paying of this bill, and the change for a sovereign[1] on the
salver superbly waved away.

"What sort of a play is it?" he asked, as the cab moved
off.

"I believe it's first-rate," said Percy. "It's by Franklyn,
you know."

Certainly Percy was changed: he was oddly abrupt
when he spoke, and fell into silences. Reggie caught him
once examining himself in the little slit of mirror on the
side of the cab. Just when the lighted entrance of the
theater came in sight he turned to Reggie full of some
fierce emotion.

"Look here," he said. "Don't say one word during the
play, will you? I really want to attend. I . . . I've got a reason."

Reggie wondered vaguely to himself during those inspiriting moments before the curtain goes up — when the
music warms the emotions, and strange lights come and
go upon the curtain. Something was certainly the matter
with his friend. Merely to have become a gentleman of
wealth and leisure would not wholly account for the unmistakable change.

He had scarcely seen him more than once or twice since
Percy had first left the City. Once they had met for lunch
in the old place, and Percy had been voluble. Once they
had run into one another on the steps of St. Francis',
Kensington. But he had never seen the other quite in this
mood before, excited yet taciturn, nervous and uncommu-
nicative. There was an air of determination about him,
too, which was new.

Well; it was not his affair at present. That was plain.
Perhaps he would be told more afterwards. They were to
drive back together to the house in Wilton Crescent where
the caretaker was to provide them both with a light supper, and Percy with a bed.

Then the curtain brightened at the bottom. The over-
ture ceased. Then, as a bell tingled the orchestra began
again a few soft chords.

---

[1] A gold coin worth £1; half a week's wages for Reggie.

(2)

At the end of the First Act Percy sat silent and motion-less as Reggie proposed a cigarette. He proposed it again. Percy shook his head.

"No. But you go. I want to sit still."

At the end of the Second Act Percy got up without a word and made his way out. Reggie found him smoking furiously in the bar a minute or two later.

"Well?" said Reggie.

"It's all right, isn't it?" said Percy with superb calm. "Have a drink?"

At the end of the Third Act Percy again sat silent and shook his head, so Reggie too sat still, waiting for conver-sation. But his friend took up the program and studied it with such earnestness that obviously nothing must be said.

At the end of the Fourth and last Act he sat quite silent once more till a couple of stars came forward to take a re-call. One was the Gentleman of Fortune himself; the other was a Miss Farham. Then he clapped earnestly and strenuously, till they disappeared again.

"Come along," said Percy. "Let's get out of the crush."

"It's a very remarkable play," said Percy with high judi-ciality as they sat together speeding westwards. "Don't you think so?"

"Oh, yes," said Reggie; "but don't you think just a little near the edge? That third act, you know."

Percy lifted his eyebrows in careful disdain.

"By the way, I know Miss Farham, you know," he said in a completely steady voice.

"Miss Farham! You mean —"

"Yes. I know her rather well. Don't you think she was very good?" (But he did not think fit to mention that Miss Farham was the girl he had met in the train.)

It is exceedingly hard for an amateur not to over-act his part. Percy's serenity was of so monumental a character, that even Reggie perceived it. And since he was not a fool in all respects, he instantly connected Percy's emotional-ism this evening with Miss Farham. He saw, too, that he must be very careful and discreet.

"I thought her splendid," said Reggie: "and it must have been a very difficult part."

Percy nodded.

At supper his silence came on him again. There was cold chicken to eat and hock to drink. (These were the provisions that Mrs. Brandreth-Smith had specified to the caretaker.) And Percy ate and drank in the intervals of walking about the big somber room. Now he came into the ring of candlelight, now he passed again into shadow. Reggie, like a good little boy, ate away perseveringly at the table and made small talk, till he had quite finished. Then he leaned back and lighted one more cigarette.

"I say, old man," said Percy, suddenly stopping in his walk; "have you quite done? I don't want to be inhospitable, but I'm beastly tired."

"Right," said Reggie.

"How are you going to go?" asked Percy, following him out into the hall.

"Walk to Victoria — and then train. . . . Well, goodnight, old man. Thanks awfully."

Reggie walked to the station feeling just a trifle injured. Really, he thought, his friend might have been a little more confidential. And, certainly too, he might have at least mentioned the weekend scheme. But of course he was very grateful for his evening.

(3)

Percy resumed his walk up and down the room; but he walked considerably quicker, and made no effort at self-control.

He was excited as he had never been excited before in all his life; and he was not thinking about Reggie at all.

The process, of course, was a very simple and ordinary one. It had begun, as has been related, in a very *bourgeois* manner in the train, when the boy had first fallen over the bag; and there had followed experience after experience to emotionalize his impressions. His initiation into religious sentiment, his new ideals, then the sudden rolling open of the Gates of Fortune — all these things, acting upon a nature that was exceedingly susceptible, had charged it all with fire. His long drafts of excitement had done for his sentiments very much what his half-bottle of champagne just now had done for his body. . . . And, it must be remembered, Miss Gladys Farham was a magnetically attractive person.

A yet more tense stage had been begun in the little tea party at the theater. He had felt her anger then, and perceived (he thought) her real fineness of character. She had behaved with stimulating perfection; it seemed to him that he had gained a knowledge of her depth of character which he could, perhaps, have learned in no other way. Finally, she had implanted in him, at the very moment of his leaving, a little barbed point of jealousy. He had not forgotten the "friend" who would see after her when he was gone.

There had followed three weeks of excited brooding. He had written to her once, begging again her forgiveness for his foolish want of tact, and she had answered in a tiny sensible little note that told him nothing. Her personality had seemed with him all the time. He had wandered about the house and park, trying to see her in its frame: he had dreamed of her both by day and night. It was the regular old tale over and over again; he had been melancholy and boisterous, barely civil, and again suddenly affectionate. But he had not said one word to a living soul. . . . It was this that distinguished this affair from previous ones. Percy was becoming a man.

And now this evening had crowned it all.

Miss Farham was, as has been said, a real emotional actress, in spite of her immature age; and possessed that heaven-given temperament that can "get over the footlights." And this particular play was not only really well suited to her, but bore some kind of parallel too to what Percy knew of her own history. She was a "betrayed" woman in the piece: the radiant dominating girl of Act I, became, by the end, a somber brokenhearted woman. The very shot is heard, at the fall of the curtain, by which she kills herself . . . (or the door bangs which announces her departure into the night. I forget which).

The thing was very nearly appalling to Percy, who knew at any rate that she herself had been treated badly in real life. He saw, or thought he saw, a kind of sketch upon the stage of what might, conceivably, be her final history. He had found, at the close of the piece, his program crushed into a ball in his left hand. . . .

It is an intoxicating mixture that is composed of Pity and Admiration and ordinary clean human love; and it appeared to rage in Percy's veins like fire. It was not that he had not looked at the arguments against his dream: he understood that he was too young (in the world's opinion); he realized, partly at any rate, how exceedingly contrary to his newly opening social ambitions this particular step would be, and how still more against those of his mother. But those very ambitions, too, helped to intoxicate him further. It appeared to him that three hundred a year of his own was wealth. And, finally, dashed into all this was the emotion of religion — his sense of the great kindly Power he had found. This, at least, should be enough to counteract worldly arguments. He longed to lift her out of her miseries . . . as might a fairy prince. . . .

(4)

The ex-policeman caretaker came up from the back-stairs to see if the young gentleman was gone to bed yet, and to put out the lights. But the young gentleman was still walking, and apparently wakeful. "That you, Simmons?"

"Yessir."

"Oh — er — I don't want to keep you up," went on the young gentleman, dimly discernible, standing beyond the supper table. "You can lock up and go to bed. I'll put out these lights."

"Yessir. What time in the morning shall I call you, sir?"

"Oh — er — nine. I'll breakfast at half-past. I want a bath. And I'll have a taxi here at twenty to eleven."

"Very good, sir. Goodnight, sir."

"Goodnight, Simmons. . . . Oh — er — Simmons. If . . . if I leave a letter in the hall tonight, you'll have it posted first thing, won't you?"

"Yes, sir. On the slab, sir."

"That's all right then. Goodnight."

"Goodnight, sir."

(5)

"The young chap seemed restless-like," said Simmons to his wife when he got up to the bedroom.

"Eh?"

"I said the young chap seemed restless-like," repeated Simmons. "There was a letter my lord must have posted."

Mrs. Simmons uttered an inarticulate comment. She had been nearly asleep.

"Eh?" said Simmons.

"Oh! Don't bother me," said his wife. "I've had enough already with the chicken and the hock and that."

"You'll have more than that, my lady, when her ladyship comes up to town. I never see such a woman for fuss as the old girl."

He began to take off his coat.

"They're too new for me altogether," remarked Mrs. Simmons dreamily. "Give me the old crusted lot as never looks at two sides of a sixpence."

"Well, it's easy enough so far," went on her husband, winding up his watch. "But it's the old girl that wears the breeches, and no mistake."

Such were the comments of the Menials. It is pleasant to reflect that Percy, downstairs, in the midst of his fine frenzy, yet found time to reflect how freely and easily he had talked to the ex-policeman, and with what an offhand air of authority.

Chapter VIII

(1)

Reggie twice went past the motionless figure that sat in the aisle, without recognizing him. And the third time he remembered.

He had been promoted now to the position of church sweeper, and was intensely proud of it; for his sole companion was a friar. He had asked for the privilege more than once, but the Father Guardian had explained evasively to the very trim-looking clerk what a dusty business it was; and it was not until Reggie had exhibited a really extraordinarily regular punctuality in his other duties that he had been allowed at last to take off his coat in the sacristy, turn up his trousers and his sleeves, gird himself with a baize apron, and on Monday and Thursday mornings, from seven to half-past, first to throw down tea leaves in the south aisle, and then (noiselessly, as Mass was being said at the high altar) to sweep them up again.

On this Thursday morning, then, twice he passed Mr. Main, perceiving only that he was in the dress of a cleric, and never connecting him for an instant with the bleak-faced curate whom he had observed drinking tea once or twice in the drawing room of Percy's home. Then his mind roused itself; and, as the priest left the altar, he remembered that this must be Mr. Main. But what in the world was the curate doing in the Franciscan church? He became interested; he placed himself, near the font, sweeping with vigor, and, as the clergyman came past, went up to him.

"Mr. Main, isn't it?" he whispered shyly. "I'm Ballard — Reggie Ballard."

Mr. Main looked at him blankly.

"Er . . . yes . . . of course —" he began, obviously at a loss.

"We met at Hanstead — Percy Smith — don't you remember? I'm Reggie Ballard."

Then Mr. Main advanced a lean-fingered hand.

"I remember," he said. "And how do you do, Mr. Ballard?"

"I'm just sweeping up for the friars," explained Reggie eagerly. "That's Brother John the other side — I . . . I didn't know —"

He hesitated.

"Yes," said Mr. Main. "I'm looking round. I . . . I understood that this was the church where — May I speak to you a moment somewhere?"

Reggie eagerly assented; and led the way round into the sacristy, genuflecting with immense particularity and with such unexpectedness that the curate stumbled violently against him, and followed murmuring apologies.

The priest, as they entered, was just folding up his amice.[1]

"May I speak to my friend here, Father?" asked Reggie, consumed with excitement, and with delight too at showing his entire familiarity with these holy men.

The friar smiled pleasantly.

"Why certainly," he said; and went out, with a small inclination to the clergyman as he passed. Mr. Main's eyes wandered vaguely round the great bare well-used room, with its countless inexplicable articles — the long low cupboards on which lay piles of strange garments, each in a group by itself; the tall pinewood presses; the little sink and basin) the pair of censers hanging over a smoke blackened gas-brazier; the roller-towel by the basin. It all looked so very shabby, and yet so well used and so exceedingly businesslike — not in the least resembling the bright and spotless vestry at Hanstead, with the Glastonbury chair,[2] the neat writing materials, the register of services, and the rows of starched white surplices.

"I . . . I am glad I met you —" he began.

"Sit down, sir," said Reggie, beaming, and drawing out a couple of wooden kitchen chairs from their places against the wall.

---

[1] A liturgical vestment that goes across the shoulders of the celebrant.

[2] A 19th century term for a style of Medieval chair, based on a chair believed to have been made for Richard Whiting, the last Abbot of Glastonbury.

(2)

"I . . . I wanted to ask about Percy," said the clergyman, after another wandering glance round the big room. "Is . . . is he received into the Roman Church yet, do you know?"

Reggie's face fell a little. He had hoped that here was an Enquirer.

"Not yet," he said.

"I understood from him that this was the church where . . . where he first heard a sermon, that . . . that —"

Reggie made haste to interpret his hesitation.

"Yes," he said, "he came here with me. He's under instruction here, you know."

"Yes . . . I . . . I understood that. There is a . . . a monk here, is there not, who —"

"Father Hilary — yes —" said Reggie eagerly. "I introduced them, you know — but he's not a monk, he's a —"

"What name, if you please —"

"Father Hilary," said the boy.

Mr. Main nodded with compressed lips, and let his melancholy eyes rest a moment on Reggie's face.

"You're up here very early, sir," said Reggie, still tremulous with expectation.

"I am spending a couple of days up here," said the clergyman slowly. "I'm going back to Hanstead this morning — a little business, you know. That's all."

Reggie waited.

"Have you heard lately from . . . from our friend?" asked the other presently.

Reggie made an effort to be loyal.

"I went to a theater with him a few days ago," he said.

"And . . . and he's happy?"

Reggie, to tell the truth, had found himself, since his visit to the theater, becoming more and more aware that Percy was disappointing him. They had been very intimate friends indeed in the City. And there was not the slightest doubt that they were no longer so intimate. It seemed more and more odd to Reggie, to take a single example, that Percy had not said a word more as to the weekend idea. In imagination, he had taken it for granted — and at Percy's word too — that he would go, as soon as the Brandreth-Smiths had settled in, or even before. At the same time he felt himself rather ungrateful for not having better appreciated Percy's taking him to the play.

"Oh, he's happy, I think. Of course he's got a lot to do, you know, down in the country."

"I meant, rather, about religion," said the curate.

Reggie made haste to reassure him.

"Oh, yes," he said, "so far as I know. Yes, entirely, of course."

Mr. Main's eyes wandered again round the sacristy.

"And you, too?" he said suddenly, turning to him again. "You're a convert, I think?"

Reggie drew a long breath.

"I . . . I can't tell you how happy," he said. "It's . . . it's impossible —"

Mr. Main nodded gently, again, three or four times.

"It's . . . it's perfectly gorgeous," went on the boy, rapturously, for his religion was to him, indeed, the passion of his life, and the one subject on which he could be eloquent. It was, not yet, very deep, perhaps; it manifested itself, largely (as has been said), in small exterior matters such as his private altar at home, the brown habits of the friars, the dusty incense-laden smell of the church; it inspired with a strange romance even such servile tasks as throwing down tea leaves in the aisles and sweeping them up again. But it was entirely genuine; it formed the material out of which all his daydreams were woven; his supreme ambition was, of course, to be a friar — an ambition suspended, however, so far as he could see, by the very explicit orders of his confessor to take no kind of practical action in the matter so long as his mother at Wimbledon was in the least dependent on him. But this check made him all the more zealous; meanwhile he could do menial tasks, and get up an hour and a half earlier than he need on Mondays and Thursdays, and draw little pictures of hooded heads on his blotting paper when he was not writing down uninteresting facts about ships on their way from Australia to the Port of London.

But his eloquence was spasmodic. He made little gestures: he said how "ripping" the friars were, and how "gorgeous" the ceremonial was. And Mr. Main looked at him, and away again, and back again.

Then the door opened.

"Why — here is —" began Reggie, rising. "Good morning, Father. — This is Father Hilary, Mr. Main."

(3)

Reggie was much too agitated and excited to observe intelligently the meeting of these two. But it seemed to him afterwards that the manner, at any rate of the curate, had been curiously significant.

Mr. Main was on his feet nearly as soon as Reggie, and seemed to have an odd air as of terror and defiance — so far as his almost expressionless face could manifest such emotions. He stood stiffly, and bowed as stiffly, in return to the friar's salute.

"Er — this is Mr. Main," explained Reggie. "Father Placid said I might see him in here. I . . ."

"Quite right," said the friar gently. "But I shall have to disturb you, I'm afraid, in a minute or two. I'm saying the eight o'clock Mass, you know."

He looked apologetically towards the clergyman, who remained as if petrified.

"I only looked in —" continued the friar, making a movement towards the door.

"I . . . I must be going," said Mr. Main suddenly and harshly, wheeling round on Reggie.

"Oh! But I'm sorry," explained the friar. "Take your friend through into one of the parlors," he went on, turning to the clerk.

"No; no," cried the clergyman abruptly. "I . . . I must go."

He pushed forward a hand towards Reggie, stiffly and awkwardly, and then let it fall again: and Reggie saw how he turned once more to the friar and stared on him.

It was not until later that Reggie realized the extraordinary contrast between these two figures. The one might have stepped straight out of an illuminated manuscript; the other could have stepped from nowhere except from a London street of the twentieth century. The one had a kind of perfect suitability about him — (Reggie was always bewildered when he met Father Hilary sometimes in secular clothes) — the folds of his heavy habit, his cord, his thrown-back hood, his radiant bearded face and bright eyes — all, from the effect of sheer simplicity, made a pic-

ture of a perfect art. And the other, handicapped of course
by his singularly unattractive face, was rendered as hopelessly conventional as can be imagined, by his black overcoat, his loose trousers, his flattish creased boots, and his
silk hat that he held still in his left hand. These two, then,
faced one another — the friar still and passive, so to
speak, the clergyman no longer defiant but tensely attentive and observant.

There was a tiny awkward silence.

Father Hilary broke it.

"I am glad to have met you, Mr. Main," he said. Then he
wheeled and slipped out.

Reggie heard his companion emit a long breath like a
sigh, and, looking quickly at him, saw an expression on
his face that he could not interpret at all. He hastened to
interpose.

"Well, I'll see you out through the house," he said, "if
you really must go, Mr. Main. I've got to be going too,
really."

He could see that something was the matter. He was
not at all clever, but so much he did understand. He was
still puzzled as to why Mr. Main was here at all; but he
supposed it must have originally been that he was curious
to see the place where Percy had first come across Catholicism. And he thought it to be a rather delicate and
exciting compliment to his religion that the clergyman
should have been thrown into such agitation through an
encounter with a friar.

When he had hung up his baize apron and was putting
on his coat, he tried again to make things easy. The clergyman was still standing motionless, looking once more
vaguely round the unfamiliar sacristy.

"I have to catch the train at High Street," said the boy.
"Perhaps you're coming my way."

Mr. Main appeared to wake out of a kind of trance.

"And where do you get your breakfast?" he asked solemnly.

"Down in the City," said the boy — "on Mondays and
Thursdays. You see it's too early—" And he explained that
he could not expect breakfast at six o'clock in Wimbledon.

"You're going my way?" he asked again.

"No; no," said the curate decisively. "I . . . I must go and get my bag."

(4)

Reggie was completely puzzled as he went down City-wards.

The clergyman had said no more, until they parted at the friary door. He had nodded absentmindedly as the boy had led him through the house, pointing out such objects of interest as the plaster statue in the corridor, a brown mantle hanging on a peg, and the little barred peephole in the door whence visitors could be observed by the porter.

Then, on the steps outside, he had suddenly laid his long fingers on the boy's blue overcoat.

"Father Hilary was the name — you said?"

"Yes — Father Hilary."

The clergyman removed his fingers briskly.

"Well — I'm glad to have met you," he said — "Mr. — er — Mr. Ballard, perhaps you will do me the favor of not mentioning that you met me here —"

"Oh! Certainly not," agreed Reggie hastily, yet suddenly taken aback.

"You — you see it might cause misunderstandings. — Well, goodbye, Mr. Ballard, goodbye to you."

Obviously, then, Mr. Main too must have that delightful and exciting sensation of having done something rather wrong in entering a Catholic church; for Reggie was still young enough to enjoy the sinister reputation of his religion. And it seemed to him now, as he rattled towards the Mansion House, wholly agreeable that this should be so, and, especially, when an Anglican clergyman was so affected.

Yet why had Mr. Main come to the church at all, and at such an hour? Was the motive of curiosity really sufficient? And yet any other motive appeared to Reggie as simply inconceivable, when regarded in the light of cold common sense — especially the idea (which had first occurred to him in the excitement of the encounter in church) that perhaps Mr. Main himself might be an Enquirer. For what in the world could there be in common between religions of which the picturesque friar was the symbol on one side, and the stiff conventionality of this clergyman on the other? One would as soon expect the Bishop of London to turn Mormon, as Mr. Main to turn Catholic.

It must be just curiosity after all, then, Reggie decided, as he climbed the steps up to the street level — curiosity and a sudden impulse to seek an uncharacteristic adventure.

Chapter IX

(1)

Mrs. Brandreth-Smith was enjoying herself vastly. She awoke each morning with the sense of a strenuous and important day before her, in which she should control a large number of people and affairs. And the best of all was that she was not *nouveau-riche* in the ordinary sense of the word: she was an exile who had come home. Was she not a Brandreth? Did not the county acknowledge her? Had not Lord Marridon himself expressed his gratification that Marston was still to be in Brandreth hands?

"That young chap, you know," he had said confidently, "who we all thought was to have it, was really rather a cub."

She had smilingly murmured something that might be interpreted as deprecatory or appreciative. "It 'ud all have gone to the Jews, you know,"[1] he had continued. "It means a good deal to us, you know, that it should still be Brandreth property."

And it was from the seed of these words that a further vast and audacious project had sprung up in the lady's mind. But she saw it must be put through quickly, if it was to come off at all.

She had a further satisfaction in the knowledge that she was not only doing her duty, but doing it well. Her husband was perfectly acquiescent and obedient: he had capitulated in a manner she had hardly dared to hope, and was beginning to show, even, a certain independent life of his own along the proper lines. She had heard him rating the gamekeeper in a perfectly respectable manner, and he had told the butler, in her hearing, that the smell of smoke was not any more to come up from the direction of the pantry. (He had shaved off his little whiskers too, and looked at least naval, if not positively military.)

---

[1] Lord Marridon means that the previous heir-presumptive was a spendthrift and would have mortgaged the estate or sold it to repay loans made by moneylenders at high rates of interest.

Her children, too, were behaving as was expected of them. Helen had made friends with Mabel Marridon and actually took an interest in her dresses. Percy had taken to shooting with avidity and had desired, three or four times, to go up to town on affairs which (with the exception of the Father Hilary business) she approved. He had been twice up to his shooting school and his tailors, once to a theater, and only yesterday had gone up again to see the priest and stay the night in town. But, best of all, he hadn't yet made any fuss about getting Reggie Ballard down to Marston: she felt that would not quite do when he had first mentioned it; and had evaded. At any rate she must insist that Reggie was not to come when there were any other guests. She had other views for Percy now. He must make new friends more consonant with his new position.

On this particular morning she had a further cause for importance. Mr. Bennett and his wife were coming down to stay a night and inspect the place before finally accepting the offer of the living: and this, perhaps, more than anything, brought home to her the greatness of her position. Up to the present the clergy had been her social superiors; henceforth they would lunch or sup with her on Sundays, meekly, as she required. It gave her an astonishing sense of power, to be able to bestow a living at her own high pleasure. . . . She looked back on Hanstead now, as a glorified scullery maid in Heaven might regard memories of a mean lodging house on earth.

The midday train brought first Percy, and next the second post. Percy looked a little white, she thought; but he gave her an intelligent account of the Wilton Crescent arrangements, and reported progress in the shooting school. He said nothing about the priest.

The second post, too, brought her a new pleasure, for it contained a letter from a friend in London in answer to one of her own, bringing circumstances within her knowledge whose manipulation would give her another opportunity for exercising social power. It was important enough — (though very sad of course, too) — to warrant discussion at the luncheon table when the servants had gone away after coffee.

"James," she said, tilting her head A little, "I have had news of the Matthieson-Howleys."

The doctor bent his eyes on her, while Helen looked up sharply.

"They mustn't be called upon," she said. "Winnie tells me there's a queer story —" she glanced at Helen.

Helen flushed.

It was she who had discovered the new inhabitants of the "Nook," in Marston Village, and had reported a conversation she had had over an unrehearsed cat-hunt on the part of her new terrier Jim and the Matthieson-Howleys' cat. She had reported Mrs. Matthieson-Howley as quite charming, and had suggested that an acquaintance might be followed up.

"Are you sure it's true, Mother?" she said rebelliously.

"It is enough that I say so," said her mother, folding up the letter again which she had held up just now as a guarantee of good faith.

The doctor nodded.

"Who are the Matthieson-Howleys?" asked Percy languorously.

"They are at the 'Nook'," said Mrs. Brandreth-Smith." I don't say there is anything specifically wrong; but — well: I think I have said enough." She rose.

(2)

Helen made her way after tea to the smoking room to find Percy. She felt she must have sympathy. He was sitting in a deep chair, his hands resting along its arms, doing absolutely nothing: he just moved his head and eyes a little as she rustled in.

. "I think it's perfectly hateful of Mother," she said, sitting down sharply opposite him. "There's nothing whatever against them really. Why shouldn't I —"

"What are you talking about?"

"Why, the Matthieson-Howleys. He's only divorced his wife: and why shouldn't he? And he's married again. Why shouldn't he? The law allows it, and he was married in church all right."

Percy sat up.

"Why, what's the matter?" he asked abruptly.

"Mother says we mustn't call upon them. (And she's simply a dear). Mother says we must be very careful indeed in the country, at any rate at first. She says you've got to draw the line somewhere: that it might be all right in an ordinary way in town; but —"

"Do you mean you're not to call upon them because of that?"

Helen was astounded at his vehemence. He did not usually show zeal in such affairs. Yet he was all awake now, and looked indignant. She felt encouraged.

"Yes. Isn't it perfectly hateful? Did you ever hear such —"

Percy was on his feet.

"And that's absolutely all that she's heard against them?" he exclaimed. "When they've only done a perfectly legal thing — do you really mean that?"

"That's absolutely all," she assented again.

"That's rot; you must have misunderstood. Look here, I'll go and ask Mother myself."

"Oh! Do, Percy. And do try to persuade her —"

But Percy was gone.

(3)

"No more wine, thank you," said Mr. Bennett politely "One finds one glass quite enough."

His wife and he had arrived by the "tea train," and had reached the house soon after five. The rest of the evening till dinner they had been closeted with their hosts.

Dinner had displayed them as variously affected, respectively, by the atmosphere in which they found themselves. Mrs. Bennett was completely herself, staidly and brightly dressed, pleasant, humorous and attractive: Mr. Bennett, in a tightish black silk waistcoat buttoning out of sight, and a swallowtail coat, was urbane and deferential. Mrs. Brandreth-Smith's composed bearing, her augustness and authority, had their subtle effects upon these two — making them both a little subdued. It was evident that they would make an excellent Rectory party, and that they intended to do so.

It was immediately after Mr. Bennett had proclaimed his abstemiousness over the port that he remembered for the first time a piece of news he had.

"By the way," he said to his host, "I never told you about poor Main."

"No."

"Well: he's told me that in any case he will not attempt to stay on at Hanstead, even should my successor wish it. There's some mystery behind; I think it must be connected with his wife. . . . I can't make it out. And yet one knows for a fact that he has not communicated with the Bishop about any other work. I don't understand it at all. I thought perhaps that you —"

"Not a word! Not a word! And why do you think that Mrs. Main — eh?"

"Well: she's been strange lately . . . one hardly knows to express it. Very polite and pleasant, and yet it almost seemed to one ironical too."

Percy fidgeted with his wineglass. It seemed to him a very unimportant matter.

For he was obsessed by the injustice connected with the tenants of the "Nook." He had managed to get a word with his mother at dressing time and had found that matters really were very much as Helen had reported. There was nothing at all against them except the fact that the man had divorced his wife and married again: and when the boy had asked indignantly whether such a thing was not perfectly justified both legally and ecclesiastically, and if so, what was wrong, his mother had answered that it "was not quite nice, anyhow," that there were some clergymen and even some bishops who did not approve of remarriage after divorce (though she made haste to say that she did not agree with them); and that people in their own position must be more careful than others to set an example.

"I don't like to have to remind you, my dear boy," she had said finally with that odd new authoritative air of hers, "that I and your father are the best judges as to who are proper persons for you to be acquainted with. We are in an entirely new position now, you know — you will learn all these little shades of feeling better by and by. I have not a word to say against these people: I have no doubt that they are most excellent and good: but people who get mixed up in such affairs must be prepared to pay the price. . . . Now you must go, my dear boy; or I shall be late for dinner."

(4)

Mrs. Brandreth-Smith's heart indeed swelled within her in pleasurable sensations this evening.

It was an immense delight to her to sit and talk to Mrs. Bennett, while Helen unwillingly played the piano out of sight in a recess; and to feel how completely old relations had been reversed. At Hanstead, though she had bravely asserted to herself that the wives of the doctors and the clergy were entirely of equal rank, she did not find that everyone agreed with her. Mrs. Bennett, on occasions of rare dinner parties, was always given precedence. But here there was no question at all as to which was the superior, Mrs. Brandreth-Smith of Marston Park or the wife of the clergyman whom Mrs. Brandreth-Smith was presenting to the Marston living.

She talked with an excellently well-bred patronage — not in the least ostentatious, it must be understood; and Mrs. Bennett, in her high-necked dress and garnet necklace, sat and meekly listened and agreed enthusiastically with the parochial plans that were set forth.

"You must just run in and out, my dear," said Mrs. Brandreth-Smith, "as if this were your own house. It's such a pleasure to me to think that old friends will be so close. And Mr. Bennett must just set to work, with his wonderful organizing power, and transform the village. I am sure he will. His . . . his music, and his classes, and his Band of Hope and so on. And you must both just ask us for anything you want — quite freely and frankly, you know."

What a pleasure it all was, too, when the door opened and the men came in, talking, with the white shirt-front of her husband glimmering in the subdued light across the great Georgian room, and Mr. Bennett's hearty (and yet slightly deferential) laugh resounding at some joke.

Tall lamps shone through red shades here and there: a dozen candles in sconces, also protected by red shades, glowed high up above the polished wainscoting: the tall portrait of Mrs. Brandreth-Smith's own great-great-aunt, in a Gainsborough hat and white dress, towered above the mantelpiece — (really, her very own great-great-aunt!).

The thin shoes sounded sharp on the smooth-polished floor, and turned silent on the deep-piled carpet: the piano-notes rippled out from the recess where Helen was still playing. It was all opulent and secure and assured. . . . A bell sounded, as solemn as a church, tolling to call the servants to supper far away. The wind whispered, scarcely heard, behind the shuttered and heavily curtained windows.

"Why, where's Percy!" she asked.

"Don't know," said her husband. "Slipped off for another smoke, I expect."

She frowned slightly. She was beginning to see that Percy would need a little management, especially if he was to fulfill the high vocation she was designing for him.

"And now what do you say to a rubber, Rector?"

She indicated a card table laid out, with candles and packs.

(5)

But Percy was not thinking about smoking.

He had gone through a very emotional day or two since his visit to the theater and the note he had written afterwards; and it was this emotional restlessness, and nothing else — least of all any great desire to see Father Hilary — that had driven him up to town again, to go to the shooting school and the priest, and, in a spare half-hour which he squeezed in, to walk past the theater where Miss Farham's name was billed. She had not answered his letter as yet; but he quite understood that she might want a day or two to think it over, and was not at present depressed by her silence.

But the fever ever was on him, and running high. Her personality was beginning to be as present to him in all that he experienced, as sunlight is the medium by which a summer garden is seen. Indeed this was different to previous experiences of the kind. He knew that well enough.

So, while the sedate and dignified party sat round the card table, he walked to and fro in the billiard room — up and down the long strip of deep carpet, between the table and the leather-covered seats. The fever was so high that

solitude alone seemed bearable. . . . And yet he did not
know what he wanted, nor what he intended. He was only
aware that in a completely new kind of way a fel-
low-creature whose Christian name was Gladys — (he repeated the name in a whisper again and again) — seemed
necessary to him. . . .

So he walked, and images and thoughts and desires,
and the past, the present and the future, defiled before
his imagination like illusions seen in delirium.

Chapter X

(1)

The ex-policeman-caretaker in Wilton Crescent was not wholly worthy of his office. He took enough care of Percy's note to place it in his pocket, but not enough to remember it for nearly a week. He then found it, displayed it to his wife, who advised its immediate posting; and thenceforward silence. It was only "the young gentleman," she said. All this was carried out; and the ex-policeman prepared an elaborate statement to be produced, if necessary, to the effect that he had certainly placed it in the pillar box when he first opened the door to take in the milk, on the morning on which he had found it lying on the slab in the hall.

Two persons, therefore, were a little astonished, each at the other's silence: Miss Farham was surprised that not a word even of congratulation had reached her from Percy; and Percy was astonished to receive not even an acknowledgment of that which was considerably more than a word of congratulation.

Finally Miss Farham found it awaiting her in her flat late at night, undated, of course, except by the postmark; but such were its contents that she did not suspect any delay. It ran as follows:

"How can I tell you how impressed I have been? You are marvelous. And what you told me the other day makes me miserable. I hate to think that you are in trouble, and in such sordid trouble too. I must risk offending you once more by asking for the last time whether you will not give me the right to help you. When you went out towards the end of the last act I was nearly brokenhearted. Is there no hope for me at all?

"Yours devotedly,

"P. B. S."

She read it through twice. Then she put it aside; and sitting down, still in her cloak and hat, began to open the others. They were precisely what she had expected them to be. Three were demands for the settlement immediately, of bills: the fourth was a receipt for a small account she had managed to pay. Then she took up Percy's note again. She was completely puzzled by it. It had seemed as clear as daylight to poor Percy, when he had written it in his excitement — an excitement generated by three glasses of hock on the top of a considerable emotion; he had wanted just then two things; first, simply to be allowed to help her so far as he could in her pecuniary straits, and, secondly, more of her confidence. It was later that his desires had become more complicated. They had sprung up, in their dim consciousness, after the writing of the letter, like weeds on a warm spring day. But to her it was not so simple. She could not, for the life of her, decide whether the two phrases "the right to help you" and "Is there no hope for me?" did or did not signify something a good deal more considerable.

She read the note through for the fourth and fifth time; and when she at last laid it down her fingers trembled a little; for she could not forget that Percy was wealthy, at least in prospect. And there were other causes too for her emotion.

She went straight to her desk and sat down at it, switching on the little electric standing-lamp.

"Dear Mr. Brandreth-Smith," she wrote,

"I do not understand your note. Will you kindly come and call upon me here any afternoon next week except Saturday; between three and five?

"Yours sincerely,

Gladys Farham

And she directed it to his country address.

(2)

Meantime poor Percy's imagination had seized upon the delay and interpreted her silence into a thousand fantastic forms. He knew nothing whatever of human nature; at one time he imagined that she had cast him off forever; at another that she was giving his suggestions serious consideration; at another that she described the whole story with jeering laughter to her "friend," whoever this might be. The one thing that he never contemplated even as a possibility was that she had not heard from him.

As was perfectly natural, therefore, the idea of proposing marriage to her, which he had just managed to resist at the close of his emotional evening in Wilton Crescent, became insistent, in spite of the disagreeable incident with regard to the Matthieson-Howleys. . . . His state of mind reached a kind of climax after a half-sleepless night on the very morning he received her little note.

He had awakened about six, and found himself unable to sleep again; and had lain there, turning miserably from side to side in the dark, contemplating himself and her, *da capo,* from every possible aspect and point of view. He saw her now defiant, now kindly, now broken and unhappy: she seemed to him now and again even sinister and cruel. It is incredible, sometimes, how men and women will, respectively, misunderstand one another and read an endless elaborateness into situations of extreme simplicity. It was a windy morning outside, and, in the silence of the house, the sudden gusts against his window appeared to him terrible and threatening and suggestive of evil. There was not a detail of his mind which did not seem to be in relations with her. There were moments when she seemed wholly tragic; there were moments in which he remembered her kindliness and humor. He was only a boy still — easily moved and disturbed; he had met one of infinitely stronger personality than himself. She dominated him wholly. . . . It began to appear to him as if his fate stood or fell with hers; existence seemed meaningless without her. Oh! it was not the real thing; it was feverish and untrue; but he did not know that. It seemed to him to have the genuine air of torture; to be so overpowering and masterful as to have extinguished all lesser emotions.

He turned and stared at the little wood and brass crucifix which he could faintly make out in the gloom above his bed: he groaned to it once or twice. Then again he shut his eyes and turned away. His religion seemed pale and colorless beside this passion.

He dozed off a little later, dreaming again of her. He awoke to find the room flooded with light and her note on the tray beside his bed.

(3)

At three o'clock that afternoon he stood by the door of her flat and pressed the bell.

His excitement was enormous.

He had come down to breakfast completely self-restrained and quiet. It had appeared to him that her note had been like a cool hand laid on his hot forehead. It solved nothing and told him nothing, except that she was not irreconcilably angry; and that the relief of that was complete, yet not sobering. Rather it seemed to him to open the door, perhaps for the last time. Yet even now he was not certain that he would do more than look through it. Again there had presented themselves to him all the objections he had already rehearsed. . . . It was enough, until he saw her, that he should see her.

He had been, then, quite quiet at breakfast. And when he had asked for the dogcart to take him to the station, as he had promised to see Father Hilary some time this week and did not like to put it off any longer, his manner had caused no uneasiness. His mother had said that the dogcart was going in anyhow, and had told him not to miss the six o'clock train in the evening. She had manifested only the usual air of faint pity which she always showed now when he mentioned the priest.

The door was opened by a maid who showed him through into an empty drawing room and said she would tell her mistress.

The room was just such a pleasant place as may be seen anywhere in the possession of a nice girl, except that the innumerable signed photographs which plastered one wall seemed excessive. It was white and light and airy; carpeted with dark rugs, furnished in chintz and oak: there were three or four mirrors, a couple of sofas, and a cage of singing birds. Yet to this poor boy it appeared a Paradise of delight. It seemed amazing to him that this should be her room . . . amazing that any mere place could be in such intimate relations with one who was the emotional center of the world's life. A book lay face down and open on one of the sofas; he did not even dare to look at the title. He stood, motionless, with parted lips on the white hearthrug, afraid to move.

Then a door abruptly opened and she came in, a graceful figure. His heart stood still, and then raced.

(4)

She was quite grave, and rather white, and very self-controlled and dignified: her eyes were quite steady and questioning as she gave him her hand. In the other she held a scrap of paper.

"You'll forgive me asking you to come here," she said. "But I really thought we must have a proper talk. I don't understand at all. Sit down, please." (There was even a touch of severity in her tone.)

He sat down in silence.

"Here is your note," she said. "I don't understand in the least what you mean by it. What do you mean by 'a right to help you' and 'having hope'?"

He put out his hand for it. She gave it him and sat back. He read it through.

"Why didn't you answer it sooner?" he asked.

"Sooner! Why I answered it the same evening it came."

"What?"

"It came—let's see—by the last post on Tuesday —"

"Tuesday — why, I wrote it a week ago."

"It came on Tuesday," she repeated.

He drew a long breath of relief, and stared at her.

"Why, I thought you were angry. I . . . I can't tell you —"

She jerked her head in a queer little impatient way she had.

"Oh! Don't let us discuss that," she said. "I asked you to come to explain it. Please tell me exactly what it means."

From the moment she had come into the room the last assault had begun. Her presence was to him so dominating and absorbing that his imaginative memories of her seemed shadowy and colorless after all. It was not her dress that he noticed — an hour later he could not have said anything about it, except vaguely that it was largely blue and had some fine needlework about the throat — yet her dress too, no doubt, contributed to his conquest. It was scarcely even her face, or her great quiet eyes or the

masses of her hair, or her slender capable ringed hands or
her dainty shoes, though his eyes wandered and rested on
these. But it was that curious thing that is called magnet-
ism, that quality which made her an actress of ability —
that atmosphere that is neither solely physical, nor solely
mental, nor solely spiritual, but a combination of at least
two of these things. It was this of which he had caught a
perfume in her very room, which he had breathed in
deeply and strongly from the instant she entered, and
which now saturated and dominated every thought and
hope of his heart.

He looked at her again without speaking. He was
charged with it all as a drunken man with wine — and it
was intensified a hundredfold by his memory of her acting
ten days ago. For very delight of the sensation he waited;
and his inebriated will marshaled his other forces to their
places.

"Well —" she began: and stopped suddenly as she
caught his eyes on hers.

Then he spoke — quite quietly, though his voice trembled a little once or twice.

"Listen," he said. "You know who I am and what my position is. You do not know, probably, that I am completely
dependent on my mother. She could turn me out tomorrow if she wished, or could stop my allowance. My people
are rather old-fashioned, too. They would look upon the
stage as beneath them altogether, especially just now.
They are trying, you know, to make a position for themselves in the county. Well, I must tell you all this first . . .
and . . . and put myself entirely at your mercy. . . ."

He dropped his eyes from her face. She sat as still as a
stone.

"Well; knowing all this, I want to ask you whether you
will marry me . . . as . . . as soon as it becomes possible."

He lifted his eyes again to her face, and saw how still
more white it had become. Her long lashes lay on her
cheek: he had not an idea of what she would say. Even at
this moment, beneath his intoxication and recklessness,
he could hear (so to speak) the loud clamor of prudence
and common sense. But he despised and mocked at the
arguments. He felt a man as never before: for the first

time since he had known her he was conscious of strength
and a real virility: he was a man, now, and she a woman. .
. . He was aware of a kind of triumph, and that this was
independent of her answer.

Then she lifted her eyes to his, and he saw that they
were full of tears.

"Yes," she said, "I will."

(5)

The wheels of the rolling train that carried him homewards sang in his ears a kind of deep full-throated chorus
of joy. The black wet night outside glowed with the splendor which his own imagination cast into it. The warm
lighted compartment in which he sat alone, was but a
kind of phantom symbol of the new life in which he
moved. The whole universe about him was as a whirling
singing globe in the midst of which he rested inviolate and
content. . . .

They had been so sensible and businesslike, these two,
when the first few raptures had passed, and coherence
had returned. She had told him of her life, and had promised to review her money matters once more and see what
was the very least which would do — she hoped that perhaps thirty pounds would set her free for a year. And he,
on the other side, had been very explicit indeed about his
parents, and had even related the incident of the Matthieson-Howleys: and she had listened with divine patience
and become, once more, still more adorably grave. And,
together, they had decided that not a single step of any
sort should be taken for at least six months, that no living
being must be told, and that neither should make any
move at all without the consent of the other. All that was
to be allowed was that he should begin to lay the foundations, if he could, for some kind of independence to be secured to him, and that she, henceforward, should be extraordinarily careful in the matter of expenses.

They had even talked a little on religion — these two! —
For Religion had come down again on Percy like a flood. . .
. It appeared to him exquisite and wonderful that God had
allowed such a joy to come to him. She was to call upon
Father Hilary some time — say at the end of Lent — and
while absolutely keeping secret any intention of hers to

remarry — for fear that details might leak out — was to begin to talk over the possibility of Instruction. It would be yet more exquisite and wonderful if they could be married as Catholics. . . . And she had appeared to consent to all this, and indeed to approve of it. . . .

All the way, then, in the train, and up in the brougham which his mother had sent as it was a wet night, life sang and triumphed in Percy. For the second time in his experience he had found the Secret of Existence; and now he perceived how the two were complementary one to the other, how the Love of the Creator which he had discovered in Catholicism was echoed and verified, so to speak, in the love of the creature. His friar-ideal seemed to him now a poor nerveless kind of thing: he smiled at its memory. . . . Of course he would have to tell Father Hilary — not, indeed, that he intended to be married, outright; but rather that his — well, his new responsibilities seemed to him very important; and . . . and that, well for the present, anyhow, he thought it but right to put away his first enthusiastic ideas. It was astonishing, he told himself, how a convert will get ideas in the first flush which need the correction of experience.

All then was glory with him as he came home, and sprang out of the brougham and into the warm bright hall.

Helen was crossing it as he came in, and stopped when she saw him. (How dull and ordinary she looked, he thought.)

"I say, have you heard about the Mains?" she said. "Are you just back?"

"Heard? No, of course I haven't."

Her face was all aglow with the excitement of giving startling news.

"Come in here," she said; and drew him into the drawing room. "It's too frightful!" she said, with scarcely repressed glee. "Mr. Main's become a Roman Catholic."

"What!"

"Yes: he has. Mr. Bennett's written to Mother. And that's not all. Mrs. Main's written a book: and . . . and it's all about Hanstead."

"But —"

"It's all poking fun at the poor Vicar and . . . and lots of people. Mother's in it, too. I've got it upstairs, locked up. She doesn't know."

He looked at her, and even his exaltation was penetrated by the astonishingness of the news.

"And . . . and old Main's a Catholic."

She nodded, with dancing eyes.

"Well done, old Main!" said Percy. "I didn't think he'd got the pluck. . . . I say, lend me that book, won't you? I won't tell a soul."

End of Part II

Part III

Chapter I

(1)

It was the night of the annual Marston Servants' Ball, held always, according to immemorial custom, on the first Wednesday in January. It was a tremendous affair, and was to begin at ten o'clock and to end with breakfast about seven next morning. There was but one shadow upon the festivities this evening, and that the attack of influenza that had prostrated the master of the house. However, as Mrs. Brandreth-Smith explained with magnificent generosity to Underhill on the morning of the day, that should make no difference; Master Percy would take his father's place; and all should be as usual. (As a matter of fact it admirably suited her ambition of making Percy realize his own importance.)

Preparations began the very instant that dinner was over. The Family retired as usual to the drawing room, together with their guests who had been good enough to consent to come over and dine; and a band of men, gathered in the stone passage on the way to the kitchen, precipitated themselves upon the dining room. It was a point of honor in the house that not the faintest interruption should be caused to the sacred routine of Family Life. Coffee was served as usual by Mr. Underhill and one of the men; the card tables were set out; Helen and Mabel Marridon performed at the piano. . . .

And, at ten o'clock precisely, Mr. Underhill appeared in the door of the drawing room and announced to Madam that all was ready.

(2)

It was with a pleased excitement — (which of course he would not acknowledge to himself) — that Percy, ushering Mr. Bennett immediately in front of him, followed the four ladies across the hall. It really seemed to him that Greatness had descended on his head, as a crown from heaven. At dinner he had sat in his father's place and conversed with Miss Marridon; he had found her a very charming

girl indeed. Among other subjects he had discussed *A
Gentleman of Fortune* — (which Miss Marridon had also
seen at His Highness') — and had mentioned in the most
casual manner in the world that he knew, slightly, Miss
Farham. Did not Miss Marridon think she had acted very
well? . . . Yes; just so . . . He thought so too. Very well indeed. . . .

After dinner his duties had been explained to him.

The ball was to open with *Sir Roger de Coverley*.[1] (He
did not know how to dance it? Very well; The girls and he
must practice it at once. . . . They had done so.) And he,
Percy, was to dance it with Mrs. Gladwin, the housekeeper; and his mother would perform the same condescension towards Mr. Underhill. After that ceremonial, he
was, officially, free until supper at one, when he was to
escort Mrs. Gladwin, on his arm, downstairs to the Servants' Hall, and respond, at the close of that meal, to the
health of the Family. After supper he was at liberty to go
to bed. It was thought that the servants would enjoy
themselves with more *abandon* when the majestic
presences had been removed. Until supper, as has been
said, he was officially free; but it would be taken very
kindly if he would dance with a few of the servants — one
from each department, for instance — the kitchen, the
still room, the house proper, the stables, the laundry, the
farm, the keepers' households; and of course he might
dance with his sister, if he liked, and Mrs. Bennett, and
Miss Marridon Yes . . . all that would be perfectly in order, so long as he did not dance with these exclusively.

(He had booked Miss Marridon at once for a waltz and a
polka; Mrs. Bennett for the lancers;[2] and his sister,
vaguely, for something called a schottische.[3]) The elder
ladies would probably retire about eleven or half-past.

The dining room presented an exceedingly festal appearance as the little procession came in. All the furniture
had been removed, except for a single line of chairs that
ran round the walls; and from these chairs arose, as the

---

[1] A traditional "country dance."
[2] Another "country dance" in the style of the Quadrille.
[3] A partnered country dance, believed to be based on a Bohemian folk dance.

Family entered, a line of menial guests. At the further end, opposite the windows, rose a small platform, and upon this was a company of four musicians — two stringed instruments, a cornet and a piano. From side to side from the tops of the tall portraits hung streamers of green-stuff and ribbons. The door into the billiard room was open, and faces peered in, smiling. The low murmur of voices stopped as Mrs. Brandreth-Smith entered. There must have been at least a couple of hundred persons, all told, from the houses round, from the village, and from Marston itself. It was an inspiriting sight to the young man who was for the time the host, and who, some day would be host in reality. The hostess beckoned to Percy as she majestically took her seat, and he slipped up beside her.

"Do your best, my boy," she whispered. "Remember you're head of the family today. And dance with Mabel too, won't you?"

Sir Roger de Coverley was a great affair. Percy had sufficiently grasped its principles to be fairly at his ease as he led out Mrs. Gladwin — a small severe energetic looking woman of about fifty, with a neat black cap with violet ribbons and a dress that creaked as she moved.

"You must correct me if I make any mistakes," he said smilingly. And an anxious smile had come and gone on her face in answer — as sharp as a gleam of sun on a heavy day.

Once the movement had begun too, the dance itself was inspiriting. A kind of elementary gaiety seized on him, as the music clashed and beat and the figures whirled. Delightful little vignettes too, whose comic element translated itself into pleasure, flashed before him. The vision of his mother, majestic yet gracious, a skirt grasped in one hand, with her other hand enfolded in Mr. Underhill's large white glove, prancing down the middle; Mr. Underhill himself — this time like a slightly drunken Dissenter[4] (if such a thing can be imagined), capering beside her, guiding her with an appearance of being about to hand her over some dangerous ground — entertainment

---

[4] Methodist.

and deference wedded in unspeakable incongruity; the Rector, whose slightly swelling outline was emphasized by his black silk waistcoat and his rather tight trousers, in pumps with his toes turned out, escorting Mrs. Blenkinsop, the coachman's wife, under an arch of arms; Helen, clasped by James who held her as if rescuing her from danger, firmly yet politely; Mabel whirling in the arms of Mr. Blenkinsop himself — Mrs. Bennett, very natural-looking with the faintest wrinkle of alarm between her eyes, dancing with Charles — all these visions, that caught his eye from time to time — brought out on his face, and kept there, a smile that was completely genuine. The music beat and clashed; the whirl went on; and Percy, intensely aware of his high position, began to be carried away, in spite of himself, by the solemn simplicity of the sight and the movements.

(3)

"I'm so hot, I don't know what to do," he said to Mabel an hour later. "And how dreadfully funny, and dreadfully nice it all is. . . . Oh! Did you see Mother when *Sir Roger* stopped suddenly?"

She smiled in that pleasant way she had. He thought he had never got on with anybody quite so quickly as with this girl. . . . She was as easy as a sister — easier than Helen in fact. He had gathered too, from a sentence or so, that she was rather religious too, in a way (though he did not know what way); and even that seemed to commend her to him. This was the end of their second dance; the room had become like an oven, and they had slipped out into the hall by mutual consent, and were sitting here now on an ottoman whence they could watch the brightly lit dancing through the great double doors.

He had got to know her better at lunch, a week ago; but this was the first time he had seen her in evening dress; and she really was charming. (Helen had said he would like her; he remembered.) She was little and fair and fresh, and surprisingly at her ease always; she had a little almost triangular face like a cat, fresh blue eyes with darkish lashes, and very white teeth, throat and arms.

"I think your mother's splendid," she said. "I am so glad you're keeping up the Servants' Ball. I don't know how the neighborhood would get on without it. . . Got your speech all ready?"

Her face creased up into delicious dimples of amusement.

"Oh Lord!" said Percy. "Yes, I suppose so. Let's see. I begin by saying what a pleasure it is to see so many friends — (slight emphasis on 'friends') — about me. That I am quite unaccustomed to public speaking, but that it would be impossible, merely because of the — er — slight indisposition of my father, to let this . . . this occasion go by without a few words of welcome from . . . from — from who? I forget."

"From those —" prompted Mabel.

"Oh, yes — from those who have found, though strangers, such a cordial welcome in the neighborhood. Then there's my mother's pet bit. I don't like that. But I suppose I must say it."

"Go on," said Mabel. "You're doing it beautifully."

"Well," continued Percy. "It is however with great satisfaction — oughtn't I to say 'gratification?' — (that's the Royal word always, you know!)."

"You can't say 'great gratification.' It wouldn't sound right."

"All right — well — with great satisfaction that I remember that although personally we are strangers, our family at least are not. We have been known in this neighborhood — I know all that, Miss Marridon."

"Well, how do you end? The last sentence is the most important, you know. Otherwise you might not ever be able to leave off; and what in the world should we all do then?"

"Oh — all that about the faces I see about me; and that I wish them a good appetite and a goodnight. Then I sit down."

"Storms of applause," said Mabel.

(4)

Percy really was enjoying himself vastly. It appeared to him that he had never before realized exactly how much his change of fortune signified. A few months ago he would not, indeed, actually have danced at a Servants' Ball in the capacity of guest; but he would have been near enough to the position in which he might have done so, to have resented violently the idea. But to dance here now, as host; to feel so confident of his position and of the obviousness of his condescension, as to be able to hold Mrs. Gladwin round her hard cylindrical waist, without the suspicion of any thought except that of his own goodness and friendliness — this seemed to establish him eternally on the high hills. (And it was just what his mother wished, too.)

He liked Miss Marridon, too, very much indeed; and the lofty security of them both under these queer circumstances, made him feel very near to her; he found himself talking with an ease which he had never experienced before in female society. They danced again together once before supper; and he had the pleasure of seeing her only a couple of places off, escorted by James, when he sat down at last at the head of the table. He had half-thought, while they sat out together in the hall, of confiding in her about Gladys Farham; but had concluded, finally, that perhaps she would not understand.

The supper was a vast success.

The great Servants' Hall, stone-floored and steel-pillared, was hung from wall to wall with streamers. Two long tables ran the length of it, piled here and there with crackers. Over the fireplace, amid a bower of greenery, was a Turkey-red shield bearing the inscription (in cotton wool) "Welcome To All." A dozen men took it by turns to wait; and halfway through a very black-haired man (Mr. Given by name — who wound the clocks, as Percy learned from his lady) — sang a comic song to the accompaniment of Charles on the zither.

The speeches were magnificent.

First, Mr. Underhill rose from the head of the second table.

"Mr. Percy, Miss Helen. . . . Ladies and Gentlemen," he began; and then delivered a most excellent little discourse, saying all the right things, and none of the wrong ones. He commented, with regret, on the absence of their generous host, but hastened to add that Mr. Percy, "as they had learned that evening, was in more senses than one, a host in himself." (Silence followed this sally, and

then loud laughter. Mr. Underhill permitted himself a
discreet glance of deprecation towards Mr. Percy, mingled
with respectful humor.) Everyone was brought in; Miss
Marridon's name was received with strong applause, and
she smiled very charmingly in response. The Rector and
his wife — (though not present) — were referred to as the
"yet more recent strangers at the Rectory whom we already regard as our friends." Helen was "the young lady
who has already won all hearts." Around Mrs. Brandreth-Smith's name, alone, was there cast no halo of
words; she was mentioned indeed, with gratitude, but her
personal augustness, apparently, was sufficient glory. He
ended by proposing the health of the Family and the
Guests.

Then Sharpe stood up — the lean body-servant of Mr.
Brandreth-Smith, and a recent addition to the household
— and did his duty in a businesslike and unflowery manner. He proposed Mrs. Gladwin's health, coupled to that of
Mr. Underhill, reminding the company that all the actual
arrangements for their comfort and entertainment — arrangements rendered possible, of course, as Mr. Underhill
had remarked, only by the generosity of Mr. and Mrs.
Brandreth-Smith — had been made by the personal exer-
tions of the two whose health he proposed.

Then a gamekeeper proposed the health of the household generally and responded to the health of the guests.
Mr. Underhill rose again and "in Mrs. Gladwin's name
and my own" begged to thank the guests for their presence and their cordiality; and finally Percy rose to his feet.

It was absolutely the first time in his life that he had
ever addressed an audience. He leaned his hands on the
table; he fixed his eyes, after a moment or two, upon a
flowerpot before him; and repeated his sentences. More
than once the room swam into mist before him, all except
Mabel Marridon's motionless face; and he settled his intention (so to speak) upon her from beginning to end. He
felt, vaguely, that it was very important that she should
carry away a good impression of him — he did not quite
know why. And he acquitted himself quite creditably.
There was loud applause as he ended, and sitting down,
with a slippery hand took up and drank off his glass of

port. Then he glanced up at Mabel and smiled tremulously; and she smiled back at him frankly.

"Well!" she said to him, as he led her out to dance ten minutes later.

"Did I make a fool of myself?" asked Percy.

"You spoke extraordinarily well," she said.

He lay long awake that night, or rather in the early morning, and his whole being throbbed and beat with romance.

He had danced vigorously until nearly two o'clock (Mabel went to bed half an hour earlier) — and although he affected to be amused, particularly when she was there, at the social graces and solemnities of the dancers, he enjoyed himself quite enormously and quite seriously. The dances were what are called old-fashioned; and in waltz after waltz he whirled round housemaid after housemaid; in the lancers more than once he faced Mr. Underhill and Mrs. Gladwin; and in Highland dances he whooped with the loudest of them. A kind of permanent grin became fixed on his face, relaxed only when he rushed off to get cool and refresh himself with claret-cup and a cigarette.

The fever of dancing and music, then, got into his blood; and, as he lay in bed between the curiously cool sheets, his head ringing with music and rhythm and voices, Romance — of the kind that is produced by such means — held high dominion over him.

It was a complicated sort of romance. Gladys, of course, was the personality on which everything centered; again and again during the night he had half-closed his eyes in order to imagine that it was with her that he was dancing; he had pictured her coming in through the great double doors, herself the mistress of the house; he had rehearsed little speeches that might be made to her, and the answers she would give; yet, as he lay now, with every pulse beating — hearing even from his dignified and remote room, gusts of music from beneath rise and fall again into silence as doors opened and shut — it was under the aspect of Mabel that she presented herself — Mabel's face and hands, the little clear voice speaking in his ear, as it had spoken when they had waltzed together — and yet underneath Mabel he perceived Gladys.

Once or twice before he slept, he wondered whether it was not a little too complicated to be perfectly loyal. . . . Then he dozed off, and the phantom whirling began again.

In spite of the heaviness that lay on his eyes almost like a physical external pressure, he jumped straight out of bed and ran to the window, so soon as he heard the sound of wheels and understood what it meant. Romance gilded the thought even of servants driving away in the chilly dawning, back again to duty.

The back door was just within range of his window, where the brakes were drawn up; and in spite of the cold he watched with absorbed interest the cloaked and hooded figures climb up into the carriages. Underhill was there, presiding, resembling a very dissipated host. Percy could see his crumpled shirt-front, and made out, with immense delight, a large pink paper cap, obviously from a cracker, which crowned that austere and venerable head. Once, as the second brake drove off, the butler gravely executed a few Highland steps on the cobbled stones, flinging up a large hand in the proper manner, in farewell to the waving jolting figures in the brake.

When the last brake was gone, Percy looked out an instant at the park, so solemn and pure in the gradually broadening light. The heads of great trees were on a level with his window, and beyond them again the grayish green slopes of the winter landscape. Slow, pale mists were rising and dispersing from the direction of the river, drifting like phantoms behind the copses. And, somehow, this vision so apart from the hot excitement of the night, this grave and splendid world turning slowly to meet the red winter sun — this frost-bound silence and magnificence, worked on him like a suggestive background to the vivid thoughts with which his weary head so whirled — thoughts of Gladys, and Mabel, and his own wealth and power — as he thought them — even his religion; he pictured a lonely priest, so great was his romance, passing across that park to a little church aglow with candles and a divine presence. . . .

Oh! But he was to meet Mabel at breakfast. He drew the curtains together again, leaving the shutters open, and went back to bed to think about it.

He awoke again, an hour later, to find the morning fully come, and James, inexpressibly correct and self-contained — such a vivid contrast to the capering white-gloved James of last night — placing his clothes on the chair.

"Hope you had a good time last night," said Percy genially.

"Yes, sir; thank you, sir."

James was a little pale under the eyes. Percy reflected he would be paler yet before night.

"Aren't you awfully tired?"

"No, sir, thank you, sir. That is, not particularly, sir."

Oh! The world was very good, thought Percy. . . . He would meet Mabel at breakfast.

Chapter II

A h!" said Father Hilary as he came into the parlor, holding out his hand. "How are you, Mr. Main?"

It was the evening of the Servants' Ball at Marston; but of course neither of them knew anything about that. It was a fortnight since Percy had been to the Friary; and he happened not to have mentioned it.

Mr. Main looked more dreary than ever, now that he was no longer in clerical clothes; he bore a faint resemblance now to a very respectable manservant who had fallen on bad times. He was in a dark gray readymade suit, with a stick-up collar and a black made-up tie that hid all trace of a shirt below; his boots creaked a little as he stood up, and had a curious crease across the toe, as if they were an inch or two too long. He smiled bleakly as he took the friar's hand; and the smile disappeared again instantly. But he did not look wholly unhappy.

"How have things gone with you?" said Father Hilary, sitting down and spreading his hands over the fire.

"Well, Father; I went to all those addresses you gave me. And I'm sorry to say they hadn't anything for me."

"Let me see — you've been in the Church a month now?"

"Yes, Father. I'm very anxious, you know —"

The friar nodded.

"I quite understand," he said.

Mr. Main rubbed his long hands together between his knees.

"There are one or two things I didn't explain before," he said. "May I —"

The friar nodded again.

"Why certainly," he said. "Tell me everything."

Mr. Main put his lips together once or twice before speaking. Then he began.

"Well, Father; I told you I had saved a little money. That was true. But it's very little. Not more than thirty or forty pounds when all my bills were paid. I found that there were one or two that my wife — that I hadn't settled when I left Hanstead. They're settled now. . . .

"Then I didn't tell you that my wife had written a book —"
The friar looked up sharply.

"A book? Why —"

"Yes, Father. It's a very clever book too, I'm told. I've
not read it —"

"Not read it?"

Mr. Main seemed to have a difficulty in speaking.

"It . . . it was accepted at once; and my wife was paid
pretty well for it. But it . . . it was a book I could not approve of, Father. It . . . it was a very unpleasant description of some of our friends."

Father Hilary glanced at him.

"Yes, Father; there is no question about it. I . . . I read
enough. My wife brought it out in the face of my express
wishes."

He paused.

"Yes?"

"Well, Father, that's one of my difficulties. I've ruined
my wife, she tells me, by . . . by becoming a Catholic. She
has no sympathy with my views." (His face twitched grotesquely once or twice.) "And . . . and yet it seems I shall
have to live on her writings, and . . . and on the little
money she has."

Father Hilary drew a breath, and remained motionless,
staring at the fire.

Father Hilary was still quite a young man, but he had
that extraordinary quickness of intuition that so often
comes to those who have sifted themselves to the very
bottom of their souls. If a man has no reserves towards
himself, he frequently finds that others have no secrets
towards him.

This man had come to him a couple of months before;
and in a very short time he had learned to what type he
belonged — to the clumsy, slow, sensitive, obstinate type,
whose sense of duty is their sole motive. Little by little,
too, he had learned some of the circumstances in which
this man was placed, the really extraordinary difficulties
he would have to face, and the astonishing heroism with
which he would face them. . . . And now he suddenly perceived that the difficulties were ten times greater than he
had dreamed, and that this dull man had borne them in

silence, and would have continued so to bear them, had he not been forced to tell them at last. . . . The priest's face grew even more tender; and for a full minute he did not speak.

"Tell me," he said at last. "I gave you four addresses to apply to. Two were scholastic agencies."

"Yes, Father. They told me I was too old for their vacancies; and I had no athletics. And the lady you sent me to said that she would remember my name, but that the demand for secretaryships was very great. And Mr. Barlow, the businessman, told me that he was very sorry, but that he had no vacancy in his office. . . . You see my difficulty, Father, don't you? I have been trying to look at it from my wife's point of view; and, of course, in one way I understand it. It's quite true that when we were married, I thought that, as a clergyman, I was justified in doing so; and that I should always be able to provide my wife at least with a home. And now you see, Father — Well; it's the other way."

He spoke quite quietly and unresentfully. Father Hilary had seen only this afternoon a horse fall in Church Street, under a heavy load, and lie there, with patient, uncomplaining eyes. He remembered this, now.

And yet he dared not pour out his sympathy; for he knew perfectly that it would not be understood.

This kind of man simply was not looking for sympathy; he took his burden as an obvious and inevitable thing; he must just struggle with it; and if he fell he did not expect to be sympathized with, but, if possible, to be lifted to his feet once more and be allowed to go on pulling. If not, he must just lie there.

"I understand perfectly," said the friar as unemotionally as the other, striving to say the plain thing as he knew the other would wish. "I see that it must be very painful and difficult for you to be supported by your wife. . . . You say that she has no sympathy at all with Catholicism?"

"No, Father. I tried to explain to her once or twice, but she would not hear me. So I followed your advice and said no more. I left one or two books about too; but she put them away at once."

"How have your old friends treated you?"

The bleak eyes blinked once or twice.

"They have not been very kind, Father. It . . . it was said that I had taken to drink."

The friar smiled.

"They haven't said you have had a fall off a bicycle, then?"

"Why, no; Father. I don't ride a bicycle."

"That's all right then. The last clergyman convert I had was supposed to have injured his brain by a fall. Unfortunately, it was quite true that he had had one. You see, they must say something, mustn't they?"

A glimmer of a pained smile went over Mr. Main's face and passed again.

"Are you still in your old lodgings?" asked the priest.

"No, Father; the rent was too high. We live in two rooms now, in Chelsea. I will leave you my address before I go. My wife is hard at work on another book, too; she tells me."

Again the whole vision broadened and deepened before the priest's mind. He saw the miserable household of two — the snarling, reproachful, clever wife, that would not listen; the desperate shifts they were put to; the dull honest heroic man who had followed his conscience exactly at the most inconvenient moment conceivable. And he perceived too that there was very little hope that the circumstances could ever be otherwise. Who in the world would take a personal interest in a man like this? And himself — what could he do for him? He sighed.

"Mr. Main," he said, "I simply don't know what to suggest. But I want to say this . . ."

He hesitated.

"Yes, Father?" said the patient voice.

An uncontrollable emotion of pity seized the friar's heart, at the sound of the voice, and at the sight of the long solemn face that looked at him.

"Mr. Main," he said, "Christ is laying His Cross on you — It is a great honor —"

There was a pause. He could not go on.

"Thank you, Father," said the patient voice. "I will try to remember what you say. I have tried to think it was that."

(2)

It seemed to Mr. Main, as he walked southwards towards Chelsea, that he was being on the whole very prompt and businesslike. He had done all the things recommended to him, and regarded them as so many steps towards success.

A man cannot be refused forever. . . . Well; he had got through half a dozen of the failures; that was half-dozen steps towards victory.

Meanwhile his present life had to be borne; and it was not very easy. It seemed to him singularly painful that he should have to live on the proceeds of a book of which he entirely disapproved; and yet it seemed that this would be inevitable within a very few weeks. He had opened the book once, covertly, when his wife had been out; and had closed it again more horrified than ever, yet more at his own sense of guilt than at anything he had seen.

His rooms were in a little lane off Beaufort Street; and on his way he turned in to the little bare French chapel for a few minutes. A dozen candles in white painted stocks rose above the poor altar; and beside two shrouded kneeling figures beyond the screen rose two more. In the midst of the candlesticks above glimmered a white disc in a gold frame. . . .

When he came out again, he had an idea; and the prospect quickened his steps a little. He had not yet heard from the boy who had once consulted him on spiritual matters — the boy whose own convictions had perhaps hastened him in his own resolve. Mr. Main had suffered from what some people call "Roman fever" for a considerable time before Percy had been to see him; he had been tormented, that is to say, with the doubt as to whether the Roman Church were not the one and only Church; and Percy's visit to him in order to speak on this very point had been one, at least, of the goads that had driven him to action. He remembered often in these days the circumstances under which that doubt had first come to him — years ago, soon after his ordination to the ministry. It was a tiny incident, wholly insignificant in itself — simply his suddenly calling upon a new family in his district and finding the priest there. It was nothing that had been said; the priest had been courteous and begged him to sit down; and he had done so, in confusion. And then, in the five or ten minutes that followed he had been amazed by the relations that appeared to prevail between this curious clergyman — (the first priest he had ever spoken with) — and those radiant ramshackle Irish. There was not the faintest touch of that air of constraint which he himself regarded as inevitable between a minister and his people; and yet there was a reverence, coupled with this extraordinary familiarity, of which he had known nothing in his own experience. That had been absolutely all; yet it had startled him. He had wondered what the secret was.

Well; all that was long passed now. Meantime here were other problems to be solved. Why then, he asked himself, should he not write to Percy, announce his own conversion, and at the end — perhaps in a postscript — inquire whether there were any prospect for him of work in the cocoa business. It could do no harm; it might conceivably lead to something — more especially as the thought had come to him just now during his prayers. . . .

He determined to try.

A smell of oil greeted him as he pushed open the door of the sitting room; and he saw his wife's back at the little writing table between the fireplace and the window; an ill-trimmed lamp stood on the corner of the mantelpiece. She was writing.

"Well, my dear?" he said as he closed the door.

She turned round, her face vacant with thought; a pen was poised in her fingers. Her brows closed down disagreeably. She jerked her head towards the table.

"I've had supper," she said. "You're late."

Then she turned back to her writing.

He took off his coat and hung it on the door-peg with his hat, and propped his umbrella in the corner; it slid down at once and crashed to the floor. The woman turned with a swift hiss of displeasure.

"I wish you could be more quiet," she said.

"I'm sorry, my dear. Are you writing?"

"Looks like it," she said.

"May . . . may I know what it is?" he said tactlessly, with the best intentions. (He had not even now learned that silence is the best treatment for overstrained nerves.)

"I'm afraid you wouldn't approve," she said icily, still with her back to him. "I've begun my new book at last."

He said nothing. Her mood was apparent even to him. He made a careful sign of the cross, glad that she was not looking at him, and sat down to the cold meat and cheese that was laid with a few plates and a tumbler at the central table. The position of the lamp was excessively inconvenient; but he dared not remonstrate.

It was a typically dismal room of the lodging-house type. There were disused gas-chandeliers, trimmed with pink paper, on either side of the spotted gilt framed looking-glass that crowned the mantel shelf. The mantel shelf itself wore a kind of short petticoat of dark magenta pinked at the edges and embroidered with a yellow wreath There were three or four oil-pictures on the walls, representing snow-mount-ains at sunset, and waterfalls. Tall rep curtains, depending from a gilt tin cornice, shrouded the windows; and the opposite wall was chiefly occupied by immense folding doors of deal painted to represent walnut; these divided the room from the bedroom at the back. There was a set of horsehair furniture, with antimacassars pinned on the backs of the two armchairs.

He had finished supper, and still sat brooding over his plan of writing to Percy, before she moved or spoke again. Then she pushed back her chair suddenly and came and stood by the fire. He turned and was astonished to see a kind of friendliness in her dark eyes; but her face looked white and pinched.

"Well, old boy," she said; "had a good supper?"

His own face lifted a little with pleasure.

"Excellent, thanks. All I wanted, anyhow. . . . How's the book?"

Her eyes contracted and then lightened again.

"It's going," she said. "Pull your chair up to the fire, and talk to me."

These sudden moods came on her sometimes; and they were as welcome to him as sunshine. Each time he hoped that it was to be permanent; each time she relapsed again sooner or later into her nervous bitterness. But he continued to hope.

He wheeled his chair round now, and put his feet on the fender. She continued to stand over him, leaning on the mantelpiece.

"Well, my dear," he said, "I've been to Father Hilary again. He'll write to me later, I think. But he hasn't any more suggestions just now."

She moved suddenly to the armchair that was on the further side of the fire.

"Tell me about Father Hilary," she said. "All about him — what he looks like; what time he gets up in the morning, what he has for breakfast, what he does all day. All about him."

She nestled down into the slippery lap of the chair, and stared at him.

A great flush of pleasure swept over him. It was the first time she had ever invited information of the kind; and in a minute or two later he was in full career. He described all that he had seen of the friar, the parlor, the monastery, the church; he attempted to sketch the Religious Life to her so far as he understood it.

"Tell me some more," she said, and he saw her black eyes gleam in the firelight.

"My dear, I know no more."

"Well, tell me some more about your Church. Did you go anywhere else after seeing him?"

He hesitated.

"Well, I went into the French chapel just now —"

"Ah! Tell me about that. Could I go there too?"

"Certainly, my dear. The doors are open all day. They have —" he hesitated — "they have Perpetual Exposition there, you know."

"Perpetual what?"

He repeated it. And then he tried to tell something of what it signified. . . . He was overcome with pleasure. It seemed to him an astonishing answer to his prayers that she should so question him. She listened in silence — intent and attentive. . . .

"That's all?" she said.

"That's all I could say in a few minutes, my darling; but —"

Then she jumped up; and the terrible elfish light which he knew so well — indescribably terrible and pathetic in this faded thin woman — shone in her eyes. She clapped her hands slightly.

"That's just what I wanted," she said. "Just what I wanted."

"My dear, why do you want —"

"Why, for my book, of course," she said. "It's going to be about all that kind of thing."

Chapter III

(1)

It was on the last day of January that Percy had his first experience of a public shoot. He had found himself tolerably proficient at the shooting-school, and had killed quite thirty rabbits at Marston as well as half a dozen pheasants (out of a large number) that had been carefully driven over him one by one by the keeper. He accepted then with sufficient confidence a verbal invitation given him through Mabel to go over to Cleever and have a last day in the coverts.

"My brother's coming down," she said. "You haven't met him, I think? And there'll be one or two others. But it won't be anything much, you know."

"All the better for me," said Percy.

"I expect you're all right," she said, with a dancing humor in her eyes that Percy found pleasant.

He presented an extraordinarily correct appearance — in fact a little too correct — as he climbed out of the dog-cart at the entrance to Cleever gates at half-past ten on the following Monday. His cartridge-bag was a little new, perhaps — but then even experienced sportsmen must get new cartridge-bags occasionally. And his gun twinkled in the sunshine with the subdued glow of really good varnish. He was in a brown shooting-suit, with the proper pleats at the shoulder blades, and neat leather patches on the shoulders; these showed distinct marks of use. He had neat leather cylinders to cover the tops of his boots; his stockings presented a good rich pattern where they were turned down over the button box-cloth that ended his knickerbockers; his cap had a kind of circular flap that could be let down in case of rain. He wore a glove on his left hand, and carried a fawn-colored ample shooting-cloak over his left arm.

A group of beaters, with a keeper in velveteen and a couple of retrievers, solemnly saluted him; and he as solemnly returned it.

"Er — at about half-past four," he said to Roger the groom. Roger also saluted him in silence, and waited to see if more were required of him.

"Mr. Marridon coming?" asked Percy.

The keeper saluted again.

"Just coming down the road, sir."

Two figures, in fact, with two more behind, were advancing down the straight drive that united the big iron-work gates, where Percy stood, with the austere flat face of Cleever Court set among the trees.

Percy opened his gun and peered down it; patted his cartridge-bag; took two or three steps to and fro; and did all those things that a young man does when he is a little ill at ease and wishes not to appear so. He had been rehearsing in silence, all the way from Marston, a few broad irrefragable principles learned from a little book bound in red; and. he now repeated these mentally to himself.

Never under any circumstances whatever point your gun at a human being.

Never under any circumstances whatever fire down the line; or into thick cover unless you are perfectly certain that no one is there.

Never follow a bird round with your gun.

Put your gun at least at half-cock on crossing any obstacle; and take out the cartridges if you are obliged to use your hands, or to jump.

And so forth. . . . He perceived that it was exceedingly important that he should make a reputable first appearance in public.

(2)

Percy managed rather well the moment at which it was necessary to turn to greet the others.

"Mr. Brandreth-Smith?" said the latter of the two sportsmen.

Percy agreed that this was so — perceiving that the two who followed were valets, each carrying a gun. (He wished he had brought James.)

"I'm Marridon," said the other; and murmured a vague introduction of the second man of which Percy caught only the word "Colonel."

As they turned together over the grass that led to the first coverts that they were to shoot, Percy was rapidly accumulating impressions.

Marridon was a bigly made man with a tanned red face, a small clipped moustache, and red hairy hands that wanted clipping; he spoke brusquely and shortly, and did not seem at any great pains to put strangers at their ease. The Colonel was an incredibly thin personage, with a large white flying moustache like a double saber, and cross-looking eyes; he walked with a little fling as if he was being insolent to somebody. Percy felt his heart sink a little; he thought he was not making quite the man-of-the- world impression that he had intended.

"There'll be nothing much to shoot, Colonel, you know," said Marridon. "I've warned you."

The Colonel grunted.

"You're no end of a sportsman, I hear," went on the other, suddenly looking at Percy as if he were insulting him.

Percy made a deprecatory noise.

"I've only just begun," he said. "But I'm very keen."

"Don't be too keen," said the Colonel abruptly. "Dangerous, that! Eh, Jim?"

The two laughed shortly; and Percy was in a tempest of confused resentment.

He felt very lonely and helpless ten minutes later. He was placed in a ride in the woods with tall trees before and behind; and no one at all was in sight. But he had been given to understand that his host was round the curve thirty yards to the right, and the Colonel the same distance, just beyond the corner to the left. A thousand thoughts tormented him; he perceived a hundred things that should have been otherwise; he had no shooting seat of aluminum, no manservant; he ought to have understood that when the squat beater with a beard had approached him (without saluting, this time) it was to take his cartridge-bag, and that this was usual; and he had said that he preferred to carry it himself. He shouldn't have said that about keenness; he ought to have grunted, like the others.

Again, he hadn't the slightest idea how the pheasants would come over in those trees; at home he had always stood before in a nice clear space outside a coppice where it was possible to see all round him; here it would be a kind of miracle if he caught more than a glimpse of any living creature. He did not know whether he might turn and shoot behind him; whether he might fire into the covert in front, if, by good fortune, he saw a rabbit; nor if he might fire down the ride. He felt entirely helpless; and he knew he dared not ask. Besides, it was too late; he had been given injunctions not to move.

All was as silent about him as woods can be on a bright day in January. There was no wind; the leafless twigs formed about him a filigree of incredible intricacy. A bird hopped in the covert and gave forth a single tweet; and the boy's heart leaped into his mouth. He wished it was lunchtime; he wished he was home again; he wished violently that he hadn't been such an ass as to come out on the last day when his reputation might be ruined with no hope of recuperation. . . . He wondered why Mabel hadn't come out, when she had expressly said —

Bang!

And then *Bang! Bang!*

He gripped his gun and stood trembling.

(3)

He carried a single rabbit by its shattered hind legs when he joined the others twenty minutes later.

It had been a terrible time; and he set his will like a flint to drive through his story. The first four pheasants had passed him without his venturing to fire at all, so grimly were the principles he had culled from the little red book embedded in his mind. Of the first, indeed, he had not been aware at all, except as of a tumultuous chuckling firework that had burst out overhead, traveling, it seemed, at about a thousand miles an hour. The other three, though he had seen them coherently for however short a space of time, had appeared to him either too much to the left or too much to the right to justify a shot.

The fifth he had fired at; and had had the satisfaction of seeing a little handful of twigs leap into the air a good two yards behind her tail. Then he had fired twice at rabbits as, after a dart across the ride, they vanished in the undergrowth behind him; then at two more pheasants; and then, at last, his chance came.

A rabbit suddenly appeared from nowhere, and sat up, with his ears cocked, plainly visible between two larch stems, straight in front. Percy had cast agonized glances to right and left; his ears told him that the beaters were still far away; then he had lifted his gun slowly and taken aim; the rabbit dropped on all fours and crouched. Percy fired; the rabbit skipped sideways and lay still.

As he came up after the drive he saw seven pheasants, a smaller brown bird with a long bill, of which he dared not ask the name, and two rabbits. This was Marridon's contribution alone. The Colonel, who had passed him as he was getting his rabbit, flung down a couple of pheasants, and his man servant, who followed immediately, no less than five rabbits.

"Awfully sorry," said Percy. "I . . . I couldn't see very well. But I think I must have wounded three or four."

"Eh?"

"I think I must have wounded several. I . . ."

"Where did they come down? Did you mark them?"

"Oh! I don't think it's worth while —" began Percy; but Marridon turned away abruptly.

"What next, Kimber?" he said sharply to the keeper. And Percy perceived that his lies were seen through. He also remembered, too late, that it was not considered correct to wound birds, and still less to brag of it.

(4)

"I shot vilely," he said to Mabel after lunch, so soon as the two were walking together to the next covert.

They had lunched in an old timbered barn. Mabel, and a very thin girl who wore spats, and whose name, of course, he could not catch, had met them there; and they had all eaten hot mutton-pies out of a tin cylinder, potatoes in their jackets, cold tart and cheese. Jim Marridon and the Colonel had drunk a quantity of whisky, and had become almost genial by the time they had finished. Percy too had drunk a couple of glasses of sherry and felt much better.

Mabel looked simply charming in her fur toque and boa. From these her face peeped out, delicately pink, with her

eyes brighter and lighter than ever; and, below her short
tweed skirt, her neat gaitered feet.

"I expect you were first-rate," she said encouragingly.

Percy shook his head mournfully.

"But your brother was awfully good to me at lunch," he
said, "in spite of it."

(Mr. Marridon had, in fact, warmed by whisky, remarked with genial irony that Percy would make a good
sportsman yet; and even this had cheered the poor boy.)

"Well, I shall see for myself," said Mabel.

Conversation, in the intervals of shooting, is capable of
becoming strangely intimate. There is no time for frills
and periphrases. Things must be said quickly, or not at
all. Further, there is a kind of primitiveness, a sense of
companionship in the wild that favors intimacy. And,
lastly, the sexes are in their original relations to one another; the man is performing, and the woman is admiring;
the brave is hunting, and the squaw, so to speak, waiting
as if to cook.

When Mabel, then, suddenly remarked that Colonel
Maitland was supposed to be a Catholic, Percy made a
half-confidence.

"Really," he said. "I'm interested in that myself, you
know."

"What! You aren't one!"

Percy hesitated. He wondered that Helen hadn't said
anything about his plans.

"No," he said; "but I'm interested."

A gleam of sudden vindictiveness shone in the girl's
eyes.

"I can't bear them," she said. "It . . . it isn't English. All
their priests, and all that, you know. (Look out! They're
coming)."

While Percy addressed himself to his gun and fired two
shots without result, he had had time to think.

"That's the sort of thing I've been doing all the morning," he said savagely.

"You shot behind those," said Mabel judicially.

Percy reloaded.

"Why is it un-English?" he said.

"What? . . . Oh — Catholics. Well, you know, their foreign pope and all that! Why should an Italian be over my soul?"

"Our Lord was a Jew," said Percy, with an effort.

"That's different," said Mabel.

Again a loud crowing from the shadows in front brought Percy up tense. He registered a violent resolution to fire three yards in front of the approaching bird. . . . There was a loud bang; and a large cock-pheasant fell with a delicious thump ten yards behind him.

"There!" said Mabel, "I told you so."

When Percy had sufficiently recovered from his gleeful astonishment, he returned to the charge. He felt, somehow, that it was exceedingly important that he should know exactly what Mabel thought, and . . . and put her right, of course.

"I don't feel that a bit," he said. "Now, Colonel Maitland —"

"Oh! He doesn't count," said the girl. "He never dreams of going to church or to confession or to anything like that. His wife's an Anglican, and so are his children."

"But I can't see why you object —"

"I don't mean it's exactly wrong," said Mabel, "though my father would have a fit if he heard me say so. We're all very low church, you know. But . . . but it's so second-rate. If Colonel Maitland was a proper Catholic, I don't suppose we should have him here, you know. . . . It's second-rate; that's all I mean. Like . . . like marrying an actress."

Percy caught his breath.

(5)

Percy was very silent indeed as he drove home in the dusk.

It was not that Mabel had introduced an entirely new set of ideas to his mind; rather it was that she had put into words, with a startling appropriateness, exactly those ideas which, almost formlessly, had been materializing round him ever since he had come into his kingdom. The appropriateness had been more than startling; she had linked together as subject and illustration precisely the two very acts which Percy was contemplating.

And the worst of it was that he saw precisely what she meant. To marry an actress, to become a Catholic — these were "not wrong"; but they were "second-rate." They were out of harmony with that smooth, well-oiled, august system of English country house life into which he was beginning to be initiated. A man of assured position might do either, without hopelessly insulating himself, — just as eccentricities are permitted to geniuses; but a man whose position was yet to be assured was in another case. He reflected on the Matthieson-Howleys. These were not considered entirely respectable — not respectable enough, that is, to be called upon from Marston, even though they might be consorted with in the tangle of London. Yet old Lord Barchison who lived on the other side of the county was welcomed everywhere, exactly as if it were not known at all that Lady Barchison was in a lunatic asylum, and that another lady had, for all practical purposes, taken her place in the smaller of his two houses.

He was very silent then, as he drove home with two brace of pheasants under the seat. . . . It was only a few weeks since he had engaged himself to Gladys Farham. . . . Besides, what does it matter what people think?

Chapter IV

Helen was coming back from a helpful afternoon at the Rectory — helpful, that is, in that she had been reading aloud, under her mother's orders, to a Mothers' Meeting, in the absence of Mrs. Bennett, indisposed.

She had disliked it quite intensely; yet it was one of those duties, it appeared, which she must expect to fall to her lot from time to time.

"You must remember, my dear," her mother had said, "that you are in a completely different position from that in which you were at Hanstead. We all have new responsibilities now; and you must just learn to shoulder yours."

"But I don't like Mothers' Meetings," said Helen rebelliously. "At least, I'm sure I shan't. I mean, I don't think they're any good."

Mrs. Brandreth-Smith smiled on one side of her mouth.

"My dear, you must allow me to be the judge of that. You have your duties and responsibilities now like the rest of us. And one of those duties is to do what you can to be friendly and pleasant to your poorer neighbors and the tenants, and so on."

"Oh! I thought they were meant to be religious — Mothers' Meetings, I mean."

"And one of the duties of religion is to be kind to our neighbors. . . . At three o'clock then, Mrs. Bennett's note said."

But she had her reward; for, as she came up the steps into the hall at dusk, Mabel ran out to meet her.

"I thought you'd never be back," she said.

"Oh! How nice of you to come!" cried Helen.

"They told me where you were. I thought I must wait. The brougham's going to call for me at half- past six, on its way back from the station."

In spite of all Mabel's visits, and the friendship vowed between the two, Helen was still entirely aware that she was never wholly at her ease in the girl's company. More, she was also aware as to the cause of this; for she was quite sharp enough to see that Mabel's attitude to life was one thing, and her own another; Mabel had grown up in a kind of wordless creed as to behavior and judgments on things and views generally; while she herself had them all yet to learn. She was learning very quickly, but she was not yet quite sure of herself. For instance, she did not burst out in abhorrence of Mothers' Meetings as she would have done to any of her own friends at Hanstead; she thought she'd better find out first what the other thought of them.

"How did you get on?" asked Mabel, as they came up the stairs into Helen's own room.

"Not very well," said Helen. "I . . . I've never been to a Mothers' Meeting before. They . . . they looked at me such a lot; and it was rather stuffy; and I didn't like the book."

Mabel laughed deliciously as she nestled back into the sofa.

"I know the sort," she said. "Poor dear!"

Helen was encouraged.

"It really was awful, you know; all about clergymen and earnest young men and Sunday evening, and about some-body's 'temptation' to marry a wild young gamekeeper. . . . Mabel!"

"Yes?"

"Do you really think that's the way to look at things?"

"How do you mean?"

"I mean all that sort of thing about good and bad and clergymen, and what happens if you aren't confirmed. It . . . it seems stuffy to me somehow."

Helen's voice had broken out into a sort of tentative pathos. Her Bohemianism, such as it was, had found itself terribly compressed by her new surroundings. Even amid the splendors of Marston there recurred from time to time visions of her little white and brown house among its orchards, its copper fire-hoods and its shelves of plaster casts. But at the same time she was not sure how far Mabel would sympathize.

To her dismay Mabel looked at her uncomprehendingly.

"I don't understand a bit," she said.

Helen took up a small smoke-colored kitten who had just disclosed himself by unrolling in the shadowy corner of the small sofa on which the girl sat.

"Oh! Don't you," she said. ("Yes, darling; how very lucky I didn't sit on you!) I mean . . . I mean . . . oh! I don't know what I mean."

A small and solemn expression was on Mabel's features when she glanced at her again; and then, for the very first time Helen began to perceive that there was at least one corner of the other's mind into which humor and lightness had not yet penetrated.

"But you don't mean you don't believe — oh! You know."

The words were vague enough; but Helen entirely understood and perceived on what a precipitous edge she had been standing. It was a complete surprise to her to find Mabel like this; she had very nearly — but fortunately not quite — taken it for granted that this delightful girl was delightful all through — (delightful, that is, in the sense in which she understood the word) — and now she understood that, as has been said, there was a solemn corner which was sacred. She made haste to prevaricate.

"Oh! My dear! Of course I do. But . . . but I only meant the way it was put. That was really all. I mean, I think one can be good, without talking exactly in the way in which the people in that book talked. That was absolutely all."

There is no gravity in the world like the gravity of the adolescent; for the adolescent, whether boy or girl, has not yet succeeded in unifying things. To young persons like these two who had discoursed on Life and Being in the pleasant little fire-lit sitting room, till the gong sounded for tea, emotions and philosophies and articles of belief are complete sets of things, like bricks in a builder's yard; each is whole and entire in itself; they have not yet been merged into a common building.

Mabel, therefore, who in other matters was human and light and easy, in such Matters as these was solemn, and even — (if the truth must be told) — a little priggish. She discoursed of the articles of faith, gravely and reverently, in complete little sentences, with a peculiar tone in her voice; and Helen listened and made resolutions not only to be very careful in future, but to conform her views so far as she could to those of her friend. It seemed to be good form to think like this; therefore she would think like it.

(2)

Percy was distinctly sociable at tea; he seemed to brighten up wonderfully and to display qualities and graces which were not always so evident. He rang the bell for more hot water at the first hint from his mother; he sat on a low chair and uttered the kind of polite banter about toast and little cakes covered with sugar that is usual on such occasions.

"I say, Helen."

"Yes?"

"How did you get on with the Mothers' Meeting?"

"It was all right," said Helen gravely.

"What was the book you had to read?"

"I . . . I think it was called 'Emma's Temptation'."

"Oh! Good Lord!" said Percy. "And —"

"That's enough, my boy," said Mrs. Brandreth-Smith with dignity.

"But I say, Mother," protested Percy (who did not propose to be treated quite like that before Mabel), "you said yourself you didn't care much for that kind of book."

"I meant," explained his mother with dignity, "that it would probably not be the kind of book I should choose for my own reading. But I have no doubt it was excellent for the Mothers' Meeting."

Percy presently asked what Helen was going to do after tea.

"Mabel and I have got to talk," she said. And a gloom fell upon the boy, that was quite unmistakable.

And indeed they talked. They carefully did not light the candles upstairs; Helen poked the fire into a blaze and sat down on the hearthrug, clasping her knees; Mabel sat again on the sofa and nursed the kitten.

Once more then they discussed on high matters — of Life and Being and Friendship and Religion; and Helen glowed with an intoxicating mixture of sentimentality and pride so subtly mingled that she did not know whether she loved a peer's daughter for being so intimate, or whether she loved her friend for being a peer's daughter.

Mabel really was attractive; she had the daintiness and
humor of a little cat such as that which she nursed and
stroked under the ears; indeed she faintly resembled the
cat even facially; and the gravity and reverence which she
displayed on certain subjects added a distinct charm, now
that Helen had determined to like it. But through all
Helen's appreciation of her friend there ran a strong
thread of what must be called snobbishness; Mabel was,
by every law of breeding, immeasurably her superior, and
yet condescended to sit here in the twilight and talk of
deep and intimate affairs.

It was Helen who first brought up Percy's name.

"Poor Percy caught it at tea, didn't he?" she said rather
nervously. "Mother's like that, you know, she can come
down hard when she wants to."

("Darling!") said Mabel parenthetically to the kitten.

"I say, Mabel. . . ."

"Yes?"

"How did Percy shoot? Tell me, really."

"Oh! He shot all right, for a first time," said Mabel. "He
shot rather well."

"I'm glad. Percy hates to make an exhibition of himself."

"We talked quite a lot," went on Mabel easily.

"What about?"

"Oh, it began with Colonel Maitland, who's a Roman
Catholic, you know."

Helen sat up.

"Who's he?"

"Oh! A man who shoots with us a good lot. He's rather
nice."

Helen felt excited. It was nervous work talking about
popery under the circumstances. She had not even yet
told her friend what the facts were about Percy; and she
half-wondered to which side she owed most loyalty.

"Well; what did you talk about?"

"Oh! We talked about the Roman Church. I said what I
thought, you know."

"What do you think about it?" asked Helen rather
breathlessly, turning round to look straight at her friend.
A flame shot up from the hearth, and by its light she saw

the solemn expression in full occupation of the little cat-like features.

"I disapprove of it very much indeed," proclaimed Mabel. "Of course, I didn't say so quite like that. I told him I thought it un-English and . . . and that sort of thing, you know."

"Did you really?"

"Yes; but of course I feel much more deeply about it really, than that. I . . . I can't bear it. I once heard a Mr. Railton speak — he had been a priest and gave it up. He said the most frightful things."

Helen was making quite a quantity of discoveries today; and for the first time in her life she had met that really serious and almost vindictive hatred of Catholicism which appears now and again in completely unexpected surroundings. She questioned her friend even more closely; she asked exactly what it was she felt so strongly about in the Catholic system, and got nothing but the fact. Somehow or other it was in the girl's blood; she could no more give adequate reasons for her repugnance than Percy himself — maybe — could have given for his violent attraction towards it. There it was, as impregnable as rock under shallow soil; and Helen was amazed at its immovability.

"My dear," said the other presently — (she had put down the kitten five minutes ago, when conversation had become really serious) — "My dear; I simply can't tell you what I feel. I . . . I suppose it may be partly bringing-up. . . . I don't know. My grandfather left the Church of Rome, you know, when he was a young man; and then I can't forget what Mr. Railton said at a meeting once. But it's not only that. I . . . I simply can't bear it at all."

Then Helen's last layer of discretion broke down.

"Mabel —" she began. Then she got up from the hearth-rug, sat down by her friend and took her hand.

"Mabel —"

"Yes?"

"I want to tell you something. Will you promise not to tell? I oughtn't to, you know; but I simply must."

Mabel looked at her.

"Yes. What is it?"

"You really promise on your word of honor not to tell?"

The girl nodded.

Helen drew a trembling breath.

"Well; it's about Percy," she said. "He didn't tell you anything, did he?"

The girl shook her head.

"I don't know what you mean."

"Well; it's this. Percy is 'under instruction,' as they call it. He means to be a Roman Catholic. You've promised not to tell anyone, you know."

Chapter V

T|ell Miss Marridon I'll be with her directly," said the
Rector, hastily rising from his sermon manuscript,
and preparing to change his alpaca jacket for his
long coat.

His cup, just now, was overflowing altogether.

First, he had become a Personage in a manner that
would have been impossible in Hanstead. Now Mr.
Bennett was a sincerely zealous clergyman, as has already been remarked; but he was human, and no one in
the world except a mortified saint (which he was not, and
never dreamed of claiming to be) is actually displeased at
the fact of becoming rather important; besides, if one has
real ambitions to be of use in the world, as he certainly
had, it is impossible to regret what he would have called
"one's increased sphere of usefulness." Here then was
one's increased sphere of usefulness readymade, for the
tenants of the Marston estate asked nothing better than
to be looked after temporally by the Squire and spiritually
by the Parson, provided that not too much was demanded
in return. Neither were there any fads or cranks to be
dealt with; there was no opposition whatever to the moderate changes he had thought it right to introduce into
Marston church — the substitution, for example, of colored altar cloths for the perennial red velvet one, of embroidered stoles for black scarves, and the addition of such
musical compositions as Gadsby in C. There was a Young
Men's Club already in existence heartily Tory and loyal
and all the rest, with a reading room match boarded with
red pine, one billiard table, and a set of block- tin
tea-urns. And everything else was to correspond. A good
quarter of the church was occupied by the Squire's household; the very gamekeepers (of whom not less than one in
three was expected to put in an appearance each Sunday)
had a reserved seat at the west end of the north aisle; and
a decent congregation could always be reckoned on; for
the Family came, in edifying decorum, through the little
door from the park, every Sunday morning about five

minutes before eleven, and the Squire read the lessons. One single drop of bitterness, however — yet only one — floated on this cup of sweetness; and that of course was supplied by Percy's defection.

The announcement by the trim maid — (a communicant, of course) — that Miss Marridon wished to see the Rector, brought the memory of some of these pleasures up again. It was really pleasant to be so much sought after — (this was the fourth visitor since breakfast) — and especially pleasant when the caller was Miss Marridon. The Rector had heard really quite unpleasant rumors as to the unpunctuality and general mild laxness of the Vicar of Cleever; and he wondered whether it might not be quite conceivable that Miss Marridon had called for some kind of consolation or advice.

So he put on his long coat and went across into the drawing room, really anxious to be of use.

Mabel stood up to greet him. She looked very fresh and girlish, and all that.

"It is charming of you to drop in like this," he said. "That is what one likes so much about the country. . . . Now do sit down, Miss Marridon. I hope Lord Marridon is better." (His lordship suffered a little from rheumatism, especially in winter; so inquiries after him were usually so worded.)

Mabel made the proper remarks; and the right sort of counters were played on both sides for a couple of minutes. Then the girl came to business.

"May I come straight to the point?" she asked. "Thank you so much. . . . And everything I say is in confidence, isn't it?" The Rector hastened to reassure her; his expression became very helpful, and just a tinge of his church pronunciation appeared in his voice.

"Of course," he said, "of course. I quite understand. Entirely confidential, as you say."

"It's about Mr. Percy Brandreth-Smith," she said, with just the faintest flush on her cheeks. "You were the Vicar of Hanstead, weren't you? So of course you know all about it."

His face became suddenly very intelligent.

"About his spiritual troubles? Certainly, Miss Marridon. I think I may say that I know all that is to be known."

"I only heard about it the other day," she went on rather hurriedly. "And in confidence. But I suppose I'm not breaking it by talking to one who knows already? Am I?"

The Rector hastened again to reassure her. He said that confidences to a Parish Priest were themselves sacred, and that there could be no breach of trust.

' "Well," said Mabel, quite frankly, "I was wondering whether nothing could be done. It seems dreadful that he should . . . should go over to Rome — without everything being tried first. And his people seem to be doing nothing whatever!" (She spoke with a vigor that astonished the other.)

The Rector shook his head, and his look became even more melancholy.

"I assure you everything has been tried. I will say this for him that he was very willing indeed, at any rate at first to hear both sides. There was one unfortunate incident, certainly. . . . Perhaps you heard of that?"

"I have heard nothing but the fact," she said.

"Well," continued the Rector, still in his church voice, "perhaps it was a mistake; but I did it for the best. I . . . I got down an ex-clergyman of the Church of Rome — a Mr. Railton —"

"Why I've heard him speak myself," cried Mabel.

"Ah! Indeed. Well I am sure Mr. Railton is a most estimable man; and very courageous too, to come out from his Church into fuller light. But, you know, just a little extreme in his views, as converts always are, on both sides. Well, Mr. Percy seemed to resent it all very much indeed. One had, in fact, great difficulty in persuading him to listen to one again. But he did — one is bound to say that, in justice. I assure you everything has been tried; though I'm sure it's very good of you, Miss Marridon, to interest yourself like this. It is a great pain to his parents — both staunch Church people, as you know."

She listened without moving to his talk.

"Then there's absolutely nothing that I can do?"

He smiled paternally.

"Well, of course, Miss Marridon, every little helps. One wouldn't say for an instant that there's absolutely no hope that it may yet not be too late. But one is bound to say —"

"Don't you think, Mr. Bennett," she interrupted without, apparently, being aware that she did so, "don't you think that sometimes more may be done just by ordinary conversation, than by arguing directly? Please don't think me impertinent. I know it sounds so, talking like this to a clergyman; but I don't mean it."

Mr. Bennett's head was a little on one side; and his church voice still more evident.

"Yes, yes. . . . It may be so, Miss Marridon. It often is so indeed. One sometimes does see that a helpful word or two, dropped here and there in season, and indeed out of it —"

Once more she interrupted; and the flush was more pronounced than ever.

"I mean that it's so dreadful to think of this place as being in the hands of Romanists. The whole . . . the whole thing would be so spoiled, with their chapels and their priests. . . . I can't bear the thought of it. . . . I . . . I wish I could do something."

He nodded gently, ten or eleven times, and began to murmur "Yes," over and over again as his way was.

She looked at him with a kind of despair; he seemed to her very unhelpful. She rose.

"Well, thanks very much, Mr. Bennett. I am afraid you don't think I can be of much use —"

"Oh! No, no! I wouldn't say that. But, you know, really everything has been tried. I am sure we shall all be most thankful if anything could be done."

"I quite see," she said. "Thanks very much."

(2)

When she was gone again, saying that she would find her way up to the Park, he walked up and down a little in the Rectory garden where he had said goodbye to her.

Certainly the situation did seem rather painful and difficult — more painful and difficult, perhaps, than he had quite realized. Certainly it would be very trying indeed to have, as she had said just now, Romanist "chapels and priests" all over the place — chapels that were rivals to his beautiful old parish church, and priests who did not acknowledge him as a brother.

Mr. Bennett was an exceedingly good man — let that be quite clear — and entirely convinced that the only really sound and reliable form of Christianity was that of which he was a minister. Obviously, then, he desired the triumph of the Church of England everywhere, and especially in the district over which he was set. Ordinary Dissenters were bad enough; there was a new red-brick Congregational chapel in Marston village the sight of which really spoiled his pleasure whenever he went to visit his flock. But Romanist Dissenters were a thousand times worse, since they actually claimed to compete, in a manner in which no Nonconformist minister even desired to compete, on the very same religious lines as himself. They actually claimed a Priesthood, and denied his, while he could not deny theirs. They were even so daring as to assert — as a cheerful party of tourists whom he had met once in his church, asserted — that the old buildings of the Church of England were once Romanist places of worship, and not, as he knew perfectly well, Anglican, from the very days of their erection. And, in support of their claim, they pointed to such remnants of the old architecture as the Seven Sacraments engraved in symbol round the font, and one half of the old holy water stoup that still survived in the porch. Of course there were answers to such arguments; and he had them at his fingers' ends; but it was trying that such arguments could be used at all.

What it would be, then, when the Squire of Marston was a Romanist, it was impossible to conceive. There would be no more coming through the little door that joined the churchyard and the park, at five minutes to eleven on Sunday morning; no country gentleman, in white spats, to read the lessons; no going up to the Park on Sunday evenings for supper, and saying Grace there.

Thoughts such as these had, of course, come to him before, but Mabel's visit had resuscitated them again in a more vigorous form than ever.

His wife came out to him presently, as he paced up and down, with a shawl over her shoulders.

"Well, my dear?" she said.

He nodded to her absentmindedly.

"Where are you off to?" he asked.

"Just round to change the flowers in church," she said.

He found himself strolling along with her presently. But he said nothing of Mabel's visit; and while she went straight through to the vestry where the altar vases were kept, he remained in the nave.

When she came out again twenty minutes later, he was still there, wrapped in thought.

"Been looking round?" she asked brightly. "That pillar wants looking to, by the way."

"I have made up my mind," he said. "That old stoup looks unsightly. I've often noticed it."

"You aren't going to take it away!"

"Well," he said firmly. "It must either be restored properly, or else walled up. It looks very bad like that."

"Restore it! But you couldn't put holy water in it."

"No, my dear, I know. But it would show — er — continuity, don't you think? . . . But that's not the chief thing. There's a nice empty bit of wall there. What do you say to an engraved brass tablet with the names of all the Rectors of Marston?"

"Since the Reformation?" she asked innocently.

The emphasis of his answer was almost indignant.

"No, my dear; the names of the Rectors from the very beginning, so far as we can identify them; and perhaps the names of the bishops of the diocese, too. It's very important to show, you know, that there was no break at the Reformation; and that it's just the same old church from the beginning."

"Oh, I see; yes, very nice, indeed. When did you think of it?"

He evaded a little, yet without sacrificing any strict truth.

"I saw one in an old church near here the other day. I think it would look very well; and be very teaching, besides."

She agreed.

Chapter VI

However dramatic may be a woman's temperament, until the age of thirty at any rate, there is always a place of complete reality somewhere underneath. Until after that age, there simply has not been time to dramatize the whole, or to get rid of the underlying character.

Miss Gladys Farham's character had been reached at last; at any rate she thought so, and that comes to the same thing. And it appeared to her now as if she had arrived at a reality which she had only guessed at before. Her first marriage seemed to her a dream; she had been an ignorant girl whose ignorance had been rapidly disillusioned; and she had taken refuge, after her divorce, in a sham kind of cynicism. And this cynicism had showed itself for the fraud that it was; and she had become a girl again, with a strange kind of motherliness woven into it, as gold into fine silk.

Her conversion was as real as anything of which she was capable. A photograph or two disappeared from her walls; her dress showed modifications which I am not competent to describe; the tones of her voice lost a particular kind of ring that they had, up to now, occasionally manifested.

It may seem remarkable that all this had been effected by Percy; and it would be safer to say that it had been effected by her conception of Percy. She had taken at once to this ardent slim boy who had such an assurance and such an engaging innocence; and she had viewed him, with the aid of her dramatic nature, as a kind of Parsifal who knows nothing, and can therefore accomplish anything. She did not now trouble to inquire how far his sudden access of wealth had illuminated him in her eyes; for even an illumination cannot reveal what is not there to be revealed. But, from the moment in which he had told her of his good fortune, he had taken on a significance that she had scarcely been aware of before; he had become, so to speak, adequate and possible. And when he had, in a sudden fit of manhood, spoken to her as man to woman, she had answered him genuinely and sincerely.

Her friends remarked on it.

"What's happened to you, my dear?" asked the very young-looking girl whom Percy had once met in the little room behind the stage.

"Happened? What d'you mean?" asked Gladys, who had had a letter from Percy an hour before.

"You're different," the girl had said vaguely, looking at her questioningly. "You look as if you'd —"

"Well?"

"I don't know."

These things, then, had borne fruit in her. There was no pose whatever in her acts of simplification; no conscious-ness at all of effort. She moved more gently; she spoke more quietly; she wrote little notes now and again to her lover, and posted them all together once a week; she opened his letters, with a distinct shock of pleasure, and kept them carefully, with his photograph, in a locked drawer of her writing table. Out of the same drawer she had previously taken two photographs of another man, and these she had burned honestly. She was in love with Percy's youth, if not with his soul — with his temporal aspects, if not with his eternal being. She had found, she believed, reality at last. And if all this seems impossible, let it be remembered that a dramatic temperament is not only exceedingly susceptive, but creative also.

(2)

It was halfway through February that she wrote an in-sistent little note to Percy demanding to see him at once. She had great news to tell him, she said; and whether it was good or bad depended on his view of it. When could he come up? But it was not till a week later that he came.

She thought he looked a little rundown; and said so.

"And why couldn't you come before?" she asked lightly.

He said that there were a hundred things to prevent. He told her that she had no idea of the extraordinary rush of tiny duties and engagements that could not be put aside. She saw that he was still a little preoccupied.

"Well," she said; when he was on her sofa with a cup of tea. "This is the news. What would you think of it if I went to America for not less than three months?"

"Eh?"

"To America," she said. "I've had a tremendous offer. They want a company for *A Gentleman of Fortune* to tour the States; and they've offered me really big terms. You see —"

"To America!" said Percy thoughtfully.

"Yes, my dear, let it soak in before you say anything more. Because I've got something else to say too."

"For three months?"

"For not less than three months," she corrected. "It may be six. It may even be a year. But —"

Oddly enough there was not that sudden fall of countenance she had expected. She had thought that he would protest instantly, and that she would have to explain all the advantages of the offer. But he seemed to take it merely thoughtfully. Was it conceivable that he was thinking the same thing as herself?

"It might even be a year," he echoed. Then he drank his tea.

"You see," she said, "it might mean a lot. If a play does happen to catch on, it leads on to other things. . . Percy."

"Yes?"

"I want to say two more things — rather difficult. At least I want to say one, first, and then perhaps the other. Will you promise not to be angry with either?"

"Why, of course."

"The first is this." (She got up and sat down again at the other end of the sofa on which he sat. She looked wonderfully young and fresh in her bright gown, with her feet crossed before her; and her eyes sparkled.) "The first is this. Is it utterly and entirely out of the question that I should go on being on the stage after our marriage?"

"*What?*"

She was astonished at the vehemence of the single word. But there was something delightful to her too in the implication that it must be he and he alone who must always provide for her.

"Yes; you're a dear to say it like that," she said. "But I want you just to think."

"I have thought. It's absolutely impossible. Look here, Gladys —"

"One minute. I see I must say the second thing. But first — Have you given any hint whatever to your people —?"

He shook his head. He looked drawn and anxious. . . . But she thought she knew why.

"There, you see; you know it would be hopeless. Well, I want to know what prospect there is of our ever being able to be married. We're no nearer it, than —"

"But we agreed to wait," he cried nervously. "Don't you remember —"

"Yes; yes; I remember everything. But the point is —" (she moved a shade nearer to him) — "the point is, *Why should we wait?*"

Again that spasm, as of a sudden shock, passed across his face. But she went on before he could speak, leaning towards him as she spoke.

"Percy, dear; I've thought of an idea. We must be sensible, you know — too sensible to have any conventions. . . . Do you remember how you said that once, and what it was that you said at the same time? . . . Well; I say it now. And you mustn't be offended. I've thought it all out; and I really think we can manage, if only you'll let me go to America. Percy, dear; I happen to love you very much indeed, you know. And . . . and I can't see why a wife shouldn't help her husband. Oh! Don't be high-minded and ridiculous, *please!*"

She had slipped down on to her knees, half-serious, half-laughing. It had cost her a lot to summon up her resolution; she knew he would hate what she had to say — hate it, that is, with one part of him; but . . . but perhaps he might love it with another. She took his hand in both of hers.

"My dear; listen to me quietly. Say I go to America. I get fifteen pounds a week and all expenses. I come back, say in a year, with . . . with how much — say five hundred pounds. Well, that's something, isn't it? We're married quietly — oh! ever so quietly, by one of your little secre-

tive priests. No one knows — not a soul. And then I go on
living here, just as before; and you're down at Marston or
wherever it is. And I go on acting; and they've practically
promised me twenty pounds a week. And not a soul
knows; and . . . and I go on saving as hard as I can; and so
do you. . . . And then in time — Oh! Percy, isn't it better
than waiting forever?"

His face was as white as paper.

"They'd find out," he said hoarsely.

She flung herself back on her heels.

"Well; and if they did! They wouldn't . . . But if they did!
Aren't we independent?"

He sprang up and went past her. He began to walk up
and down the room.

(3)

He was in a torment of indecision.

So long as he was away from her, down at Marston; so
long as he moved about in that solemn inexpressibly comfortable life, or talked with Mabel; or assimilated little by
little the warm atmosphere of County Tradition and all
the rest; it was possible for him to regard his engagement
at least detachedly, to admit other considerations and to
contemplate other alternatives. But here, in her presence,
in the very room in which he had undergone the fiercest
emotion he had ever known, where, drunk with that emotion, he had driven his will to do his purpose — here, with
the girl herself kneeling before him, and the touch of her
hands on his, and the strange look in her eyes — the passion came back in a wave. . . .

He fought it, as if with teeth set. He told himself he
must be cool and sensible. He must not allow the allurement of this secretiveness, and the infinitely more attractive allurement of the secretiveness which she proposed,
to blind him to common sense. For it was this last suggestion of hers that had completed what the sight and touch
of her had begun. When he had had her in his arms, first,
half an hour ago, and kissed her, he had by no means lost
control of himself. He felt "sensible" without feeling the
need of telling himself to be so. Yet now, to think that he
might come here as her husband; to think that this room
of hers might also be his; and that yet there might be no

need for him to leave his home life — this tossed his poor
heart to and fro in a storm of longing.

And then, again, cold reason asserted itself. It told him
that the thing was a dream; that it could not be kept a secret; that all would come out; and that then indeed his
ruin would be complete.

And then again Desire seized him; and he cried out interiorly, as certain kinds of souls will, at the intolerable
injustice that he should have to bear such complications,
and be so torn this way and that between his desire and
that which he was already beginning to call his "Duty."

But all that Gladys saw was a high-minded young man
and lover striving between his love for her and his pride
aroused by her offer.

(4)

It was a quarter-past five before he arrived at last at
the Franciscan Friary where he had made an appointment for another instruction from Father Hilary at five
precisely.

His interview with Gladys had ended just as any psy-
chologist who knew them both would have predicted. He
had been pale and manly; she feminine and full of en-
treaty. He had said that the whole thing was so new and
startling that he must have time . . . he must have time;
and that they must both be very sensible and considerate.
And she had gone so far as to wave a telegraph form before him, and beg that she might wire, *Accepted,* to her
manager. That had brought him up sharp. He had forgotten America.

Then he had said that that was an entirely separate
question, anyhow; and had demanded whether it might
not be better that she should accept that in any case?

And she, in a flare of feminine unreason, had declared
that that was not so, at all; and that she flatly refused to
go to America unless he gave his consent to the whole affair. It must be all or none.

Once more he had entreated her to be reasonable; and
she had replied that she would be nothing of the kind.

Then the clock had struck five; and in sudden boisterous
despair he had declared that Father Hilary would never
forgive him if he missed him this time again. Well, Gladys

had demanded, But what about America? She must answer by noon next day. Then he had seized and kissed her, suddenly and uncontrollably. . . .

He would send a wire, by latest, tomorrow morning. He promised so much.

Already the mood was ebbing, ever so slightly, as he found himself in the parlor; and cold common sense was coming back. The bleak walls of the little room; the bare table, with a single book explanatory of the Catechism, lying upon it, the associations of the place — all these things helped to steady him on his swaying pedestal. The lay brother who opened the door to him, said that Father Hilary had been here at five, but had been called away to church. Would Mr. Brandreth-Smith wait a few minutes? He did not think his Reverence would be long.

Certainly Percy's first ardors of religion had waned; yet, somewhere, far down in him there was a very well fixed determination to persevere. The instructions he had received had shifted the weight of conviction from the emotion to the intellect; and, much as he might resent certain disadvantages that might follow, it must be said in justice to him, that he intended, quite coolly and deliberately, to continue, and, in due time, to be received into the Church. (It had only become just a shade more difficult after Mabel's remarks.)

This at least was an unmistakable duty — so he said to himself. And the very fact that, with regard to the Gladys-complication, he had, at least interiorly, swerved a little, drove him with the more vehemence to be faithful to this. His marriage with Gladys might or might not be his "Duty." But there was no question about this.

This, then, is what he said to himself. And he said it once or twice as he took a turn or two up and down the room. Then he sat down; took up the book and began to turn its pages.

(5)

Father Hilary was detained longer than he had expected; and ten minutes later came swiftly along the corridor and through the swing-door into the extra-claustral part of the house, with his habit swinging and his sandals clapping. He did not, however, propose to apologize, since he had waited ten minutes himself beyond the time that Percy had appointed.

He came straight in, smiling, and stopped. For a very tremulous-looking person was there to greet him.

Percy was standing sideways to the fireplace, with his hands hanging down and a very curiously agitated look on his face. A book was open on the mantelpiece.

"Father —" he began instantly; and then remembered himself. "I . . . I'm afraid I was a little late. I'm so sorry."

"Why — what's the matter?" asked the friar kindly.

"Nothing . . . nothing, Father. I . . . I've got to catch the six-ten, you know."

"Well, we've got nearly half an hour, if you'll take a taxi."

Percy sat down instantly, like a mechanical figure.

Ten minutes later the priest stopped. He saw that something was wrong; but also saw that he was supposed not to see it. Percy had been obviously unconscious of practically everything that the priest had been saying. So Father Hilary tried an ancient device.

"There," he said. "And now you ask me some questions. Anything you like. We often get at difficulties better that way."

Percy instantly awoke from his stupor.

"May I? . . . Well, there are one or two things . . ." (He indicated the book on the mantelpiece.) "I . . . I was looking at that before you came in. I . . . I saw one or two things I didn't know before."

"Yes?"

"I . . . I was looking at the instruction on Matrimony." (He smiled, in a ghastly attempt to seem at ease.) "And I'm not sure that I quite understand —"

The friar stopped himself just in time from saying that that had better wait till they got there.

"Yes?" he said again.

"You'll think me fearfully stupid, I expect. But . . . but the book seemed to say that Matrimony was indissoluble — that . . . that it lasts till death, whatever happens."

He was managing his voice quite well; but his face betrayed him. Father Hilary looked carefully into the fire. He could not conceive what the matter was.

"Yes. Our Lord said that, you know. 'What God hath joined together' — you know."

"But . . . but didn't Our Lord say something about, except for fornication. I . . . I always supposed that meant that in a . . . a real divorce — I mean where one of the married people has . . . has been unfaithful, and a proper divorce has been made, that both were free."

"No," said Father Hilary dispassionately. "Certainly the Church allows divorce —" (he corrected his phrase). "I'd better say Judicial Separation, for that sin, under certain circumstances; but that never means that either of the two can marry again in the lifetime of the other. They remain husband and wife in God's sight."

"But the laws allow —"

"The Laws of the State, yes. And, apparently the laws of the Church of England too. . . . At least clergymen can and do remarry divorced people. But the Catholic Church says No, always."

There was a pause. Again Father Hilary refrained from even glancing at the boy.

"But . . . but isn't that fearfully hard, sometimes, on the . . . the innocent party?" asked a voice that was beginning to quaver. "Suppose a good girl has been married to a beast of a man, and has divorced him —"

"Oh! Yes," said the priest gently. "God's laws are very hard sometimes. So it is very hard if the man is a convict or a lunatic. But even the laws of England don't at present allow divorce for that. You see —"

Percy interrupted, without apparently being conscious that he did so.

"Then . . . then a Catholic can't under any circumstances marry a divorced person — I mean, an innocent divorced person."

"Not so long as the husband is alive."

"And . . . and suppose someone who had already done so, wanted to become a Catholic, could he . . . or she —" (he added with a jerk) . . . "I . . . I want to get it all clear."

"Not unless he, or she, separated from the other."

There was a dead silence. The little clock on the mantelpiece ticked gently and ruthlessly. A cab rumbled by outside. The fire fell in with a little crash.

Then Percy stood up. . . .

"Er . . . Thanks very much, Father. . . . I . . . I think I shall have to go. It's rather late."

The friar too rose and held out his hand.

"Well; goodbye," he said. "When will you come again?"

"Next week. . . . I'll . . . I'll write."

Chapter VII

(1)

Percy sat alone in his room at Marston that same night, thinking, thinking.

He had got through that evening, as a man gets through a nightmare. His mother had looked at him half a dozen times during dinner; and had told him afterwards he had better go to bed early; and he had jumped at the release. He had said he felt stupid and tired, and perhaps a little feverish. No; he'd sooner not take any quinine; he didn't think it was influenza; but if he felt no better in the morning he would stop in bed for breakfast. Then he had wished goodnight to everybody; gone upstairs to his room and locked his door, got out a couple of books that Father Hilary had lent him and studied them again. Then he had put the books carefully away, blown out the candles, and sat down before the fire.

The horrible thing was that, far down in his soul, he knew that there was a deep spring of relief that by and by would flood him. But he would not recognize that he knew it. He was aware, on the contrary, that he ought to be entirely overwhelmed and heartbroken; and in order to fulfill this duty he repeated to himself little sentences.

"Ah! My poor Gladys.... It's too much ... it's too hard ..."

He did this fitfully. There came moments when he writhed himself backwards, his face against the cushioned back of the chair, his hands twisted together — moments when his conventions told him fiercely that he ought to be miserable, and when even his emotions — his memories of Gladys this afternoon at certain instants — came to help his conventions. In one such spasm he practically believed that it was all infinitely pathetic; when, reviewing exactly what Gladys had proposed — that she should support him — he caught some glimmer of the fact that she really cared for him; when he viewed again, imaginatively, the amazing prospect she had held out to him, of a secret marriage; and then, against all this he saw himself pale but determined, clinging to his cold faith, in preference to warm love, obedient to principle rather than passion. At this point his eyes filled with real tears; and moaning softly that "God was cruel" he saw himself magnificent, pitiless and patient.

It was not altogether surprising that he had not been aware before of this little flaw in his plans. He had known nothing of Catholicism whatever, except so far as his instructions had gone; and it had been a complete and overwhelming surprise when he had first read, this afternoon, and then verified, the impossibility of his marriage with Gladys. He knew that English Church people contracted such marriages, and that the law of the State permitted them to do so — (for instance there were the Matthieson-Howleys). And he had thought vaguely that, although perhaps such a marriage would not be considered ideal by the Catholic authorities, there would be no insuperable objection; and that anyhow it could be set right afterwards, somehow.

It had been really paralyzing at first. He saw simply, in the parlor in Kensington, that he could not do both — could not fulfill both his engagements; and it had not been until, settled down in a comfortable first-class carriage, he had begun to shift back again into the Marston atmosphere and prospects, he had perceived what an exceedingly graceful and, indeed, almost heroic retreat this dilemma offered him.

"The poor girl!" he had murmured, even then.

And the pose had grown on him. He stepped into the brougham at his journey's end with a world-weary air; he had stepped out of it, viewing himself as a sort of martyr; his deliberate repressed dignity at dinner had been mistaken for incipient influenza; and now, in the wavering firelight, he gave himself up to a superb series of sentiments. . . .

He leant forward presently, sighing; drew out his cigarettes, and, with the help of the tongs and a small coal, lit one and leaned back again, with the air of one who takes a little necessary refreshment, even though a world is shattered about him. As he did so, he remembered the need of a telegram to her next day; and sat still, suddenly.

(2)

He must be very businesslike and practical, he told himself, presently. He must not consider himself at all — her, only. It was no time for indulging in regrets; he must be practical and think only of her — of her highest good, that is, of course.

At first there appeared objections to every course that presented itself. If he told her to decline the contract she would lose, so to speak, both worlds. If he told her to accept it, it would be to give her the impression that he consented to her plan. If he guarded, explicitly, against this false impression, she would decline to take his advice. In any case but one (and that was impossible), she would remain in England. And if one thing was absolutely clear to him it was that Gladys Farham must get away to America — for her sake, of course — for the sake of her highest good. Perhaps . . . perhaps . . ." he said, it would help her to forget.

And then at last the fine solution suggested itself of sending her a wire telling her to go, and of following it up later, when the contract was finally signed — say in three or four days — explaining his heroic decision, and bidding her a long farewell. Of course he would not suggest seeing her; in fact he must decline to, in any case. It would be fairer, so, to the poor girl.

Then one more thought suggested itself; and it is impossible to say that the contemplation of his own heroism (with the desire that others should contemplate it too) was wholly absent from the thought. It was that he would write to Father Hilary at once, tell him the circumstances, and . . . and ask his prayers, of course. He would urge Gladys, too, to go and see the friar herself. That would prove, if any proof were needed, his own entire sincerity.

It cannot be denied that Percy had begun to enjoy himself considerably by now. It is not often that a young man has an opportunity of sacrificing this world to the next in so heroic and yet, simultaneously, in so comparatively painless a way. There was some pain, of course, and there were instants when this pain really hurt — instants, for example, when, both lulled and stimulated by his cigarette and the warm-lit darkness, he perceived suddenly

and very nearly visually, the look on Gladys' face as she
had kneeled before him in her semi-mock entreaties this
afternoon, and compared with it the look he could imagine
there when the facts were made plain.

But he saw that it was his duty to put such unmanning
visions away. He must be strong — strong, he told himself
with emphasis. He must think of his Duty, and his Religion. . . . He must distract himself, in the weary days that
must follow the Great Renunciation, with little coun-
try-duties, and friends — Mabel, for example. . . .

(3)

He went to the writing table at last, with a firm and unfaltering step. . . . He would put it once and for all out of
his own power to recede from his duty. He could write a
telegram to Gladys, terse and unmistakable; and a letter,
also terse and unshrinking, to the friar . . . Father Hilary
would understand, at least. . . .

Then he would put these outside his door for James to
find at eight o'clock — in time for the postman to take
them both; with a direction not to awaken him till half-
past eight; and thus, when he was awakened — always
supposing, of course, that he did manage to fall into a
troubled sleep about the dawn — all would be over, and
the die cast. (Beautiful language and phrases of this kind
did, actually, pass through his mind and even his lips; for
he was struggling furiously to keep on the high-water
mark, and not to face himself in the depths.)

The telegram was soon written.

"Accept immediately. Writing presently."

He looked at it with a sorrowful resolve. . . . No; he
would not sign his name. It was better so. She would understand.

Then there was the letter to Father Hilary.

This was more considerable. He took a large sheet of
foolscap to give himself room to turn, so to speak; and bit
the top of his pen.

"My Dear Father," he wrote. Then he paused.

The stable clock was striking twelve before he read the
fair copy over for the last time; and his eyes filled with
tears. It was beautiful, he thought — dignified, reserved,

virile, and yet through it rang the wail of a broken heart that would not yield.

Let it be understood plainly that this boy really did not know that he was deceiving himself. Truly, as he read the letter for the last time, he believed it expressed his deepest self; that he loved Gladys as he said, and that it was the demand of Faith, and no other motive, that had prevailed at last. He even believed, now, that he had passed through a terrible struggle of indecision.

The letter ran as follows; —

"My Dear Father,

"I do not know whether you understood this afternoon the significance of the questions I put to you. In any case, let me tell you now that it was of myself that I spoke.

"Until this afternoon I have been engaged, secretly, to a girl who herself had hoped to become a Catholic later on — a wonderful girl. You would know her name if I mentioned it. She is well known.

"Well; that is all over now. I am writing to tell her of the blinding shock of the discovery I have made; and that her marriage is impossible, at least so far as any good Catholic is concerned; since she has a husband living — a man whom she divorced a few months, I think, after marriage. . . .

"Father! I cannot tell you what this means to me. Nor can you ever know. I am a broken man. Nor can I dare to say what it will mean to her. . . . I shall do my utmost to urge her to go abroad immediately, for of course we must not even meet again. I understand that, Father! Do not fear for me.

"Father! I ask your prayers. . . . I cannot come again next week. You must give me a little time. . . . I will write again when I can.

"Your brokenhearted child in Xt.,

"P. B. S.

"P.S. — Destroy this, if you please, at once. My parents know nothing of the affair."

No wonder Percy was moved. He sat again in the firelight, and his tears became broken flashing mirrors before his eyes. . . .

Then, again with a firm and unfaltering step, he put the telegram, the letter and the directions to James, all outside the door; shut the door, locked it, and flung himself on his knees before his crucifix.

Chapter VIII

(1)

It was on the following day that Mr. Main, carrying out his great resolve, arrived at Marston Station by the morning train. He had destroyed his first letter. It seemed to him that he could not plead his cause adequately with a pen; and he had, of course, hesitated a good deal from pleading it in person. Besides he had written that letter in a burst of misery; and he thought it too bitter. But the days had gone by; his little fund was running low, and no answer came to his other applications. He was becoming desperate. He must risk everything, he said; risk even meeting his old friends; but he would do his best to avoid this. He would send up a note somehow, and ask Percy to come out and see him. He had the note already written in his pocket, signed, "Yours faithfully."

He was a desolate shabby figure as he trudged up the lane towards the lodge gate. He was in the same ready-made suit in which he resembled a manservant; the same boots, with a crease across the toes; the same overcoat, turned up at the collar, as the skies were drizzling a little; the same soft hat. It would have been too violent a change for him — so to speak — to have been attired in a more glaringly lay costume.

Marion was in full-blast once more. She was writing desperately, eagerly, almost hungrily; and her drawn face showed the strain of it. She had even read little bits to her husband, and he had submitted drearily. The story, so far as he had any coherent idea of it, concerned a priest who left the Church and lived happily ever afterwards. It was written really rather well, and was almost perfectly calculated to give a convert extreme and poignant pain.

He was thinking about it as he strode up the lane; he was wondering painfully and conscientiously whether or not he was justified in allowing her to make one or two minute slips in Catholic technicalities.

Then, as he pondered, he looked up and observed what from his inquiries he identified as the lodge of Marston

Park. A woman was cleaning the doorstep of the Corinthian porch.

"Er — can you tell me, please," began Mr. Main in his clerical voice, "whether this is Marston Park?"

The woman turned quickly and straightened herself; but her manner changed as she saw the shabby nondescript figure.

"Yes, it is," she said.

"Er . . . and would you be good enough to tell me if Mr. Percy Brandreth-Smith is at home?"

She looked him up and down. (She was the same woman that had bobbed so charmingly to Percy upon his first arrival.)

"That's not my affair," she said. "The Park's the proper place to ask."

A small stout boy of nine or ten years old appeared at the door of the lodge, and eyed the stranger. Mr. Main had an inspiration.

"Do you think," he said pleasantly, "that if I gave your little boy sixpence he would run up to the Park for me with a note; and bring back the answer, if there is one?"

The woman looked at him again; then she relieved her feelings on her son.

"Where's your manners, Tommie," she said. "Take the gentleman's note, d'yer hear?"

Mr. Main beamed as the boy advanced down the steps to the gate.

"There! My little man," he said, in the full clerical way. "And there's your sixpence. And tell Mr. Percy if he's in and asks, that I'll be walking up and down outside the lodge."

He patted the boy's head with his lean fingers.

(2)

Bitterness came down on him again tenfold, yet not one spark of resentment, as he walked up and down in the drizzle. From the top of the slope above the lodge he could catch a glimpse beyond the trees of the church spire and the Rectory roof where his old chief, he knew, was now established.

But it was his relations with Tommie that had struck the first note. He had spoken to him and patted him on

the head, quite in the old manner — that old manner that
had caused him, not so very long ago, after all, to answer
Mr. Bennett's advertisement for a "Curate in priest's orders; good with men and boys. No extremes. E.P. Colored
stoles. Staunch churchman. Apply, &c." He had picked
that out carefully, from the columns of the *Church Times,*
thinking that it might just suit him, and that a little hard
work in congenial surroundings "with men and boys,"
might silence the anxieties that had begun to trouble him
with regard to the whole position of the Church of which
he was a minister.

Well; that was over. He must not pat little boys' heads
any more like that, nor call them "my little man." That
was a clergyman's way. The woman had looked at him
quite oddly when he had done that; and had even called
him "Sir." But he had refused her offer to wait in the
lodge. It seemed to him that it would be on false pre-
tences. So he walked up and down in the drizzle; and at
his third turn refrained from looking again at the church
spire. . . .

The first he knew of Percy's coming was the woman's
head thrust out from the gate. She nodded violently to
him from thirty yards away; and he made haste towards
her as she vanished.

He was just in time to see her bob to Percy as he slipped
off his bicycle and ran it up the steps of the portico.

"I'll . . . I'll just leave it here, Mrs. — er," he said
vaguely.

She bobbed again, with an anxious side glance at the
muddy track the wheel left on her newly cleaned step.

Then Percy turned.

"Why —!" he said, and came forward smiling and
hearty. (The woman at the lodge determined to err in future on the side of politeness towards doubtful strangers.)

(3)

"You see," said Mr. Main, when they were well out of
hearing, when the first few obvious questions had been
asked and answered, and the main object of his visit revealed — "You see, I thought I might venture to ask just
the favor of a letter from you to your old firm. I . . . er . . . I
am not finding life very easy."

"But I don't understand, really," said Percy, in a perfect fever of friendliness. "Of course I'll give you a letter or any mortal thing I can. But do you really mean you'd consent to be a clerk or, as you say, a . . . a traveler for a cocoa firm. Why, your education —"

Mr. Main smiled bleakly.

"I fear that does not qualify me as a clerk," he said. "I very nearly obtained a position as a private tutor with an old Catholic family, but —" (He hesitated.)

"Well, why not? That's just the very thing, isn't it?"

"The fact is that I am too old; and . . . and too much of a parson still, I fear. I . . . er . . . unfortunately overheard part of a conversation that was not intended for my ears. I . . . I gathered that those were the principal objections."

"What a vile shame!" snarled Percy. "And have you tried other things?"

"I may say that I have — unsuccessfully. So I thought —"

Percy seized his arm; and poor Mr. Main's heart glowed within him at the kindness.

"But my . . . my dear Mr. Main; you really must come up to the house; and see the Rector too, and lunch with us. We'd be delighted —"

Mr. Main shook his head solemnly.

"Your own kindness, my dear Percy — (if I may say that once again) — is far more than I had hoped. I am sure I had better not risk —"

His voice broke suddenly, horribly and grotesquely. Percy, shocked beyond measure, could not resist one glance at him; and saw how that large lean face was working as if in a dreadful parody of a laugh. . . . He shivered and set his teeth. . . .

"Well, look here," he said. "If you won't, you won't. And of course I'll write the letter, and do anything in the world that I can. I'm . . . I'm very much touched that you've come to me. I . . . I wish that I could do more. Won't you let me —" (He bit his lip suddenly.)

There was a sound of a noisy swallowing in the lean throat beside him. Then the solemn clerical voice answered.

"My dear Percy . . . I am ashamed . . . you have done me good. And . . . and will you send the letter to the address I will give you? No, nothing else; nothing else upon my word."

"But —" began Percy) who had visions of writing him a small check.

"No, my dear boy — No. I'm . . . I'm very fortunate in finding such a good friend. I may say that it is with Father Hilary's full approval that I came to see you."

Percy nodded.

"Have you seen him lately? I hear you're still under instruction."

"I saw him yesterday," said Percy. "I . . . I hope to be received soon after Easter perhaps; or the early summer. I'm not able to get up to town much, you know."

(4)

Percy went back again as soon as the stable bell begun to ring for luncheon, still unable to persuade Mr. Main to come with him; and indeed he wondered at his own daring in having asked him. And Mr. Main had set off downhill again to the station, saying that he would get something to eat at the railway inn, and once more repeating his gratitude.

Percy had leaped at the opportunity of doing something to serve his old acquaintance, with an ardor which he scarcely understood himself.

With the cold light of morning had come something of a reaction against the emotions of last night. He had been awake by seven, and had listened, palpitating, for James' arrival at his door, and his departure again with the telegram and the letter. He had even sprung out of bed, half-intending to call him back. But he had hesitated; and a quarter of an hour later had seen the postman go down the back drive.

' His uneasiness had increased with the morning. Certainly he had committed himself now, and the particular set of motives with which he had acted still insisted to him that he had done the only right and sensible thing. But something stirred within him that would not let him rest. Whenever he faced it, it fled before him like flying specks before the eyes; it could not answer for one instant the plain argument that he had to choose between Gladys and his Faith, and that no man with any conscience could hesitate. Yet it recurred, so soon as he had done his emphatic self-answering.

Helen had been with him in the smoking room when the
thumbed note had come up from the lodge.

"By George!" said Percy, as he opened it. "Old Main!"

"What?"

"Er — tell him I'll come directly," continued Percy to the
butler. "No; wait; I'll go myself. My bicycle's in the yard,
isn't it?"

"What is it?" asked Helen.

"Tell you when I come back."

Percy's haste to be of service, and his zeal when he met
the ex-curate, was wholly instinctive then, and (so to say)
reactionary. Down in that sphere of himself of which he
knew nothing, there was forming a strong conviction that
he was behaving like a cad. As has been said, this, when
it showed its head and he tackled it by logic, fled down
again and vanished. Yet it was there — this uneasy sense
that he was not really choosing at all between Gladys and
his religion, but simply between Gladys and his own comfort. He fortified himself with words, reassured himself by
argument, but in the light of morning his emotions did
not help him; and he leaped, therefore, at this opportunity
of helping Mr. Main as a kind of additional reassurance to
himself that he was really a good fellow and nothing but
conscientious.

At lunch, of course, Helen did precisely the wrong thing.
She was indignant at being left in the smoking room uninformed, and hastened to revenge herself. She waited until
everyone was seated; and then began.

"Did you see Mr. Main?" she said.

Percy looked up abruptly and angrily; and his parents
with him.

"Yes, I did," he said, in rather a loud voice. "I was going
to tell you, Mother. I had a note just now from Mr. Main,
and went out to see him. He wouldn't come in."

"Mr. Who?" asked his mother icily, who had caught the
name quite distinctly; and who had also read by now, with
indescribable indignation, Mrs. Main's portraiture of her
in "A New Arcadia."

"Mr. Main, you know," said Percy, "from Hanstead. He's become a Catholic, you know."

Mrs. Brandreth-Smith closed her eyes an instant.

"I think we had better discuss Mr. Main at some other time," she said. "But I am not surprised at his coming in such a furtive way; and I am extremely glad that at least he had the good taste not to present himself at this house."

Then silence fell. It was evident that Mrs. Brandreth-Smith had read the book of which Helen still had a concealed copy in a locked drawer.

Chapter IX

Gladys Farham was a little puzzled at not having received Percy's promised letter. But she was extraordinarily happy.

She had gone off to her manager's and signed the American contract within two hours of having received the telegram; she had lunched out all alone in a restaurant to which Percy had once taken her, in a kind of ecstasy; and had tested her stability, so to speak, by the admirable composure with which she had been able to encounter Jim Marridon at the end of her lunch.

She was putting on her gloves when she looked up and saw him coming towards her. He sat down instantly at her table.

"You're all alone," he said. "How's that?"

Jim Marridon was one of those large, rather silent and rather rude persons, who have nothing whatever to exalt them amongst men except that extraordinary gift that is called Personality. His intellectual activities were limited strictly by such literature as the *Sporting Times;* his artistic aspirations rose no higher than musical comedy. He was entirely stupid, except as regards the lower reaches of human experience, in which he had a certain shrewdness; he possessed a number of little rather cynical principles which, unfortunately, were quite often justified. He did not believe, that is to say, in the disinterestedness of any human being on earth; he was persuaded that no woman really took any interest at all in anything except men. The type is quite a common one, and quite a successful one in its own plane, especially when it is accompanied by that which I have called Personality. Its examples are seen everywhere. They sit with mask-like faces in the stalls of the Gaiety Theater and at the supper tables of the Savoy Restaurant; they remain, slow speaking and oracular, in the smoking rooms of country houses until the small hours of the morning; they solemnly appear in divorce-courts with an air of irreproachable respectability; at certain hours of the day they exude a faint aroma of whisky, of which they talk a good deal, with allusions; they have a curious, but quite rigid code of morals and behavior, which scarcely resembles at all that of Christianity. But, on the other hand, sometimes they settle down into admirable fathers and husbands, become very careful indeed for the welfare of their children, and attend Divine worship in the country, with portentous and punctual gravity.

Jim Marridon, then, was precisely one of these. If he were placed in a selected row of his fellows it would be almost impossible to distinguish him from the rest. He had, to the full, the set eyes and the rigid mouth under a clipped moustache, and the little indescribable details of gait and language. But he had Personality, unquestionably. People cared, somehow, very much as to whether he were pleased with them or not, although they could not have justified their attitude for a moment; they would hasten to propitiate him if he were annoyed, and would glow all over with satisfaction if they succeeded and he approved.

Now he had laid the slow siege of his kind to Miss Gladys Farham for nearly a year, and had given her to understand, without any unforgivable openness, that she might command him in anything reasonable. God, who made him, alone knows why he had selected her; it was usually the musical-comedy kind of person to whom he was attracted. He had been privileged to meet her at supper a few times; and it may be supposed that he found in her moods a kind of pleasant foil to his own solemnity.

Gladys had always been a little afraid of him. She had shown this on more than one occasion by a sudden flare of rudeness to him; while at other times she had concealed it under extreme pleasantness. . . . In any case she was delighted now, as she nodded to him, to find that he no longer affected her at all. She felt completely on a different plane from that on which he energized.

"Oh! I don't know," she said. "I suppose because there's nobody with me."

No expression passed over his face to show that he was either amused or annoyed at her flippancy.

"And what have you been up to?" he said.

She drew on her left-hand glove completely and began to button it. He appeared to watch the process.

"Well," she said, "I've just signed a contract to go to America."

"For long?"

"I don't know. Not less than three months. But it may be more."

"Is *A Gentleman* of *Fortune* going, then?"

"That's it."

"Soon?"

"We sail on Wednesday week."

He lifted his eyes to her face as she began on the second glove.

"Can't I come and see you first? Can't we do something together?"

It was astonishing to her how unimportant this suggestion seemed to her now. On the half-dozen occasions when she had driven or supped with him it had seemed to stand for more than it presented; it was all part of the game that sometimes ended in marriage and sometimes did not — the game she had seen played by others more than once, with various endings — the game which she had once played herself, in the case of her first marriage with such astonishing ill-fortune. But it seemed to her all very trifling and foolish now; she had done with such follies; she felt exalted clean out of its atmosphere altogether.

"No," she said coolly. "I've got too much to do."

He dropped his eyes again to her glove. Then he took out his card.

"Look here," he said. "Perhaps you'll change your mind. If you do, let me know. I'm staying at my club."

He put his card before her and stood up. She looked at it carelessly, and then a thought struck her. She wondered if he knew Percy. Their places in the country must surely be rather near one another.

"By the way," she said. "Haven't you some neighbors called Brandreth-Smith?"

He nodded.

"Some new people. Yes. Do you know them?"

"I've met one of them."

"Which? The girl?"

"No, the boy."

He laughed a little.

"That young cub!" he said. "He was out shooting with us the other day. At least that's what he said he was doing."

A spasm of sudden and intense anger seized her. She drove it down; she must not rouse any questionings at all. But she must have her little revenge.

"Well," she said, "I mustn't keep you."

She stood up, smiling, wholly disregarding the card, nodded to him, and moved off. Yet she was entirely aware of his anger, of his hot slow displeasure, and of that which I have called his Personality. She knew perfectly well that he wished to be friends with her very much indeed, and that her manner had been to him like a slap in the face. And she did not care in the slightest, she told herself.

(2)

When the third morning dawned, and there was no letter from Percy in her box, she became a trifle perturbed. She had promised herself last night that it would be here. Then she remembered that she had thought that perhaps he meant to come instead, and again felt content. There were not many more days, and some of them at least would be pretty full since she was to sail today week. It would be charming if he could manage to get up to town for two or three of them, and perhaps see her off, at least from Euston. But there was an element of pleasure to her, in her new relations, in the thought that she was waiting upon his plans.

It was one of those sudden mornings of spring that occasionally herald Easter; and the sunlight streamed into her pretty room as she sat at breakfast, softened by the delicate muslin curtains through which it came, lighting up the sprigged china, the daffodils behind the teapot, and the two or three pieces of really nice silver that she had. She half-shut her eyes, to see it with the greater pleasure; it was as dainty as a picture.

She, too, was as pretty as a picture; and she was not entirely unaware of it. Her masses of dark hair were looped out loosely, shadowing her clear face and her big bright eyes . . . she put out her ringed fingers once or twice and looked at them, and particularly at that on which was the diamond and ruby half-circle that had been Percy's.

Her contentment was very nearly complete. It would have been quite complete if his letter had come; yet it was very nearly as nice to contemplate pleasant reasons for the delay. Perhaps he had some plan, and would presently burst in upon her, with it. Perhaps he was arranging, on some excuse, to stay at the house in Wilton Crescent, and would be with her every day. Perhaps — why, there were a hundred possibilities!

That which, possibly, gave her the most joy was the very point at which Percy had so obviously hesitated — the arrangement that, after her return from America, it would be upon her money that the two would chiefly depend. Money was a very big symbol with Miss Gladys Farham; she was not at all avaricious, but she was quite aware of what it could do, and of the discomfort that accompanied its absence. It was delightful to her, then, to feel, first that the tables had been very completely turned since the day when Percy had first proposed to help her with her debts, and that it was she who for the present at any rate would be the provider; and, next, this very thought chimed in harmoniously with the strong element of motherliness that lay in her relations towards him. It was this motherliness, probably, that gave her love for him its peculiar clean sweetness; she combined it somehow, in her extremely feminine nature, with that other, apparently mutually exclusive, emotion of desiring to look up to him and be protected and ruled by him. It is an odd combination, but extremely common; and it resulted, in her case, at any rate, in an emotion towards this boy that had really and truly, for the time being, at any rate, changed her character. She was aware of this — that her standards had changed, that her hardness had practically gone, and that such views of life as those represented by Jim Marridon were entirely and completely distasteful to her.

She heard the latch of her letterbox click suddenly; she rose instantly and went out into her tiny hall. Then she came back, smiling, with Percy's letter in her hands. He must have caught the last post, then, after all.

She forgot the remainder of her breakfast; and sat down in the sunshine on her sofa to read what he had to tell her. A canary burst into sudden song.

Chapter X

(1)

Percy, if the truth must be told, was feeling very considerably satisfied with himself, though he still thought it proper to affect an air of melancholy.

For, first, he had been of service to Mr. Main; at least he had done his utmost to be of service, since he had not only written a very warm letter himself to the firm in whose employment he had been, but had prevailed on his father to write one too. And he had had the most grateful letter from Mr. Main in answer.

Next, he had behaved, he thought, with singular resolution in the affairs of Gladys. He had had a line from Father Hilary, telling him of course exactly what he expected, that there was no other course open to a Catholic; and he had then sent off his previously drafted letter to Gladys herself — full of the most beautiful sentiments. In this he had drawn a fine picture of his own grief — a grief, he had remarked, which was doubled by the thought of the sorrow he must be giving. (He had, actually, said this!) He had referred to sacrifices which others had been forced to make in the same cause of religion; and hoped that Gladys herself, too, would rise to the occasion. (He did not put it quite like this; but these were the sentiments he conveyed.) Finally, he said that he was quite certain that they must not meet again — "it was better so . . . no good could be served" . . . Only distress could be caused; and he had ended with further expressions of grief and of his own desolate heart.

The letter, then, was entirely correct from a logical and intellectual point of view. Every word of it, and, more, every argument was perfectly defensible. A man who really had Catholic principles could not possibly act otherwise, nor justify his act more completely.

It was now thirty-six hours since the letter had been dispatched; and no answer had come from Gladys; although it should have come if she had replied by the next post.

(2)

It was a charming morning as Percy strolled out in the middle of it into the big gardens to the northeast.

These were as severe and formal as the house they adorned. A huge lawn, with two or three groups of cedars, ran along the whole side of the house from the edge of the carriage drive to beyond the laundry — a small temple-like building tucked away amongst shrubs — and was bounded by a paved terrace; this again led down by a couple of spacious openings to a further long strip of shaven turf, bounded again by a low wall. And, from the whole, the park sank away in rich slopes to the village and the high-road.

It was up and down this lower strip of lawn that Percy was pacing when Helen and Mabel came upon him.

He looked all that he should. The little mistakes of dress — so indefinable, yet so evident — with which he had begun his high-life, were all smoothed away. His clothes no longer looked too new or too careful. He had dropped his beautiful waistcoat and wore a proper Norfolk jacket instead, suitable to his years. Its belt was unbuttoned, and he carried his hands in his knickerbockers pockets; he wore nice low, strong shoes with leather fringes coming out of them. Here, then, in the spring sunlight, with his pleasant boyish face and bright eyes, his smooth complexion, and his curly hair, hatless, wearing as he did just now a little air of melancholy — he really looked very well indeed. He resembled a gentleman in every possible detail.

"Hullo!" said Helen over the wall.

Percy turned. Then he saw Mabel's little triangular smiling face under a big hat. He smiled back.

"You're over early," he said. "What's up?"

"Oh! Five-thousand things," said Mabel.

Percy knew precisely the kind of things she meant — all the innumerable small affairs that girls work up together — things like the decorations of churches, or poker-work, or the dressing of charity-dolls, or mysterious confidences, or exchanges of literary efforts — all the indefinable crop of business and secrets that make their appearance when two girls become friends. Mabel came over pretty often now; sometimes she stayed to lunch, and sometimes not.

"I want you to look after her for a bit," said Helen. "I've got to see Mrs. Bennett."

"I shall be delighted," said Percy. "Come and walk along here, Miss Marridon; the grass is quite dry."

"I'll be back in five or ten minutes," said Helen. "Or a quarter of an hour at the latest."

Percy had reached now, he thought, that pleasant stage of intimacy in which one can be abrupt. He said nothing for four or five paces. Then he began.

"I've been thinking about what you said over at Cleever. Do you really think that, Miss Marridon?"

Mabel looked startled.

"About what?" she asked, "I forget."

"About . . . about the Colonel, you know; and his religion."

"Oh, yes! . . . of course I do, Mr. Brandreth-Smith. It's only that in his case he doesn't put his religion forward at all."

"A man came to see me the other day," said Percy pensively. "He was the curate in our old home at Hanstead. Well; he's become a Roman Catholic; and he's having a fearfully hard time."

Mabel sniffed delicately.

"Don't you . . . don't you think that's rather fine?" asked Percy tentatively. "He's lost everything and gained nothing, you know. His wife gives him an awful time, I expect."

"And has she lost everything too?"

"Why, yes; her position and so on, of course. They're in lodgings somewhere."

"I think it's extraordinarily selfish of him," said Mabel deliberately. "You don't really think it's fine of him, do you?" (She began to grow excited.) "Just because he thought he'd like to change his religion, he's . . . he's sacrificed his wife and all her happiness. What did he marry her for, if he couldn't keep his word to her better than that?"

"His word?"

"Yes; his promises, and all that she expected too! What right has he to do that? . . . Mr. Brandreth-Smith, you can't really think that's fine of him . . . do you? Why should he think about himself, more than about her?"

He had never seen her so serious and excited before. Her eyes had grown quite grave, and her face worked a little. She resembled a kitten that suddenly behaves like a cat; he said nothing for a few seconds. He was really surprised. He did not know her as Helen did.

Mabel was of that quite distinct and recognizable class, that on the subject of the Church of Rome, and on that only, becomes very nearly fanatical. Largely it was her education, and the influence of her father, who, with tolerably loose views on the subject of works, was very Evangelical indeed upon that of faith; and partly, to her very individualistic temperament, the idea of religious obedience was absolutely distasteful. Catholicism, then, to her, was the single subject for which nothing could be said. Religion, to her, was almost everything that Catholicism was not. But she was quite sincere too in her arguments just now, and entirely unaware that she was moved by prejudice. It seemed to her, honestly and genuinely, that a religion that could not take the second place — as in poor Mr. Main's case — was simply not religion at all. It was exactly unchristian. And her knowledge of Percy's own position gave her a deliberate and pointed force in all that she said.

"But," Percy began, a little uneasy that something was wrong, "it seems to me that if a person's conscience tells him a certain religion is true, he's bound to follow it whatever happens."

"But how can a religion be true — how can he even think it true, if it makes him cruel to his wife? That's not Christianity!"

Percy was silent.

His mind was revolving vehemently. At one instant there came on him a violent impulse to tell her everything — everything, at least, with regard to his religious views. (He did not propose to tell even her about Gladys) Then a no less violent impulse swayed him to do nothing of the kind. After all, why should he lower himself in her eyes?

He did not forget how she had compared a conversion to Catholicism with marrying an actress. . . . Well, at any rate, he had not done the second.

So he compromised, once more.

"Miss Marridon," he said, "do tell me what you mean by religion . . . I . . . I really want to know."

She turned her face on him, and an odd startled look, almost shy, took the place of the little glow that had been in her eyes just now.

"Yes; do tell me," he said. "I really mean it."

"But . . . but how can I say it all in a minute or two? I really —"

"I don't mean exactly everything you believe. But . . . but the whole thing."

She drew a breath, as they moved on again over the noiseless grass.

(3)

"So there you are," cried Helen, ten minutes later. "I'm fearfully sorry for being so late."

Mabel was beside her almost before she had finished speaking. It had been a very intimate conversation indeed; and the reaction had come.

"Yes, my dear, you are late. We shan't have time —"

"You must stay to lunch. Come along. Goodbye, Percy."

Percy nodded; and as the two disappeared behind the low wall, was in time to catch a quick glance from the girl he had talked to so long. The glance certainly seemed eloquent; but he could not have put into words — scarcely into thought — exactly what it signified. It seemed to mean a great deal more than it possibly could.

For a minute or two, as he continued to walk up and down, he could think of nothing except of the girl herself. Indeed, she had revealed herself, it seemed to him, as never before. Up to the present they had talked purely on the tops of things; there had been plenty of *camaraderie,* and sympathy, and mutual understanding and all the rest of it; but it had been as if they had played at ball, catching and tossing, swiftly and easily. Now they had dropped the ball and come together.

A very real and vivid person, he thought, had been revealed to him; sane, cool, comforting, yet curiously stimu-

lating. As she had talked, more and more had her pleasant conventionalities dropped from her, and her intimate
self emerged. Her eyes had grown large and serious, and
even eloquent; she had talked with little quick gestures of
her hands, glancing at him — it seemed — as if unconscious of everything except her subject. He was nearer to
her, he knew now, than ever before. And once more he assured himself that all this was "quite different" from any
previous experience of his.

Then, presently, as though lit still by her presence, the
extraordinary sanity of her Gospel (as he thought) began
to fascinate him. . . .

She had not, naturally, touched on dogma. Dogma had
practically no place in her Gospel at all, except perhaps
subconsciously, far away down, in mysteries. Her religion
rather consisted in an Attitude — an attitude, primarily,
to her neighbor. One must be good to people, she said;
kindly and charitable; that was the First Great Commandment of the Law; and, compared with this, all else
was secondary. After all (she had asked in effect), what do
we *really* know of anything except that? Of course Christianity was true — no reasonable person denied that —
and one must repeat the Creed and go to church; and
there was heaven no doubt, to which (as a matter of private opinion) she held that everyone would go some time.
But these things were, so to speak, extras; or, at least,
they were not one's first business. One's first business,
one's real religion, was to perform the duties of one's station; one must be good, of course, too; and one must be
kind and pleasant. And anything that interfered with
this, she had argued (with a memory of poor Mr. Main,
and of other circumstances too, within her knowledge),
could not possibly be right or true — was not, in fact,
Christianity.

This, roughly speaking, was the Gospel she had
preached just now, with her quick little gestures and her
bright grave eyes. And her sincerity had been undoubted.
That had been a tremendous point in her favor. She appeared really to care; and to find inspiration in such a
faith.

Now Percy knew perfectly well that the scheme was open to a number of criticisms. He was perfectly aware that it did not rest on anything but an individualistic point of view, quite natural indeed in a properly brought up person, and yet not seriously defensible. But he would not formulate these criticisms. He just regarded it, and it seemed wonderfully attractive.

In a word then, he saw the two Ideas of Christianity which were still within his choice. There was first Catholicism — that large, definite, coherent scheme of which he knew quite enough to understand its coherence. . . . Yet here, in this morning sunlight, on this rich lawn, shadowed by the great house that was his home, in these smooth circumstances, all colored as they were by ten thousand tints and shades — to him, soothed now and tamed, as it were, by the alluring facts of his life and his money and his future, surrounded by a hundred suggestions, where all was rounded off and complete, where every wheel was oiled — against this background, to him still glowing from the intimacy of this delightful girl, whose very talking with him, flattered and excited him — to such a person, in such circumstances, the Idea of Catholicism, with its peremptory orders, its clear-cut statements, its rigidity and its demands, loomed out as something forbidding and unlovable.

Then again, too, working upon him underground with a force he never suspected, was the patient, untiring plan that his mother had pursued ever since they had first come to Marston. It was astonishing how subtly she had worked — how, in point after point, she had given him to understand that Catholicism was not at all wicked (for that would have stimulated him), but not quite well-bred; that it was in slightly bad taste; that it would be a handicap to him all his life. And there was not a soul near him to help him the other way. His father and sister, the Rector and his nice wife, the very servants of the place — all these people formed a kind of group from which he appeared to himself interiorly excluded. He remembered a sentence that the ex-priest had uttered months ago, about the Church being the enemy of domestic ties. For an instant, even now, he recoiled at the memory of that man, yet half its horror was gone. Besides, even though the man did have a disagreeable personality, his words might be reasonable enough. Surely there was something inhuman in the Catholic demands!

And, on the other hand, the Gospel he had just heard seemed precisely suited to his life, and even to have in it a certain inspiration. If men really lived up to it, what more could be wanted; if all men were kind and charitable, and went to church and didn't bother much about dogma, would not the victory of Christianity be, after all, complete? What need was there, after all, to drag in the gaunt structure of Catholicism across this smooth and pleasant countryside? The one was reasonable, suitable and quiet; the other was arresting, inharmonious and hard. What was there, after all, in the intellectual completeness of Catholicism, that it should necessarily be preferred to the moral and human completeness of the Gospel according to Mabel? . . . .

And Helen, when the two had got out of earshot of the terrace, had turned to her friend with a dancing light in her eyes.

"Well; did you rub it in?" she said; "as Mother asked you?"

"I told him exactly what I thought," said Mabel.

(4)

"I want to speak to you an instant, Percy," said his mother after lunch a couple of days later.

He followed her listlessly into the little morning room that opened out of the drawing room where Mabel and his sister were again over their coffee.

"Your father's caught a chill again, as you know. It's too tiresome. And the doctor told me just before lunch that he must take much more care than he did last time."

"I'm sorry," said the boy, still with that dreamy air, as he sat down in the window recess.

"Well, there it is; and the Rector's dreadfully upset, because of the bazaar, you know, on Easter Monday."

Percy looked up quickly.

"I'm to open it, you know," she went on. "But who's to do the speaking? . . . Percy?"

His heart was beginning to beat a little.

"Yes?" he said.

"I wish you'd do it instead of him," she said abruptly. "I heard how well you spoke at the Servants' Ball . . . and . . . and you know the bazaar's for the Church certainly, for a new lectern the Rector wants and . . . and a stove for the vestry. But I don't see that need stop you. It's . . . it's for the place as a whole you know. And it's so important that we should be well-represented there; and so I thought —"

Percy moved his head abruptly; and she stopped. Then she began again, with an oddly mingled air of authority and complaint. She talked about "unreasonable prejudice," "narrow mindedness," "the good Rector," a "position in the county."

But Percy scarcely seemed to hear her. His pleasant, bright eyes, a little melancholy, now were resting on the far-off blue hills beyond the rich rolling slopes of the great park.

"All right, Mother," he said quietly, as she stopped at last. "I'll speak if you like."

Chapter XI

(1)

Down here in this side street of Kensington, one might almost think oneself in some country town except for the low steady murmur, as of a rolling sea, that beat in ceaselessly from the High Street a hundred yards away. Here, strangely enough, the principal traffic was on Sundays, when Father Hilary preached; the roadway seethed with vehicles; but on this Friday evening in June it was empty enough.

A rather shabby figure in a readymade suit and soft hat came briskly down the turn from the High Street, swinging a stick. He pulled out his watch as he came, and pursed his lips to look at it. Then he put it back and came on.

The church was nearly empty as he turned into it. There were scarcely half a dozen people there — dark motionless figures — motionless as Catholics usually are in the presence of their God; and content, it seemed, to sit there in the half-dark church, without book or beads, regarding the pale sanctuary and the little leaping light in the red glass.

Except for the curious sounds echoing from the gallery near the high altar — sounds of many male voices alternating with one, on a rapid monotone, the whole place had an air of being out of the world altogether, in some strange parenthesis, outside of which considerations of time and place clamored in vain. And even the rapid chanting from the gallery, and the single bright loophole in it that slashed the darkness, seemed, after a while, elements in this air of apartness. For these sounds too, as the friars recited their office, appeared as if on a different plane altogether from ordinary voices and ordinary music; they had nothing whatever in common, for example, (except their physical laws), with such compositions as Dr. Gadsby's Service in C. . . .

The shabby figure turned into a seat by a pillar and presently, as the church darkened yet more, faded into its background.

(2)

It seemed to Mr. Main, as he sat here, that God was being extraordinarily good to him after all; and it was this
thought that was chiefly projected by him in thanksgiving
against the remote background of this place.

Two particular points stood out as supreme instances of
the Divine Mercy — the first that his money was not yet
wholly exhausted, so that he had not been obliged, up to
the present, to use any of his wife's; and the second that
the letter had come from the cocoa firm in the City, that
very afternoon, bidding him present himself on Monday
morning as an accepted aspirant to the post of Commercial Traveler.

It seemed to Mr. Main very nearly miraculous that
these two things had so fitted one into the other. He had
made more than one Novena for this very intention, and
now, actually upon the ninth day of his last Novena it had
been accomplished. He need fear nothing further now; the
one supreme dread that he would be forced to throw himself, not merely upon his wife's mercy (for that might very
well be a humiliation demanded of him), but upon the
money gained by the publication of a book of which he did
not approve — this dread was forever removed.

Henceforth he would earn his own living, and would be
able, even, if he were at all successful, to lay a little by in
case of illness or unemployment.

So he had come here to tell Father Hilary of God's marvelous mercy to him.

Meanwhile the time and the place and the strange
chanting and Mr. Main's own soul conspired together in a
stream of thought that ran through Mr. Main's mind.

He saw now, he thought, as never before, how "all
things work together for good" if one will but trust God.
Here was he, who had flung himself and his wife upon the
world six months ago, with no provision but the very
smallest, rescued now and set upon the rock. His education had been useless to him; a grounding at a grammar
school in Latin grammar, arithmetic, a little history, and
a little geography, followed by two years in a provincial
University, followed again by one year's instruction in the
History of the Prayer Book, Waterland on the Eucharist,

the first three hundred and fifty years of Church history, with some commentaries on the Bible and the Thirty-Nine Articles — this course of erudition was not calculated to lay the foundations of a fortune. Neither does a little experience as a curate in suburban parishes very considerably brighten the prospect.

It was with these weapons then that he had faced the world six months ago. Yet here he was now, secured at least for the present against starvation, and in the employment of a thoroughly sound and reputable firm. . . Mr. Main's cup seemed overflowing. . . .

After a while he began to regard other figures of his world; and these seemed to him scarcely real. It was perfectly true that his late Vicar and Mrs. Bennett were persons on whom another kind of prosperity had fallen in floods of blessing; but this bleak-faced man's mood was such that, at present, at any rate, envy no more presented itself to him in their regard, than with regard to the King of England; they were as creatures of another world than this; they had principles, and possessed talents, which, as the country was constituted just now, were almost certain to win such success as they enjoyed . It seemed to him, in a strange sort of way, entirely right and proper that these strenuous and sincere people should live in a Rectory and have a well- warmed church and strong patrons and a more or less submissive congregation of tenants and dependents. It was part of their life. And, in the same kind of manner too, it had begun to seem to him that a converted curate who happened to have no particular gifts — (and Mr. Main was getting quite clear on this point) — should almost necessarily receive snubs and live in dingy lodgings; it almost seemed natural to him that he should have such a wife as Marion. These things were part of his bargain, as Mr. Bennett's Rectory was part of his.

So, too, when he looked generally back upon Hanstead, with its mayor and its pump and Mr. Barnes the undertaker and its parish personages — these figures appeared to him as if seen through a telescope; they moved in their appointed courses, and enjoyed the prosperity proper to their case. But he could no more, just now, regret or envy that life than he could regret his childhood. The thing was passed, for him, inevitably.

For his astonishing good fortune intoxicated him (if Mr. Main's exalted moods could ever be called by that name). After all, was he not a Commercial Traveler, with all traveling expenses paid, a minimum of thirty shillings a week, and possibilities in the way of Commissions? . . . And he was a Catholic, too. . . .

He bowed his head again upon his hands presently; and a fragment of an old psalm came to his lips.

"We went through fire and water; and Thou hast brought us out into a wealthy place."

(3)

"Well!" said Father Hilary, ten minutes later in the parlor, smiling as usual, "what news now, Mr. Main?"

Mr. Main put his hat and stick carefully down on the little table. He too was smiling as hard as he could, which meant that his solemn mouth widened like a gash in his face, while his kind short-sighted eyes looked as usual.

"My dear Father," he said as he too sat down, "the best of news. I am successful at last."

"Well? In what way?"

"You remember I told you I had been to young Mr. Brandreth-Smith — and how kind he was, not only in writing for me, but actually in getting his father to write?"

Father Hilary nodded. He knew now that Mr. Main must not be hurried; he must be allowed to lay down all the preliminaries and circumstances as if he were to preach a sermon — say on the life and character of Ahab.

"Well!" continued the other, now solemn and judicial, "I went to the firm in question — the firm of Martenson and Cabell — and saw one of the partners — Mr. Cabell, in fact. He was very kind, though a little impatient, I thought, once or twice. Well; he asked me a number of questions; in fact I had to fill up a paper. . . ."

So it proceeded. Every detail must be related; the arrival of further papers, a request for guarantors; and then the silence that followed. It must have been nearly five minutes before the crucial fact was announced; and the letter that proclaimed it spread before the priest.

"That, Father," said the other, "arrived this afternoon. And I am to enter upon my duties on Monday."

The priest read it through, returned it, and held out his hand.

"I congratulate you, Mr. Main, with all my heart."

And he saw the tears in the convert's eyes, and the broad gash-like smile upon his lips. Mr. Main was very deeply moved indeed.

The priest had learned by now an extraordinary respect for this man. He had found him a trifle slow, at first, and had even been guilty of what he would have called interior impatience; the proselyte had been so excessively conscientious, so very exact and so very deferential. And then, little by little, the priest, accustomed to deal with men, had begun to understand. . . .

First he had perceived the almost startling absence of what are usually called Gifts; and had understood one set of reasons, at any rate, for the singular failure that Mr. Main appeared to have made of his life. Never once had the proselyte appealed for pity; in fact the other had seen that pity would have been thought almost an insult, and certainly uncalled for. And next he had perceived that the amazing insuccess of Mr. Main as a clergyman really and truly had nothing whatever to do with his change of faith. He did not wish to become a Catholic in order to make a better job of his earthly life; in fact he seemed with astonishing complacency to take his ignominies in clerical life as the normal and usual accompaniment of such a life. Nothing whatever had influenced Mr. Main's movement except the conviction, built perhaps originally on somewhat incoherent grounds, that the Church of Rome was right and the Church of England wrong.

And then respect had grown into admiration. Not only had this elder man submitted to the teaching of the younger, as a child to his father; but he had submitted too with the same unquestioning acceptance to the circumstances of his life. He had not complained; he had just related these circumstances so far as was necessary. . . . The peculiarly disagreeable attributes of the wife to whom he was bound; the poky lodgings; the snubs and the disappointments — these had been discerned by the priest as shadows moving among Mr. Main's careful little sentences.

The man appeared to him with at least some of the characteristics of the saint. He was very slow, quite stupid, utterly conscientious and unquestioningly patient. And it was necessary therefore to be very careful in talking to him.

(4)

"And there's another thing," said Mr. Main when the proper congratulations had been given and received — "another thing just a little on my conscience. I . . . I daresay it's not my business at all; and in any case, Father" — (he lifted solemn eyes to the priest's face) — "in any case I do not wish even to appear to pry into what I should not. If I should seem to do so, kindly do not answer me at all; and I will promise to draw no conclusions. Or, better still, just tell me to mind my own business."

Father Hilary bowed as solemnly in return.

"But I do not think there is any likelihood —" he began.

Mr. Main lifted a lean hand with a clerical gravity.

"Wait till you have heard me, Father," he said. "It concerns young Mr. Brandreth-Smith."

"Yes?" said the priest, without a movement.

"I have heard very unhappy rumors about that young man — that . . . that he has given up all idea of becoming a Catholic. Well; I had better say outright that it was my wife that informed me. She also informs me that . . . that he has engaged himself to be married to a young lady of his neighborhood."

The priest made a quick movement. But again the long hand checked him.

"Wait till you have heard me out, Father; and then say what you think proper. Now I do not ask with any motive but this. I have known him for a considerable time; I think I may say that I had a little influence with him; and . . . and I think he regards me with feelings of kindness. If those things are true, Father; and I may say that they have worried me more than a little, I have been wondering whether you would think it my duty to write to him, or even to go and see him."

Father Hilary drew a sudden breath. To put it gently, —
he did not think it likely that Mr. Main was quite the man
to be of service. But he did not say so; he waited.

"I will abide by your decision entirely, Father, I need
hardly say. If you tell me no, I will take that simply to
mean that I need do nothing. I shall not draw any conclusions at all as to whether or no the reports are true. I
shall simply put them out of my mind — that is unless
you wish me to know the facts so far as you may happen
to know them yourself."

He had finished. That was clear. There was an air in his
tone as of a peroration concluded. He now waited for orders.

The priest sighed and sat back.

"I think you have been most discreet, Mr. Main," he
said, "in the way you have put things. Nothing could be
more delicate." (It was necessary to say things to Mr.
Main, he had learned, which with other people might be
taken for granted.) "And I will tell you all that I know —
all, that is —" (he corrected himself), "that I am at liberty
to tell. I tell you," he proceeded carefully to explain, "first
that you may know what you ought to know, when these
stories are referred to; and next that you may give him
the benefit of your prayers. I am sure that attempting to
write to him or see him, would be useless."

He paused; and Mr. Main gravely assented with a
movement of his head.

"Let me see — it is June now. Then it was over four
months ago that I had a letter from Mr. Smith which, I
thought at the time, did him a good deal of credit." (He
paused; then he went on briskly.) "Yes, I think I am
bound to say that we must take that letter to have been to
his credit. It appeared to show that he was willing to
make a great sacrifice for his faith. I mustn't say any
more about that. The contents of the letter were very private. But I feel it's only just to him to tell you so much.

"Well, then; oddly enough, ever since that time I have
never once seen him. I wrote to him twice, reminding him
of his instructions; but it seemed that he always was too
much engaged. That made me uncomfortable. I wrote to
the priest in whose district Marston stands; but I found

from him that Mr. Smith had never once been to see him,
and that he — the priest — scarcely liked to call under
those circumstances. (I am bound to say that he lives six
miles away, so perhaps it was natural that they hadn't
met.)

"Well; I wrote to the young man once more — a week
later; and last week only I had an answer. I am sorry to
say that it corroborated the first part of the rumor you
speak of. In it, he tells me that he does not propose to continue his instructions; and that he finds — let me see —
that he finds it was only emotionalism that brought him
to me in the first instance."

Mr. Main was motionless. Then he spoke, still without
moving.

"You think that was true, Father?"

"I am quite certain it is not true," said the friar quietly.
"And I do not think that he thinks it true either. But of
course I may be wronging him."

"Thank you, Father. I . . . I will do as you say."

"There's one thing more," said the priest. "I don't know
whether you know young Ballard, who was a great friend
of his last year? Well; I asked after him from young Ballard, who is an acolyte here; and I find that he has heard
nothing whatever from his friend. He went with him to
the theater once; and since then has heard nothing. I
think he is a little hurt, you know. They were great
friends. But I hear that Mr. Smith is with his family in
London, now. As regards the engagement you speak of, I
have heard nothing of it. But I should not be likely to, you
see, under the circumstances."

Mr. Main gravely inclined his head. His face was very
grave and judicial, and his lips a little pursed.

"Thank you for your confidence, Father. I shall now
know what to think."

In this manner, then, sat and talked these two persons
of no importance; — the young friar of no birth or position
at all — a popular preacher, indeed, just for the present,
but that would not last long; and this failure of an Anglican curate, an uncomfortably angular man, who was
proud and pleased to be a traveler in cocoa. So they sat
and discussed, without any sense of proportion, a young

man of wealth and position, about whom the world had ranged itself very happily indeed. But people in ignoble circumstances never do have any sense of proportion, or of their own impertinence.

Chapter XII

(1)

Outside the house it seemed as if Nature as well as Art had done her utmost to make the great day a success. It was not yet ten o'clock; and the full August heat had not reached its zenith; yet even now, above the terrace where the chairs stood ready, and the little tables and the bandstand, amongst which buzzed earnest men in black trousers and green baize aprons, the air shook and shimmered from the refracted light. The beds between the cedar trees were one blaze of radiance; the tall trees themselves reared against the burning sky heads that were at the very height of luxuriant green; birds skimmed from shrubbery to shrubbery, at present undisturbed, gathering their last meal before the midday siesta, and before, too — if they had but known it — the invasion of the entire County into their wide domains.

Art too — at least that form of Art which can be provided by a wholesale London decorator — had done her utmost. Large striped tents, with canvas doors at present hooked back, enclosed the edges of the lawn at either end, and hung out drooping flags from their pairs of poles. From the eastern door of the great house ran already a strip of carpet, and other cylindrical bundles awaited their unrolling. Across the gardens too, where, like dignified though not very wealthy relations, lay the church and rectory embowered in trees, rose a flag post from which hung the standard of St. George — ("Which, one must always remember," said the Rector, "is the proper flag for England"); and about the lych gate,[1] through which the Family proceeded to church on Sundays, appeared other strips and streamers of bunting.

It was a scene of extraordinary opulence and prosperity, and even of beauty. There is nothing in the whole world which so combines to produce the appearance of these things, as a really first-rate English country house. When

---

[1] A gateway covered with a roof typically found in English country churchyards.

such a place as Marston, then, lays herself out to be
splendid — when beneath an August sky, cloudless from
horizon to horizon, and behind the bunting and the carpet
and the chairs and the bandstand and the tents, there
stands a glorious Georgian mansion that is the very last
word in classicism — a place of shallow steps and Greek
columns and circular windows and curved balustrades —
all entirely perfect of their kind; when absolutely no expense has been spared, and its mistress is a dominant
woman of large ideas who will have things her own way
— when all these powers conspire together, the effect is
indescribably great.

Within, too, the house promised at least an equal glory.
Doors stood open, and busy persons hurried through them
in all directions; banked about the foot of the great curv-
ing staircase were positive shrubberies of flowering
bushes; chairs stood in pairs, one on the top of the other
in ranks and battalions — presently to be grouped suitably — in every space of the great hall that was not a thoroughfare; a sound of footsteps and talking came through
the open doors of the drawing room where the furniture
was being arranged for the reception of a big crowd. And
upon all this looked down the solemn gigantic portraits of
dead and gone Brandreths, watching it seemed these tremendous preparations for the wedding festivities of their
present heir.

(2)

In the morning room, resembling Napoleon on the eve of
a battle in which his victory is predestined, sat Mrs.
Brandreth-Smith herself, with Mrs. Bennett, who rashly
adventuring herself here on an errand from the Rectory
was ordered to remain, while a man took the message
back to the Rector.

"My dear, I positively must insist on your remaining.
Helen is useless to me, and I was forced to let her go over
to Cleever last night; and there is not a soul who under-
stands anything here except myself. I was really ashamed
at breakfast; it was no better than a picnic. Underhill has
completely lost his head."

So here sat meek and helpful Mrs. Bennett, distracted
with the thought of what her husband would do without

her, yet unable to resist. For she too, like all the world, like the poor Major himself, now struggling into the prescribed white spats, with a buttonhook, overhead — (he had received some species of a commission in some auxiliary force of His Majesty's dominions last month) — like Underhill, and the Rector, and the gamekeepers and the schoolmistress — she too had capitulated to the masterful adequacy of the great lady, and now revolved round her like a planet about a central sun. The Rectory must look after itself for the present; she must sit here and be talked to. For Mrs. Brandreth-Smith, like a true strategist, had perceived that she herself must be a fixed point. Presently she would make a Progress through house and gardens; but just now it was essential that everyone must know where to find her. So she sat here, and discoursed, with a roving eye, interrupting herself to deliver distinct answers to all who came for direction.

Her successes had, indeed, been extraordinary. She had not made a single mistake in the complicated processes of taking her place in the County. Her instincts had been as unerring in all things as in, for example, the case of the Matthieson-Howleys, who had abandoned the Nook three months ago in despair and fled to hide themselves again in the crowds of London. For instance, it was she who had decided that her husband must not undertake the Harriers (since he was still but imperfectly acquainted with the art of riding), but must subscribe largely instead; she who had fixed the number of pheasants to be reared; she who had maneuvered the coming of the Flower Show to Marston, on which occasion with brilliant delicacy of intuition, she had selected for the presenting of the prizes the very lady who had hoped to have the Show at her own house, thus completely satisfying everybody. She had not made a mistake; more, she had not neglected an opportunity; and her reward was come, in the supreme achievement of having planned, conducted and concluded the engagement between her only son and Lord Marridon's only daughter.

Of course the swiftness of it all was the sign of her genius. Many mothers could have managed the business ultimately, under the circumstances, but few in so short a time. It was not a year since they had come to the place.

Mabel, of course, was by no means a supreme matrimonial prize; her father was not particularly wealthy, and practically the whole estate would pass to his son. But in every other respect she was desirable She was an Honorable; she was quite pretty; she was very good; she was socially quite first-rate; she was thoroughly well-known in the neighborhood. It was good enough for Mrs. Brandreth-Smith.

Her handling of the reins, of course, cannot adequately be described here. It is enough to say that it had to be very delicate. For, first there was Percy to drive; and when one reflects on Percy as he was nine months ago, her adroitness is evident. First, he had to be taught how to carry himself, how to dress, how to shoot, how to ride, how to dance — even how to think — how, in a word, to get rid of the Old Man of the City and how to put on the New Man of the County. She had done this quite perfectly — seldom by a direct touch of the whip. Of course he had been trainable, yet it was none the less credit to the trainer. Next there was the matter of his religion — his regrettable tendency to Romanism; and in the managing of this more, perhaps, might be set down to the pliability of Percy than to his actual handling by his mother. Yet she had been very adroit; she had surrounded him by suggestion; she had made it just a little inconvenient (but not more than a little) for him to go up to see his priest; she had soothed and comforted him with luxury; she had never once abused his faith; yet she had instilled into his atmosphere on every possible occasion a continual stream of the most delicate and tactful hints that his proposed religion would be a real drawback in the future. Lastly, and supremely, she had actually employed Mabel herself in the business, thus accomplishing two strokes in one — she had thrown the two together upon intimate lines — (since spiritual flirtations are the most promising of all) — and had, simultaneously, put her own views through lips which were more likely to prevail than her own. It was Percy's responsiveness that had done the rest.

The matter of Mabel had been far easier. First, the lady had encouraged Helen's friendship with her in every possible way; then she had hinted to Helen her future hopes

— again more by suggestion than direct statement; then she asked Mabel over on every occasion when Percy would be likely to see much of her, and had praised her emphatically in her absence. All this she did, long before Mabel knew the story of Percy's unhappy religious entanglement. Certainly it is the horses that pull the carriage along; no amount of skilful handling of the reins and whip can take the place of the flesh and blood between the shafts. Yet the most ardent flesh and blood in the world will not pull the carriage safely and swiftly through crowded traffic unless there is a competent driver upon the box. Percy and Mabel both thought that it was themselves who had arranged the marriage and talked over their respective parents. Mrs. Brandreth-Smith knew better. She had squared Lord Marridon frankly and straightforwardly by the generosity of her proposals with regard to the settlements she would make upon the pair, if the marriage took place at once.

"And why should they wait, after all?" she had asked pathetically. "I'm sure they know their own minds — the dears!"

(3)

She was deploring presently the one single shadow on all this sunshine.

"Such a pity," she said, "about her poor brother! I had hoped he would be best man."

"Have they heard anything for certain yet?" asked Mrs. Bennett, who like so many very good people, took a strange interest in iniquity.

"Simply that he's gone with this woman abroad — an actress, you know. She was making quite a name for herself, I hear, on the stage, and was actually on the eve of sailing for America — Miss Farham, you know."

"They're not married then?" asked Mrs. Bennett softly.

Mrs. Brandreth-Smith shook her head lamentably; but her lips were tight and severe.

"They don't know —" she said. "It may be so. It may not. They've been gone five or six months now. They were last heard of in Italy. They must be simply living on moneylenders. It's terribly sad in any case. Not even here at his sister's wedding I . . . (She broke off to issue an order.)

"No, Charles, I distinctly told Underhill *not* to take the Persian carpet from the landing. He must find something else. . . .

"Well, and so Percy's got young Blakenham as his best man. I am only thankful that he didn't want that young clerk — Ballard, I think his name was. But he never even suggested him. . . . Percy is really behaving very well indeed."

"And he's very happy?" asked Mrs. Bennett in her soft voice.

"My dear; of course he is. . . ."

("Please, Madam, Hubbard has sent up to know whether the landau or the brougham is to come to the door first."

"The brougham — I said so distinctly.")

"And they get to Como tomorrow night," mused Mrs. Bennett romantically.

(4)

And as for Percy as he stood regarding himself, for the last time as a bachelor, in the tall mirror of his walnut wardrobe upstairs — regarding his patent-leather boots and white spats, his silky-looking gray trousers, his white waistcoat, his exquisite frockcoat, his lilac tie, his boyish face and curly black hair — who shall say all that he thought?

The mind of an average man — above all when he is scarcely more than just a man — is all but infinitely complex. Yet if there is one thing that rises dominant and rigid out of the myriad motives and desires and faculties that twine and intertwine beneath, it is the power of an astounding self-deception.

For, since Percy was just now quite content and intensely excited, it is practically certain that he believed himself to have acted quite properly during the last year. Certainly he had made mistakes — in fact two — yet even these had been sincerely made. One was when he had determined to be a Catholic, and the other when he had asked Gladys Farham to marry him.

These mistakes he had hastened to set right. As regards the second of the two he had practically no scruples at all. He had acted, he believed, resolutely and bravely, and even kindly. From the point of view at which at that time he had stood, he could have done nothing else. Had not Father Hilary told him so? And had not the appalling escapade of Gladys since that date abundantly showed him how right, even from the human point of view, his instinct had been?

And, as regards the first of his mistakes, which he had last remedied; on that, too, he had no scruples. He thought he saw himself now, like a little mad figure (as he looked back) — emotional, inexperienced and boyish. It was the knowledge of life, he thought, that had taught him better. Certainly it was a remarkable fall of the dice that had caused him to sacrifice Gladys for the sake of his faith; and then, quite tolerably soon afterwards, his faith for . . . well, for a Larger Life. Yet he was not responsible for that sequence. Surely a man, he had told himself, while he had still been a little uncomfortable about it all, four or five months ago — surely a man must take each step as it presents itself! One can only move one step at a time! . . . There was a hymn that said so, wasn't there?

But now he was content enough that all was as it should be. Those heart-storms of the past were over—those heavings of great waves that run out of the illimitable distances and toss the journeying craft to and fro, those great winds that blow where they list and come no man knows whence, and go again no man knows whither. And he had kept his head, he thought, during the tempest; at least, if he had lost it for a little, he had recovered it again, and let down his anchor and ridden out the swirl and the rush. If he had not — well, if he had not, even now he might still be driving before it, in the company of such mad souls as Father Hilary — (to think that he too once thought he would be a friar!) — or with poor narrow-minded Mr. Main who actually preferred to be a Commercial Traveler than a curate! — or with Reggie Ballard, clerk and acolyte, who lived at Wimbledon, and went to the City every day, and to St. Francis' every Sunday. (What a bounder poor Reggie was, by the way!)

He looked slowly round the room. There were the tall white-framed windows; the inlaid dressing table all set out with silver things; the wardrobes; the boot cupboard;

the thick black mat at the fireplace; the deep carpet. . . .
(By the way, he had forgotten his pencil case.)

He went to the little Japanese cabinet that stood on a
side table — (it was the one little thing he had brought
from his old bedroom at Hanstead) — and pulled open one
of the drawers. A bunch of keys, a pocketknife or two, a
pair of tiny tin candlesticks, from a Christmas tree,
smeared with drippings of pink wax, some coppers and
three or four other things were there. He pushed these
aside to find his pencil case, and, among them, a little
brass and black wood crucifix. But he did not notice it.

Well; surely all this was better. The comfort and the
wealth and the secured position — these were the elements of his life now — his responsibilities as a future
landowner, and as a husband, and a father — these were
the stars by which he must guide his course.

He was excited? Yes; and, naturally, and yet ironically
enough, too, it was the future that excited him. It seemed
to him that Life was going to begin — as his father had
solemnly and uncomfortably told him last night in the
smoking room. It did not even occur to him that possibly
Life was over; that he had had his chances and lost them.
On the contrary, he was quite convinced that they were
just opening out, really, for the first time.

His repeater struck like a tiny cathedral bell in his
pocket, as he moved back again towards the door. That
was eleven, he reflected; and his mother had told him to
be down by then.

So he opened the door and went slowly out.

Chapter XIII

(1)

The wedding was an entire success. It was at once a symbol and a transfiguration of what may be called County Life. The obedient tenants of the two estates formed a beribboned crowd that occupied the entire space between the two lych gates and the church porch; and the carriages and the motors in the road outside were four deep.

Within, the church was an almost perfect harmony of earth and heaven. Earth, so to speak, was composed of all the important people for twenty miles round as well as of a considerable little mob from London who traveled down in a special train; and Heaven was represented by Mr. Bennett in a shiningly clean surplice cut according to the real Old English pattern, white stole and Oxford hood, a choir that sang *Lead, Kindly Light*,[1] and an organ that appeared to consist chiefly of *Vox Humana* — or as young Mr. Blakenham humorously called it, *Nux Vomica*.[2]

The center of attention was, as might be expected, the bride and bridegroom. The bride looked entirely charming, coming in on her father's arm — (he also wore white spats, and, with his black crutched stick, made a very distinguished figure); and still more charming as she knelt with Percy at the chancel step. The sun shone in punctually as they knelt there, and clad them in radiant colors projected through the persons of Saint Simon and Saint Jude who, in an attitude of benediction, presided in the window by the pulpit. It shone also on the new brass tablet in the porch, that contained the list of all the Rectors of Marston from the very beginning.

---

[1] A famous hymn composed by Blessed John Henry Cardinal Newman, whose conversion to Catholicism in the early 19th century shocked the Anglican religious establishment.

[2] A drug distilled from the poisonous seeds of a tree found in Asia and Australia. No longer used, it was administered as a tonic dissolved in alcohol as a tincture in minute quantities for digestive problems. Larger doses cause convulsions and death.

The Rector delivered a characteristic and appropriate little address (a copy of which was handed in the vestry afterwards to the reporter of the *County Gazette,* from which journal, indeed, many of these details are drawn). His eyes were moist with honest pride and sincere emotion as he contemplated that member of his flock — now in full wedding-glory — who had caused him so much anxiety in the past; and he made to that past the most delicate little reference in the world.

"One must always remember," he said, "that the path of life is set about with rocks and hidden shoals; now it is the impetuous ardor of youth that beckons the traveler away, now it is some pointed shaft from without that finds entrance between the joints of his harness. Now it may be some passing fancy, now some intellectual fallacy, that beats upon the citadel of the young Churchman. But, no matter, brethren —" and so forth. The metaphors were mixed, but the meaning unmistakable; and to convey thought, after all, is the highest function of all language.

In short there was not a shadow on the scene, except that little patch of gloom to which reference has already been made. And even that was largely dispelled by the private communication made by Lord Marridon to the Major and to Colonel Maitland, in the vestry, between the blasts of the Wedding March, to the effect that after all at present there was really no reason to believe as yet the horrible rumor that Jim had actually married the girl. There was not a Christian who heard that reassuring little message on that day, who did not breathe the more easily for it. Of course it was very shocking, but anything was better than that Miss Farham should make an honest man of him.

But for that, then — and Jim's absence — all was perfect.

The bells played the melody of a hymn as a preface to the joy-peal — a melody, it is true, which required a B flat bell and did not get it; yet (as in the matter of the Rector's metaphors) the sentiment was unmistakable.

The crowds were indubitably loyal; and took full advantage of the Rector's indulgent concession, for once, to the use of confetti in the precincts of the churchyard; and the

procession, out to the brougham that was to conduct the
bridal pair up to the house, was a very hearty matter indeed.

So too, as the hours went by, until the final departure of
the newly-wedded couple at four o'clock, there was not a
hitch to trouble the hostess' mind. Underhill, though looking harassed, had recaptured his head, it seemed, to such
effect that he was explicitly congratulated by his mistress
next morning. The band played loudly; the ices did not
melt before their time; no one appeared hot or cross; the
Major moved about with a subdued air that appeared
completely well-bred and easy; Lord Marridon was gracious; Mrs. Brandreth-Smith actually held a kind of little
court all of her own in the morning room, with a successful sort of insolence that was its own justification; and at
four o'clock precisely her son stood, in a beautiful gray
suit, hat in hand, at the foot of the magnificent staircase,
with personages ranged about him at the proper distances, to await the descent of his bride.

Certainly he was a little excited; but no more than was
suitable. His complexion was still that of a boy, but his
eyes were those of a man, and he bore himself at once
resolutely and modestly. His Life was going to begin, it is
necessary to remember.

For he had gone through a considerable crisis; and had
emerged from it, victorious, precisely in that way which
probably every person present on that occasion would
heartily have applauded. He had had his emotions —
what boy does not have them? He had had his dreams of
austerity and Quixotism and honest human passion, and
had trodden them determinedly down. He had even fancied that Faith could be so great as to draw a man from
his father's house into a far country, not knowing whither
he went; and he had had the moral courage to remain at
home. He had learned that prudence was the higher form
of valor, if not actually its better part; and he had been
self-controlled enough, therefore, to write a letter for the
breaking of a girl's heart, instead of being weak enough to
face her and tell her the truth with his own lips.

Heaven therefore was rewarding him. Here he stood —
a prodigal who had done his repenting comfortably at

home — the heir of two houses and fifteen thousand a year, a reasonable, prudent, sensible young man, and the son-in-law of a peer.

And here came Mabel, delicious, triangular-faced, and bright-eyed, down the great staircase to join him. . . . She looked simply sweet.

(2)

But in London streets that day of August glory was turned to the breath of an oven. The pavements gave back that same heat — that makes country lawns and the shadow of cedars so delightful — flattened, dulled and oppressive. Long since, in the less-frequented thoroughfares, the morning freshness of the watercarts was gone up in vapor, and the dust lay heavy and stifling. Along the sunny side of every road, blinds were drawn, awnings were let down, and the laurels in the little iron-railed gardens shimmered as with leaves of painted steel; along the shadowed side every window was flung wide to let the baking heat escape, which, from long before noon, had soaked down relentlessly and ceaselessly from the gray heat-haze overhead.

It was along one of these streets in Chelsea that (just at the time that in far-away Marston, Percy stood, cool and smiling and modestly triumphant, waiting for the coming of his bride downstairs) there trudged, keeping in the shade so far as was possible, a hot and dusty figure in a readymade suit, hat in hand for the sake of coolness. The other hand carried a small shiny black bag.

He looked a little older, even, than he had looked two or three months before; because even two or three months of ceaseless journeying in local trains — (third-class to save the difference) — of carrying small tins of cocoa in a black bag, of ingratiating oneself with grocers and provision-dealers in arrogant little country towns and suburban districts — even three months of this life take the elasticity out of a man. His hair had retired a shade or two further back on his high temples; the lines at the corners of his mouth and eyes were a trifle deeper.

He did not look unhappy; but, undoubtedly, he looked resolute; for he was picturing the home to which every step brought him nearer. He would be there in a quarter of an hour now. . . . Marion, if she had awakened from her afternoon nap, or if she were not too much engrossed in proof-correcting, might perhaps be getting tea ready. Or she might not. One could never tell. At any rate, there would be Marion; and the hot little room, and the disused gas-chandeliers, and the dusty carpet and curtains, and the untidy table, and the smell of cabbage.

All this he was picturing to himself. Yet that was not all; for he was imagining, too, what would be the most tactful way of introducing the piece of news he brought with him. It was true that he carried in his pocketbook a written testimonial, bearing witness to his stainless probity, his perseverance, and his willingness. But he carried also in his memory the sentences to which he had listened that morning from the lips of the junior partner of Messrs. Martenson and Cabell.

"I'm afraid it's no good, Mr. Main. I haven't a word to say against your punctuality, or your zeal, or anything else of *that* kind. But, you know, it's a gift that's wanted, for the success of a traveler; and if a man hasn't got the gift — why he must just try something else. I'm very sorry, Mr. Main; indeed I am. But it's kinder to tell you straight out. . . .

"Then — at the end of the month, Mr. Main. . . ."

The End

Robert Hugh Benson Titles from Universal Values Media

A WINNOWING

Mixing such seemingly incongruous elements as social satire, near-slapstick, and obsession with death, *A Winnowing* flays Edwardian society in terms that bring to mind the comedy of P. G. Wodehouse, and the black humor of Evelyn Waugh.

ISBN 978-1-60210-005-3   224 pp. $20.00

NONE OTHER GODS

This gentle, yet profound satire relates the story of Frank Guiseley, a young man who drops out of college and tries to force God to instruct him personally on what God wants him to do. People of all faiths can appreciate the growing frustration and bafflement Frank experiences until he finally stops trying to make God listen to him, and starts listening to God.

ISBN 978-1-60210-006-0   312 pp. $20.00

THE COWARD

A young man is faced with challenges and manages to fail at every step. He becomes convinced he is an irredeemable coward, and only then begins to find courage. In a damning indictment of close-minded Edwardian society, a supreme act of courage on the young man's part is mistaken for yet one more craven act.

ISBN 978-1-60210-007-7   312 pp. $20.00

INITIATION

Initiation explores the different types of pain with which people are afflicted, spiritual, psychological, and physical, none of it deserved, yet all of it leading to greater self-awareness and growth in understanding of what it means to be human. Despite the theme, the novel is both entertaining and profound.

ISBN 978-1-60210-009-1   360 pp. $22.00

LONELINESS?

Loneliness? examines the life of a woman who sacrifices everything to be accepted by people who can see her only in terms of her singing ability and the roles she plays on the stage, and who is abandoned by them when she can no longer fit into their preconceived ideas. *Loneliness?* may be Benson's least known, yet one of his most insightful — and entertaining — novels

ISBN 978-1-60210-010-7   298 pp. $20.00